HARSH REALITIES

THIEVES' GUILD: BOOK THREE

COMING SOON

6e

BLATANT DISREGARD

THIEVES' GUILD: BOOK TWO

BLATANT DISREGARD

THIEVES' GUILD: BOOK TWO

C.G. HATTON

www.6e.net

First published in paperback in 2012
by Sixth Element Publishing
Arthur Robinson House
13-14 The Green
Billingham TS23 1EU
Tel: 01642 360253

© C.G. Hatton 2012

ISBN 978-1-908299-40-6

Printed in Great Britain.

www.6e.net

For Hatt

The piece of junk in geostationary orbit around Sten's World was not the nicest of places to be running from a determined bounty hunter. LC fumbled another magazine into his pistol as he ran along the walkway between sectors. The incident in the bar had shaken his nerves more than he realised. He'd thought they were close again but not that close.

He ducked into the half cover of a doorway to catch a breath and let Thom, an acquaintance of only a few hours, catch up with him.

"This is crazy," Thom said, dropping in alongside him. "Have we lost them?"

"I don't think so," LC said, grinning. "These guys are some of the best. We should make it back to the ship though. Don't look so worried, kiddo."

Thom scowled. "I'm not that young."

LC smiled.

"Why are they after you anyway?" Thom said.

LC looked up from checking the charge on the pistol and shrugged. "Gambling debts. Don't ever play poker with the Gadini brothers." He nudged Thom with his elbow and snatched a glance back down the corridor. "C'mon."

As they left the alcove, LC walked backwards for a few steps. The walkway was empty but something didn't feel right. He stopped and edged against the bulkhead, motioning Thom to do the same. He stared at the access stairs where a tangle of pipes were hissing steam. A shadow moved where it shouldn't have done. Metal glinted in the light of the stairway lamp.

He cursed silently and lifted his pistol, aiming towards the stairs. He was greeted by a hollow metallic clatter and saw a small object tumbling towards them. He blinked, then yelled, shoving Thom off to one side, trying to get down himself as the blast threw him into the wall.

He almost laughed as sparks of sheer agony flared behind his eyes and his cheek and left arm crunched into the cold metal of the bulkhead. He staggered around.

It was a strange feeling to be looking down the wrong end of a gun barrel through the effects of a concussion blast and he couldn't focus, either on the end of the barrel aimed at him or the figure standing half in shadow behind it.

So this was it after all. He began to lift his hands in grudging surrender and flinched back, his knees almost buckling as a shot resounded in the narrow space. The gun and its owner dropped. LC took a step back, swaying, blotting blood from his cheek with the back of his hand, waiting for the second shot, not quite trusting that this was a reprieve.

The corridor remained quiet, his guardian angel anonymous.

LC stumbled backwards and stooped quickly to help the kid to his feet.

Thom was closer on his heels this time as they ran on towards the docks.

1

"Where is he?"

The room was dark, the Man's face in half silhouette only partially illuminated by a single candle flickering off to the side.

NG stood by the door. Tired didn't describe how drained he felt. There was a jug of wine on the desk, filled to the brim, white vapours swirling upwards in gentle spirals. Two pewter goblets stood poised beside it.

"We don't know," he said.

The Man gestured for him to enter, leaning forward to light another candle.

NG sat. A chessboard was set up in the centre of the desk, intricately carved pieces waiting patiently for the battle to begin. The Man poured wine into the two goblets, careful not to spill a drop.

The darkness was smothering and it was impossible not to feel completely isolated from the entire universe in there, insulated and cut off from the whirlwind of war that was brewing outside.

"This is the most precarious of times, NG." The Man lifted the goblet and paused in a toast. "Strength and determination."

NG raised his own goblet and took a sip. The fumes were intoxicating, the wine hot.

The Man drank then said quietly, "We find ourselves in the midst of a maelstrom not of our making. Our people by their very nature and through no design of our own have found themselves drawn into a drama of cataclysmic proportions."

"Anderton and Hilyer had no idea what they were caught up in," NG said, sounding more defensive than he intended.

"Yet they are now key to the very future of mankind."

LC was running out of places to hide. There were too many armed unknowns milling about the orbital to relax and tensions were higher than he'd ever seen before. Coming to Sten's World had seemed a good idea at the time but if he was honest, he hadn't had much choice. After Palmio, this was about it. And from here, there was nowhere else except the scuzz bucket mining colonies and not exactly where he'd planned to retire once the gig at the guild was up. He'd always known life at the guild was too good to be true, and the Alsatia had never quite felt like home. Even so, he hadn't expected it to end so suddenly and in such a crap way.

He stopped running once they reached the main concourse to the docks, the tell-tale cramp starting in the small of his back as the adrenaline wore off. By the time they could see the security barriers, the shakes were starting to set in and the bone-deep ache that had become all too familiar in the last few weeks was sending its spikes of pain through his joints. Security at the barriers was never high on Sten's World but after the run-in with the bounty hunters, he was still on edge and he held his breath as they were asked to show ID. They were given a curt nod and pushed their way through.

They walked through the docks and it was hard not to panic, feeling the stiffness in his limbs spread and the buzzing in his head increase as they encountered more people.

"Thom, relax would you?" he said quietly, irritated that the kid was looking back over his shoulder constantly, twitchy as hell. If he wasn't careful, he was going to start attracting attention they didn't need.

"I can't believe that guy was going to shoot us," Thom whispered.

LC bit his tongue. Shoot you, he thought. He was fairly sure the bounty on his head was higher if he was alive. But he'd just met the kid so there was no need to spook him out even more. He shook his head instead and rubbed his eyes.

The ship was berthed at the freighter terminal. It was a relief to make it to the airlock. He leaned a hand against the bulkhead, feeling the chill of the hull suck away some of his rising temperature, and tried to keep his breathing shallow to ease the pain.

Thom frowned at him. "You don't look too good, Luka."

"I'm fine."

"No, really, you look like crap. You want me to get help?"

"I want you to get the door open."

The pressure in his head spiked and LC squeezed his eyes shut, pinching the top of his nose. He needed to get somewhere dark, quickly, or he would pass out right here in the docks and any freaking bounty hunter passing by would be welcome to haul his butt in for whatever price he was worth these days. Twenty six million, he'd been told. Twenty six each for him and Hilyer. It was hard to believe. Never before had a guild operative had a price put on their head, now two of them had been targeted. And for a job they'd had no choice but to take.

Just thinking of it made him feel queasy.

The airlock opened.

LC let Thom lead the way, glad to hear the door cycle shut behind them. It wasn't ideal but this freighter was the quickest way out of here and signing on as crew had been his only option. Just to keep one step ahead until he could figure out what to do.

The freighter was supposed to be shipping out that night. It was the only independent vessel due to leave for the mining colonies within the next three days and he couldn't afford to risk hanging around any longer. The station at Sten's World was a shit-hole at the best of times and right now it was getting way too hot. It wasn't easy to stay anonymous when everyone knew everyone and gossip travelled faster than light. He knew he'd been careless. Two bounty hunters had already tracked him down and he knew there were others.

He'd come here because of Olivia and he knew now that might have been a mistake. It left a cold spot inside to think he wouldn't be coming back.

The owner of the freighter had promised him they were booked to take on cargo and go, no messing, and the guy had seemed as eager as him to get away. No questions asked and not an ounce of curiosity about his background. LC just needed to get on board, wait out the shakes and get the hell out of here.

"Hey Luka."

He stopped at the door of his cabin; a few steps from sanctuary and a yell stopped him short. He turned slowly, and forced a smile. He'd only met the pilot of this rust bucket once and that had been enough.

"Gallagher wants you dockside, buddy," DiMarco said with a smirk. "You'd better get your ass back out there."

He wasn't used to taking orders and it took a measure of control not to tell the son of a bitch to go screw himself, but he needed the ride out of here and this was Gallagher's ship. And to give him credit, Gallagher had come across as a decent guy – one with terrible judgement in picking crew, but decent in the same way that Mendhel had always been with them. For a guild handler, Mendhel was always too patient for his own good, handling all his field operatives with infinite humour and stubborn protectiveness and a decency that had got him killed. A cold knot formed in LC's stomach at the thought and he blinked at DiMarco through a headache that was threatening to overpower him.

"Where?" he said softly.

DiMarco grinned as if he'd won a round. "Dockside administrator's office. Something's come up. We've been delayed."

The painkillers he'd grabbed hadn't worked and when he finally found the office, he knew he was looking flaky as hell. He had a vial in his pocket that would get him arrested if he was stopped and searched, but he was reluctant to use it until he knew what was going on. He'd left nothing on the ship that he would miss if he had to run. His possessions were pretty much down to what he was wearing and the only money he had left was on an unregistered credit stick hidden in his boot. He had no idea where he'd go but he was not going to get caught here, not after everything he'd been through.

He tried to clear his head as he approached the admin area. It was noisy, a lot of people and a background clutter of indistinct voices and muttered words. As far as he could see, the only guards hanging around were the same ones as earlier, making routine checks, nothing out of the ordinary and no one taking any undue interest in him. He stuck his hands in his pockets and strolled casually, feeling the weight of the gun tucked into the small of his back and hoping he wouldn't need to use it.

Gallagher was in the waiting area of the admin office, pacing up and down and tapping impatiently at his leg with a data board. LC paused at the door, watching and trying to gauge whether the guy had sold him out. There were no guards in there and no one flashing the silver badge of a bounty hunter. Gallagher looked up at the sound of the door opening and waved him over. He looked stressed.

LC walked in, the headache peaking to a new level.

Gallagher welcomed him with a pat on the shoulder and steered him towards a desk where a tired-looking clerk was shuffling data boards.

"I'm not in the mood, Gallagher," the guy warned without looking up.

Gallagher sat, gesturing LC to take a seat beside him, and placed the board on the desk. "This is the guy I was telling you about," he said. "Luka Cole. I've known him for two years. He'll vouch for me. Right, Luka?"

The clerk looked up suspiciously and stared from Gallagher to him and back. LC tried to sit up straight.

"ID?" the guy said finally and held out a hand.

Oh god. LC calmly took out his documents and passed them across. It was his last set and it was hard not to jump up and run out. He kept his breathing slow and even, heart rate steadying with the effort despite Gallagher's nervous energy spilling over next to him.

The clerk ran the papers through the system for what seemed like an eternity. No alarms went off, no guards came running. He looked up. "You've known him for two years?"

LC looked from the clerk to Gallagher, not sure who the question was aimed at, and nodded when the clerk pushed back the documents and asked the question again, this time directly to him.

"Gallagher," the clerk said, taking up the board, "I swear if this gets back to my supervisor, I'm dead meat. You're crazy going out with this guy, you know that?"

Again, that last was directed at him so LC smiled. "We go way back," he said simply, playing along with whatever it was that Gallagher was pulling. He could feel Gallagher wind down a notch as he said it.

The clerk shook his head. "You're all mad." He scribbled on the board and held it out. "Sign here."

LC dutifully signed, careful to match the name on the documents, not caring a damn what he was signing or why. He pushed the board back across the desk.

"You're cleared for Harbin 7," the clerk said to Gallagher, "but that's all I can manage."

"But," Gallagher protested.

"No buts, Bill. I'm pushing it getting that for you. You have the ship and you have a run to Harbin."

Gallagher leaned forward. "Come on, I know there are runs out to Erica," he said, trying to hide an edge of desperation in his voice.

The clerk leaned onto the desk himself so that they were nose to nose, and he whispered so quietly that LC could hardly hear what he was saying. "I know your psych report is fake, Bill. No one here in their right mind would let you take a crew back out there but I've known you a long time, and if Mr Cole here has known you that long and is happy to take his chances with you, then I'll let it go. Take the run to Harbin, come back safely and we'll see what we can do from there."

Gallagher sagged and the clerk pushed back from the desk. "Good luck, Gallagher," he said. "I really mean it. There are a lot of people here who feel for you. No one would ever wish what happened to you on anyone. But take it easy, yeah?"

Gallagher picked up the board and stood. LC followed, leaning on the back of the chair for a moment to catch his balance. He didn't care what this guy had going on or whatever the hell it was that everyone was so sorry for, he just wanted to get away and right now, get back to the ship and crawl into a dark space.

Gallagher shook the clerk's hand. "I appreciate it, bud," he said and walked away.

The clerk caught LC's eye. "Look out for yourself. He's not ready."

"I'm sure he'll be fine," LC muttered and turned to go.

The clerk laughed behind his back. "Yeah, well, watch out for those little green men."

Gallagher was waiting for him outside. "Cheers for that, Luka. Come on, I have to go meet our new navigator."

LC hesitated. He was fairly sure that Gallagher wasn't going to sell him out, but there were too many people around and it was too much of a risk to stay out here. And his head was still pounding.

"What's up," Gallagher said, and peered close. "You don't look well. You're not sick, are you?"

Shit. The man would be well within his rights to change his mind if he decided he didn't want some unknown onboard with an illness that could spread through his crew.

LC shook his head. "I'm fine," he said, knowing full well that he didn't look fine. He was too hot and he could feel a flush in his cheeks.

Gallagher didn't look convinced.

"I swear, I'm fine. Why do we have a new navigator? What happened to the guy I met yesterday?"

"He called in. Told me he fell down a staircase and broke his damned leg. And people say I'm unlucky. But I've got a replacement and we should be clear to leave as soon as we get the cargo loaded. God, it'll be good to get out of here. I don't know what the hell you're running from, Luka, but I've had enough of Sten's World to last me a lifetime." Gallagher smiled at him, a small rueful smile from one conspirator to another. "Don't worry, I'm not going to ask. It's your business. Just keep my engines running."

LC glanced around. The docks were getting busier. More ships must have come in and for a small station, there were a lot of people suddenly milling around, too many people who could be looking his way. He knew he'd been making mistake after mistake since he'd left Hil after it had all gone to shit at the lab. He was hoping like hell that this wasn't another one.

"I should get back to the ship," he said.

"We should both get back to the ship, but one beer won't hurt. One for the road, right?" Gallagher slapped him on the back. "Come on, let's go meet Sean. I think you'll like her."

2

NG sat quietly, breathing in the vapour from the wine in front of him, feeling it extend insidious swirling tendrils deep inside.

It was difficult to sit there, knowing everything he did about the situation unfolding outside, knowing how many loose ends were still unravelling.

The light from a single flickering candle cast an oasis of orange, shadows dancing on the Man's face, his expression completely unfathomable. It was stiflingly hot in there, environmental control set high with a depth of humidity that made NG glad he'd ditched layers before coming in. A bead of sweat ran down his back.

The situation was more dangerous and more momentous than anyone could have realised.

He took a sip of the wine, waiting for the next line of questioning, seeing it go one of two ways. The potential here for immense progression was almost unimaginable; the possibility of outright disaster could mean instability across human occupied space that the guild couldn't begin to control, could possibly never even attempt to amend.

He set the goblet on the desk and waited.

The Man looked up, eyes sparkling. "Never, ever despair, NG. We thrive on the very essence of chaos and all its auspices. Embrace the turbulence for it is that which gives us the unparalleled opportunities with which we play." He leaned forward, considering the chessboard for a moment. The board was set with white in front of NG.

"Tell me more about Luka," the Man said, reaching for the wine. "From the beginning. Why did your young prodigy run? And tell me, NG, how did he manage to elude us?"

Walking into Danny's Bar, LC felt like he could have been transported half way across the galaxy. He was half expecting to see Polly behind the bar and her pet enforcer Tavner watching from the door. There was already a heated argument in full flow at one end of the room and raucous laughter from the other. He followed Gallagher through the crowd of bodies to the bar, scanning the room with well practised ease.

Gallagher pushed his way in and made room for both of them, catching the attention of the barman with a wave. Two beers and two whisky chasers appeared. It seemed to LC like a lifetime since he'd had a beer and the bottle was cold and very welcome. The buzzing in his head had peaked into a din that was making his eyes hurt, but it was blending in with the background noise of music and chattering voices all around. He could just about shut it all out and enjoy the beer and it was tempting to wonder if he could drown it out completely with enough alcohol.

Gallagher nudged his arm to get his attention and clinked the shot glass. LC smiled vaguely and downed the whisky in one, feeling the heat of the liquor as it slipped down his throat. It was good quality, far better than a place like this should stock.

"Danny keeps the best stuff for us old-timers," Gallagher said loudly in his ear, as if he'd read his mind.

They pushed the empty shot glasses away and an older guy pushed his way past the staff behind the bar, grinning at Gallagher and sticking out his hand in welcome.

Gallagher shook his hand and patted LC on the shoulder. "Danny, this is Luka, my new chief engineer."

Danny nodded in acknowledgement. "I heard you got the Duck," he said to Gallagher, refilling the two glasses and adding a third.

Gallagher picked up the whisky. "She's old but solid. No AI so I've had to hire me a pilot and a navigator, can you believe it? But I've got a good feeling about it. We've got a run to Harbin. I'll find a way to get out to Erica from there. We leave in the morning."

They clinked glasses and LC picked up his too, joining in, trying to follow the conversation while he watched the mirror behind the bar, tracking the flow of people as they crowded in and then moved away again with their drinks. The back of his neck was tingling and he edged round slightly so that his back wasn't entirely exposed to the room behind.

"You're mad," Danny was saying to Gallagher, almost shouting over the noise.

"I know. That's what they said!" and they both laughed.

It felt surreal and he would have thought that two more fast whiskys added to the first and most of a bottle of beer would have at least begun to take an edge off the headache, but for all the effect it was having, he might as well have been drinking water.

He turned his back completely to stand leaning up against the bar. Gallagher and Danny were talking about old times and the spec of the ship, not what Gallagher had wanted from what he could pick up but LC really didn't care what type of shields it had or how slow it was. He listened politely, not even hearing half the words unless he made an effort, and he matched them for each shot of whisky that appeared in his glass.

By the time Danny disappeared to go get another bottle, they'd had seven each and Gallagher was cheerfully inebriated.

"We'll show them," Gallagher said, leaning in to yell it in his ear.

"I'm sure we will," he shouted back, not caring in the slightest whatever the hell he was on about. "Where are we meeting this navigator, Gallagher?"

He didn't hear so LC had to yell it again, wincing at the volume of his own voice.

"Right here. She's late but I'm sure she'll find us."

Danny returned and they started again, talking about old times and old friends and the state of the colonies. LC's ears pricked up at the mention of war and he leaned in to try to hear what they were saying but he could only catch occasional words, and it just seemed to be the usual rumours of the escalating tension between Earth and Winter that he'd been hearing since all this crap had started. The thought of heading back to the safety of the Alsatia was more tempting than ever but Hilyer's warning had been clear. Don't trust anyone at the guild.

He rubbed his eyes, tired and strung out and about done being surrounded by this many people. Looking around the place for anyone suspicious was hopeless; they all looked suspicious. He tried to spot anyone alone, or anyone who could be working in pairs, but there were too many bodies milling around and no bounty hunter with any sense would flash a badge in a place like this. He was about to turn back to make an excuse to leave when he saw heads turning to follow a woman who was heading straight for them. She caught his eye and smiled. Gallagher must have seen her reflection in the mirror because he turned and grinned, and pushed past a couple of people to steer her into their space at the bar.

"Danny, Luka," he said, "this is Sean O'Brien. She's our new navigator."

She had a holdall with her that she tucked up against the bar at their feet, happy to join Gallagher and Danny in yet another one for the road. LC opted for a beer, feeling uneasy that each time he turned back to the bar, she seemed to be watching him in the mirror. He drank the beer quickly, still keeping an eye out as the place got more rowdy and more crowded. Sean slipped into the conversation easily, charming both the older guys and still attracting glances from the other men around them. A couple of times her hand found its way to LC's shoulder or lower back as people pushed past them, forcing them to close up against the bar. It wasn't completely unwelcome but it set him on edge and as soon as he'd finished the beer, he put the bottle on the bar and caught Gallagher's attention.

"I'm going to head back to the ship," he said. "Nice to meet you, Danny."

Danny shook his hand and LC turned away to ease his way through the crowd.

"Hey lady," a voice jeered behind him as he was a few steps away. "Why are you wasting your time with these losers?"

He turned back to see Sean smiling at Gallagher, pointedly ignoring the guy. LC was about to turn away again when the guy pushed forward, bumping into Sean and jabbing a finger at Gallagher. "This jerk's a lunatic, did no one tell you that?" he slurred loudly.

LC needed to disappear quietly and everything in him screamed at him to do just that, to slip away and get out of there. He didn't need to get involved.

The guy raised his voice, "You're not fit to fly a freaking shuttle-bus," and pushed Gallagher in the chest.

LC took a reluctant step back towards the bar. He could see Danny twitch and gesture to one of his staff. Gallagher objected and Sean stepped aside, putting a hand out to stop the guy. The drunk pushed forward suddenly, taking hold of Sean's arm. One of his buddies stepped in and shoved Gallagher, who yelled, resisted and got a fist in the face.

LC cursed under his breath and tried to push his way back to them, feeling people surge behind him as emotions flared. A body bumped into him. Someone yelled and he was jostled aside. He could see Sean talking, too quiet to hear, to the guy who was still leering at her. Gallagher was swearing, getting more heated. Danny was calling for them to break it up but too many people were shoving back and yelling and anything anyone else could have said to calm it down was getting lost.

Someone grabbed hold of LC's jacket from behind. He tried to shrug them off and when they wouldn't let go, he thrust an elbow backwards, fast and hard, felt it hit home and pushed away. He pushed through and stepped in between Gallagher and the two guys, shouldering in to separate them.

"Back off."

"Says who?" the first guy said with a laugh, too loudly. He still had hold of Sean's arm but she was tensed and looking from him to Gallagher as if she was trying to figure out what she could get away with. The drunk pushed her away suddenly and LC saw the glint of a knife. The pain in his head vanished, the buzz gone, and for the first time in hours, he could focus clearly.

He reacted, stepping in and reaching to deflect the blow as it came up in a slash. He caught hold of the hand and twisted, swinging his elbow into the guy's face.

Sean called out. The guy grunted and dropped the knife and in that instant, LC was aware of the guy's buddy behind him and in that fraction of a second before it happened knew what the guy was about to do. He turned, caught the movement out of the corner of his eye as the man stepped in, another blade flashing, and LC instinctively blocked with his left hand, no time for anything fancy, the knife slashing through his palm as he caught hold of it.

He kept the grip on the knife, balancing his weight on his back foot as both men lunged forward. Sean moved deftly to stop them reaching Gallagher who was still shouting and LC was vaguely aware of people pressing in behind him when a figure loomed up behind the two drunks, catching them both around the neck. With one smooth motion, the two men's heads crashed together, the figure letting go to let them drop to the floor.

Danny was pushing in then, arms up, saying, "Enough!" in the sudden quiet. The press of people eased off. LC turned to check on Sean and Gallagher, the pain of the gash in his hand kicking in and the buzz in his head returning with enough force to make his eyes water.

Gallagher was talking to Danny, apologising; Danny saying not to worry, they were idiots.

The big guy who had floored the drunks leaned in to Danny, said something quietly and turned to go. LC started to go over but Sean took hold of his hand, holding him back. He flinched as a spark flared behind his eyes at her touch. She called to a guy behind the bar for a cloth and pressed it into his palm, staunching the flow of blood.

"Is it always this exciting?" she said with a smile.

"Don't ask me," LC muttered, wrapping the cloth tight around his hand. "I've only been here a couple of days."

The music started up again and the conversation rose as people realised the excitement was over and got back to their free time.

Sean looked back at Gallagher. "We should get him to the ship."

LC nodded. There was something disconcerting about her, an intensity he didn't like being close to. Since the lab it had been easier to avoid people all together. He didn't know what the hell he'd been thinking to sign on as crew. And he didn't have the faintest idea about engines. He just needed to get away. The faster, the better.

She touched his shoulder and he saw a look of curiosity in her eyes that left him feeling queasy. He was pretty much at the end of the line. Christ, could it get any worse?

3

NG took a moment to decide where to start. The Man knew a lot of this and a lot more besides. The gathering of intelligence was the lifeblood of the guild but he always wanted to hear NG explain the details, the minutiae of operations at ground level, because he said he liked to get a feeling for those insights firsthand.

NG took a sip of his wine. "We must consider that it was Mendhel who brought LC to us," he said slowly, "in difficult circumstances and at a very young age. Mendhel has always been the only handler who could work with him. Losing Mendhel has been hard for us all but for LC, it was devastating."

The Man was watching intently, drinking in every word, the shadows shrouding the small room seeming to mirror a growing darkness outside.

Mendhel had been one of their best handlers and for someone of that standing to have been killed, by people who knew far more about the guild than any outsider ever should, was unprecedented. NG knew without needing to pry into the Man's mind that the question wasn't so much why Anderton and Hilyer had taken it on themselves to run the tab but why they hadn't returned to the safety of the guild when it went wrong.

That wasn't an easy question to answer. Someone had dared challenge the Thieves' Guild and had given their operatives no choice but to comply. Once that choice was made, circumstances had tumbled out of their control.

The Man leaned forward and topped up the two goblets. "The audacity of our enemies sets the bar by which we exist," he said and gestured towards the board, an invitation for NG to commence. The flame of the candle wavered.

"They set the bounty at a figure we couldn't ignore," NG said.

He moved a pawn. "And given the price on his head and the heat that attracted, it wasn't surprising that LC ran to the Between if he suspected that the guild had been compromised."

He woke with a jolt, disorientated, and for a moment couldn't place where he was. Rumbling echoed through the bare metal bulkheads next to his bunk and it was hot. So not the Alsatia then. He grabbed his pistol from under the pillow, sat up suddenly and banged his head on the hard surface of the lockers above. He almost panicked disentangling himself from a sheet that was so thin it might as well not have been there and looked around a cabin that was dark but for the soft red glow of night lighting.

He was on the Duck, he realised, calming his heart rate and listening to figure out what had woken him. The hull of the ship was reverberating. That was all. They must be loading cargo. He sat with the pistol a reassuring weight in his hand. His palm was itching. He'd cleaned and bandaged the gash and it felt like it was healing already.

The headache was gone. He was hot but that was because the cabin was hot. And the shakes had gone so it was over, at least for the moment. The gaps between episodes seemed to be getting longer and it was weird but some of his old aches, pain he'd lived with for years, were easing off. He stretched out his left leg and massaged the knee. It was fine, only a faint twinge of the ever-present ache he'd had since he dislocated it falling off a roof when he was a kid.

He rubbed a hand across his eyes and looked at the band on his wrist to check the time. It was the middle of the night and he was wide awake. He'd never downed so much alcohol with so little effect and if he hadn't seen the state Gallagher was in, it would have been tempting to think Danny was watering down his whisky. Another two or three beers, he thought, was what he needed to help him get back to sleep. He dressed, tucked the pistol into the small of his back, pulled his shirt out over it and wandered out to find the mess.

He walked through the Duck's main deck, a dark and claustrophobic level crammed with tiny living spaces. The ship spared no energy on superfluous lighting or fancy environmental control, like it didn't care too much about the humans it needed to keep it flying. Gallagher had said there was no AI so it was just a hulk of a hull with cargo space premium and temperamental engines. Thank god Thom actually was an engineer. The kid was more than capable from what he'd seen and they might even make it to their destination intact, and once at Harbin or Erica or wherever they were going, he'd split and find another ride out. Keep running for now, at least until he had a plan.

He touched a hand to his pocket, no need to pull out the tiny object that was stashed there, just a touch to reassure himself it was still there. It was his only lead, the only clue as to who had sent them into that lab, who'd taken Anya and killed Mendhel. Pen Halligan had told him about the corporation and slipped the implant into his hand as he'd left. "The woman who sent you after that damned package is dead," he'd said. "Hilyer pulled this Senson out of her. We can't get a damn thing off it. See if you have any luck."

He hadn't. Yet.

Before the lab he would have bust it wide open in seconds. Before the lab he never used to wake up in the middle of the night shaking. He still couldn't face the thought of having to admit to anyone what had happened. If Hil hadn't been there backing him up, there was no way he would have got out alive. LC owed him a lot, his life, more than anyone could have asked. He could still feel the heat of the explosion behind them. And whatever the hell it was that he'd been exposed to in there, his body was still adjusting.

He needed a beer.

The door to the mess was ajar and he could see the flicker of a screen in the darkness inside. Muted sounds and voices almost made him turn away but the last thing he needed to do was sit in a hot cabin, wide awake and going insane.

DiMarco was in there, sprawled across one end of the L-shaped seating that took up two walls of the cramped space. One of the station's news channels was playing on the screen alongside three music streams and the pilot was flicking idly between them. He looked up as LC walked in.

"Hey, look who it is," he said. "Throw me a beer, will you?"

LC got two beers from the fridge unit by the door, threw one of the bottles across to DiMarco and sat down, putting his feet up on the low table in front of the sofa.

He could feel the pilot looking at him and smirking, but he just leaned back and closed his eyes, letting the mix of voices and music wash over him.

"I heard what you did for Gallagher in Danny's Bar," DiMarco said. "I had you down for the quiet type who'd run from a fight but the skipper says you're a regular hero, Luka. Fancy that."

LC ignored him. The beer wasn't bad and it was cooler in the mess than in his cabin so he could put up with the company for a while.

DiMarco turned up the music and flicked backwards and forwards between videos. "Fast reflexes, Gallagher said."

LC had his eyes half closed and sensed more than saw the empty bottle thrown at his head. He caught it easily, not entirely sure why DiMarco was being such an ass.

The pilot laughed. "What are you running from, Luka?"

"I don't know what you mean," he said casually, placing the bottle on the table and leaning back.

"Come on. This place is the back of beyond. No one ends up here except burnt out miners, drunken freighter pilots and scum with something to hide."

"And which one are you?"

DiMarco laughed again, louder this time. "That kid Thomas is out of his depth. He won't last long. The woman – she's something. I'll figure her out. You? I don't know where the hell Gallagher picked you up from, but I'll find out, Luka. No one is ever who they seem to be. You don't get to keep secrets on Sten's World."

LC leaned across and pulled two more beers from the fridge. He threw one to DiMarco. He was starting to get a headache and the beer wasn't doing much but he wasn't going to give the pilot the satisfaction of spooking him out of the mess.

"How long have you known Gallagher?" he asked, more out of a need to divert attention from himself than any real curiosity.

DiMarco shrugged. "Long enough to know he has more than one screw loose. Trust me, I'm not piloting this bucket for him out of choice. The guy's crazy."

He sat up suddenly and peered at LC. "You don't know, do you?" He laughed so hard then that it looked like he was going to choke. "Oh man, this gets better."

LC smiled and drank down the rest of his beer in one. He really didn't care. Whatever these people had going on was nothing compared to where he'd come from. They had nothing on him and he wasn't going to get involved. He'd been in crap situations before and he'd always got out. The more that assholes like DiMarco ribbed him, the more it helped him focus on that. He'd looked after himself alone for years as a kid before the guild had picked him up and then near enough ten years fighting to get to the top and stay at the top which had taught him plenty about taking care of himself. Hil and the others thought he had it easy, that he didn't have to work at it, and that was an image he was happy to sustain. But it wasn't entirely true. And compared to some people he'd had to deal with, DiMarco here was an amateur.

The pilot was still looking at him with a feral grin creasing his thin mouth. He stood up, swaying slightly, and pointed at LC. "You need a real man's drink," he said with a laugh. "Stay there."

LC leaned back again and watched DiMarco stagger out of the mess. He scratched absently at his palm and pulled away the bandage out of curiosity. The knife wound wandered in a jagged line across his hand, red inflammation around it, but the gash was starting to seal already. He clenched his fist, opened and closed it a few times. He'd thought it might need medical attention but it was healing fine. In the time he'd been running since the lab, he'd taken a few knocks but he'd thought it had been the pure adrenaline that kept him going. The episodes of shakes and aches, bone-deep pain and agonising headaches that hit suddenly had kept him preoccupied enough not to think about the scrapes he'd had.

He looked at the wound. It was weird that it was healing so fast but not unwelcome. He heard footsteps approaching and quickly rewrapped the bandage around his hand.

DiMarco stumbled back in and set an unlabelled bottle and two shot glasses on the table. The bottle was a third empty already and the liquid in it was a murky green colour. The pilot laughed to himself like he had a private joke going on and poured the alcohol into the two glasses.

LC picked one up quite happily. So far the beers and Danny's best whisky hadn't touched him. He wanted to get back to sleep. If this was what it took, he was curious to try it.

DiMarco leaned across and clinked glasses. LC saw that the pilot paused to watch him drink first. It burned its way down into his stomach and had a nasty chemical aftertaste, the fumes making him cough. "Jesus, what is this?"

DiMarco laughed and downed his own, grabbing the bottle and refilling both glasses.

"This, Luka my lad, is the best moonshine Sten's World can offer. You haven't lived until you've survived a session on this stuff."

The pilot passed out before they reached the bottom of the bottle. LC sat quietly for a while, enjoying the peace, and considered finishing off the rest to see if it would make a difference. He felt stone cold sober.

He rubbed his eyes, trying to decide if he was tired enough to go back to sleep and reckoned he was more hungry than tired. Sitting with DiMarco and listening to his stories of the station and its black market, the gossip about Gallagher and the pilot's theories on why Earth and Winter should leave the Between alone and go screw themselves had just about pushed LC to his limit. He'd zoned out, refused to be pushed into talking about himself and let the guy drink himself into oblivion. If Gallagher was a madman who thought aliens had shot him down on his last trip out to the mining colonies, then that was his business. And hearing about the politics of the three big families that ran the organised crime of Sten's World had felt like minor small town gossip compared to what went on throughout the Alsatia. The massive guild cruiser had intrigue seeping out of every deck although the field-ops rarely had anything to do with it. It had never interested him so long as he was free to go out and run the tabs that kept the Thieves' Guild thriving. Except he wasn't free to do that anymore. It was tough but he had to remind himself that Mendhel, his buffer against the Chief and the rest of the guild, never mind the rest of the universe, was dead.

LC poured himself another glass and raised it in a silent toast to Mendhel, the man who had rescued him when he was thirteen years old and about to be shot for being on the wrong side of the line in a freaking war zone.

4

*"The effects of Mendhel's death will be felt for a long time to come,"
the Man said solemnly. "The guild feels any loss keenly. Mendhel
was one of our brightest stars." He held his hand poised over a pawn,
motionless for a long while before sliding it across the board. "Tell me,
NG, what do we know of this freighter captain?"*

*It seemed an innocuous enough question but the meaning behind it
was daunting.*

*"William Gallagher is one of the old timers," NG said. "Solid
reputation, decent man by all accounts. LC was fortunate to fall in
with him."*

*The Man nodded. "I understand this chance meeting may prove to
be most serendipitous," he said.*

*"Gallagher tells a fairly convincing story of having been attacked
by aliens," NG said. "We have people investigating. Gallagher did lose
a ship, that's not in dispute. By all accounts, he was lucky to survive.
Legal have dismissed the claim of alien aggression as myth. Media and
Science are more interested because of where it happened. We have
other evidence from that sector."*

*The Man picked up a small pot and rubbed his thumb and fingers
together over it, dipping in to take out a pinch of black powder. "Earth
and Winter are fast to dismiss the events that happen in the Between,"
he said. "It will be their downfall."*

He managed to get a couple of hours sleep and it was quiet when
he woke. He sat up too quickly, banged his head again and was
reaching for the gun before he focused and saw where he was.
He got up, realised he felt better than he had in a long time and
worked his way through a set of stretches, as much as he could

manage in the confined space. He missed the Maze, missed the full on challenge of the Straight through the field-ops' training ground. He'd not really had the chance to stretch his legs fully since before they'd found out that Anya was being held hostage, before the fiasco at the lab.

He was sitting back on his bunk, struggling to concentrate enough to use any kind of technique to control his breathing and lower his heart rate, when someone hammered on his door.

"Rise and shine, Luka buddy," DiMarco yelled, sounding even more rough and obnoxious than usual. "Gallagher wants us on the bridge."

LC didn't reply. He didn't like working in a routine and he wasn't used to working as part of a team. It was tempting to ignore them all but a niggle of conscience reminded him that he kind of owed Gallagher for giving him a ride out of Sten's, and being here on this ship was a hell of a lot better than being stranded on an orbital that could fast become bounty hunter central.

He showered and dressed, tucking the pistol into the back of his waistband and checking the knife in his boot before he left the cabin. The Duck was a hefty ship, much bigger than the small guild ships the field-ops got to work with, tiny in comparison to the Alsatia but still big enough that it took him a while to make his way down to the engine room. Thom was already in there running through a routine of pre-flight checks.

LC leaned around a huge block of machinery and waved to get the kid's attention. "Gallagher wants me up top," he said. "You alright in here?"

Thom looked up, a dirty smear across his forehead and a rag in his hand. "This ship has two Denholm 64s combined with a Lewis A drive," he said, fidgeting and way too serious for LC's liking.

He'd never been this close to the workings of a ship before and he didn't really want to get any closer. Ships flew, whether they were big or small, and he really didn't care how. "Is that a problem?"

"The Lewis is Wintran."

Like that meant something. Didn't the Wintrans make the best drive systems? LC shrugged. "And?"

"And the Denholms are from Earth. They shouldn't be compatible."

It wasn't even tempting to ask what the hell a Denholm was. LC rolled his eyes. "There'll be an interface," he said. Of course there would be.

He told the kid that he'd be back before they had to warm up the drive, for whatever good that would do, and made his way to the bridge. Sean was there with DiMarco and Gallagher, going through the boards and arguing out a route. They all looked stressed and a headache began to pulse behind his eyes as he approached.

"Luka," Gallagher said, turning around. "You're with me. You two," he said, turning back to the boards where Sean and DiMarco were scowling at each other, "come up with a solution. I don't care how."

Sean looked disgusted but as Gallagher stalked out, her expression changed. "Wait," she said.

LC felt a tentative query reach out to his mind, the implant he hadn't used in weeks engaging with a feeling that made him blink in confusion as it competed with the buzzing in his head. He allowed access and heard Sean's voice in his mind as clear as if she was speaking aloud.

"Thank god," she sent through the remote. "Are you getting this?"

"Yeah," he sent in reply. "How did you know?"

She smiled, relief evident. "I guessed. I think Thomas has an implant, Senson, high spec too, but Gallagher and DiMarco don't. Keep this private. Listen, Gallagher's in trouble. I think he wants you to go back onto the docks with him. He's caught up in something – don't let him make it worse. I need to stay and babysit hangover boy here through some jump calculations. Be careful, okay?"

He nodded and backed away to follow Gallagher. Going back on the station was the last thing he wanted to do.

"What's up?" he said, catching up and matching stride with the older man. "We're due to leave, aren't we?"

Gallagher slowed. "I trust you, Luka. I don't know why but there's something about you." He slapped a hand onto LC's shoulder. "I've got a problem and I need an extra pair of eyes with me. DiMarco is a drunk and Thom is a good lad, but he's young. I want Sean on the bridge so that leaves you. And like I said, I trust you. You have good instincts. Just keep your eyes open and watch my back."

"What are you expecting to happen?" LC asked cautiously, not really wanting to know and definitely not wanting to go out there.

Gallagher looked uneasy. "I arranged a business deal with Mal Donnelly to buy the ship. Good terms. I know, I know what you're thinking."

He wasn't thinking anything other than trying to figure out a contingency plan if they ran into trouble.

"We have a legitimate cargo and permits for a round trip to Harbin," Gallagher continued, speaking quietly so that he was almost whispering. "Problem is, Donnelly is demanding we take a detour on the way. He won't sign the release with the office until I agree and I can't mention it to anyone, so we don't have enough fuel, we don't have the right permits and Donnelly wants to see me now on the docks. I reckon he's going to insist we take an extra item on our inventory."

He stopped and turned to face LC. "I need this ship, Luka."

And LC needed a way out. From what DiMarco had said, Donnelly was a bully, more mouth than muscle but with the backing of a family that no one on Sten's World dared cross. It was small time, back of beyond crap and it was hard not to snap at Gallagher to just do what the guy wanted and be done. Whatever it was, he was sure he'd handled worse himself.

"It'll be fine," he said. He'd break into the damned office and steal the permits they needed if that's what it took to get away from here.

"Agree to anything they say," LC said quietly as they walked across the docks, trying to ignore the dull buzz in his head.

"Don't worry, it's not like I have a lot of choice," Gallagher said. "Shit."

LC followed Gallagher's look and saw what was bugging him.

Crates were being loaded into the ship, guys in black combat gear standing guard and cradling an array of weapons as others checked inventories and supervised the operation.

"I thought you said the cargo for Harbin was on board already."

"It is," Gallagher said. "See that small guy with grey hair? That's Mal Donnelly's man, McCabe. We're screwed. Look, Luka, don't say anything to antagonise them, okay? I'll sort it out. Just watch my back."

Watching his own back was more of a priority and it was way too public out here. He was heading towards a contingent of armed thugs who were brazenly flaunting their own weaponry, amidst the suddenly disinterested station security who were equally well armed, and that was nothing compared to the thought that in amongst all these people could be someone watching him and waiting for the right moment to take him down.

The back of his neck was prickling and he tried to be nonchalant about checking all directions, all exits from the docks and his own route back to the crew access of the ship. It was second nature to him but he wasn't normally this paranoid about it, not in the way Hil could be. God, he missed Hil and he missed Mendhel. He'd never realised how much he relied on them to be there, right at his side. Even when he was out on tabs by himself, he always knew that they'd be there when he got back.

It felt like a lifetime ago.

As they approached, two of the guys in black dropped what they were doing and came to intercept.

"Where's Donnelly?" Gallagher said, blustering with bravado.

"Mr Donnelly doesn't oversee cargo shipments," the smaller of the two guys said in a withering tone, looking them both up and down.

Gallagher looked like he was losing his nerve already. "He said he wanted to see me."

"Mr McCabe will see you when he's ready." The guy signalled to his buddy. The big man stepped forward and gestured for them to raise their hands.

He was big but he didn't look like much – no balance and LC

reckoned he could floor the guy if he had to. Gallagher nudged him in the ribs though and he turned reluctantly, arms up while the guy frisked him, finding the pistol straight away and as it was pulled clear of his back, it was hard to stay calm and not think that this could be a trap. If Donnelly had found out who he was and how much he was worth, this could be it. Right here.

The suit leaned in close and whispered in his ear, "You must be new or stupid to be bringing a weapon into a meeting with Mr Donnelly's crew."

LC stood his ground but stayed calm. Not so long ago he wouldn't have been able to resist a cocky comment but in the circumstances it seemed wise to stay invisible. Staying on the ship would have been wiser but what the hell; if Gallagher lost out here, there'd be no ship.

And no ride out.

The two guys kept them waiting then the first one turned and said, "Mr McCabe will see you now," and they were waved over towards the grey haired guy who had stepped away from the loading operation and was watching from the sidelines.

They walked side by side and LC could feel that Gallagher was fuming, muttering, "They can't do this to us. This isn't what I agreed to. Believe me, I would never agree to take cargo for Donnelly."

LC was looking around, gauging angles and numbers.

"Danny told me not to trust him. God, how could I have been so stupid?"

"It's not stupid to have the guts to want to keep on trying," LC said quietly.

Gallagher looked confused. "Jesus, did I say that out loud?" he said, embarrassed.

McCabe looked up as they got near. He was holding a thin data board to his chest, tapping it gently. The guy had two men standing behind him, both armed and watching them approach with fingers twitching on triggers. A third who was standing at McCabe's side was familiar, not openly brandishing a weapon and a faint smile twitching the corners of his mouth as he watched them approach. LC recognised him instantly as the big guy who'd stopped the fight in the bar. He looked out of place somehow, not as hostile as the rest, and LC had got the impression he was a regular at Danny's place so to see him here in this company was surprising.

It was disconcertingly hard to read the scene. It wasn't clear what they were expecting and it was difficult to keep his mind clear and on track when the noise in his head was becoming overwhelming. He was so used to just knowing what to do, how to react without needing to think in whatever situation he found himself that this sense of indecision was debilitating. He blinked and tried to concentrate on the four men in front of them.

Gallagher strode up to McCabe. "What the hell are you doing?"

"We're loading cargo, Gallagher, surely you can see that."

"I can't take cargo for you, McCabe. No way."

McCabe smiled again and held out the data board. "Yes, you can," he said. "And you will."

Gallagher took the board and flicked through the screens on it, his anger turning to disbelief. "This isn't the document I signed."

He reached the last screen and sagged visibly. He looked up at McCabe. "This isn't the document I signed," he said again, his voice quiet.

"That is your signature, Bill."

LC was watching the two bodyguards, who'd both taken a step closer. The big guy was standing quietly, calm and impassive.

"McCabe," Gallagher said quietly, "you're going to kill us with this."

McCabe looked unimpressed. "Without this, Gallagher, we will kill you. You owe Mr Donnelly now. And this," he gestured to the stack of crates, "is your first instalment. The mortgage on the ship has been signed, your papers are in order and you will take this cargo to a location that will be specified once you have left dock."

He looked at LC suddenly. "I heard you scraped yourself a crew together, Bill," he said, sneering and LC knew beyond a doubt that the guy had no idea who he was. He relaxed.

McCabe took the board back from Gallagher and smiled. "One more thing," he said. "Mr Donnelly doesn't completely trust that you'll take good care of his consignment. I'm coming with you."

Gallagher tensed and shook his head. "That's not necessary. I don't take passengers."

"You don't have a choice."

"I'll speak to Donnelly," Gallagher said. "He didn't say anything about this."

McCabe held the board up between them. "You don't have a choice, Bill," he said, quiet and malicious.

The two bodyguards planted their feet, shifting the weight of the stubby guns they were carrying. The big guy from Danny's Bar took a small step closer himself, staring at LC, and shook his head, a tiny almost imperceptible movement, in a gentle warning.

LC got the message, stepped forward and placed a hand on Gallagher's back. "It's fine," he said to McCabe. "Just let us know when you're ready."

As he turned to manoeuvre Gallagher away, the implant engaged and Sean whispered inside his head, "Luka, we need you back on the ship."

"We're coming," he sent back. He had to get off this dockside. And hope that Gallagher could keep his act together long enough with these small time crooks to get them away from here.

5

A pinch of the black powder trickled from the Man's fingers into the wine. Steam rose as the two substances reacted.

"As volatile and hostile as the Between has become," the Man said, picking up the jug and swirling it carefully, "I take it that our operative conducted himself well. Why did we not extract him, NG, as soon as you knew where he was?"

Clouds of vapour rose in a billowing surge. The fumes were potent, a heady mix of intoxicants blending with the humid air in the chambers.

NG moved another pawn, classic King's Gambit, trying to anticipate the strategy the Man would adopt. He pushed his goblet forward. "We didn't know for sure. He was smart to join the crew of a freighter. Those ships spend months in space. Half the colonies they service aren't even listed." He knew he sounded defensive again and bit his tongue.

The Man smiled as he poured the wine. "Don't be hard on yourself, NG. We train our people to survive and improvise. We expect a lot from them. LC Anderton is one of our very best, is he not? Don't be surprised that he evaded us. He has a talent for it."

They gave him his pistol back and he kept it held loosely in his hand, dangling down by his thigh, until they were through the airlock and walking back onto the ship. It was strange how safe it felt, how much distance a set of two doors could put between him and a universe full of crap.

LC tucked the gun back into the small of his back as they walked. Gallagher was still chuntering about McCabe. He blocked him out and called silently to Sean. "What's the emergency?"

"Are you back onboard?"

"Safe and sound."

"Thom needs you in the engine room," she sent, sounding relieved. "He said he needs a hand if we're going to be ready to leave on time. What happened out there?"

"I'm sure Gallagher will explain," LC replied, bemused that it felt like no one could manage anything without him. What was it all of a sudden? Usually when he needed to bug out in a hurry, there was an extraction team waiting for him and nothing to do but snooze until he got back to the Alsatia. He didn't work well with people depending on him. "Tell Thom I'll be right there."

He made his excuses to Gallagher and wandered down to the engine room. It was dark except for a pale blue light flickering deep inside the vast space, casting shadows on the tangled mass of pipes and chambers. He climbed down and followed the light to the centre where a small control room nestled amidst the machinery. Thom was sitting in there, leaning on the main panel with his nose almost touching the screen.

LC approached quietly and watched from the doorway without a word as the kid intently manipulated some kind of device, both hands straining with the effort, finally groaning and dropping his head onto the panel.

"Hey, what's up?" LC said cheerfully, leaning against the doorframe.

Thom sat up suddenly, with a look that was half embarrassment and half relief crossing his face. He gestured towards the screen.

"The life support recycling unit is shot," he said with frustration. "It blew when I fired it up and I can't get the remote to reach the pod to replace the control module. You want to try?"

LC squinted at the display. "You can't get the what to do what?"

"The remote," Thom said. "It's a piece of shit. The module keeps slipping."

LC nudged past him and dropped into the second chair, swivelling round to peer at the screen. "Pretend I know nothing," he said, "and explain to me exactly what you're trying to do."

Thom turned and looked at him, his expression switching to a mix of hurt and indignation. "You don't have to test me all the time. I know what I'm doing."

"I'll know that when you show me I can leave you to get on with it," LC said, resisting the urge to laugh. "Come on, show me what you're doing."

Thom talked him through it patiently, flicking through schematics and finally bringing up a real-time shot of a remote drone. "There's no AI," he said.

LC nodded like he was encouraging the younger engineer to carry on explaining something that he already knew. It was absurd and if Gallagher knew what was going on, he'd get thrown out on his ear. But Thom seemed oblivious to it and the faster he could get the kid back to work, the faster they'd get out of here.

"So we have to control remotes manually," Thom continued, "to get into the enclosed units we can't reach. But the remote is being a bitch."

LC watched while Thom tried it again, and again. He could see straight off that there was no way the remote was going to manage it, no matter how careful anyone was to operate it. The kid was about to try again, give him credit for not giving up, but LC had hit the limit of his patience. He looked back at the schematics, one glance enough to sear the entire system into his memory.

He stood up. "Wait here."

The life support unit was massive, an inner core sealed against contaminants and an outer compartment of moving parts and huge conduits. LC found the main access panel, eased the lockpick away from the edge of his wristband and quickly broke open the locks, ignoring the warning notices declaring mortal danger.

There was a sharp intake of breath behind him.

"Don't say it, Thom," he said, climbing through, "and don't start anything up, for Christ's sake."

The compartment was crammed full, an intricate and elaborate three-dimensional jigsaw of machinery and pipes that had just enough gaps and spaces for him to climb and struggle his way through. Knowing the route was one thing, getting there was something else. It was difficult going, about as tough as anything he'd ever done and he got stuck twice, almost lost an arm when a hefty rotor shifted suddenly as he leaned on it, and irrationally thought he'd run into electrobes when he imagined the band on his wrist tingled in warning. It was ridiculous. The ship had no AI so there couldn't be any of those damned things in here. And anyway the bio-readings on the band hadn't made any sense to him since the lab so they were pretty much meaningless and he didn't even know if the warning mechanism still worked.

He took a tentative breath, balanced precariously as he was. The meagre amount of air in the compartment was stale and tinged with an acrid scent of chemicals, but nothing hit his lungs the way electrobes would. He felt fine. He felt more than fine. He clenched and unclenched his left hand. If the crap he'd picked up at the lab had that kind of effect on an open wound and could neutralise shocking amounts of alcohol, he reckoned it could probably fend off the side effects of electrobe poisoning. No wonder people wanted to get their hands on him to get hold of it. A curse, the guy in the lab had called it but then the man had been half mad and laughing and had somehow got the drop on him. LC could still feel the cold of the jab against his neck, sprawled half stunned on the floor amongst shards of broken glass, with a madman screaming in his ear. He'd managed to yell out to Hil before passing out and that was all he could remember except for disjointed memories of the heat of an explosion behind them as Hil dragged both their asses back to the ship.

When he tumbled out of the unit clutching the burnt out control module, Thom was still standing gawping.

LC got to his feet, dusted himself down and handed over the scorched module. "There you go."

He hung around the engine room watching Thom work until the power plant, main engines and auxiliaries were fired up and all systems were online. There was no AI but it all seemed pretty much automated. They reported in then he told Thom to go rest up, offering to take first watch because he wanted some time alone and down here was probably the best place to get it.

He sat in the tiny control room with his feet up on the panel, flicking through display screens of all the information they had access to and breaking into the encrypted areas that were supposedly restricted. It was all low security, manufacturer's defaults designed to prevent the unqualified from tampering. There wasn't anything thrilling but he got a good look at the ship and its systems, noting a few bolt holes for future reference and checking out the cargo with nothing other than passing curiosity. He reckoned Gallagher's legitimate cargo was full of domestic supplies and McCabe's crates had the look of narcotics from the outlines on the scans he could access. It looked like McCabe and two of his guys had booked in as passengers, taking spare crew quarters. He made a note of where so he could avoid them.

He poked into a couple more areas, casual boredom more than anything, and was about done when he was bumped abruptly out of the system. He sat up and stared at the console. Three attempts later and it was impossible to resist a closer look at what was ditching him out. He engaged a direct connection from the implant and went slowly, spotting a couple of traps and nudging back when it threatened to fire a spark his way. The link was clear and smooth, far better than he would have expected from a rust bucket with no AI, and he was sure the protections were more sophisticated than a cargo freighter out here should ever need. But it had nothing he hadn't broken before.

He got through the barriers that had stopped his manual search and hit a black wall. Total void. The sudden backlash that hit his neck and spiked into his head knocked him back physically as well as mentally. He wasn't sure if he blacked out completely but he opened his eyes to a screen that showed detailed maps of the crew deck as if that was where he'd left it. Flickers of light danced on the edges of his vision. The engines were still running and no warning klaxons were screaming out. If it hadn't been for a sting of warmth where the usually cool implant nestled below the skin on his neck, he would have thought he'd imagined it.

He rubbed his neck, feeling around the sore spot, and looked at the screen, tempted to go back in and crack it. He had about an hour before they were due to leave. But Thom would be back before then and it wasn't worth the hassle of trying to explain to the kid what he was doing. He seriously doubted that a ship like this had anything of value to hide anyway. It had probably been a blip – it was old enough and decrepit enough to have obsolete systems that didn't match up to other sections of its operations.

LC flicked the screen back onto routine maintenance and went for a run around the engine room. It wasn't the Maze but parts of it weren't far off.

Thom reappeared after his break even more eager to prove himself as an engineer which suited LC just fine. They worked out a system of six-hour shifts and doubled up on the first to see them safely out of dock and through jump – in case of any problems with it being such an old ship, LC had said. He watched what Thom was doing until he was fairly sure he could blag his way through a solo shift, sent the kid off to take first rest and sat through his watch in the control room, watching numbers scroll and hoping the life support unit wouldn't blow again. He'd never appreciated what it took to keep a ship flying. The guild worked with AIs on some of their smaller ships and as far as he knew the Alsatia had a whole legion of staff to keep the cruiser moving. He'd never had anything to do with it. And sitting here watching all this, it was a responsibility that he didn't want so instead he ran scenarios through his head, trying to figure out what he could have done differently and always coming back to the fact that Mendhel had been alive when they'd left him on Earth.

He pulled the stolen implant from his pocket. He'd tried to get into it a couple of times but his head had been too screwed up to get anywhere and he was wary about damaging it.

He sat back and stared at it, tumbling the tiny device over his fingertips. He was getting tired of running and he'd hit the end of the line at Sten's World. This implant was his only way of finding out who had taken Anya and right now, he had no chance of hacking into it. He tossed it up into the air, catching it deftly and pocketing it.

By the time Thom came back, LC was feeling jittery and ready for a change of scenery even if it meant the risk of running into people. He showered away the dirt of the engine room, grabbed a snack and tucked himself securely in the mess with a beer. DiMarco was on the bridge, flying the ship, so there was no moonshine but the beer was doing the trick. He didn't know why he hadn't thought of it sooner. It was the sugar, he reckoned, that was keeping the shakes and aches away. Pure carbohydrate and after four beers, he felt almost normal again.

Until Sean appeared at the doorway and the buzz in his head reminded him that he was far from normal.

"Hey," she said with a smile. She wandered in, took a fruit juice from the fridge and sat opposite him. "How's Thom doing?"

"He's fine."

She smiled again. "He told us what you did with the life support unit. I think you impressed him."

He downed the rest of his beer and leaned forward to put the bottle on the table, making a row of five empties, uneasy at what he was hearing. "He's easy to impress then."

"Gallagher's concerned it might happen again."

He shrugged. "It might. We're watching it." He knew he sounded hostile and he had no openly obvious reason to be.

She didn't seem to take offence, reaching over and flicking on a music channel. "How's the hand?"

He scratched absently at the bandage. "Painful," he lied. "How's DiMarco?"

Sean laughed. "He wasn't impressed that you out-drank him. You want to watch yourself with him."

LC smiled. He had to watch himself with everyone. He stood up, made his excuses and dropped the empty bottles in the disposal chute on the way out. The brief conversation had started a pounding in his head.

He was half way down the corridor when Sean called out behind him, "Hey, LC."

He turned, automatically responding to his guild nickname and freezing in horror as he realised his mistake.

6

The swirling dance of the vapour rising from the goblet was almost hypnotic. NG wrapped his hand around its stem, feeling the warmth of the wine working its way through the twisted metalwork.

The Man leaned forward. "Tell me about the laboratory."

NG let out a breath he hadn't realised he was holding. "We understand it was a research facility. Bioweapons. Earth. Off the radar. Nothing they'll admit to."

"Pah. The arrogant isolationism of man has no bounds. Imagine what these creatures could accomplish if they dared collaborate." The Man raised his goblet and drank deeply.

"Science and Legal are squabbling over the ashes," NG said. He could feel from the fumes hitting the back of his throat that the concoction was stronger than anything he'd been offered in here before. It felt as if the Man was testing him. "LC and Hil were lucky to get out alive."

The Man moved his pawn to take NG's, the first casualty. "They should have come back to us."

NG looked at the pieces on the board, each handcrafted with incredible skill, each casting a flickering shadow that gave the illusion of pent up energy, each piece eager for the chance to move. "They should have. We could have lost LC for good if O'Brien hadn't managed to catch up with him before they left."

Time slowed as he stood there, rooted to the spot, looking at her.

"It's about two hours to the rendezvous," she said softly and disappeared back into the mess.

She knew.

He made his way to his cabin, locked the door behind him and sat on his bunk, hands shaking. The noise buzzing around in his head was always worse when he was with people, and it peaked the more people there were around. He'd thought he was going insane at first, hearing snatches of words inside his head, and for a while he'd thought the implant could be malfunctioning, but it was only lately, when it was directed at him or about him, that he'd realised he could hear what people were thinking. It had given him the drop a couple of times and saved his neck twice on the orbital at Sten's World, but to see Sean looking at him and know she was thinking about the guild and people he knew, and wondering if he could have changed the colour of his eyes, was too much.

She didn't know for definite – that was the only saving grace right now. She had doubts that it was really him. He just needed to lie low and split when they got to Harbin. Whoever she was, she wasn't going to be good enough to follow him.

He rubbed his eyes, the headache beginning to wear off. He stood up and couldn't resist wandering over to look in the mirror over the small sink in the corner. His eyes were lighter than they used to be. He'd noticed it at Olivia's place. She'd teased him and asked what drugs he was on. Sean must have seen an image or a description to know they were different now and that meant she must be after the bounty.

Crap. He was stuck on a ship in deep space with a bounty hunter and reacting like that when she'd called him LC wouldn't have done his case any good if she was having doubts. He hadn't had any choice but to use his last set of ID – he hadn't been able to get anywhere near any of his drop boxes to pick up any more. But yes, using an ID with the initials LC might not have been smart.

He rubbed a hand over the back of his neck. His hair was shorter than it had ever been – Pen had told him to get it cut, if nothing else, he'd said. Why his eyes had changed, he didn't know but since the lab, he could see better in the dark, could heal inhumanly fast and now it seemed he was also immune to the effects of alcohol. And he could hear snatches of what people were thinking. As clear as if he was connected via an implant as long as they were close to him. God knows what the downsides were going to turn out to be

– apart from the excruciating cramps and agonising pain, he could drop down dead any minute. If Sean made a definite decision that it was him, he was sure she wouldn't hesitate in arranging an accident and stuffing him into cold storage for the journey back to claim the bounty. Right now his only advantage was that she had no way to extract him and clearly didn't want to share the profit.

He checked the time. Two hours. Then they'd be heading for Harbin and he could get away. No problem.

He didn't intend to fall asleep but he was exhausted. He was woken suddenly by Thom calling through the Senson and managed to get back to the engine room before they started to manoeuvre for the deep space rendezvous that McCabe had arranged. The conversation with Sean hadn't changed anything. He knew he had to get away. Hiding out in the engine room at least gave him a place to disappear until they reached a port with other ships. He reckoned he could start to double back at some point and try to figure out a way to find out what had happened to Anya. The idea of going back to the guild was one that he'd long since abandoned. He needed to talk to Hil before he could even risk thinking about that.

LC slipped into the control room, muttered something to Thom about checking the cooling system and disappeared into the depths of the engine room. There were more than a dozen blind spots down there where a guy could hide away without being seen, nowhere near any moving parts and cosy enough to spend a few hours away from any prying eyes and intrusive noise. Machines didn't think and being able to sit quietly with only his own thoughts for company gave him a chance to play the games with his breathing and heart rate that they were all trained in. He hadn't practised in weeks and it was no wonder he was so jittery.

The gentle nudge at the implant was so soft that he didn't notice it at first, only recognising it the second time when she pushed a bit more insistently. It was tempting to ignore her, but she tried again with enough force to have woken him if he'd been asleep.

"Jesus, Sean, what do you want? We're working down here."

"I think we've got a problem," she sent, almost whispering even though, wherever she was, no one else would have been able to see she was speaking to him. "We're almost at the rendezvous point and McCabe is insisting that Gallagher goes onto the other ship with him. I don't trust the man and it's obvious that Gallagher doesn't, but he won't let up."

"So what's the problem?" He didn't see it. It wasn't so much that he didn't care but he didn't have time to care. Whatever these people had going on, he was just hitching a ride.

Sean took a moment to reply, then, "Gallagher wants you to go with him."

She'd sounded genuinely anxious and if he'd thought it was more about the safety of his neck than the twenty six million price tag attached to it, then he would have been touched.

He paused at the entrance to the cargo deck. Gallagher was standing with McCabe and his two bodyguards, both of them huge guys in black fatigues, weapons holstered.

LC walked up to the group, not quite sure why he was there until he reached Gallagher and picked up on the relief the man felt simply at having someone at his side, someone armed who could handle themselves and watch his back. He smiled, realising for the first time that Gallagher might not be so ignorant about his lack of engineering skills after all.

Gallagher gestured towards the two guys. "Luka, this is Hal Duncan and Aaron Richardson. You know McCabe."

LC nodded. He recognised Hal Duncan. He was the big guy who'd stopped the fight at Danny's Bar. He looked out of place here, standing there confidently bored enough to be thinking that this was run of the mill. Richardson was more twitchy. Both of them looked like they'd done more than their fair share of military service.

McCabe was standing perfectly still and thinking nothing that he could distinguish. He'd never actively tried to read someone's thoughts and standing there waiting for the two ships to couple, he couldn't resist. It was like trying to use the implant to reach out to an AI or computer, only there were no obvious accessways, no gateways to break through or query. It was hard not to slip into using the implant itself but he was fairly sure no one else here was equipped with one. If McCabe was plotting anything, he wasn't openly thinking about it. He was picking up a vague buzzing that was giving him a headache but nothing specific, not even a hint of emotion.

The ships nudged together gently, more gently than he was sure DiMarco was capable of so it was probably the other side doing the manoeuvring. The hull rang slightly as the connection was made and after a moment, the lights on the cargo bay airlock turned green.

McCabe gestured for them to lead and they walked through and into the other ship to be greeted by heavily armed men. LC tensed. They looked an awful lot like mercenaries.

Gallagher spun around but McCabe silenced him with a raised hand. "Routine, Gallagher. My people are simply going to check the condition of the consignment before we let you go."

He waved them away from the airlock and they stood off to one side, Gallagher quietly fuming and Duncan and Richardson standing calmly with them as they waited.

It took a while for the crates to be transferred. It was freezing, cold enough to make their breath frost into white clouds. LC blew on his fingertips, glad to be cooling down, feeling like his temperature was getting somewhere near normal for the first time in as long as he could remember. He could see that Gallagher was getting more irate though, cursing each time another load was brought through and McCabe went through a show of checking each batch.

Finally Donnelly's man signed off the last of the crates, looked over at them with a smile that was way too much the wrong side of smug to be anything other than a sign that they'd been screwed, and nodded to his people. What was surprising was that Duncan and Richardson knew nothing about it. LC picked up the first hint of trouble as the mercenaries picked up the signal to draw weapons.

He shoved Gallagher into cover, pulling out his pistol and firing at the same time as McCabe's mercenaries opened up.

Duncan and Richardson jumped back, Duncan yelling and

pulling out a cannon of a gun that he aimed right at McCabe. LC felt his hesitation and in that moment, Richardson took a hit and fell. A cold pang of intense pressure popped in the very centre of LC's entire being, taking his breath away. His vision darkened, a black spark of nothing flaring behind his eyes.

He fired instinctively, an FTH round that took down one of the guys next to McCabe, as Duncan dragged his buddy behind cover.

The deck lurched suddenly. The bastards were going to pull away. Gallagher was shouting abuse at McCabe and it was all LC could do to keep him in cover and return fire at McCabe's guys. He hit another one. The guy fell, still firing, shards flying off the crate next to LC's face.

He risked leaning out to take a look. McCabe was backing away, his men covering his route from the cargo deck.

The ships shifted again.

"We have to go."

Gallagher nodded.

Duncan glanced their way. "Go," he yelled and LC moved, dragging Gallagher along with him towards the airlock.

The deck dropped out from under them as they ran, both of them stumbling. Warning sirens began to scream. Shots pitted the bulkhead in front of them, shattering the lights around the door, and the boom of a gun returning fire echoed behind them.

LC skidded up against the door and punched the button to open access, turning to aim back into the open area. Only a couple of McCabe's men were still there, firing from the cover of crates. Duncan was kneeling to check on his buddy, cursing softly. LC didn't need to look to know the guy was dead. His heart was still hammering from the shock of feeling it, that instant of void like a tiny burst of vacuum hitting the depths of his mind.

The adjoining door stayed shut.

"Sean?" he sent, urgently then, hoping she was still there to hear. He hit the button again, firing at the crates to keep their heads down.

If the ships broke away, they were screwed.

"Luka, hold on," she sent calmly.

Hold on to what, he almost yelled back. There was a bump that knocked them off their feet and the door opened with a hiss.

"Tell me when," Sean sent and LC yelled at Gallagher to go.

Duncan was firing steadily and he stood up, Richardson's body hoisted over his shoulder, and began to back towards them. LC switched targets to cover him and as soon as they were in the airlock, he hit the button to close the door. It slammed shut with a shudder that reverberated through the deck.

They turned and ran.

He yelled a go to Sean as soon as they set foot on the Duck, the airlock cycling shut behind them. She didn't reply but the ship lurched beneath their feet as the engines fired and broke them lose, the entire bulk of the vessel complaining. LC grabbed for a hold but nothing came to hand. He tumbled across the deck and crashed up against a crate. He curled up and rolled with it, hearing curses and muffled grunts behind him.

He could feel the pull of the acceleration as the ship moved, rumbles echoing through the cargo deck. A distant boom vibrated through the hull.

It sounded like an explosion. LC cringed and struggled to get to his feet. "Sean?"

She didn't reply. Another impact and the ship rolled. He staggered, clinging to the side of the crate, trying to see where Gallagher and the big guy had ended up.

Sean's voice was quiet and strained when she did answer. "Hold on, Luka. They're firing missiles at us."

LC almost laughed out loud. He'd run half way across the galaxy and he was going to die because a small time double-crossing crook wanted to make a fast buck on a drugs run. Christ, he should have told McCabe who he was and taken his chances.

Another explosion rocked the ship. He stood up and shouted out to Gallagher.

"I'm fine," Gallagher yelled back.

LC looked around. They needed to get off the cargo deck.

He'd taken two steps away from the crate when Sean whispered inside his head. "Oh my god, LC, grab hold of something, we're going into jump."

7

"The sheer scale of human greed baffles me," the Man said, disdain dripping off each word. "Earth and Winter stand aloof, dictating laws they cannot police to colonies they cannot control. Decent men driven to desperation and scoundrels given the perfect impetus to profiteer. I despair."

NG risked a sip of the wine and felt his head spin as the substance hit his bloodstream. He gave the Man time to rage, feeling the anger intensified, anger that the guild had been put in this position. That tiny hit of intoxication fuelled his foolhardiness. He drank more, recklessly, sharing the frustration. They worked hard to set plays into motion, throughout the galaxy. And one move by an individual that dared the effrontery to take on the guild itself had jeopardised so much.

He moved his bishop.

"They can't see past tomorrow," he said. "We can because we know. How can we expect them to see past their immediate gains when they can't even imagine what may be coming." He drank again. It was hard to be the single human in the whole galaxy who knew, who had seen in the mind of the being sitting there in front of him the horrors of the attack to come. The Man was manipulating humanity at the very heart of its genetics and complex social interactions in order to prepare it for an onslaught that was as inevitable and impending as the next breath.

The Man looked up, eyes piercing. "Their selfish pursuit of gain may well destroy them before we have a chance to act."

It was dark. LC lay still, too many parts hurting to pinpoint anything specific. Usually a jump through hyperspace was a fast, vague discomfort spent securely restrained within the confines of a chair to cushion the body against the forces of the manoeuvre. That was the first time he'd ever done it in freefall and the last time he ever wanted to.

The ship felt steady. He could feel a constant, quiet hum through the deck beneath him. They were moving and no one was shooting at them.

A sudden cramp squeezed the muscles in the small of his back and a throbbing ache moved into his neck. Oh crap.

He closed his eyes.

The touch at his elbow was soft and when he heard Sean speaking quietly, he didn't know if she was talking out loud, using the implant or thinking to herself. He didn't know how to respond and it felt too much like effort to open his eyes so he lay there and waited for the deck to stop spinning.

"Luka," she said again, touching his cheek that time, a warm soft caress.

He shivered and looked up. He was still on the deck of the cargo bay.

"Where's Gallagher?" he asked quietly, not liking the echo he was hearing as he spoke.

"He's fine. So's our guest. A bit battered but they're up on their feet." Which is better than you are, she was thinking.

He took a deep breath. "Help me up," he said. "I need a beer."

"You might have a concussion," she said gently. "You took quite a knock to the head. Is anything hurt?"

My ego, he thought. But as much as he felt sore all over and the shakes were threatening to start, he didn't feel like there was any serious damage.

He sat up, blinked away a swirl of vertigo behind his eyes and looked around. His gun was lying just out of reach. He leaned over and grabbed it.

"I'm fine. C'mon, help me up."

She took hold of his arm and helped him up onto his feet. He felt a cold sweat break out as he tried not to keel over and throw up.

"Where are we?" he whispered. "And why the hell did DiMarco throw us into jump without any warning?"

"He didn't."

LC felt his knees start to go. "Let me sit down," he mumbled and half fell back onto the deck. Sean eased him down and sat behind him so he could lean back, shivering. She wrapped her arms around him and the warmth was welcome so he didn't complain.

"What do you mean, he didn't?" he said. "Why…?"

"Neither of us initiated it," she said. "Something overrode the controls – we had no say in it, believe me. DiMarco is furious."

"So where are we?"

"On route to Poule, of all places. The ship jumped itself to within two hours of the station. Gallagher swears he knows nothing about it. There isn't an AI as far as he knows. He's going up there now to talk to DiMarco." She felt his forehead. "What are we going to do with you?"

"Give me a minute." Apart from Hil, the only people to see him like this had been Pen and Olivia. He hoped to hell it wasn't going to be as bad as then. He tried to control his breathing and felt his eyes starting to close.

Sean shook him gently awake. "I don't think sleeping is a good idea. Come on, let's get you up top."

She was thinking about Zach Hilyer and it was weird to eavesdrop. He caught a fleeting image from her of Hil lying in the dark. Pen had told him they both had a price on their heads for what they'd done. He'd thought Hil was safe there on Aston with Pen and it was chilling to think that a bounty hunter could have caught up with him.

"I need a beer," he said again.

She laughed, pleased with herself for some reason he didn't understand but he didn't really give a shit why.

"You need something," she said, smiling. "I'm not sure it's alcohol."

He managed to make it to the mess without passing out. Sean was still thinking about Hil, images flashing through her mind, and it was creeping him out to think that she might have cashed in on him already.

She left LC with a blanket, a squeezy pouch of drinking water and a sheet of painkillers, and disappeared, saying she was heading to the bridge. Once she'd gone, he sat quietly for a moment then staggered to his feet, threw the tablets in the garbage chute and grabbed three bottles of beer.

He was half way through the third and trying to think what he knew about Poule when Gallagher and Duncan walked in, in the middle of a heated exchange about McCabe and Donnelly, Gallagher holding a cold pack to his head.

LC winced with the onslaught of emotion that he caught from the two of them.

Gallagher misread the look on his face. "Jesus, Luka, you look like shit. Should you be drinking?"

He actually felt a lot better. Tired though. He was aching all down his right-hand side and the knot in his lower back hadn't completely gone yet. He was half hoping DiMarco would appear with his moonshine.

"That was a hell of a tumble you took across the cargo deck," Gallagher said, sitting down. He had a bruise himself across his forehead. He rubbed it. "Damned if I know what happened. DiMarco thinks I'm lying but I swear, there's no AI. I couldn't really afford the Duck as she is, never mind if she had an AI."

Duncan sat down and rested his arms on his knees, rubbing a hand across his eyes. "We have to get back to Sten's World," he said wearily like he knew he'd lost the argument already. "Donnelly needs to know what happened."

Gallagher shook his head. "We took too much damage. We're limping into Poule as it is. One of our main engine vents was hit." He looked at LC. "Thom said he's working on it but he can't fix something or other until we stop. I told the kid to manage. I didn't think you'd be in a fit state to go down there and help. Here, you look like you need this more than me." He threw across the cold pack.

LC caught it and held it against the back of his neck, feeling the chill spread through his strained muscles. He balanced his beer on his knee and leaned back, shifting slightly to ease the aches. Thom would have to manage – he didn't want to move. "So what happened?"

"According to DiMarco, the shields were down," Gallagher said. "Completely. One more hit and we would've been toast. He had nothing. With thrusters out, we couldn't manoeuvre and we were too close to their mass to risk jump."

"But we did."

"DiMarco says an AI butted in and jumped us out. We were too close to the other ship. He's right. It wasn't safe. But I swear, there's no AI. He's quit."

LC almost choked on a mouthful of beer. "He what?"

"Quit, stood down. Stomped off the bridge and said he wouldn't fly with a bastard AI for a lying bastard like me." Gallagher shrugged. "There's no AI. The guy's off his head. I knew he was a drunk but he was the only licensed pilot I could find who'd fly without an AI. Ironic, isn't it?"

Duncan looked up. "So who's flying the ship now?"

"Sean at the minute – our navigator," Gallagher said. "She said she can get us to Poule. The jump took us within two hours of the station. We're already catching grief from the controllers for breaking safety parameters. For god's sake, of all the places to jump us to." He paused and rubbed at his forehead again. "I don't know what we're going to do after that."

LC closed his eyes.

"Donnelly's going to be pissed, right?" he heard Gallagher say.

"Aaron was his nephew – he's going to be more than pissed," Duncan said quietly.

LC heard the pop of a bottle top. Another beer would be good, he thought vaguely, but couldn't bring himself to lift so much as a finger. The sofa in the mess was more comfortable than the bunk in his cabin.

He could still feel the emotion from the two men sitting alongside him, with snatches of phrases here and there and a mix of conversation interspersed with private thoughts. Gallagher was worried about the repair bill and terrified of McCabe. Hal Duncan was more enigmatic, angry but a simmering anger that was understated like he didn't want to bitch about his boss's business in front of strangers.

LC wasn't even tempted to join in. He let the words flow through his mind and let his breathing slow, heart rate dropping about as low as it could go. He relaxed completely. They were in deep space, well into the Between, as far from the incident at the lab as he could be, and with people who were only concerned with the politics of petty small time gangsters. He was fairly sure Sean wouldn't try anything while Gallagher was there. For some reason she didn't want to blow her cover. She probably didn't want to share the bounty.

The voices faded.

What could go wrong?

He opened one eye. The crew's mess was dark and quiet. Someone had taken the beer bottle and thrown a blanket over him. The ship was still. They weren't moving.

He felt a hand touch his arm and sat up with a start.

"Hey, it's just me," someone whispered. "We've got a problem."

LC ran a hand over the back of his neck. "How long ago?"

"Just a few minutes," Thom said. "Sean's been trying to get in touch with you. She's furious."

He rubbed at the cool spot where the implant lay beneath the skin. He didn't understand why he hadn't woken up. He'd slept through the whole docking procedure.

A headache was starting to throb at his temples. "Why didn't Gallagher realise something was wrong?"

Thom shrugged. "I think he did. He wanted you to go with him but Sean said let you get some rest. You were crashed out, Luka. She said you must need it. She offered to go instead but Gallagher said he'd be fine."

"And the station just said he had to report to the office?"

"We couldn't get any response to our request to book in for repairs," Thom said nervously, cracking his knuckles and pacing up and down in the small space of the mess. "Gallagher said he had no choice but to go onto the station to sort it out. I went back to the engine room to sort out that son of a bitch coupling unit and the next thing I know, Sean's calling me and saying he's been arrested. I didn't even know she had a wire and suddenly she's yelling at me out of nowhere."

A wire was what the Earth military called an implant. LC hadn't heard it called that in a long time. Thom didn't look like a soldier but it was possible the kid was a drop out. Plenty of kids from Earth ditched out on their year of conscription by bugging out to the Between. But drop out grunts weren't kitted out with expensive personal communications gear.

Curious.

He looked up. "Where's DiMarco?"

The look on Thom's face was a picture. His immediate thought at the mention of the pilot almost made LC laugh.

"Arrested," Thom said. "He left the ship and got picked up straight away."

LC tried to get his head straight. All he knew about Poule was that it was an even worse place than Sten's World – a tough as they came corporate-run mining colony that used convicts as labour, without caring too much who'd convicted them or for what, and a vicious strain of vodka that was rumoured to be toxic if drunk neat. DiMarco would be right at home.

Why they'd refuse repairs and arrest half the crew, he didn't know. He only took notice of current affairs when they had the potential to impinge on a tab and even then he didn't do the kind of research some of them did to get to know the ins and outs of where they were going. He always tended to wing it.

"Where's Duncan?" he said.

"On the bridge. He's trying to find out what's happening."

LC sat for a moment, reaching out to find Sean. She was furious and even through the link her voice threatened to spark the headache up again.

"This place is a shit-hole that has no idea how the rest of the universe operates," she fumed.

LC summoned every ounce of patience he had. "Where are you? Is Gallagher alright?"

"I'm on the bridge. They've impounded the ship and they're holding Gallagher and DiMarco in an interrogation room up in the station. God, these bastards have no idea."

"Sean, it's Poule – what did you expect? You should have woken me up."

She didn't reply and for a moment he thought she'd gone but then she said, "Luka, just come up to the bridge. Something hinky's going on. God, these people are stupid bastards."

"Why have they arrested Gallagher?"

"How the hell would I know?" she snapped back. "Oh, for god's sake, I have to go. Just get up here."

The connection disappeared abruptly. LC looked at Thom. "You have any ideas?"

Thom shook his head. "The only thing I've ever heard about Poule is that it's a shit-hole."

"No kidding."

Field-ops didn't usually get sent to places like Poule; they rarely ever contained anything of value. And if they did have to go anywhere this precarious, they usually had an extraction team or two watching their ass. He felt painfully alone and at the same time surrounded, almost claustrophobically, by people who for some reason were depending on him to pull a trick out of the bag and save them. It was upside down. He didn't work well with people. Even Hil, who'd always obsessed about chasing him for that top spot, had never asked him for anything. And he'd never asked Hil for anything – until that last run.

"Luka?" Thom said, expectantly, as if LC was the only one who could sort this out.

He sat for a moment grinding his palms over his eyes then stood up. The aches had pretty much gone but he felt like he could sleep for another week. "Let's get up to the bridge."

Thom nodded and headed for the door.

There was a clatter from the end of the corridor. LC paused, aware suddenly of a distant buzz in his head. There were people out there where there shouldn't have been.

"Thom, wait," he whispered, too late to stop the kid from stepping out into the corridor.

There was a yell then a shout to stop, and he could see Thom glance both ways, hesitantly raising his hands.

LC froze. He could hear weapons and the clatter of armour.

He grabbed his gun from the table and looked up. He already had a route mapped out in his head. He clambered onto the shelf above the sofa and thrust open a panel above his head, hoisting himself up and into the ventilation shaft, and dropping the panel gently back into place as the first of the intruders pushed their way into the mess.

He watched quietly as they searched the area, declared it clear then left. They were wearing uniforms with insignia he didn't recognise. Private militia probably, the kind of mercenary units the corporations hired. The chances that this had anything to do with him were slim but not totally impossible. Twenty six million was a lot of money and Pen had warned him that there were parties interested who wouldn't normally pursue a bounty.

He waited until they were gone and then eased his way carefully into the main shaft. The schematics he'd pulled up in the engine room had shown a ventilation system that wormed its way through the whole ship with access to the engine room and the bridge. If he went to the engine room, they'd have to tear the place apart to find him. If he went to the bridge, he could find Duncan and Sean.

He tentatively reached out to Thom, hoping the kid was smart enough not to react. An implant wasn't a run of the mill piece of kit and if Sean was right, whatever reason the kid had for having one should mean he knew how to use it.

There was no response.

He tried Sean.

"We know," she replied curtly. "We're tracking them but I can't find a way to stop them. If this ship does have an AI, I'm damned sure I can't find it. Can you get up here? We've managed to isolate the bridge."

He kept the link open and climbed through into the central core. "How many are on board?" he asked at one point, pausing as he heard movement in the ship below him.

"Five," Sean replied. "Two have Thom at the airlock. The other three are searching. Hal's trying to figure out what the hell they think we've done but we're having trouble getting access to anything. Oh shit, Luka, move, they're closing in on you."

He ran, ducking under pipes, squeezing through vents and climbing anywhere he could get a handhold, reckoning that the engine room might be a good idea after all. If he could reach the control room, he might be able to get back into the ship's systems.

He worked his way round and sat quietly above the main access. If they were using thermals and bioelectrics, the equipment in the engine room might cause enough interference to screw their sensors.

"Sean," he whispered through the link, "where are they?"

She didn't reply and for a moment he felt strangely abandoned. He always worked alone and he wasn't used to having anyone there for him so it was weird to find himself depending on her. He shook it off, broke the connection and sat and listened.

He finally decided he was clear to move and as he got to his feet, he felt just enough of a sense of someone behind him to roll out of the way as a flashlight lit up the conduit and a small object clattered past. He ducked away as the concussion flash went off, catching the edge of it and half falling down a ladder to get away.

There were voices then, behind and up ahead, and he had no choice but to drop down into the corridor. He landed, got his balance and turned to run. An armoured figure at the corner down the hallway had a gun aimed at him already. He cursed and as he turned away, an agonising shock hit him square in the back. He fell to his knees, managed to stagger to his feet and took two steps forward before another shot hit him in the chest.

8

The Man swept his queen across the board, aggressive play to place NG's king in check. "The state of the colonies in the Between will be crucial in the coming times." He sat back, hands together, fingers laced over his chest and paused, eyes almost closed, thinking. "Tell me about Poule."

NG sipped at his wine, trying to figure out the cascading consequences of the potential moves he could make. The Man didn't tolerate an opponent that did not commit. It was as difficult as trying to work out what to say. He'd been horrified to learn that LC had been drawn into the cesspit that was Poule. The corporations pushed the limits of human decency and the normal bounds of civilised operations in places like Poule.

"Last we heard it was being run by United Metals. Wintran. They acquired it from Zang in a hostile, and violent, takeover some time back." He put the goblet down next to the candle, the vapour rising in a twisting swirl with the smoke from the wick. He paused and waited for the Man to look up. "We have no influence in that sector."

The Man swept a hand over the chessboard. "We normally have the luxury of choosing where we play our pieces, NG. It's when we don't, when other forces interfere, that our operatives show their true instinct for survival."

It felt like his heart stopped with the impact. He fell back, neurons sparking uncontrollably, and lay there, excruciating pain spreading through every inch of his body.

They ran up, footsteps echoing through the deck. "Son of a bitch took two shots to go down," one of them said, nudging him in the side. "And he's still not out."

He still had a loose hold on the pistol but he couldn't get his fingers to obey and tighten on the trigger. They kicked his hand and the gun skittered across the deck. He'd never been hit with an FTH before but Hil had bitched about them enough for him to recognise it. He could feel the effects wearing off already but before he could fight back, they rolled him over, one of them grabbing the back of his neck and pushing him down. They roughly pulled his arms behind his back, clamped something around his wrists, hauled him to his feet and told him to walk.

He called out silently to Thom and Sean, trying to get a reply from someone.

There was nothing from Thom.

Sean just hissed, "Give me a minute."

She sounded stressed.

Whatever, it sucked and he wasn't going to get caught this easily. He tested the restraints. They felt like simple plasticuffs, the kind anyone else needed a knife to break and the kind he could snap out of in seconds, but as he twisted his arm slightly, one of the guys shoved him brusquely and wrapped a fist around his wrists, catching both in one firm grip.

They marched him to the airlock where Thom was waiting, similarly restrained and looking miserable, flanked by two other uniforms, more mercenaries from the look of them.

He could see a patch on the side of Thom's neck that explained why the kid hadn't answered. LC tried to give Thom an encouraging look but the kid just slumped his shoulders and shook his head, like he knew he should have done better.

LC was pulled to a halt and one of the grunts waved a broad wand up and down to check him over. It beeped at his wrist and the guy roughly twisted his arm to check that the band there was harmless. It beeped again, higher in pitch, as it passed over his neck.

They slapped a patch over the implant, negating it completely and isolating him from any contact but the constant buzz in his head from the proximity of the group. He couldn't pick out anything specific and he didn't try. They were working to orders and didn't care about anything other than securing the ship and taking the crew up to the security deck on the station. It wasn't routine.

He tried to shrug free from the guy holding his arm and got a slap to the back of the head. He shifted his feet slightly, subtly adjusting his balance, and looked sideways at the guy holding him. "Don't you people knock?"

"Funny," the guy who seemed to be in charge said, taking a step closer then turning to the others. "Watch this one."

Someone grabbed LC's shoulder and thrust him forward into the airlock. They crowded in behind and he felt the ship's artificially controlled gravity vanish with a lurch, his weight suddenly gone and his feet off the floor, stomach turning. There were shouts and curses, weapons raised, and for a minute he thought that was it. The hand on his shoulder squeezed hard but as quickly as it had gone, the gravity was back, magnified and as one they all crashed to the deck.

The pressure was almost unbearable. Someone landed on top of his legs and their weight was immense. No one could move to even complain. He felt the panic from the bodies lying around him and pulled out all the tricks he knew to slow his own breathing, taking as much oxygen as he could from the limited breaths he could manage. He couldn't see Thom but he could sense the kid kicking in a concerted effort to stay calm; someone somewhere had trained him well.

It felt like it lasted an age then as it began to lift, he heard a quiet command to stay still and twisted his head round to see Hal Duncan standing in the corridor, covering them with a massive pistol aimed steadily at the centre of the group.

"Cole, Garrett, get up," he said quietly.

The gravity was still higher than usual and it was tough to get free, get to his knees and struggle to a stand. The guys in armour had it even harder and even though a few of them were wriggling, they weren't going to jump up and grab their weapons in a hurry.

LC made it to the doorway. Stepping through was like falling into a cloud. He gasped in a breath and twisted his hand in a dextrous movement that freed it from the plasticuff with a snap.

Thom crawled through and got to his knees as he made it into the normal gravity. LC pulled the knife out of his boot and took hold of Thom's wrists, freeing them from their bindings.

"We need to go," Duncan said, backing away from the airlock.

"No arguments there," LC muttered and followed him, keeping the knife in his hand and casting a glance back at the militia pinned to the deck. He didn't care who they were so long as he was free.

The airlock door slammed shut behind them trapping the intruders and isolating the ship from the station.

When they reached the bridge, LC took the seat at the main control panel. He'd already torn the patch off his neck and he hooked straight in to the ship, no messing. If there was an AI, he wanted to find it.

"What are we doing with those guys?" Thom asked behind him.

Duncan edged into the seat next to LC. "They can stay where they are."

LC hit the barrier he'd encountered earlier and winced as it shut him out with a spike. He tried again and the surge that was fired back at him sent his vision spinning into black for a moment. He sat back with a soft curse.

"What are you doing?" he heard Thom say and heard Duncan hush him gently.

He tried a different route and came up against the same wall, nudging it this time and sending a query spiralling around it. The guild had experts in the best systems available. They built some of the most sophisticated systems out there and they trained the field-ops in how to break them. Half the tabs they ran were to acquire insubstantials, information, data, nothing you could fit into a neat package, but more valuable than most of the kit they were sent after. He'd been taught by the best and he was one of the best they had.

This system was like nothing he'd ever encountered.

He took a risk and delved deeper, reckless and careless, ignoring the fact that he had no safe route out.

Time stopped.

LC closed his eyes and felt the shift. It let him in and opened up access to the entire ship and the whole station. Something was wrong. The security level on the station was too high.

He nudged. Information suddenly streamed at him faster than he could process. He tried to slow the flow and felt it fight him, as if something was saying, you wanted this, well here it is. He tried to track through the station to find Gallagher and DiMarco but he was dragged back to the docks, an array of data from every ship berthed there flowing in so fast that he couldn't distinguish one vessel from the next.

He switched again and tried to infiltrate the station, this time easily homing in on Gallagher and a whirl of security data that was too much to comprehend. He concentrated, got the information he needed and pulled back abruptly to the Duck, probing gently at the ship itself and nudging towards its heart, querying the core systems. It was delicate going and just as he felt its curiosity, the connection froze.

He realised with a jolt how precarious his position was and when he tried to back out, it stopped him. He felt it take hold and then he couldn't move, couldn't so much as blink. His internal temperature started to rise and breathing got hard.

He pushed back. "What the hell are you?" he thought at it, mentally or through the implant, he wasn't sure.

"This is quite a risk you're taking," a soft voice whispered. "Why?"

"I don't like being told I can't go somewhere," he replied, feeling his blood pressure rise.

"I could kill you."

"I don't care."

"I think you do. Who are you?"

"Why did you bring us here? Why here?"

"Why not?"

It increased the pressure and it felt like every blood vessel in his head was going to burst. LC tried to back out again. He pulled away gently then broke free suddenly, giving it no chance to react.

He jerked back in his seat. "Holy crap," he muttered.

He was sweating and hot, shaking. Thom was hovering and Sean was staring, a curious expression on her face and a weird mix of regret and anxiety in the emotions she was throwing out. She was thinking it was a shame and LC looked her in the eye, biting his tongue not to ask what it was she thought was such a shame.

"Did you find them?" Duncan said.

LC shook his head. "Gallagher's in a detention cell but I can't see DiMarco anywhere. Station security is being run by a unit of mercenaries and they're twitchy as hell about something." He stood up, unsteady on his feet for a moment. "DiMarco was right," he added. "There's an AI. Is that how you fixed the trick with the gravity down there?"

Duncan shook his head. "It wasn't us. That was your tech guy."

"What tech guy?"

"Tall guy, really pale. He said he'd fix it if I got down there to cover you."

"We don't have a tech guy." LC turned to Thom. "Do we?"

"No," the kid said. "But we thought we didn't have an AI. Why has Gallagher been lying to us?"

"He hasn't," said a voice at the door.

They turned. LC squinted at the figure standing there, disturbed that he hadn't felt anything. He thought he was getting pretty good at sensing the presence of people, even if he didn't pick up any direct thoughts or emotions. He got nothing from the guy, who looked almost shy, hesitating to enter the bridge.

"You're the tech guy?" Thom said, walking over, confrontational. "Why didn't Gallagher introduce us? We need to know if an AI is going to screw around with the engines when we're working down there."

"Thom," LC said, cautiously.

The kid was full flow and didn't stop. "Why didn't Gallagher tell us he had someone on board working with an AI? We could have been hurt. It threw us into jump with no warning. Luka here," he waved at LC, "was hurt."

"Thom," LC interrupted and looked at the newcomer. "Gallagher doesn't know you're here, does he?"

He still couldn't sense anything from the guy; even tentatively reaching out with the Senson there was nothing. Beside him, Thom was getting more agitated.

The guy shrugged nervously. "I didn't have anywhere else to go. I was still on board when Gallagher bought the ship. It's a big ship and he didn't look too hard." He glanced at Thom. "I was just trying to help."

"How could Gallagher not know about an AI?" Thom said, still defiant.

The guy seemed uncertain like he wasn't sure how much to say. "He assumed the ship didn't have one at the price he paid and, like I said, he didn't look too hard at what he'd bought. I'm Elliott." He stuck out his hand.

LC reached forward reluctantly and shook it. The guy's hand was cold, pale and cold. "Luka," he said. "Thom and Hal. That's Sean."

"I know," Elliott said. He gestured towards the console. "May I?"

Thom got out of the way to make room and they let the tech guy hook up with the ship and start to feed data onto the screens. A lot of the information was familiar and it had taken LC a hell of a lot more effort to get it. He watched with a detached curiosity.

One of the screens showed a view of the ship's main airlock with the five guys who'd come on board, sitting or pacing up and down, looking furious.

Duncan leaned over to peer at the monitor. "What are the chances those guys contacted anyone?"

"They didn't," Elliott said with quiet confidence. "And they're shielded now. They're not going anywhere until I let them loose."

LC stood back, watching them flick through the screens. He didn't know what to make of Elliott and felt vulnerable without a gun to hand. It was disturbing that he couldn't sense anything from the guy. Worse than that, it felt like there was a void sitting right there in front of him.

He rubbed the spot at the centre of his chest where he'd been hit by the FTH. It was still sore and the back of his head was pounding.

He was tired, unsettled by the encounter with the AI and he couldn't help distrusting this tech guy who'd turned up from nowhere.

He looked over at Sean who was still watching him. She was thinking about Hilyer again and trying to figure out how she could have been wrong – they were so alike. She was wondering where LC Anderton could be and was angry with herself for wasting so much time here. She'd decided she had the wrong guy. No wonder she was so pissed.

LC choked back a laugh, turning it into a cough that turned into a real cough, sending sparks piercing through his head. Somehow he'd managed to fail an ID check on himself. If they could make it back to Sten's World, she'd split and he'd be free. He could jump on a ride going anywhere, get back to Pen. It was tempting to try to persuade them to take the ship and go, just bust out of there right now.

But for some reason, he felt obligated to Gallagher. The guy reminded him of Mendhel in that unassumingly easy way he was happy to accept LC's abilities and more than willing to overlook his blatant disregard for protocol and procedures. LC knew fine well how much of a pain he'd been to Mendhel, and somehow Gallagher gave him that same sense of security. Like even if he screwed up, he'd still be welcome.

He felt caught between lives.

"Wait up," Duncan said, tapping at a screen. "What the hell is that?"

LC stepped forward to look at the information Elliott scrolled onto the monitor.

"Orders to impound the ship," the tech guy said.

"They're running a hefty security force for a mining colony and repair dock," Duncan said. "Who is it registered to?"

Elliott flashed up another screen. "Right now? United Metals. Wintran."

Duncan pointed at another set of orders. "They've issued arrest warrants for the whole crew. Who the hell do they think we are?"

LC stared at the screen, a bad feeling gnawing at his stomach. "We need to get Gallagher out."

Elliott swung round. "We all need to get out unless you want to end up joining the volunteer labour force on the surface."

"They couldn't get away with that," Thom said.

"This is the Between," Elliott said. "They can do anything they want. Who are we going to complain to?"

9

The flame of the candle was creating a perfect corona that contaminated the darkness in the chamber with a glowing sphere. The Man sat, an imposing figure, at its edge.

"This freighter upon which our operative found himself," he said, "tell me more. It intrigues me."

"Science are eager to get their hands on it," NG said, careful to understate the fact. Science were more than eager. It had become an obsession. He moved the king to safety. "As soon as we started to hear the rumours, they started coming up with theories. As far as we know, it has an AI that is nothing like anything we've encountered before. Legal are trying to find out where the ship came from but they can't find anything, no registered history beyond its sudden appearance at Sten's World, no papers of origin, no certificates of ownership before William Gallagher. It's as if it didn't exist."

The Man considered the board, leaning forward, one hand cupped around the bowl of his goblet. "This is the Between," he said finally, moving a pawn. "Is it not teeming with undocumented ships and undesirable individuals?"

"It is," NG said, sitting back and feeling a trickle of sweat run down his back. His head was pounding. "But everything and everyone leaves a trail somewhere."

Hal Duncan disappeared for twenty minutes and came back to the bridge holding an assault rifle and a kit bag. "Courtesy of our mercenary friends," he said with a smile.

Thom stood up. "What's the plan?" he said nervously.

"How badly is the ship damaged?"

LC watched as Thom glanced at him then Elliott before he

replied. "Some of the manoeuvring thrusters are out and one of the main propulsion vents took a direct hit. There's nothing I can do about those without a dock facility. The starboard aft shield generator overloaded and needs parts we don't carry. There are a few other systems down but redundancy and back up can take care of those. Hull integrity is still good. We can still fly, sort of, but our biggest problem is that one of the primary heat exchangers was hit and we've lost a lot of coolant. I've managed to bypass a few things that have kept us running but unless we can replace it, we aren't going anywhere."

"Can we get any here?"

"Sure, this is a repair dock facility, they've got tonnes of the stuff. I just need to get it on board, but the systems are all automated and they're not just going to give us any, are they?"

Elliott stepped in then. "That won't be a problem."

Duncan nodded. "Garrett, you stay here with Elliott and work on the repairs. O'Brien and Cole come with me. We get our crew back and we leave." He looked at LC. "You have an implant."

It wasn't a question but LC nodded. How could he deny it after hooking up with the AI like that right in front of them?

Duncan looked at Elliott. "Can you establish a secure link that will reach us out there?"

Elliott smiled. "What grade is it?"

Elliott was still a blank void standing in front of him and LC couldn't read anything from the man. The Senson was an expensive piece of kit, way above anything a ship's engineer should have. He didn't know these people and he didn't trust anyone.

"Senson Four," he said. It was a Six but they didn't need to know that.

"Impressive," Elliott said. "That'll do." He nodded at Sean. "We'll be able to reach you both everywhere except security – they have that shielded. Get me access through a terminal and I can help you with station systems so far but you'll have to break into the security level manually."

Thom caught LC's eye. "A Senson Four?" he whispered incredulously.

LC shrugged. Duncan pulled a holstered pistol and a small pouch out of the bag.

"Take these." The big man was thinking through the plan to reach Gallagher like it was a military operation, curiosity and some apprehension about the new company he was keeping, as if he wasn't sure about trusting someone else to watch his back but he didn't think he had any choice. LC couldn't help but overhear regret over Richardson, snatches of emotion that Duncan was trying to push aside, that he didn't want to hear. He could pick up the thoughts clearly, the heightened emotions almost amplifying the effect. It was hard to ignore.

He took the pouch and flipped it open. It held three micro concussion grenades. He didn't need to take any extra kit and he'd never, ever needed to resort to flash bombs to get into anything but if they were there, and if it made Duncan feel better, why not? The gun was loaded with live rounds but he strapped the holster to his thigh and clipped the pouch to his belt.

When he looked up, Sean was watching him again. She was wearing a jacket over an armoured vest and had a gun strapped to the thigh of each leg. She was thinking how much she had wanted him to be the one. With no hint of the reward, simply wanting to find him. She flashed on NG and that made his breath stick in his throat. How could she know NG? She'd run a DNA test while he was crashed out asleep after the jump, he realised, listening in to a torrent of thoughts as she stood there. And the DNA hadn't matched the profile she'd been given – by NG.

Memories clicked into place, Pen saying trust no one – not even the guild. It made him feel sick.

"We go in fast," Duncan was saying. "And avoid all contact if we can. Have you done anything like this before?"

LC nodded. Not that it was anything he could explain. He was Thieves' Guild. He could get into anywhere. He'd broken into Science within his first few weeks on board the Alsatia, thirteen years old, bored and curious, no one keeping too close an eye on him yet and everyone underestimating what he could do. And that had been before they gave him any training and equipment.

He watched Duncan's face, overhearing the emotion rather than specific thoughts. Richardson had been a close friend, same unit. LC picked up flashes of a war zone that made him think of his own childhood. It was too personal and he didn't know how to shut it out. He checked the magazine on his pistol again just to do something.

"Put this on," Duncan said, holding out a vest.

LC shook his head. They were too cumbersome. He was wearing layers with enough light armour to deflect shrapnel and a vest would just slow him down. "I'll be fine."

"Put it on," Sean said, resigned like she'd accepted that she had no choice and no way of leaving without helping them.

He conceded and took off his jacket, shrugging into the vest and pulling the straps tight. Thom helped him back into his jacket. He had to bite back a flash of irritation; he wasn't used to such a team effort.

Elliott flashed up a schematic once they were ready. "These are the terminals you need to access," he said.

LC glanced at the screen and nodded.

"Any will do," Elliott said. "Get me into one of those and I can hook into the station."

Sean stood with her hands on her hips. "What's the plan to get in?"

Elliott smiled, a sly creasing of his thin mouth. It was unnerving not to be able to read any emotion from the man.

"You're all geared up ready for a fight," Elliott said, shyly. "Let's give them one."

He brought up a view of the station's main concourse, bleak holding cages imprisoning an assortment of deadbeats. He panned the view around, zooming in on the faces leaning against the bars. There was a mix of despair and outright belligerence, jeers as the guards patrolled.

"They're waiting to be shipped down to the mines," Elliott said. "There's already two shuttles full of them about to depart. Convicts, killers, deserters. Looks like UM are upping production."

Sean looked uneasy.

Duncan narrowed his eyes, guessing what Elliott was going to suggest.

"If you walk out onto that station now, security is just going to pick you up no matter how well armed you are," the tech guy said. "Give me ten minutes and I can cause enough chaos out there that you'll be able to walk right through it and they won't have time to give you a second glance."

LC nodded and looked from Duncan to Sean.

"Gallagher's a good man," Duncan said.

"Yes, he is."

"So let's go get him. Elliott, do it."

It was like running a tab and if it hadn't been for the big guy at his side and the bounty hunter just behind them, LC could have almost thought the last few weeks hadn't happened. They'd watched as Elliott coordinated a mass breakout, disrupting the station systems he could reach and setting the station security on an instant back footing. Duncan had been impressed. "Get me access to the core system," Elliott had said to LC, "and it'll be even more impressive."

They'd watched the prisoners make the most of their newly-found freedom and the mercenaries, taken by surprise, withdraw to stage a defence. The docks were chaotic at first then the fighting shifted, moving into the station as the prisoners ran riot. After that it was easy to time an exit from the ship and make a run for it.

Hal Duncan moved quietly for his size and had a calm alertness that reminded LC of the extraction agents of the guild, a confidence in their own ability that bordered on arrogance, setting them aside from the grunts of the Alsatia's Security teams.

LC reached the exit gates first and ducked beneath the barriers. He paused and scanned the area ahead, waiting to make sure it was empty, nowhere near as cocky as he had been getting about knowing where people were since he'd run into Elliott. There were too many shadows to be sure but he couldn't sense anyone nearby, except Duncan and Sean following up behind.

He waited for them then they moved on carefully. Twice they

heard voices, relying on Thom and Elliott to guide them around in a diversion to avoid a confrontation, and eventually they reached the central hub of the orbital. Poule was a typical rundown, stretched to its limit, hole of a station that was operated barely within safety parameters by a corporation that was more interested in profits than its people or the suckers they were trafficking. LC found a maintenance hatch, whispered softly to them to keep watch, and bust open the lock.

The central shaft should have been condemned and Sean looked in dismay at the dilapidated ladders that ran around its walls. LC hooked an arm around a rung and leaned out, looking up.

"The lift looks like it's stuck up there," he said quietly. "We should be okay to climb. You good?"

Duncan holstered his gun. "I don't know how the hell you can see that far but I'll take your word for it."

They climbed. It was good to stretch his muscles again after so long stuck on a ship and LC moved quickly, reaching up and hauling himself over gaps in the ladders, enjoying a strength and suppleness that felt like he'd taken a shot of the wacky drugs the extraction teams used. That stuff could make you feel invincible and he was feeling close to that now. As long as the shakes didn't kick in.

He perched on a ledge, waiting for them to catch up and reached out to Thom.

"They're pulling reinforcements from the surface," the kid sent. "How's it looking out there?"

"We're…" LC sent and bit off his next word, hearing something above, looking up and flinching as the shockwave from a massive explosion above them sent vibrations rumbling down the shaft. He tumbled from the ledge and tried desperately to catch hold of the ladder as he fell. He heard Duncan yell, twisted in midair and grabbed for a rung. His hand bounced off the first couple then he caught a hold and slammed up against the ladder, his shoulder almost wrenching out of its socket.

Sean and Duncan were both shouting to him. He hugged the metal frame for a minute then started to climb back up, trying to gauge where the nearest maintenance hatch was. He might feel invincible but he didn't want to test the theory by falling to the bottom of a lift shaft.

Another rumble echoed from above.

"Luka!" Sean yelled.

"I'm fine," he yelled back. "We have to get out of here."

"No kidding."

They emerged into a dark corridor.

"Four more levels?" Duncan whispered as they walked cautiously through an area that looked like administration offices. It was abandoned. They must have managed to evacuate to somewhere safer.

LC nodded. He was holding his gun loosely down by his thigh. It was quiet but something was niggling at the back of his mind. He almost flinched when Thom's voice came suddenly through the Senson.

"Luka, Sean, they're tracking you," Thom sent calmly. "You have to get out of there."

LC instinctively crouched, glancing around. "What?"

"They've got teams coordinated to clear the lower levels already. They're just shooting to kill any of the escaped prisoners. You need to climb."

That was quicker than they thought they'd manage. LC looked back at Sean, covering the corridor behind them and getting more and more agitated.

"We're trying to disrupt their trackers," Thom sent, "but they're carrying out a complete sweep anyway. You need to move. Go left."

They moved as fast as they could without being reckless, LC leading the way through the station. Duncan brought up the rear and it was weird to think that someone else was watching out for him.

Another tremor rumbled through the station. Thom urged them to hurry and they made it up two levels before he called out for them to stop.

"There's a team searching this level," the kid sent. "Elliott says this is the best chance we have of getting into the mercenaries' comms system. Luka, he told me to ask if you're up for it."

LC bit back a snide comment. "Where are they?" he sent back instead.

Thom gave them directions and reeled off an array of positions and strengths. According to Elliott and Thom, there was a unit using a mobile command terminal to coordinate a search of this level. If he could get close to it, he could hack in and give Elliott access to their whole system.

"Fast in, fast out," Duncan said and nudged him ahead to lead the way forward.

Once they were in position, LC hung back, waiting for the signal and by the time he was waved forward, there were two guys in the black uniforms of UM's hired mercenaries out cold on the floor. He grabbed the terminal from a desk and backed into a corner with it, sliding down to sit on the floor behind a cabinet. Sean and Duncan left him to it and went to watch the corridor.

Getting in wasn't difficult but trying not to disrupt the flow of data was tricky. He worked around it carefully and listened in to an operation that was panicked and uncoordinated. They were overreacting as if they'd been too complacent for too long.

He was vaguely aware that Sean came back in to check on him, impatient and anxious. She didn't like to disturb and stalked back out. He got the message and started to break into the command structure, rerouting approvals and creating a way in for Elliott. He made it as elaborate as he could quickly, adding some strings they could pull to create damage if they needed to and leaving a few trip wires to hamper anyone who tried to fix it.

He was still in deep when Thom yelled a warning and gunfire erupted outside the room.

"We've got enough," Thom sent. His voice was tight, every word concise. The kid had been trained well somewhere and not just in engineering it seemed. "Go, get out."

LC got out fast, discarded the terminal and ran to the door. The buzz in his head was erratic, nothing specific and he couldn't even distinguish individuals out there. Sean wasn't replying but he could hear the distinctive sound of Duncan's massive cannon of a pistol firing somewhere down the hallway.

He pulled out his gun and risked a glance into the corridor.

Sean was right outside the door. She grabbed his arm and pulled him into a run. "UM are mobilising fast," she said, breathless. "Hal is covering us but we're going to be pushed to get up to security if we don't get through now."

They ran through dark corridors, Thom trying to keep current but their information was getting more and more disjointed and eventually he sent in a whisper to them both, "I don't know which way you can go. You're cut off."

LC skidded to a halt. There was no point running into trouble. "Lift shaft," he sent to Sean and tried to get his bearings. They needed to back up. "Where's Duncan?" He'd lost track of the noise of the massive cannon some time ago.

Sean turned. "He'll be..." she said and her eyes flared. She shoved him hard as an explosion lit up the corridor behind them.

10

NG took the pawn with his bishop. The Man nodded with appreciation at the move and they both drank. NG had always suspected the wine had a narcotic as well as an alcoholic effect and he could feel the boundaries of his mind open up, awareness becoming as sharp as a razor's edge.

"Angmar Rodan is CEO of UM, I believe," the Man said.

NG sat quietly. It wasn't a question. The Man knew the name of every shareholder, director and CEO of all the top one thousand listed corporations on both sides of the line. United Metals were registered in Winter, aggressive, unscrupulous and highly profitable. It was a young corporation in the scheme of things but they were ambitious and they were focused, resisting the temptation to diversify that was looking to destabilise several of the other older names. And UM had been smart to pay enough respect, and extravagant donations, to certain key parties so the human rights campaigners would turn a blind eye.

The Man reached for the jug, swirling it to mix the infusion before topping up the goblets. "Men are fools," he said. "The Between embodies every rebellious and mutinous trait of mankind, yet the fools who fight so fiercely for their independence stand by and idly allow institutionalised vultures such as UM to encroach on their hard-won no man's land and exploit the very laxity their anarchy promotes." He brought his knight into play.

NG didn't say a word. The Thieves' Guild also exploited that grey area between the two power bases of Earth and Winter, very successfully.

The Man looked up at him. "Out loud," he said softly, reprovingly.

NG looked at the chessboard, not quite in the position he'd wanted to be. He raised his eyes. "Even before we found out that LC had got *caught up with them," he said cautiously, "we knew UM were going to be a problem. Almost as much as Zang."*

LC hit the wall and tumbled, debris raining down, sparks hissing. By the time he stopped, his ears were still ringing. He'd lost the pistol and a warm trickle was running down his face. He blinked away dust and saw Sean struggling to her feet, staring at a guy in armour who was standing over her, feet planted amidst the rubble, pointing an assault rifle at her.

"Luka," she sent tentatively.

The soldier wasn't wearing full body armour – no helmet and no neck protection. LC reached slowly into his boot and pulled out the knife, keeping every movement minimal. He braced himself against the wall, balanced the weapon with its blade pinched carefully between his fingers, gauged the distance and the angle and threw it in a left-handed, perfectly fluid motion. The knife tumbled gracefully, cutting through the air, flying a fraction of an inch past the guy's nose to clatter against the wall beyond.

The soldier turned his head, incredulous, towards the knife then back, piercing eyes glancing over the rubble to settle on LC.

His gun was somewhere out of reach. He felt Sean freeze, looking at him too. He looked from one to the other.

The rifle was still aimed at Sean but the soldier was beginning to twitch like he couldn't decide whether to switch targets to the chump on the floor. The guy took a step back to widen his arc and his back suddenly arched, a loud crack breaking the silence and a spray of blood flying out of his chest, fragments of shattered armour and bone scattering. Sean flinched as the red spray hit her across the face.

The soldier dropped, LC reeling from the punch of void that hit his mind, the man dead before he hit the floor.

Duncan walked up, long strides crunching broken glass and debris beneath his boots. "Will you two quit fooling around? We have to get out of here."

LC wiped his sleeve across his face and staggered to his feet, looking around for the pistol and the knife. He couldn't believe he'd missed, again – it had been a perfect throw – what did a guy have to do?

He spotted the gun, leaned down to grab it and stood up, sensing that Sean was too close a fraction of a second too late to react as she slammed him against the wall, palm flat on his chest, pushing hard, face up close and furious, still spattered with blood. Her mind was a whirl of emotion. She brought up her other hand, fist clenched around the hilt of his knife, holding the blade up in front of his eyes. She was flashing on Hilyer again.

"Where did you get this?" she hissed.

LC narrowed his eyes, not sure how to respond. He could see Duncan behind her watching them both and flicking his gaze back down the corridor.

"Where," she said again between clenched teeth, "did you get this?"

The knife was the twin of the one that Hil carried, a unique pair of extraordinary throwing knives that Mendhel had given them as a prize in a competition that had been too close to call. He had to force down the raw emotion that almost surfaced as he remembered that day, that moment. Sean was replaying a scene in her own mind; Hil twirling an identical knife between his fingers, saying to her, "LC has the other…"

LC blinked. Something warm was still dripping into his eye.

Her hand slid up to his throat. "Where?"

"I took it off a dead guy," he said softly.

She was assuming that he'd stolen it, thinking DNA never lies, so who the hell is this guy? But he could also feel that there was a hint of uncertainty creeping in; she knew he was left-handed and she could hear Hilyer saying, "LC can't throw a knife for shit". He almost smiled. She tightened her grip.

Duncan put a hand on her shoulder. "We have to go. This can wait, whatever the hell it is you two have going on. Cole, take point."

She stepped back and made a show of putting the knife in her belt.

LC didn't know how to handle it and he wanted the knife back. Stubbornly and absolutely wanted the knife back.

Sean was upset. He could feel her dilemma. She'd been about to abandon him for a lost cause and now suddenly he turned up with a weapon that couldn't be anything other than a link to the guy she was looking for. She was hooked back into him and she was angry because she didn't understand why, and he was pissed that he'd screwed up badly enough to attract her attention again.

He glared at her and she glared back before turning and stalking away.

Duncan gestured for him to go and they ran through the station, dark corridors echoing with heavy footsteps and the rattle of armour.

LC moved cautiously. It had been a while since he'd been caught up in a conflict like this. Usually it was get in, get out, encounter no one. The guild picked its targets carefully and only if an acquisition was significant enough would they be sent in to a situation that was already volatile.

It was only when they heard movement up ahead that they stopped. LC glanced around. They slunk up against the wall and he reached out to Thom.

There was no reply.

They didn't have time to wait.

LC quickly ran the schematics through his head, recalling the diagrams that Elliott had displayed, seeing the possibilities flash into his mind like tracks lighting up through a maze. The guild psych teams had never managed to figure out how he did it, no matter how many tests they put him through. He spotted a solution and moved, backing up and taking a couple of neat short-cuts to slip through into a maintenance area. Sean was right behind him, still fuming, wondering how the hell he was working out a route from memory, thinking about something else Hilyer had said to her. For Christ's sake, why the hell had Hil even been talking to her? It was frazzling his nerves.

He ran round and led them to an access panel.

"In here," he whispered and stepped aside to let Duncan go first, waiting stubbornly until Sean followed. He wanted her in front of him. He still hadn't figured out how to get the knife back off her and he needed to think of some way to deflect her attention away from him again.

She caught his eye as she edged past, that curious look back in her expression.

That was all he needed.

It was tight but they crawled in and worked their way through to a narrow tube with a rickety ladder. It was dry, hot and dusty inside the tube with a rusty tang to the air. Not the worst place he'd ever crawled through.

They climbed three levels fast, Duncan pausing as he reached the top of the tube. LC knew without being able to see that tunnels branched out in four directions.

They both looked down at him.

It was unsettling to have so many people depending on him. It was easy to be reckless when it was only your own neck at stake. That was the thing Hil had never really appreciated; that LC could beat him at every turn simply because he cared less. Cared less about success, cared less about his own reputation and at the very end of it all, cared less about his own safety. Mendhel had suspected and the Chief had outright accused him of it, many times. But nothing anyone could say would change anything. He was lucky to be alive and he lived every moment, but he knew, from hard experience, how precarious life could be. He wasn't going to sit around worrying about it. Except now he had other people to worry about. And a bounty hunter at his back who was suddenly very interested in him again.

"Go straight ahead," he whispered and followed as they worked their way through into another maintenance area.

By the time they found a terminal, the prickling at the back of his neck was setting his nerves on edge. They were too exposed, high on a gantry that was narrow and lit only by dim red flashes that were intermittent, suggesting that power relays to the area were damaged.

LC crouched by the black box. If he'd been on his own, he wouldn't have risked it, sitting out here like this, but he had a bad feeling that they were running out of time.

Duncan and Sean took up position on either side of him and he set to work. The box opened easily enough with a twist of the lockpick and it was encouraging to see that the system was set up for easy access, nothing too elaborate, and getting into it was fairly straight forward. He worked fast but carefully, breaking deeper into the station's core system. It was heavily guarded and getting in without setting off any tripwires or traps was a bitch.

Twice he heard gunfire, distant and echoing. He didn't move but he could feel Duncan twitch, almost physically towards him at one point and he half expected to be yanked away. It didn't happen and he shut out the buzz. There was nothing like being under pressure. He hadn't realised how much he missed having a specific target, having a tab to focus on with a definite end point. Running had sapped his spirit more than he knew.

He switched to the station's security system and tried to identify the exact cell the skipper was in.

He felt Duncan's hand rest gently on his shoulder and realised that the sounds of gunfire were closer.

"Almost," he muttered without losing the connection. He found them but the protections around the cellblock where Gallagher was being held were isolated from the main system. He almost had it when Duncan took a grip on his arm, harder that time, and whispered, "Time's up."

LC slowed his breathing, slowed time and threw everything he had to Elliott, total access to the station's core. He broke free in the same instant that Duncan pulled him away, hauling him backwards as a hail of gunfire ricocheted off the panel in front of them.

It was hard to focus coming out of a link that fast. He heard the clatter of grenades spinning along the gantry. He couldn't see them, couldn't get out of the way and he flashed on a view of crosshairs, seeing Duncan clearly in someone's sights. LC reacted, no hesitation, pushing the big man out of the way.

Something hit LC in the chest and something hot punched into his leg. His knees buckled, sparks from the grenade flashing behind his eyes.

He vaguely felt someone grab hold of his arm and pull him down as his body went into overdrive to deal with the neural reset and the throbbing heat that was pulsing in his thigh. He felt himself falling backwards and tumbled, bouncing, down a staircase.

11

"Considering the damage caused by Hilyer's recent foray into independence…" the Man said and paused. He sipped at the wine as if tasting it for the first time, gaze resting on something in the darkness behind NG. His dark eyes blinked slowly and came to rest on NG again. "How did Anderton fare?"

NG was considering his own knight. "LC has an innate complement of talents for everything we do here. He can run the Straight in the fastest time we've ever recorded. He can break into systems we've built to be impregnable. He's patient. He's determined. He survived frontline combat before the age of thirteen." NG made the move, the knight moving into position to threaten the Man's queen, and looked up. "From everything we've heard, he handled himself well."

"Good." The Man stood and left the circle of light to go to the cabinet, the motion sending the flame of the candle into an erratic frenzy. It looked for a briefest instant that it might extinguish, plunge the chamber into absolute dark, but it settled.

NG studied the board, trying to guard his train of thought. He could hear the sound of bottles clinking behind him as the Man took his time to select more wine.

The black queen glided silently across the chequered surface, withdrawing to safety.

NG drained the last of his wine, feeling the ambient temperature rise. It wasn't often that the Man resorted to such obvious displays of his abilities.

"So what happened?" the Man said from the far side of the room.

"LC isn't just good, he's lucky," NG said. "And on Poule, his luck ran out."

LC went sprawling at the bottom of the steps. An agonising heat stabbed into his leg and a painful cramp constricted the muscle low down in his back.

Duncan pulled him back and LC struggled to get to his feet, right leg refusing to take his weight.

There were yells up ahead of them.

"Got any ideas?" Duncan hissed, still firing steadily over LC's head.

Passing out seemed like a good idea. LC almost laughed. He couldn't think straight.

Thom's voice was a gentle whisper inside his head. "I'm back. What's going on? You need to move. Back up and duck left. You're about to get company."

"We've got company."

"Yeah, your company is about to get company – this is getting out of hand – and you're right in the middle. Luka, listen to me, you need to move."

Shit. LC blinked. He heard Sean relay the message and Duncan pulled him back as footsteps began to echo up from behind them, coarse yells and shouting.

Gunfire erupted in both directions as they ducked left into an alcove and pushed through a hatch.

The corridor was empty and quiet, the noise of the maintenance area they'd left sealed as the hatch slammed shut. LC leaned against the bulkhead watching as Duncan clicked a fresh magazine into his pistol. Sean and Thom were saying something, urgent exchanges that he thought he should try to follow but he couldn't focus. He had a hand gripped tightly around his thigh. It was sticky and hot. Blood leaked through his fingers.

Sean glared at him again, swore and grabbed his other arm, hoisting it over her shoulder. "Come on, we need to move before we can see to that."

They made it to the stairwell and stopped half way up, LC collapsing finally, shivering in a cold sweat, with a throbbing behind his eyes matching the pulsing agony from his leg. Sean eased him down onto the step and sat behind him, letting him lean and he could overhear her thoughts as if she was speaking out loud to him, hearing her decide he was her only link to LC, cursing that she was down to depending on a damned thief to lead her to the thief she wanted. She wasn't impressed and was less impressed that he'd got himself shot, that he was wasting her time even more.

Duncan knelt in front of him. "Check with Thom that we're clear."

"We're clear." He couldn't sense anyone anywhere near. He closed his eyes, trying to shut out Sean and her cacophony of thoughts, one hand pushing down on the hot spot on his leg. He'd been shot before, more than once, but not since the lab, and the pain taking hold of his back was almost worse than the pain from his leg.

He felt Duncan place a hand over the hand he had clamped to his thigh.

"This might hurt," the big man said, peeling his hand away and pressing something against the wound.

LC tensed and cursed. Might hurt? The excruciating sting of a trauma patch hit his leg and instead of the anticipated numb that should have followed, the pain magnified. He bit his lip, expecting numb any minute but it got unbearable fast. He tore off the patch, sagging back.

"What the hell was that?" he gasped, eyes closed tight.

Duncan pushed pressure against his leg again. "You need a trauma patch, bud, or you'll bleed out. This doesn't look good."

LC coughed. "Crap, that was a trauma patch?" He didn't understand. He'd used patches before but never felt anything like that. "Just bandage it, I'll be fine."

"You're mad."

"Yeah, I've been told. C'mon, help me here."

Thom was nudging them again by the time they got moving. LC felt sick, light-headed and ticked off, sure that getting shot had never hurt this much before. So much for being invincible.

By the time they reached the top, he was out of breath and he could feel that his right leg was soaked through right down to his boot.

The burning was getting worse and it felt like someone was pushing a hot spike through his flesh. They stopped two steps from the top and Sean let him drop to a sitting position, back leaning against the wall. She spoke quietly with Duncan and came back to kneel beside him.

"You're losing a lot of blood," she whispered. "I know you don't want a trauma patch but you need to realise you're in real danger here."

She seriously thought he was going to keel over and die right there.

He shook his head and muttered, "Another bandage. That's all I need and a beer if you have one."

She didn't smile but she did wrap another field bandage tightly around his leg, the black cloth soaked before she'd finished. The vial in his pocket was looking more and more tempting. It was an easy out, something one of the extraction agents had given him once and told him never to use.

He leaned over, hands gripping his thigh either side of the bandage, feeling the heat spread.

"I'm not joking," he said. "Beer would be good." His eyes felt heavy, too much effort to focus. It took him a minute to realise Sean was talking again, out loud, up close.

"Luka," she said. "Elliott can't break the security around the cells remotely. Can you do it from the cellblock? He says there's a command post on the security deck. Luka?"

He tried to recall the layout of the permissions that controlled the cells. They were isolated. That was why they wouldn't be able to bust them from the ship.

"Five minutes," he said finally, unsettled by the breathless catch in his voice. "Give me five minutes in there and I'll have Gallagher's cell open."

Duncan was tumbling a grenade in his palm. Sean turned to him. "Two guards are patrolling each side. How do you want to play this?"

LC sensed a hesitation in Duncan and whispered, "I'm fine."

Duncan wasn't convinced and for a second, he flashed again on

Richardson and other faces with such a sense of loss that LC had to squeeze his eyes shut.

"I'm fine," he said again, struggling to keep the pain out of his voice.

Thom sent, "Luka, you don't sound fine."

For Christ's sake, he'd about had enough of working with people. He coughed and straightened up stiffly, the knot in the small of his back emanating a constant ache as his body fought to fix itself. "I'm fine. What's the plan?"

"You wait here," Duncan said. "O'Brien will come back for you."

He didn't have much choice and he didn't argue. He sat and waited, right leg stretched out along the step, left hand resting on the pistol he placed by his knee.

It was quiet. He listened to the calm exchanges between Sean and Thom, a remote commentary as they moved in on the guards. His leg was still bleeding – the gunshot wound throbbing and the field bandage Sean had wrapped around it soaked through. Sitting there quietly, he kept his breathing steady and deep. The shakes were getting severe and he could feel a bead of sweat trickling down his back. Whatever the hell it was in his system that speeded up the healing process, it took a helluva toll on the way. This was just about as bad as it had been.

After a while, he sensed Sean's presence at the top of the stairs and waited until she moved towards him before looking up. She'd been standing there for a while. She had her hand on her belt, thinking about the knife, that it was her only lead and the only connection she had to that lead was sitting down there bleeding all over the stairs.

He looked up at her, eyes hooded.

She was also watching how he had his left hand, not right, on the gun, and she was wondering if there was any way he could be the one, thinking about what Hil had said about LC's memory, how confident he'd been about the route to take, and trying to decide if there was any way NG could have given her the wrong information.

She trotted down the steps and knelt by his side. "We're all clear. Are you good to go?"

"I want my knife back," he said.

She stared at him in disbelief. "We don't have time for this," she said. "Come on, we need to get you out of here."

LC sank into the main chair in the command post, taking the weight off his leg and back a massive relief, the pistol in his lap.

Sean left him to it and went back to watch the corridor. He waited until she'd gone before he linked in with the system.

Breaking in was far harder than it should have been and twice he broke loose, sat quietly for a moment and tried again. Trying to concentrate backfired. It always did. The more he wanted to be able to do something, the less likely it was to work. The instructors at the guild had hated him, hated the throw-away attitude and lack of concerted effort but he couldn't help it. The more he tried, the worse he got. It had to be pure instinct, laid back, take it or leave it, catch it out of the corner of your eye nonchalance, and that was when he could work miracles. His problem now was that he cared, cared more than he was comfortable with, about Gallagher, Duncan, the kid and strangely about Sean.

He leaned back and closed his eyes, shutting out the pain and blocking out the last few weeks. It came quickly then and he hooked up and bypassed a tangled mass of protections to bust into the system. It was still a mess from his last interference but someone somewhere was working hard to fix it. He closed them down, isolated cell seventeen and popped it open.

DiMarco was nowhere on this level. LC cursed and dug deeper, trying to figure out where they were holding the pilot.

He got what he needed, then pulled back and tried to figure out what the station was trying to protect. UM had increased security on the station about three weeks earlier, shipping in people to up the output of the mine and stripping station personnel to high security only. Elliott was right – they'd dropped into the middle of something. And for some reason they'd targeted Gallagher as a threat. It didn't make sense.

By the time he'd finished, he knew why it didn't make sense and a headache was banging away behind his eyes.

He didn't move, eyes still closed. He could feel Sean standing at the door. He'd stretched his leg out, resting it up on the desk. He could feel himself healing, feel the round embedded in his flesh like a red hot needle tip that was being pushed out, slowly and excruciatingly. If he could sit here quietly for a little while, he'd be fine.

"Time to go, Luka."

LC looked round. He didn't know how long she'd been there but it was obvious that she wasn't going to let him out of her sight for long.

"DiMarco's being held one level up," he said, sitting up, using both hands to grip his leg and gently ease it to the floor. "It wasn't Gallagher they wanted – it was DiMarco."

Sean scowled. "Where is he?"

He stood up. His heart rate was low and he could feel his blood pressure falling. He didn't know how he was going to make it back to the ship. If he'd been on his own, he would have found a bolthole and waited it out. Having Sean on his case, that wasn't going to be an option. And as much as DiMarco was an ass, he wasn't going to abandon the pilot to the mercenaries and a death sentence.

"I can't access it from here," he said. "I'll have to come with you. Bastard promised me a bottle of moonshine. We can't just leave him here."

12

Again, two pinches of powder went into the wine. NG could feel the fumes wind their way down his throat.

The Man poured. "Given the recent intelligence gathered regarding Anderton," he said without looking up, "Legal feels herself justified in her recent challenge."

He let that statement hang in the air, heavy amidst the pungent vapours.

NG sat up straight, not realising he'd slouched. "Legal needs to remember that these operatives are the ones putting themselves in danger every time they go out."

He rubbed his eyes. He was tired. They all were and it didn't help that Legal pounced each time Acquisitions was exposed like this. He reached for his wine. "She needs to remember what caused this. She wasn't here when the decision was made to let Mendhel keep his daughter away from us."

He moved a pawn.

The Man smiled and raised his goblet. "To the guild," he said quietly, "and all our little foibles."

NG drank, more than he intended, the wine in this mixture smooth with a delicate sweetness to it that tempered the tang of the narcotic. He glanced at the pieces facing each other across the black and white squares and saw clearly an alternative move he'd missed, obvious now.

The Man sat back. "Legal consider UM to be worth closer scrutiny."

"It's a corporation that gets results," NG said simply. "Whatever you think of their means, they get results."

Sean helped him up and out, every step shooting an agonising pain bone deep into his thigh. The entire security deck was dark, cells sealed and they moved slowly through, slower than Sean was happy with. He could feel her frustration and it was hard not to take it on, his own emotions feeling erratic.

They met up with Duncan, the big marine standing with Gallagher, the skipper holding a pistol like he didn't know what to do with it. LC couldn't help the faint smile that slipped out. How the hell had he ended up with this bunch of misfits? He thought for a second that Gallagher was going to run up and give him a hug but the skipper just clasped his shoulder and said quietly, "Nice work, Luka," while trying to suppress a distinct queasiness at the sight of all the blood.

They made their way to a stairwell and struggled up another level, Thom warning them to hurry. By the time LC stood leaning against the holding cell door, he was soaked through in a cold sweat, hands shaking as he tried to work the lockpick and find the sweetspot on the mechanism. Trust DiMarco to get himself incarcerated in an old fashioned cell with manual locks that weren't controlled from the central system.

Sean and Duncan were twitchy as hell at the delay and it took as much effort to shut them out as it did to concentrate on the door. Finally he got it. The lock clicked and Sean pushed the door open to let DiMarco out.

The pilot looked like shit, like someone had hit him in the face with a wall. He laughed. "Being the hero again, Luka buddy? Jesus, you look worse than I feel."

Duncan hurried them along, throwing a rifle to DiMarco who took hold of it and checked it, way more confident with it than a drunken freighter pilot should be. LC was picking up a buzz of emotions and thoughts from all of them, and including the commentary from Thom through the implant, it was all making his head ache.

He cut the connection and let Thom talk to Sean, trusting them more than himself right now. Each step was a challenge and a couple of times he felt himself fading out. Gallagher dropped back and took up his other arm, helping Sean to almost drag him along.

They were lagging behind and Duncan was casting anxious glances back at them, holding DiMarco back while gesturing them to speed up. He was worrying that they'd get caught out again and he'd marked Gallagher and LC as liabilities. LC could feel the tension in the man, memories surfacing of shepherding civilians through supposed demilitarised zones. LC had been herded through enough front lines as a kid, heavily armed soldiers less than gentle and bombs dropping all around. He shut it out and did his best to ignore Duncan's memories and emotions, while he concentrated on putting one foot in front of the other.

He leaned on Sean heavily. She held him around the waist, Gallagher holding him up on the other side, and they made slow progress, every step agony. He was going as fast as he could and when Sean piped up to say that Thom was telling them to hurry, he couldn't up the pace as much as he tried.

DiMarco dropped behind them while Duncan scouted ahead. A couple of times, there were loud gunshots as the big marine encountered guards. LC felt each death as a cold pop of void, like a punch to the stomach. He faltered each time, Sean's exasperation building.

It didn't help when DiMarco exclaimed suddenly, stopping to search one of the bodies.

"For Christ's sake, DiMarco," Sean hissed.

The pilot stood, dramatically flourishing a small hip flask. He unscrewed the top, took a mouthful and grinned. He kicked the guy in the head, muttered, "Thieving bastard," and tucked the flask inside his jacket.

LC almost laughed but Sean dragged him forward and a sharp pain flared in his leg. It was a relief to finally see the elevator.

Sean pulled open the lift door, tugging it aside. "We go down," she said. "Thom and Elliott have control of the main elevator. Then we find a way to cross the docks."

LC sank down onto the floor, leaning against the back wall. The lift dropped fast, sending his stomach lurching. Duncan was reloading and showing Gallagher how to check his own magazine. DiMarco stood slouching by the lift door, hefting the rifle as if he was gauging its balance and smirking down at LC.

"Can't someone rustle up a TP for you, bud? You're gonna bleed out."

LC shook his head and closed his eyes, not up to an argument. He was healing but it was tiring.

"He's had a bad reaction to a trauma patch like he's allergic or something," he heard Sean say, overhearing her wonder if that had been in his file. She had a file on him? Where the hell did she get a file on him?

"Shit," DiMarco said and added, "Luka," to get his attention.

LC opened one eye. The pilot waited until Sean wasn't looking at them then winked and tossed the flask down to him. LC caught it, screwed off the top and smiled. The liquid burnt his throat and he coughed, feeling his system snatch immediately at the alcohol to metabolise it into energy.

Sean looked over in disgust. "DiMarco, what the hell are you doing giving him alcohol? For god's sake, that's the last thing he needs."

She moved towards them but DiMarco intercepted and said quietly, "He's dying. Give him a break."

LC drank down the last of the liquor quickly before she could take it off him. His chest felt like it was on fire and the warmth spread rapidly. The knot in his back flared and he couldn't help coughing again.

Gallagher was watching them, trying to take in what Duncan was showing him, but looking at LC with a mix of empathy and awkward guilt.

"Thanks for the vote of confidence," LC muttered, well aware that he was flaking out and covered in blood. He felt a strange guilt himself, couldn't help overhearing that these people were worrying about him – Sean because she thought her only lead was about to croak it, Duncan because he felt helpless and Gallagher because he seemed to genuinely want him to be okay. DiMarco didn't give a shit but he'd given up his personal stash of hooch so that must mean something.

"I'm fine," LC said stubbornly, draining the last drop of the liquor. He tossed the flask back to DiMarco who caught it with a laugh.

Sean looked like she was about to argue but the lift stopped between floors with a sudden lurch and she was hard pushed to keep her balance.

"Thom, what's happening?" LC heard her send.

There was a quick, "Wait," then Thom sent, "Get back away from the doors – there are two autosentries set up aiming right at the elevator access. They're independent units. There's nothing we can do from here. You're going to have to deal with them up close."

"Jesus," DiMarco said as Sean relayed the message.

LC was sitting directly in front of the door. He braced himself to get up and it took Sean and Gallagher, one on either side, to get him to his feet. They hauled him off to the side, Duncan and DiMarco on the other.

"What do we do?" Gallagher said, nervous energy spilling over and sending LC's headache spiking. He was finding it hard to keep his eyes open.

Sean leaned in close and whispered in his ear, "Don't you dare die on me."

He felt her fumbling at his belt and smiled. "I didn't know you cared," he mumbled.

"I don't," she whispered sweetly. "But I need you alive. You're going to take me to the guy you stole that knife from."

She turned and LC watched, vision blurring, as she threw the pouch she'd taken from his belt to Duncan. "These will give us a couple of seconds to get out there."

The big man caught it and nodded. "Take care of him. We'll take care of the guns. Let Thom know we're ready."

The next few minutes were hazy – the lift falling, a rapid spattering of gunfire that echoed in his head as if it was far away and voices that were too loud, words that didn't make sense. More than once, LC came to, vaguely aware that they'd moved.

"Sean," he tried to say at one point and felt someone push his head down. Fingers pressed against his neck and someone said, "His pulse is weak and he's burning up. I think we're losing him."

He tried to reach into his pocket, fumbling out the vial. It spilled from his grip.

Whoever was sitting with him shifted and he felt a cold sting hit his neck. The drug hit his system and he gasped. A hand touched his lips and he opened his eyes to see Sean, up close. He blinked.

"Welcome back," she said quietly. "You should have said you had a shot of Epizin with you."

Go-juice. No one ever called it Epizin.

"I've got a feeling it's not going to last long," he replied, voice not much more than a whisper. He could feel the drug coursing through his system faster than it should and it was beginning to fade already. "Where are we?"

"Just across from the Duck's cargo bay doors. Elliott is going to open up for us but there's too much security around at the minute. UM have control of the docks again. He's trying to divert them away to give us a chance."

LC could sense Gallagher close by and could just about make out DiMarco crouching off to the side.

"Where's Hal?"

"He's setting up the diversion," Sean said. "Are you going to be good to go?"

What she meant was were they going to have to haul his butt across to the ship or could he walk it? He wasn't absolutely sure. He knew his body was healing but he could feel his entire system struggling and knew it couldn't keep up with the damage, as if his reserves were just too low.

"I don't know," he admitted, feeling himself going under.

DiMarco looked back at them and flashed a hand signal.

Sean gripped LC's arm. "We're going now," she whispered, more to Gallagher on the other side than to him.

Gallagher caught up his arm and they stood. DiMarco fired two rapid shots and an explosion lit up the entire docks area. The deck shuddered.

Duncan ran up, and ushered them out with a, "Go, go," and they followed DiMarco into the open. LC could see the Duck's cargo bay door easing up slowly. Sean had a hand around his waist and was taking most of his weight. He could feel a calm, controlled urgency emanating from Sean, Duncan and DiMarco and a sense of total bewilderment from Gallagher. He couldn't pick up any specific thoughts but he knew exactly where each person was like they were bright sparks moving through the darkness. There were unfamiliars some distance away, all preoccupied and no one focusing on them and it looked like they were going to make it, just walk on board, when something jarred at the edge of his attention.

Talking would take too much effort and he wasn't entirely sure he could form coherent words anyway, so he tight-beamed a message through the implant. "Sean, far right," he sent, squinting, trying to see what he'd caught.

She turned, midstep, and raised her gun automatically, aiming into the shadows.

A figure stepped forward, way across the dock, but looking right at them. LC could see the glint of a weapon and the guy began to shout. Sean fired and the figure fell, the yell cut off.

Duncan and DiMarco both turned, opening fire as more figures appeared.

Sean and Gallagher tried to drag LC into a run.

"Thom," Sean sent and was answered with another blast on the other side of the docks.

Shots began to ricochet around them. Sean staggered and LC couldn't help that he stumbled to his knees as her support vanished. He was done and as he sprawled, he knew he was slipping into unconsciousness and couldn't do a thing about it.

His world shrank to darkness with only voices and the sound of gunfire and the smells of sweat and smoke penetrating what conscious part of his brain was still active. He felt someone try to pull him up, heard footsteps and DiMarco up close screaming, "Jesus, girl, he's dead, leave him."

He tried to open his eyes but it wasn't going to happen.

Heavier footsteps thundered up. A hand gripped the back of his jacket and heaved. "We don't leave anyone," he heard Duncan say and LC felt himself lifted and hoisted, thrown over a shoulder that bounced straight into a run. The sound of gunfire set a background cacophony to the thumping rhythm of the ex-marine's boots, the reverberation jarring LC with every step. He was exhausted and knew he was a deadweight but he could do nothing and gave in to the downward spiral of oblivion.

Pain flashed as his head hit a wall, briefly snapping him back to awareness. He hit the deck, Duncan dropping him as the cargo bay door closed, metal on metal echoing as it slammed shut. Pain was good. It meant he was still alive.

"Go," Sean yelled.

He was aware of Thom shouting, "Grab hold of something," through the implant as the ship shuddered, docking restraints first groaning then tearing with an agonised scream of failing steel as the engines kicked in and the Duck tore free.

LC thought he should try to brace his legs, but every part of his body was refusing to move. He was shutting down.

He felt Sean grab hold of his shoulders and pull him close and in that instant he could have sworn he picked up from her a raw ember of emotion directed towards him that was pure need, beyond any superficial job she was on. She thought she was going to lose him and she was clinging onto him like she could will him to live. He tried to find her hand but couldn't coordinate his muscles to even twitch, tried to smile but slipped instead into a cold, consuming darkness.

13

"I understand this Hal Duncan served with Earth's Marine Corps," the Man said.

It wasn't often that they discussed non-guild personnel. NG hesitated before he nodded, knowing the implications this conversation could have. "Highly decorated. He was at Derren Bay."

If the Man was impressed, he didn't show it. "Dare I ask how such a prized soldier ended up playing bodyguard to a small time mobster in a place like Sten's World?"

NG had strong opinions on the subject but said simply, "His unit was caught up in the rebellion on Hanover. They survived. According to the official line that Legal managed to dig up, in the aftermath Hal Duncan was charged with treason, thrown in jail and dishonourably discharged."

"And the unofficial line?"

"The guy was a hero. He went against orders that could have been argued to constitute war crimes." NG took a sip of his wine, feeling its heat and potency nudge awake the dark corners of his mind.

The Man was still sitting back, eyes half closed, considering the battle lines taking shape between them. "It's a poor fact of any established military that they fear initiative," he said. "What is your view of the man?"

NG didn't hesitate at that. "He has the makings of an excellent extraction agent. He saved LC's life on Poule."

The last time he'd been in a state like this he was with Hil and Skye and, as much as they were all in trouble, he'd known for absolute certainty that he was with friends. This time he had a bounty hunter hovering and he didn't trust Elliott so it was hard to stay calm.

LC lay quietly, listening. He'd woken up in a cabin, the ship flying and a steady hum emanating through the bulkhead. The pain in his leg was excruciating and he felt like he'd been on a three-day bender. He was still dressed, grimy and caked in blood, jacket and armoured vest gone and shirtsleeve pushed up, an IV tube hooked up to the crook of his elbow.

He couldn't sense anyone near.

The ship lurched and a deep boom resonated through the hull.

He reached out to Sean, tentatively, and she answered straight away. "Luka, god, just sit tight. We're having a few problems getting away here. I'll be there as soon as I can."

"I thought we didn't have any shields," he thought, inadvertently sending it without really meaning to.

"We don't," she replied, "and excuse the pun but we're a sitting duck here. DiMarco's an ass but if he flies us out of this, I'll kiss him."

LC tried to sit up. His blood pressure was still low enough that his head started to swim and he sank back down. Another detonation echoed deep from within the ship.

"Sit tight, Luka," Sean sent again, her voice strained through the connection. "We'll be with you when we can."

She cut the link and he lay there, tired, hurting, possibly about to be blown out of space. He closed his eyes, thinking about that feeling he'd caught from Sean back there on the cargo deck and couldn't help but smile.

He woke up a couple of times, feeling the pull of jump, disorientated and drowsy. One time, he thought there was someone there with him but by the time he persuaded his eyes to open, he was alone.

When he finally woke long enough to take stock, the throbbing in his leg had eased and he realised he was lying in a clean bunk, undressed. He felt wrung out. This wasn't like any other time he'd had to lie low and wait out the shakes. This time had been close, he knew that. If Hal Duncan hadn't picked him up out there, he would have died, no doubt. So there was a limit to his superhuman invulnerability.

He lay still, eyes closed. He hadn't heard any explosions in a while so he reckoned they must be clear. Whatever someone had set up to drip into his arm was helping, but slowly. It was tempting to call up to Sean and ask her to send DiMarco down with some moonshine.

He listened to a quiet beeping that was keeping time with his heartbeat and tried to figure out if he could move. He was starting to think he could when there was movement at his side and a gentle tug on the tube in his arm.

"I know you're awake," Elliott said softly.

LC opened his eyes.

"You're lucky to be alive." The tech guy adjusted the IV, injecting something into the line.

"What is that?" LC asked, squinting at the pouch drip-feeding the tube.

Elliott smiled. "Pain meds and glucose. You've already gone through our entire stock of plasma."

Painkillers had no effect, he'd learned that the hard way, but LC didn't say anything. He was uncomfortable enough that Elliott was there. He still couldn't sense anything from the guy and he didn't like the look of curious interest he was getting.

"I'm not a medic," Elliott said, slowly and carefully, "but I do know that the human body can't lose that much blood and survive."

He let the words hang there and turned away to rummage in a drawer.

LC levered himself up onto one arm. He pulled free a wire that was connected to his chest and the beeping stopped.

Elliott turned back, a slight smile on his face. "What was it? A bullet? Shrapnel? It must have hit the artery, don't you think?"

LC stretched out his leg. He reckoned he could probably put weight on it if he had to.

Elliott made a show of filling a syringe with clear liquid from another vial. "Hal thought he was bringing another body back on board. None of them thought you had a chance. Yet here you are."

"Someone told me once," LC said, sitting back casually, "that I had nine lives. I reckon I've used up six of them."

"So you have three left?" Elliott injected the solution into the tube. He tapped the line and stood back.

LC straightened his arm and watched the fluid enter his vein. He felt it pulse into his system and almost gasped as a tight spasm took hold of his chest. He breathed through it and raised his eyes to look at Elliott.

The tech guy reached into his pocket and pulled out a small object, holding it out on his open palm.

LC took the distorted fragment of metal, not quite managing to avoid touching Elliott's cold, dry hand.

"The bullet that almost killed you. It made its own way out," Elliott said. "Quite remarkable. Best we don't mention that to anyone, I suppose."

LC tumbled it between his fingers, not sure what to say.

"I'm intrigued by you, Luka, but don't worry – I'm not going to give away your little secret. You know things about this ship," he said coldly, "that I would rather our dear captain Gallagher remain ignorant to."

LC narrowed his eyes. He didn't take well to blackmail.

"Breaking in like that took skill," Elliott said.

"Your AI let me in."

"Irrelevant. You got further than anyone else has ever managed, much further." Elliott leaned forward. "You're a very interesting individual, Luka Cole. That first injection," he said, flicking a finger at the IV line, "should have knocked you out cold in seconds. That last one was enough to kill a man ten times over." He let that hang in the air then left.

LC sat for a moment then lay back down. His heart was thumping – whatever the hell it was that Elliott had given him had delivered a real punch and he could feel his system fighting to neutralise it. He doubted that Elliott knew about the price on his head or the guild. It had been a mistake going after the AI like that but almost bleeding to death so dramatically in front of everyone was a development he couldn't have helped. He had a clean bandage around his thigh and someone had stripped and cleaned him up. And for Elliott to pull that stunt with the syringe, he must have suspected something and he'd had plenty of time to run whatever tests he wanted. Christ, he might even know what the hell it was.

LC closed his eyes and threw his arm over his face. This could be bad or it could be good, or it could be very bad. The problem was that too many people knew too much about him and he didn't trust any of them.

Sean nudged his legs aside and perched on the edge of the bunk. "We're about an hour out of Sten's World," she said. She was thinking about her plan to get him off the ship.

LC looked up at her through heavy eyelids. He'd pretty much slept his way through the trip and they'd all been down to check on him, DiMarco with a bottle of moonshine and Thom to say the main engine was struggling but he'd manage. The liquor had helped and the steady low rumble of the engines sounded fine from where he was. He was tired but the wound in his leg was on its way to being fixed. Elliott hadn't been back but no one else had said anything to make him think the tech guy had let on.

Sean touched his hand gently, resting on the band around his wrist.

"I know you're still recovering, Luka, but I need you to take me to the guy you stole this from." She recognised it. He could see her thinking about Hil. "This and the knife."

LC shook his head. "I told you already, I took them from a dead guy."

"Well, take me to that dead guy." She didn't believe him. He could read her thoughts as clearly as if they were displayed on a screen. Every time she'd called by, she'd been friendly, endearing almost, and he'd been hard pushed not to fall for it. She hadn't mentioned the knife and he'd managed to stay cool despite her advances. Now that he was obviously going to live, that desperate need and fondness he'd felt from her while he was bleeding on the floor seemed to have evaporated.

"Why?" he said obstinately. "What was so special about him?"

She took her hand away and looked at him. "He killed someone I cared about and I want to find him."

She was lying.

"He was dead," LC said. "What does it matter?"

Sean put her hand on his leg. It might have been healing but it was still sore. She pushed down ever so slightly and leaned towards him. "It matters to me. Where is he?"

"Probably scattered out in space by now."

She frowned. "Where was he? Where was it?"

He was getting a headache and he didn't like the not so subtle attempt at intimidation. He tried to shift his weight to ease the pressure on his leg but she stayed with him. He said the first thing that came to mind and regretted it as soon as it was out, "Abisko."

She sat back and it was obvious that she was trying to keep her face neutral.

He quickly said, "Maybe it was Abisko."

She'd been there looking for him. How the hell did she know about Abisko? She was looking at him like she was reassessing the whole situation.

"I need you to show me," she said.

LC whispered, "I'm not leaving with you, Sean."

She looked at the IV line and he thought she was going to try something, but she flashed on an image of NG and Hil, utter frustration, and the moment was gone as Elliott turned up.

"He's not up to going anywhere," the tech guy said, leaning against the doorframe, arms folded.

Sean stood up and smiled, the old charms turned on full blast. "We'll see," she said like she'd been trying to persuade him to go on a date with her and she left, edging past Elliott with a delicate touch to his arm.

LC watched, bemused. Elliott didn't quite know where to put himself. When she'd gone, he stared after her for a while then turned, a puzzled look on his thin face. "She followed you onto the ship at Sten's World, did you know that?"

"I don't care," LC said, sitting up and stretching out his leg beneath the sheet.

Elliott pulled a handful of medical supplies from the drawer. LC let him change the dressing on the gunshot wound, watching with detached interest. The flesh around the entry point was swollen and mottled still but less angry than it had been. He flexed the muscle, feeling the soreness down to the knee. He knew he needed to start moving and once done, moved to swing his legs round to get up.

Elliott stopped him with an outstretched hand. "Don't even think about it," he said. "If you want to keep this quiet, no one should see you up yet. We're about an hour out. Give me another hour once we've docked to get everyone off the ship, then get dressed and come up to the bridge. There's something I want to show you."

LC snoozed and listened to the sounds of the ship docking then pulled out the IV, got up and stood to test his balance. Even going through a simple set of stretches set his leg off aching. He was trying to work his way through pushups when Elliott called down to give him the go ahead.

He slipped down the corridor to his cabin and found his boots clean and a neatly folded pile of clothes on his bunk. He picked up the armoured vest and absently picked at a tear in the chest, right over where his heart would have been. Christ, he couldn't even remember that one. His combat pants were there too, clean but with a ragged hole in the thigh. He threw those in a corner, showered, rooted a fresh pair out of his locker and made his way up to the bridge.

Elliott was sitting at the main console, quietly flicking through screens of data. One was an image that looked like footage from a microscope, squirming organisms fighting for supremacy. LC peered at it as he took off his jacket and sat down, breathless and sweating. "What is that?"

Elliott smiled and looked over at him. "Are you alright?"

"No," he said. He gestured towards the screen. "What is it?"

"I reckon it's some kind of organism," the tech guy said, "and I reckon that is why you didn't die out there and why you have a price of twenty six million on your head."

14

"You don't believe it's an organism," the Man said softly, hands laced across his chest, making no move to take his turn.

NG shook his head, sitting back himself and resting the goblet of wine on his knee. "I don't know what it is."

"The infamous package."

NG could feel his heart pounding, the awareness of each beat intensified as he drank more of the wine. If Hilyer had known what the package was and what had happened to LC, he'd hidden it well.

"The facility they were sent to was destroyed," he said. "Reactor meltdown is the official story. As far as we know, it's not public knowledge that it belonged to the Earth military. How many people, if any, know exactly what they had in there is anyone's guess."

"And this elusive ship's technician?"

That was a harder question to answer. NG shook his head again, a small movement, reluctant to admit they'd failed to uncover anything about Elliott. "We don't know."

The Man sat patiently, dark eyes watching and waiting.

NG sat up. "Same as the ship," he said. "Legal and Media are beyond themselves trying to beat each other to find out who he is and where he came from. There's nothing, no trace at all. We don't even have any leads to follow."

LC stood up and took a step back, a cold chill hitting his stomach. He reached behind his back and pulled the gun out of his waistband, holding it down by his side as he took another step away.

Elliott swung round to look at him. "Where are you going to go, Luka? If you run now, where's left to go?"

There was none of that awkward shyness the guy had affected

when he was around the others. LC stared back at him. "How did you find out?"

"About the bounty? I tracked Sean to the ship she has stashed here in the port, the ship that's been following us since she came on board, and had a very interesting – exchange – with her AI. They don't think you're the guy they are after because your DNA didn't match a profile they're working to. But this," he swung back and tapped on the screen, "this could explain that, don't you think? Seriously, Luka, where are you going to go? I told you, I'm not going to tell anyone your secret. And if I wanted to cash you in, I wouldn't have let on, would I?"

It was hard not to turn and run, right then. The guy was a void, giving nothing away. LC hesitated. "What else do you know?"

Elliott smiled. "I know you have a Senson Six, not Four. That's covert military grade technology and as far as I know it hasn't even hit the black market yet. And I'm reasonably certain you're not military."

He turned back to the console and started tapping at the screens. "Sit down, LC, before you fall down."

LC sat, trying to control the adrenaline rush and ease his heart rate. "Where is everyone?"

"Sean is in a bar with some guy I reckon is probably another bounty hunter. I had to tell her you were unconscious again and unlikely to wake up for a while. Hal is taking his friend back to the lad's family. Gallagher took Thom to Danny's Bar and I don't know where DiMarco went. Out of all of them, watch yourself with him."

LC looked back at the screen with the image of the organism. The display was frozen and magnified. "Do you know what it is?" He was aware that Elliott was watching him.

"It's running riot in your body – don't you know?"

LC rubbed the back of his neck. It was weird to be talking so openly to someone about this. "No, I don't."

"I'm not even going to ask how you got it." Elliott paused and flicked the screen to let the footage play. "I'm no expert on human biology but on the regeneration traits alone, I'm not surprised someone wants to pay twenty six million to get their hands on you. And it looks like it's mutating."

Christ, that was all he needed. LC tucked the pistol away into the small of his back and stood up. "I need a beer. Do you want anything?"

He grabbed two bottles from the mess and was making his way back to the bridge when Thom called, a frantic tight wire request that he was tempted to ignore.

The kid pushed it again so he allowed the connection, pausing on the stairs to catch his breath.

"Luka, are you awake? We've got a problem."

The last time the kid had said that there were heavily armed mercenaries storming the ship. LC sat down on the step, easing the weight off his leg. "What is it, Thom?"

"Oh god, Luka, we're playing poker with the Gadini brothers."

LC had to choke back a laugh.

"Gallagher's drunk," Thom said. "God, Luka, what do I do?"

The kid sounded half cut himself. Danny didn't water down his whisky and if they'd had a session anything like last time, Gallagher wouldn't be able to hold a hand of cards never mind play a coherent game. He hadn't realised Gallagher was buddies with the Gadini family when he'd made his flippant comment to Thom the last time they were here. The Gadinis ran a ship repair business, strictly legit as far as he knew, and from what Olivia said they were a decent bunch of people making the best of a bad situation.

"Get a coffee, Thom," he said, standing and making his way up the stairs. They were in good hands. They'd be fine. Grandma Gadini would probably cook them breakfast in the morning. "Strong coffee with a lot of sugar, and get one for Gallagher as well."

Elliott was watching a real time video feed when he got back. LC handed over one beer and popped the top on his own, settling into the chair and putting his feet up on the console.

"What's that?" he asked, yawning, glad the guy had moved on from the technicolour nightmares swimming about in his bloodstream.

"Sean," Elliott said, switching the view to a wider angle. "Have you seen this guy before?"

She was in a bar, standing with a tall guy, well built, with stubble that looked neat and contrived rather than scruffy. "No," LC said, strangely put out that she was drinking socially with someone. "Is that him?"

"He's not wearing a badge but no one would be stupid enough to show one out here. I reckon he's a bounty hunter. There's a lot more ships docked since we were last here a few days ago."

LC downed half the bottle, wishing he'd brought a couple more. He couldn't be bothered to go back down to the mess. And when he couldn't be bothered to shave, he didn't look anywhere near that dapper. "What else did you get from her ship?"

"Apart from the information on the bounty?" Elliott said with a smile. "She has a full file on you – ID, biometrics, something about Paninski. And training records. Who was training you to do what, LC?"

He had a disconcerting knack of throwing in a complete sidewinder with very little effort. And LC had no way of knowing whether the guy was malicious or toying with him for kicks. He paused with the beer bottle half way to his lips and smiled back. "Doesn't it say?"

"She has a file on some guy called Zachary Hilyer as well. Was she after him too?"

LC drained the bottle and sat forward, dropping his feet back onto the floor so he could up and run if he had to. He kept hold of the bottle. "Does it say anything about where she got the file?"

"No, it doesn't. The whole document bundle was carefully anonymous with regard to its origins as if," Elliott sat back himself pondering the issue, "it had been sanitised for an outside audience, I would think."

LC laughed. "Elliott," he said, "hand me in or don't, just don't fuck with me."

Elliott smiled. "Why would I want to hand you in, Mr Anderton, you're far too entertaining."

It was a knife's edge as to whether this could get nasty. LC wasn't too bad at reading people but he'd already become way too reliant on his recently developed ability to sense what people were thinking, if not to hear their thoughts outright. Elliott was a complete unknown and the way he spoke, he could turn quickly and unpredictably.

LC tumbled the bottle so he ended up grasping it around the neck. "Don't take this the wrong way, but why the hell should I trust you?"

The guy raised his eyebrows and looked disappointed. "I'm not going to hand you in, LC. I don't need the money. Gallagher is my concern and I have a feeling he's going to need you around. Whatever it is you've done to earn that little price tag and wherever you've come from, I'm not interested. Sean, on the other hand..."

LC looked back at the screen. They were still talking. He wondered if it was about him but the image was too pixelated to be able to lipread or guess. She wasn't drinking but she was standing close to the guy, often placing a hand on his back.

He watched her, watched her give that familiar gesture to someone else, feeling cold inside. It was a wake up call to see it. She was a bounty hunter and she was after the twenty six million. That was her only interest in him, whatever other emotions he'd picked up from her. He'd been a fool to think she could have been feeling anything else.

They watched Sean for a while then Elliott started switching between random views across the whole station. LC fell asleep curled up on the chair. He felt just about safe enough to snooze. Elliott had a point and like he'd said earlier, if he was going to hand LC in, he would have done it already.

He was woken up by an insistent impulse hammering at the edges of his awareness. Thom tagged it with urgent priority that LC almost didn't recognise. And when he allowed the kid in, his voice was vague like he was having trouble concentrating.

"Luka, we're in real trouble. We're not at Danny's any more and Gallagher's been dragged into another game. He's been played and he doesn't know it. Oh god, Luka, he's going to wager the ship."

"Thom, calm down. Where are you?"

"I don't know but if Gallagher gets into this any deeper, he's going to lose the ship." His voice was tinged with a desperate edge.

"Thom, where you are?"

"We're in a back room somewhere with four people." The kid wasn't thinking straight, the words coming through broken and unclear.

"Thom, calm down. Where on the station are you?"

"Some bar. They brought us here," muffled, panicky, nothing like the neat controlled communications of earlier.

"Where?"

"The Reo," the kid said finally. "We're in some place called the Reo. I can't let him lose the ship. What do I do?"

LC groaned. "Stay with Gallagher. For god's sake, don't leave him alone."

Thom cut the connection.

Elliott raised his eyebrows. "They're in the Reo?"

LC looked at the skinny tech guy. There was no way he should have had access to a private tight wire link between two high end implants. "Did you hear all that?" he said.

Elliott nodded, absolutely no embarrassment at being caught eavesdropping.

That was something else to file for future reference. LC stood up and shrugged into his jacket, feeling cold suddenly. "What the hell is Gallagher doing at the Reo?"

"Thomas sounds concerned, don't you think?" Elliott said.

LC narrowed his eyes. "He should be."

"Why? He's been on this ship for about a week longer than you have. You've both known Gallagher for a handful of days. I know why you care. You have nowhere else to go. Why is Thom so disturbed? It's just a job. He's an engineer – a good engineer. He could walk onto any ship in this dock and get hired on the spot. What is it to him if Gallagher loses the Duck?"

Elliott was playing at something and LC desperately tried to resist getting caught up in it, but he did care about Gallagher, however foolish the old guy turned out to be.

Elliott whispered, conspirator through and through, "Thom has a Six, did you know that?"

Christ, how much more complicated could this get? LC knew exactly what he was getting at. The kid was obviously ex-military and way too young for the type of training he kept dropping back to. And with a Senson Six? Sean had said high end but a Six?

"So what is he?" LC said cautiously. "He's not a bounty hunter, I know that much."

"I have a feeling," Elliott said, leaning back, "that he's more interested in Gallagher than you. Or the ship. I haven't figured out which yet."

LC began to pace up and down across the limited deck space of the bridge, trying to figure out if he could walk without limping and flaking out like an invalid. "If Gallagher's caught up in a back room game at the Reo, he's lost the ship already. Those guys don't fool around. Did Thom sound strange to you?"

"He sounded drunk."

"Elliott, I may have only known Thom for five minutes but I'm telling you the kid can't drink and he'll avoid it if he can. If this is going down the way I think it is, he's been spiked."

"Spiked?"

"Drugged." LC rubbed his eyes, feeling a headache begin to pulse. He'd spent enough time in places like this to know the scam. "They'll have hustled Gallagher into thinking he was on a winning streak, spiked his drinks and increased the size of the bets. You start losing but you're too far in to pull out, then they deal you a hand you can't lose, on stakes you can't afford. They'll have thrown Gallagher the great idea that he could put up his ship as collateral to cover the cash. And if he was trying to get the money to pay the repair bill, he couldn't have refused. Especially if he was half out of his mind on the kind of crap they use to make everything seem like such a good idea."

"So what are you going to do?" Elliott said casually.

It was absurd. How much more entangled could this get? "What am I going to do? This is your ship."

Elliott shrugged, a little half twitch of his shoulders and a sly half-smile. "Couldn't we just settle Gallagher's debt? Buy the ship back?"

LC shook his head. "They don't work like that. They'll start to rack up interest on the down payment the minute they leave the table. Gallagher will be in debt to them for the rest of his life, which will be about twenty-four hours when they find out the ship's not even his. Like he isn't in enough trouble as it is. Christ, if they don't kill him, Mal Donnelly will."

"So how much do you need? How much cash do you need to get into the game?"

"Elliott…" He couldn't say it. Couldn't say that he couldn't go out there. It was a standing joke on the Alsatia that he never said no to anything but he couldn't go back onto the station. It had been hot enough the last time they were here. Sean was out there now, buddying it up with a bounty hunter chum and probably arguing about how they were going to blow the twenty six million.

"You can play poker?" Elliott said.

"Yes," he admitted. He had a freaking eidetic memory – he could beat anyone at poker.

"So how much do you need?"

"At the Reo? A hundred thousand minimum."

Elliott held out his hand, beckoning. "You have a credit stick?"

He did but he didn't have a hundred thousand.

Elliott just smiled and said again, "Credit stick?"

LC groaned and dug a stick out of his pocket. It didn't have much left on it.

Elliott took it and plugged it into the console. LC watched as it filled up with credit. Gallagher might not have much money but Elliott obviously had no trouble accessing cash from somewhere.

"There you go," Elliott said. He held it up between them for a moment then tossed it across. "Go get them, Mr Anderton. Maybe the universe does revolve around you after all."

15

The Man moved his knight. "It was known that Anderton had a contact on Sten's World, was it not?"

He left the rest of the question unspoken. NG knew exactly what he was hinting at. Why hadn't the guild had someone there watching Olivia? They could have retrieved LC as soon as he set foot on the orbital.

"We had people there," he admitted. They'd even sent a team to Kheris in the unlikely event that LC had decided to go home. "They missed him."

The flame flickered.

"Twice," the Man stated simply.

NG took a sip of the wine. It was difficult to concede that his people had made mistakes. At the time, they'd been searching the entire galaxy, for LC and Hilyer, as well as battling internal dissension and fending off attacks from outside agencies.

He swirled the cup and watched the wine splash and surge against the smooth metal surface. There was no point being defensive.

The vapours rose, the scent of the spiced wine swirling in soft eddies. Sten's World was a squalid cesspit of a colony. The guild had little influence there and their investigations had been hampered by the instinctive, shutters-down paranoia that was inbred on the orbital. He'd never understood why LC had such an affinity for the place. But it didn't take much to see why it was the perfect place to hide.

"Not so perfect," the Man interjected, "as I understand."

"No," NG said, "not once half the galaxy's bounty hunters had descended on it."

LC stood in the shadows high up on the balcony that ran parallel to the main concourse of the Avantine. Behind the bustle of the docks and the row of bars that fronted the port area, Sten's World station had an underlying business district tucked discretely behind the thin veneer of legitimate commercial activity. On the Avantine, if you knew the right people, you could get hold of anything.

It had been hard work to get this far without running into trouble and he watched for a while, letting the music drown out the buzz in his head, uncomfortable at the closeness of so many people milling around down there. The balcony was narrow, the Avantine itself not much wider, and doorways and staircases filled every space.

A girl brushed past, barely dressed in a skimpy red affair, catching hold of LC's hand as she squeezed by. "Hey," she whispered, "this is no place to be standing alone."

She had a tiny red star tattooed just behind her left ear. He let her pull him along and she took him through the nearest doorway, dancing her way through the throng of people to the bar. There was a sweet scent of narcotics in the air mixed in with the pungent stench of sweating bodies. She got the bartender's attention straight away as if the guy had been waiting for her to appear and she ordered for both of them, taking the drinks and leaving LC to pay, five times as much as it was worth.

He knew the drill and smiled, clinking glasses and not resisting as she put an arm around his waist. "So where are you headed?" she breathed into his neck.

That was the routine. You didn't walk into the depths of the Avantine – you were escorted and there was a price.

"I have a date at the Reo."

She looked at him through long blue eyelashes with disappointment. "You don't want to go to the Reo," she said, voice husky and almost hypnotic. "I know somewhere far more fun. Come play with me."

LC knocked back the rum in one and shook his head. "Olivia'll be waiting."

The girl rolled her eyes like she knew she was out of her depth and laughed. "Come on then," impatient, now she knew who he was associated with, to ditch him and latch onto the next punter.

She took his hand and dragged him through the crowd to a back door that led to steep steps winding down onto the concourse. It was weird but he felt safer in here than out on the docks. The guild had no standing here but there was still a kind of honour amongst these lowlifes. Even so, he didn't let down his guard; if they found out how much he was worth, it would be a different matter.

The girl in red took him to the door of the Reo and waited for her tip, standing on tiptoes to give him a parting kiss. He paid up and turned to the two doormen, spreading his hands to let them frisk him. They took the gun and gave him a chit without a word, standing aside once they were satisfied and letting him in.

The Reo was even more crowded and the music was a beat that thumped in time with his heart. He pushed through to the bar, ignoring the growing noise inside his head. Two more fast shots of rum staved off a trembling in his knees that was threatening to spread and he waved over for a third.

He froze as a hand ran up his back to grasp his neck and he tensed slightly before he recognised her, the familiar perfume as much of a giveaway as the thoughts tumbling from the mind that was nuzzling up so close.

"My god, Tigs," she whispered. "I thought I was never going to see you again."

LC grinned and took hold of Olivia in a hug that felt like he was holding onto a lifeline.

He had a feeling that she'd known something was wrong the last time he was here. He wasn't usually in such a state when he landed on her doorstep but she'd told him she didn't want to know, which was fine by him. She'd simply kissed him and told him to be careful, like she always did when he skipped out.

She was the one that broke the hug, holding him close still but pulling back just enough to look at him. She ran a hand gently along his cheek.

"You haven't come to see me," she said suddenly, suspiciously, and he could have sworn that she could read his mind. Maybe he wasn't the only one with this affliction after all.

"Business," he replied, still smiling. When he was with Olivia, he could forget everything – the war he'd grown up in the middle of, the guild that had bought his soul, and the damned package. Hil had never understood. If Hil wanted to hide away, he ran to the guild. LC had always run out here. When they both needed to bug out, they went to Pen and that's what they should have done this time. Gone there together instead of going after the package then maybe Mendhel would still be alive.

He looked at Olivia and the petulant put-on pout she was trying to fool him with. She was wearing a black dress that left nothing to the imagination and an elaborate string of diamonds he hadn't seen before.

He hugged her again and whispered in her ear, "You have a game on here. I need in."

She dug a hand into his ribs and whispered back, "You can't afford it."

LC slipped the loaded credit stick out of his pocket and into her hand.

She checked it and looked up at him. He'd never been short of cash – the guild paid well and the tabs he ran were some of the most lucrative. But he always stayed under the radar. The amount on that stick was at least a magnitude higher than anything he'd ever wagered on a card game before. And she knew it.

"Liv, I need you to do something for me."

She looked suspicious again and narrowed her eyes. She looked beautiful.

"What are you into, Tigs?" She didn't usually ask but then he didn't usually turn up asking to gatecrash one of her backroom games. And he could feel that she was worried about him. More than usual.

"I have two friends here that need looking after."

He told her about Gallagher and Thom and she nodded. "Will I see you afterwards?"

LC pulled her forward and kissed her without replying.

She shrugged him off. "God, Tigs, you're incorrigible. Be careful in there. And if that's not your money to throw away, don't come running to me when you lose."

She disappeared for ten minutes then came back with a smile he could tell was forced and led him through the back into a private area that was quiet except for the muted thumping of the bass filtering from the bar. The deck was bare metal, no frills. They went up some narrow stairs and onto a landing.

"Three people have crashed out of this game already," she said quietly as they walked, "including your friend. You know how high the stakes are. You should know there's a waiting list running downstairs. I had to use some hefty favours to get you in. Don't upset anyone in there." She squeezed his hand. "Why are you limping?"

She didn't miss much. She was thinking that his hand felt hot and wondering if she could get off early when he was done. He almost blushed at some of the other things he was overhearing and tried to even his step. He didn't think he'd been limping that noticeably.

She pulled him to a stop before they reached a door that was being guarded by two huge bruisers. "I don't like this but I know there's no point arguing with you. Your friends are with two of my girls — we'll keep them happy. And don't worry, they don't know you're here."

LC said, "Thank you," and kissed the side of her neck. There was no tattoo there, she didn't belong to anyone.

"You're a liability," she replied and whispered into his ear, "People are asking around after someone who sounds a lot like you, Tigs. What have you got yourself into?"

She wouldn't give him up, he knew that for certain, but she was unnerved by it. He shouldn't have been surprised that she'd heard something with this many bounty hunters around. Olivia's business was knowing everyone else's business and she did it very well. He knew that she liked having him around because he had nothing to do with this place and she could relax with him. Except now that safe anonymity might be gone for good and he could feel that she was unsettled. He couldn't tell if she knew about the twenty six million.

She stared at him then pulled away abruptly. "Go play cards, Tigger. Come find me when you're done."

She turned and walked away, heels clicking on the metal floor.

The two bouncers stepped aside as he approached, one of them gesturing him to adopt the position. He let them search without arguing. Once satisfied, they let him into a small anteroom where a clerk was waiting behind a tiny barred window. The credit stick checked out and he was handed a stack of chips. It was cold in there like the inside of an airlock and when the guy nodded, there was an audible click and the far door eased open.

He walked through into a smoky room that was warm and humid. The door clicked shut behind him and as far as he could see there was no other way out. If anyone in here recognised him, he was well and truly trapped.

LC dampened down an itch of panic and controlled his breathing. He'd never played a backroom game here before but he'd been playing poker since the age of nine when he'd been caught out in a thunderstorm after curfew and a gunship crew had taken him in after they'd been grounded. They'd got him drunk and taught him to gamble with bullets lined up in neat rows. Years after that, he'd practised the finer points of counting and manipulating the cards with Mendhel and Pen. Whatever these half-bit mobsters had going here was nothing he hadn't beaten a thousand times. And that was before he could hear what people were thinking.

He sat at the vacant seat and placed the chips in neat piles on the green in front of him. There were three guys and one woman sitting around the table. No one else in the room. And no one said a word until he was settled and looked up.

The guy holding the deck, shuffling the cards in fast snappy flicks, had slicked back black hair. He didn't stop cutting the cards as he cast a sly glance at LC and said, hard and fast, "Aces high, no holds, minimum drop two thou. House rule," he added casually, "is all or nothing. You don't walk 'til you're done."

LC nodded. There were no introductions, no names. One of the guys was nervous, twitching like he wanted to leave, sipping at a squat glass of golden liquor and wondering what had gone wrong. An older man opposite looked calm, smug almost, and he looked over at LC with way too much interest. What were the chances a bounty hunting son of a bitch would be sitting at the table? LC stared back and decided he was being paranoid.

The woman opposite the dealer was stunning. Long blonde hair and pale pink lips. She lit a cigar, blew a perfect smoke ring and slid a tumbler across the table to LC, topping up everyone's drinks. They all lifted their glasses then, no toast but to the cards, and as he drank, he could taste the bitterness, subtle and probably not something he would have noticed if he hadn't been expecting it.

He glanced around as he drained the glass. The dealer and the blonde with the cigar were the ones in control, not obviously together outwardly but he could tell they were working the trick in tandem.

The black haired guy holding the deck for that deal had the most chips, Mr Twitchy the least and as cards began to fly across the table, LC felt his head spin slightly, chest restricting and the knot spasming in his spine.

16

"Have you brought her in?"

"No." NG was cradling his goblet, trying to make the wine in his cup last, not sure he could handle much more.

The Man frowned, drinking steadily and expecting NG to keep up. "I can see why Legal considers her such a risk."

NG forced a smile. Legal could be a vindictive bitch who didn't like to be thwarted. Once it was clear that Acquisitions was out of bounds, she'd switched her attack and tried to discredit every contact Anderton and Hilyer had ever made outside the guild. "There was no reason to bring Olivia in," NG said. "We cleared her. LC was careful. She knows nothing to connect LC to us. She doesn't even know his real name."

"What do we know of her?"

That was a far more pertinent question. NG raised the goblet to his lips and drank. The wine was keeping its heat, steam still rising. He looked down at the board, tracking the consequences of possible moves.

"She runs a successful escort agency on Sten's World station. Legitimate as far as business is ever legitimate there. She's highly respected, has no enemies that would dare move against her without drawing wrath from her supporters and is very fond of LC."

"And?" the Man said, knowing fine well what NG was avoiding.

"She's the youngest daughter of Ennio Ostraban. There's no way we could bring her in, even if we wanted to."

They all pushed forward the two thousand ante.

Someone had refilled his glass. He downed that in one, feeling the liquor and whatever the hell it was they were doping him with hit his bloodstream. It was subtle but potent. After weeks of trying to get drunk, this was the one time he needed to keep a clear head. Christ, how ironic. Whatever Elliott had thrown at him on the ship had had no effect and he'd been thinking this might be the same but he could feel his nervous system hiccup at the hit. He was going to have to work fast.

Mr Twitchy laughed nervously and LC looked up to see the guy watching him. "If you're going at it like that," he said, "why don't you throw your stack over to me now, huh? Make it less painful on yourself. Hell, I could do with a break." He looked at the dealer. "What are you doing to me?"

The dealer smiled and nodded to Mr Calm on his left who tossed in one card and kept his face expressionless as he picked up its replacement. It was a king; LC could read it in the guy's mind, clear as day. They were all concentrating so intently on their hands, he could see their thoughts, that intensity of focus making it as easy as if he was looking over their shoulders. Damn, this might work after all.

LC threw in two cards and got back an eight and a three and it went on, each round followed by a round of bets. They were all going conservative, like they wanted to gauge the new guy at the table before getting back to business.

The pair running the hustle weren't house staff. It wouldn't be good for business. Olivia probably didn't even know it was going on. He'd never seen it here before. Never looked and never cared. Until it happened to someone he'd somehow come to think of as family, as much as Mend and Pen and Hil had ever been. How the hell had Gallagher managed that?

He'd smiled before he could catch it. He glanced up. Mr Twitchy grimaced at him, said, "Jesus, you're killing me," and threw in his hand. He looked like he might stand up but he just shuffled his weight and slouched down again.

LC looked again at his own cards. His hand was crap. He smiled confidently and raised extravagantly, tossing the chips casually into the growing pile.

Mr Calm folded, still watching LC quite openly. It was down to Mr Black and the woman. LC had nothing. He took a sip of the liquor. It was expensive whisky and the drug in it was pulling his senses sideways.

The blonde blew out another perfect ring of smoke that spiralled up. She considered the pile of chips in the centre of the table and looked from face to face. She was curious and bemused and LC could hear clearly that she was thinking they had a sucker here that would do them fine.

They both saw the raise and the dealer added more, challenging him to match it.

LC shook his head, smiled and folded, tossing the cards in face down and tossing back more of the liquor.

Black beat the blonde with two tens and a, "Hard luck, my dear."

"How about a decent hand next time," Mr Twitchy said, mopping his forehead with a cloth.

The deck moved left. LC kept track of the cards, despite a growing fuzzy headache pulling at the back of his skull. The tumblers were topped up constantly and he couldn't see how they were filling their own glasses any differently. It was always possible they'd taken some kind of neutraliser.

Twitchy was struggling with it. LC could feel the conflict of desperation and over eager optimism from the guy, emotions swinging as wildly as his bets. He had a reason for needing to win, something personal. Probably as desperate as Gallagher had been and LC hated the pair sitting so serenely across the table for pulling this scam. He'd cheated at games himself before but he'd never hurt anyone, at least no one who didn't deserve it.

When his glass was empty, he made a show of pushing it forward and watching the woman intently until it was filled, then knocking back half the liquor in one like he didn't care how drunk he was getting.

They thought he was a sure thing and when he accidentally knocked over his stack of chips, the two hustlers exchanged glances that they didn't think he'd noticed. Mr Twitchy laughed.

After another couple of rounds, LC decided Mr Calm wasn't a bounty hunter. There was nothing in his mind but a determined concentration on the cards. He was doing well, really well, until he took a nosedive.

He had two aces. LC had already folded and he could see the hand easily.

He threw in two cards and was dealt an ace and a seven. Three aces. His face was impeccably neutral but LC could feel the tension in the man, the dilemma of knowing that the risk was too high but something saying screw it, go for it. That's what they were all fighting against. The drug was inhibiting caution. And Mr Calm had been dealt three aces by Mr Black who'd already folded and had already dealt his partner four threes.

That was the scam right there. The hustlers were manipulating the deck and the liquor was taking away the inhibitions of the other suckers around the table. LC could feel it himself.

Mr Calm didn't say a word. He simply pushed forward his stack of chips.

Twitchy leaned forward. "All in. Jesus, man. Why can't I get that kind of hand?" LC couldn't figure out what he had riding on this game but it was something big and something the guy cared about.

The blonde winked at LC and pushed forward a matching stack of chips and for a long heartbeat Mr Calm felt doubt, despite the drug. He laid out his three aces and when the four of a kind appeared in the hand she spread, Calm simply stood up and walked away, at least one hundred thousand down and no looking back.

It was a relief that he was gone.

They played two more hands, LC folding each time – on an average hand dealt by Mr Twitchy and a hand with ten, jack, queen dealt by Mr Black. That got him curious glances from the two of them and confirmed the hustle. They'd been expecting him to bet high and would have stung him for it.

After that a hefty looking guy in a slick grey suit joined the game. Before he sat, he leaned over the table offering his hand to each player in turn. "Malone," he said.

Mr Twitchy stood up and shook, saying, "Tennison. You better have some serious balls there, Malone, this is one helluva game."

Malone laughed. No one else offered a name and he sat. He was cocky and talkative until the dope kicked in then he played on tilt, reckless and panicky.

It made LC's head throb. He turned it back at the hustlers slow and steady each time he got his hands on the deck. He was good and being able to read each hand around the table made it almost too easy.

He figured out he was playing one stacked deal against his own and it was slow going. He could feel his vision start to blur and the knot in his back was cramping as his body tried desperately to neutralise the drug.

Mr Black was the one who could throw the cards any way he wanted and he was good. The blonde was called Carrick He picked that up from listening in to Black's thoughts. She was just his scam-buddy and as well as the loaded hands, they had a system of elaborate tells they were using.

LC played steady, matching Malone's wild stakes when he knew for sure he had the winning hand and folding enough times that no one took too much notice of him. When he had the deck, he threw winners out to Tennison and Carrick often enough that the pile in front of Mr Twitchy Tennison crept back to respectable as fast as LC's own stack of chips grew.

Malone took off his jacket when he got down to thirty thou. "Hot in here," he said and moved his stack around as if he could make it grow just by spreading out the chips.

LC's headache peaked. He was overheating too and it wasn't just the room. He kept on drinking, breathing carefully to lower his heart rate, and just as he thought he might pass out right there at the table, he felt his head start to clear as his system began to cope with the drug.

He looked from face to face, reading the emotions and intentions of each person sitting there, seeing their cards and looking into their minds easily. He could strip away the layers and see their deepest secrets. He could see the contempt Carrick had for her partner, Black's fear of being caught and locked up again, and Malone's hatred for the woman whose money he was squandering. And LC didn't even need to look at Tennison to know why the man needed to win here.

It was absurd. And it was time to stop running. He knocked back another glass of whisky, feeling like he could take on the universe. It was time to find Anya and show whichever fucked up corporation had dared to screw them over what happened when you messed with the Thieves' Guild.

LC glanced at the two queens in his hand and casually folded, letting Malone take the win on two tens.

Malone slapped the table and grinned. "Good gods, about time. Now let me show you how this game is played, gentlemen."

Tennison laughed and clinked glasses with him, neither of them with the faintest idea why their fortunes had changed.

That was the way LC needed to keep it but after a while he picked up that Black was beginning to suspect something. The man was good himself so it wasn't a surprise that he should see if someone else was manipulating the deck. And the pile of chips in front of the man had diminished noticeably.

Black started to work his fingers nervously, cracking his knuckles, itching to say something to Carrick. He wasn't sure. LC could see it in his eyes and hear the uncertainty, the guy arguing with himself each time LC shuffled and dealt – no one could be that good, he was thinking.

It was hard not to smile.

LC dealt him two aces. No one else had anything worth a damn. Black eyed his hand and watched the bets, watching Carrick for a tell but the blonde folded with an exaggerated sigh and lit another cigar. Paranoia won out and Black folded, staring at LC as he ditched the hand, expecting a sting, eyes narrowing as he saw Tennison take the pot with a pair of fives.

The tension built and next time round, LC dealt a winner to Carrick, narrowly beating Malone's two tens with two tens and king high.

"Jesus, Malone, your luck schtinks tonight," LC said, leaning on the table like he was trying to steady himself, adding, "Nice one, Carrick," with a wink as he passed on the deck and held out his glass for a refill. Both the hustlers were smart enough not to react but the confusion was almost overwhelming. No one had mentioned their names and there was no way LC should know, unless Black was thinking, they had something going on and he was being screwed by his own scam-buddy.

Black looked at Carrick, then looked down at her stack of chips. She was confused but too good to show it. She licked a finger and ran it in a circle around the rim of her glass, casting her attentions over to Malone.

For the next few rounds, Black dealt himself winners and Carrick got nothing. In his turn, LC made sure only himself and Tennison were dealt anything worthwhile and the chips migrated steadily away from the two con artists. Malone couldn't keep up and when he left, no one came in to replace him.

So much for Olivia's waiting list.

Mr Twitchy Tennison started to sit back and calm down, enjoying the game. LC dealt him three, four, five, six of hearts, throwing three jacks at Mr Black.

"Shit," Tennison muttered and raised a reserved five thou, like he didn't quite trust the hand. LC could tell he hadn't been counting the cards and he hadn't been playing the odds.

LC folded and watched Carrick eye him suspiciously before she folded too. Black saw the raise and gestured across for two cards, snapping his fingers impatiently at Carrick to fill the tumblers. Whatever his double-crossing bitch of a buddy had going with the fool, he was thinking, that fool was still drinking the crap in the whisky and it was obviously having an effect.

LC smiled, paused for one long moment, then dealt the fourth jack to Black.

Tennison asked for one and LC tossed him a seven of hearts.

The two men stared at each other. LC felt Tennison's blood pressure rise as he swallowed down an urge to gloat. He tentatively pushed all in.

Black had no choice but to fold or match. LC slouched, drinking down the rest of the liquor in his glass as they waited.

Carrick was staring at LC. He knew she was seriously starting to suspect they were getting hustled and couldn't figure out why her partner was being a dick.

Mr Black ran a hand over his hair and smiled.

Touch and go. If he went all in, they had them down to one.

How could you lose with four jacks? Black was thinking about the two aces. How he could have won earlier with the two aces that he'd folded.

Carrick shook her head imperceptibly.

LC peered into his glass like he was astonished it was empty and pushed it forward, tapping it on the table for a top up. "What the hell is this?" he said, letting a slight slur slip into his voice. "This is good schtuff." He blinked and grinned at Tennison.

The woman drained her own glass and as she reached for the bottle, Black went all in. LC could hear him think there was no way the hand was crooked, he hadn't seen a thing, nobody could be that good, nobody could be that good after drinking down that much Banitol.

Shit. Banitol was nasty stuff and about as black market as you could get, banned on both sides of the line for its potentially lethal side effects.

Tennison smiled and laid out the flush with exaggerated care. Black cursed and threw in his hand, pushing back from the table, mouth twitching like he was trying to stop himself from accusing anyone.

Carrick looked stunned and was staring at the table to stop herself giving anything away.

LC sat up straight and stared at them both. "A friend of mine was in here earlier," he said quietly, his voice steady and with no sign of inebriation. "You took a marker from him for his ship. I want it back."

"Who the fuck are you?" Mr Black said.

"You're out of the game," LC said calmly. "I want the marker."

Mr Black narrowed his eyes, glared at his partner and took a plastic chit from his pocket.

"This?" he said with disdain, holding it up. "It's a piece of junk anyway."

He threw it onto the table and stalked from the room.

Carrick took the deck from LC, gathered up the cards and shuffled.

Tennison scooped up the chips. "Shee-it," he muttered, stuck for words for once.

17

*He could either play safe and move a pawn or risk the knight. NG
sat back. It was hot in there, the fumes from the wine strong and the
narcotic edge tingling at his senses. He stared intently at the white
knight. He'd been born telepathic, hadn't realised no one else was and
wouldn't have made it past the age of five if he hadn't been rescued by
the Man. Telekinesis was a different matter.*

The knight didn't move.

The Man smiled. "Did Anderton know?"

*"That Olivia is Ostraban's daughter? No. LC takes people at face
value. She keeps her heritage well hidden and I don't blame her. Sten's
World isn't the type of place to let people know you're from one of the
wealthiest families in Winter. Ostraban is making a lot of noise trying
to gather support for his chairmanship and the situation with Zang
hasn't helped. Olivia is well out of it."*

*NG stopped and bit his tongue, sipping at his wine. The Man knew
his opinion of Ennio Ostraban. There was no need to drag it out.*

"And the situation on Sten's World?" the Man said.

*"Volatile," NG said, giving up and moving the knight himself,
sweeping it up to stand face to face with its opposite. "It always has
been but trouble followed LC there and took the station almost to
melting point."*

After that it was easy to drain down Carrick. She left, serene in
defeat, touching LC gently on the shoulder as she passed, thinking
she'd catch him in the bar later, deciding that she might have found
herself a new partner.

No one else entered the room and when it was just LC and
Tennison sitting across from each other, LC stood and stretched.

His head was pounding, his leg had pretty much seized up and his back was still aching.

He shoved across enough piles of chips to make Tennison's stack up to a hundred.

"What is this?" Tennison said, sitting back with a smile. "I thought it was last man standing?"

"It was," LC said. "I'm standing and I'm calling it a night. How much more do you need?"

Tennison folded his arms. "Bloody hell, that was some game."

LC said softly, "How much?"

Tennison's eyes looked moist. "Quarter of a mil."

"Who is she?" It had been hard to tell whether it was the guy's daughter, wife or sister who was in trouble or why they needed the cash but it didn't make any difference.

"Daughter."

LC counted out the rest, leaving more than enough to pay back Elliott his hundred and leave some for Gallagher to pay for repairs.

They went back through the airlock together and swapped the chips for credit sticks.

Olivia was waiting in the hallway, anxious and pacing.

Tennison stuck out his hand before he left. "Thank you," he said, clasping LC on the shoulder. "If you ever need a partner, give me a shout. I wouldn't want to miss another game like that." He looked at Olivia, leering slightly. "He's a star, this guy, you look after him."

Olivia forced a smile.

Tennison went, heading to the bar, and Olivia grasped LC's arm, leading him quickly away in the opposite direction.

She wasn't impressed. "Are you insane?"

He opened his mouth to answer but she glared at him.

"No, don't say a word. My god, Tigs, there are two hustlers down there who don't know whether to kill each other right now or gang up with a posse to go after your head. What were you thinking?"

He needed to get back to the ship. "Where's Gallagher?"

"There's also a bounty hunter in my bar offering ten thousand a go for information." She snapped his arm and pulled him close. "It is you, isn't it?" she hissed in his ear.

"Liv."

"They're saying you were hustling in there."

"Liv, they were the ones running the hustle. I out-hustled them, that's all."

"Tigs, what did I say to you? These are not the kind of people you want to be messing with. I can only take care of you so far." She took hold of his hand, lacing his fingers with hers. "Your friends think you are lying unconscious in a medical bay back on their ship. They said you were shot."

He squinted at her, tired now the adrenaline was wearing off, and wanting very much to be either back in that bunk or back in Olivia's bed.

Her expression softened. "Gallagher's a nice man. He said he'd lost the ship. Why didn't you tell me? Is that what you were doing in there?"

LC held up the marker. "I got it back. Where is he?"

"My girls are still looking after him. They're very taken with the young lad."

Christ, Thom wouldn't know what had hit him.

Olivia swatted at his cheek. She still wasn't impressed. "How do you want to play this? You can't come back into the bar. It's too dangerous."

He pressed the chit and the credit stick into her hand. "Give these to Gallagher. And keep him busy for another hour or so. I'll make my own way back to the ship. Tell the girls I owe them."

She reached up and kissed him, long and hard, before stepping back. "Don't get yourself killed," she said softly and walked away.

Getting back to the ship was easier said than done. LC made his way slowly out of the Avantine, taking back stairs and maintenance routes through its winding levels.

Back at the docks, he stopped high on a gantry above the main thoroughfare and waited, watching for a long time. It looked busy, way too many people milling about down there to be sure he could walk in unnoticed. He had no idea where Sean and DiMarco were and no one could know he'd left the ship. It was too risky to just walk out there.

He climbed along to the loading area, easily breaking through security barriers, and settled in above the Duck's main cargo bay doors.

He reached out tentatively to Elliott, not sure what he was looking for or even whether he'd be able to get through, but Elliott replied immediately on a clear link.

"I've got you," the tech guy sent back. "You were right to be cautious. There are people asking about you all along the docks."

"Asking about me?"

"Not you exactly, but the description fits. You need to be careful."

"Where's Sean?"

"She went to her ship. How did it go?"

LC watched a cargo handler manoeuvre a loader stacked with boxes. She stopped by the Duck, ditched the load and drove it back across the dockside. "Gallagher has the marker back and enough money to pay for repairs. Are we taking on cargo?"

"Supplies. I thought you'd probably need a way back in."

LC watched the woman trundle her vehicle back with another load. "Where's DiMarco?"

"In a bar dockside so watch yourself."

He stood up and edged along to a ladder. Before Poule he would have clambered down the piping conduits in the shadows. Now he didn't trust that his leg would hold and he still felt drained so it was the ladder and the risk that someone might see.

He slid down two levels, waited until the woman was across at the ship then dropped down to the deck, slipping through an open door into a back area of grimy offices and locker rooms. He walked like he belonged there and pushed through into a changing room where two guys were arguing about someone being late.

LC palmed a security badge from a jacket and walked back out onto the dockside, snagging a data board as he went.

He made a show of flicking through screens and headed for the

Duck, looking bored and walking slowly, trying not to limp. The woman pulled up as she drove back.

"I need to check the inventory," he said, casually flashing her the badge and waving the board.

She shrugged, didn't care and didn't seem in the slightest bit concerned that she'd never seen him before. "Go knock yourself out."

The cargo bay doors started to rise as he approached and by the time he reached it, there was enough of a gap that he could duck under and through into the ship.

Elliott was waiting in the mess. LC threw the badge and the data board in the trash and reached into the fridge for a beer. He slouched down on the sofa, put his feet up and closed his eyes.

"Gallagher and Thom are on their way in," Elliott said softly just as he was settled. "You should get back to the medical bay. Don't want to give the game away, do we?"

LC bit back the comment that leapt to mind and got to his feet grudgingly.

Elliott stepped aside and frowned. "Are you okay? Your biometrics don't look good," he said and let LC lead the way into the corridor.

"I'm tired," he said, not stopping and not even tempted to be curious as to how Elliott knew what his freaking biometrics were doing. "They were using Banitol. Gallagher and Thom are going to be goosed."

He drank half the beer on the way to his quarters and the rest in the shower, standing in a torrent of cool water and letting his temperature drop until Elliott called him to hurry up. Then he perched on the edge of the bunk in the medical bay while the tech who wasn't a medic readied an IV.

"Is that necessary?"

"Probably not," Elliott said and LC watched as the needle pierced his arm, "but as far as everyone else is concerned, you just almost died and you shouldn't even be up. You need Ms O'Brien to think you're too sick to move."

"Fair point." LC lay back on the bunk. He felt worn out and his leg was aching. No shakes which was a development, but sore and tired. It wasn't going to be hard to act the part.

Elliott hooked up a pouch. "Get some sleep. The ship's secure. No one can reach you here."

He woke to the sounds of bumps, deep reverberations rumbling through the ship so they were either loading or starting repairs, which either way was a good sign they'd be leaving again soon. LC lay quietly with his eyes closed, gradually aware of a presence in the room, quiet breathing and the gentle aura of a mind that was meditating.

She was thinking about cool waves breaking on a beach of white sand, warmth and safety. As soon as he opened his eyes, she sat up and leaned forward.

It was dark and the door was closed.

"I know who you are, LC," she said quietly from the shadows.

"You don't know anything, Sean."

She stood and walked to the bunk cautiously as if she was afraid he'd leap up and bolt out of there if she moved too fast.

"I'm working for NG," she said and LC's stomach clenched in a cold knot. To hear her even say NG's name sent a chill through him.

He sat up slowly and untangled his arm from the sheet where the IV line had got caught up as he was sleeping. He reached his left hand under the pillow to rest against the cold metal of the gun there. "I don't know what you're talking about."

"LC, you have to trust me. I've been sent to bring you in. The guild wants you back and the Alsatia is the only safe place for you right now."

"I'm not the guy you're after, Sean." He closed his fingers around the pistol grip. Knowing the guild had sent her was worse than knowing she was a bounty hunter. Pen had been very specific in his warning, passing on the message from Hil. Trust no one, especially that goddamned guild of yours, Pen had said and, as much as LC knew how much Pen hated the guild, the big man had always respected their allegiance. If Hil thought they had a reason to distrust NG and the guild in all this, then something had happened to make him think it.

"I've got too much proof, LC. I know it's you. And I'm going to be the only way you can get back safely from this."

"I don't know what you're talking about," he said again.

She held her hand out to him and he could see that she was offering him his knife back, hilt first.

"Badger told me about the competition," she said in almost a whisper. "I know this is yours and I know that Zach Hilyer has the other. He told me you couldn't throw a knife if your life depended on it."

The cold knot twisted and LC looked from the knife into her eyes. He could feel that she was willing him to believe her.

"I have a retina scan match," she whispered. "I know that you're LC Anderton. The Thieves' Guild wants you back, LC. Safely. Please trust me."

The way she said please almost made him fold.

"I know that Mendhel Halligan met you on Kheris when you were thirteen. Your first name really is Luka and Latia Cole was your great-grandmother."

She pronounced it Keris. And hearing her say those names threatened to bring a lump to his throat.

LC swallowed and took a deep breath. "You're mistaken, Sean. I'm not him."

She rocked back a step as if she wasn't sure what to do then sat on the edge of the bunk, still holding the knife. "Why deny it, LC? I'm here to help you. God, and I thought Hilyer was hard work." She stared at him and he could hear her frantically trying to think up something that would prove her right. It was a lost cause. No one could know any of that unless they got it from NG. Fine, she didn't have to prove to him that she was working for the guild. That he could trust her and trust NG was another matter.

"Hil took me to Badger to find you," she said, leaning in and whispering hard. "We ate chilli together and I had to hit the damn shower unit with a wrench to keep the hot water running. You don't think you can go back to the guild because there's a price on your head courtesy of some unauthorised job that you and Hilyer ran that got your handler assassinated. What more do I have to say, LC?"

18

"We train our people well," the Man said.

NG placed his goblet on the desk. "There was nothing I could have given Sean that would have made a difference," he said grudgingly. "And as it turns out, LC was right not to trust us."

"Don't be too hard on yourself," the Man chided. "We are far reaching and have extensive resources, NG, but we are not omnipotent and we do not always have the whole picture. The decision to utilise the talents of Ms O'Brien was justified. She found him, did she not?"

"It didn't occur to me that LC wouldn't just hook up with her and come home." NG shifted his weight uneasily, feeling the darkness of the chamber all around. He knew these field operatives better than anyone. He should have known. "I should have realised that in his state of mind and considering what we knew of the circumstances and the weight of the price on his head, he'd be wary."

"To say the least." The Man leaned forward and studied the board. "Nevertheless it was an accomplishment that she found him and managed to stay with him. Would he have survived without her?"

"Considering what happened, probably not."

LC took the knife in a fast, fluid motion that didn't give her a chance to deny him. He stared at her. There was no way that Hil would have taken her to Badger unless he was sure she was safe.

"Hil trusted me," she said and sat back. She was thinking it had been a mistake to confront him and that it would have been easier to drug him and drag him onto her ship unconscious.

"I don't know anyone called Hil."

"LC…"

"I'm not him," he said. "Why do you think I am?"

Sean turned her head slightly, smiled at him and stood up. "You know, usually when I take people in, they either fight me and end up on the floor in cuffs or they decide that maybe coming in with me is their best option after all. You need to trust me, LC, because there are people very close behind me who won't stop to ask if you mind. Latest on the bounty is that it's dead or alive. My arrangement with your guild stipulates alive. Help me keep you that way.'

She was too sure of herself. God knows how she'd got a retina scan. When he was unconscious?

"I'm not him and I'm not coming with you," he said tossing the knife to tumble up into the air and catching the blade in a perfect throwing grip. "So what do you do now?"

Sean ignored his continued denial and put her hands on her hips. "It's too hot dockside to haul you off this ship now. And you're in no state to run so I'm going to stay here with you, Luka. And when you come to your senses and decide to go home, I'll be here to help you get there safely. Believe me, you won't make it out of here alive by yourself."

After she'd gone, LC lay back and tumbled the knife over his fingers wondering if it was too hot out there for him to slip through and catch a ride. He reckoned he could. He'd wait until they were about to leave then he'd split. Whether Sean was working for NG or not, he couldn't go back until he'd talked to Hil and that meant trying to get back to Aston.

Decision made, he tucked the knife beneath the pillow and closed his eyes.

The next two days were interminable. Sean checked on him regularly and he had a feeling she'd made a deal with Elliott to make sure he didn't leave the ship. He couldn't exercise properly with the damned drip in his arm and every time he tried to get up, Elliott or Sean would appear and coax him back to bed. Elliott was enjoying it, that much was evident without having to read the guy's mind. And when it was obvious they weren't going to leave him alone, LC lay back and relaxed. He'd spent time in Medical before. Two months he was stuck in there on the Alsatia after one tab and he still hadn't dropped off the top of the standings, so he could handle it for a couple of days.

Thom came to visit once the hangover had worn off and mumbled something about forgetting if he'd said anything, he couldn't remember what exactly but whatever it was, it didn't matter. LC had told him not to worry.

He was lying on the bunk trying to figure out if he could sense where people were on the ship, maybe get into their minds and influence them when DiMarco stuck his head around the door and waved a bottle of moonshine.

LC almost laughed, sure it hadn't been the power of his thoughts but appreciative of the coincidence of the pilot's timing nonetheless. He sat up and pulled on a shirt, leaning his back into the corner and pulling up his left leg beneath the blanket to sit forward.

DiMarco pulled up a chair and held out two shot glasses. "It's good to see you're still breathing, Luka buddy," he said with a grin, no remorse at how close he'd come to leaving him for dead back on Poule.

LC took the tumblers and balanced them on his knee while DiMarco filled them with the green liquor.

They took one each.

"Gan bei," the pilot said, nudging his glass and knocking it back in one.

LC followed suit and held out his glass for a refill. The alcohol hit his bloodstream with a satisfying warmth.

"Gallagher asked me to tell you we'll be leaving in a few hours," DiMarco said, sipping at his second glass. "The repairs are all done. Get this, he got caught up in a card game and won enough to pay for the shields and the main engine to get fixed. Can you believe he can't remember it but he's sure it was one helluva night. We have cargo loading, courtesy of my good self. And Thom's got the engine room covered so you can sit on your ass a while longer. We're all good to go."

It wasn't that simple and LC could feel a tension in the guy that he was covering with the flippancy.

DiMarco tossed a pack of cards onto the bunk. "I thought you might like some company. What's your game, Luka buddy?"

He was fishing.

LC took the pack and slipped out the cards, throwing them into a simple shuffle, nothing flash.

"What's the stakes?" he said amiably.

"You tell me."

"Five card mean queen," LC said, dealing out five cards each and placing the deck between them. "Aces high. Loser buys the next bottle."

DiMarco laughed. "Mean queen, Jesus. I haven't played that in years." He tapped the bottle of moonshine. "And this stuff isn't for sale, buddy. You lose, you're gonna have to do better than that."

"I'm not going to lose," LC said softly with a smile, checking his hand and reading the pilot's hand as clear as if the cards were marked.

DiMarco threw three cards into the discard pile and took three off the deck. "How about loser pays ten thou?" He rearranged the cards in his hand and raised his eyes.

LC caught the look and threw in two. The two he got back fitted nicely into his hand. "That's pretty high stakes, DiMarco."

"It's how much I turned down last night not to give you up, Luka." He threw down one card and took one from the deck, making eye contact only when he was done. "I reckon you owe me, bud."

"I don't know what you're talking about." LC placed two queens on the pile. He picked up a two of diamonds and a four of hearts. Not bad.

"I also heard a rumour about a game of poker two nights ago." DiMarco dropped three cards and looked up with a smile. "How much is it worth to keep my mouth shut on that one? I'm guessing you don't want Gallagher and Seanie to know."

LC took the opening to ditch his last queen. "I've been stuck in here since we docked, DiMarco. Check with Elliott."

The pilot laughed with disdain. "That guy. I don't trust him as far as I could spit. Look, I'm not going to make trouble for you. If I wanted to do that, I'd have ten thousand in my pocket and you wouldn't be sitting there so cosy, buddy. Someone is asking about you. I swear, I even saw a picture and it's you – hair's different and the colour was off but it is you. And they're offering ten thou a pop for information. Why are you worth so much, Luka? I knew you were hiding something. Care to share?"

LC put his cards face down on the bunk and looked at the pilot. The guy was an ass who was enjoying baiting him. It was a dangerous game.

He said softly, "Are you going to tell Gallagher why he was arrested on Poule?"

DiMarco narrowed his eyes and tossed back a shot of the moonshine. "Whatever you think you know, Luka buddy, I'm telling you, don't go there."

"Everyone has something to hide, right DiMarco, but piracy? They would've thrown away the key on all of us."

"Gallagher doesn't need to know. It was a long time ago. It was nothing. Fucked up places like Poule, they use any excuse to commandeer a ship and take its crew. Look at me, I'm a drunk. You on the other hand..." DiMarco was still holding up the glass. He pointed at LC with one finger. "You're something else. What is it, Luka buddy, that makes you such hot property, huh?"

LC was resisting the urge to go for the knife or the gun. The pilot had him trapped. He sat perfectly still, unblinking, weighing up how fast he could take the guy down.

DiMarco laughed again, genuinely that time. "I'm ribbing you, Luka. Jesus, don't panic." He topped up the tumblers. "You're all hooked up there and weak as a kitten, right? How could you have been gallivanting around the station, huh? And what the hell is it to me if someone's trying to find you? Lighten up, buddy. I didn't give you away. Are we playing cards or what?"

LC picked up his hand, trying to read what the hell DiMarco was intending. There was nothing clear. If anything, there was an appreciation there that they hadn't left him to rot on Poule but it was hidden deep and the guy was well on his way to getting drunk. Whatever, it was getting too close for comfort here on board the Duck. If they were leaving in a couple of hours, it was time to go.

He stayed quiet while they finished the game, matching the pilot shot for shot of the liquor, and playing aggressively to win fast.

When LC threw down his last card and sat back, DiMarco chuckled and stood up, taking the bottle of moonshine and walking out with a wave.

He left the cards.

LC scooped up the deck and shuffled, setting it up into four perfect suits in a series of fast, neat flicks. He placed the deck on the bed, pulled the IV line out of his arm and slipped down the corridor to his cabin.

It was definitely time to go.

He dressed quickly, pulled on his boots and was stuffing his few belongings into a bag when he heard heavy footsteps outside. He froze. A wave of hot raw emotion hit him, Gallagher and someone else, so sharp that it set off a pulsing pain behind LC's eyes.

He grabbed the gun, heart hammering, and stood staring at the door but they passed, heading towards the medical bay, the onrush of agitation and anguish fading as they moved away. He laced up his boots quickly, slid the knife into place and tucked the gun into his waistband in the small of his back. He pulled on his jacket and glanced around. There was nothing there that he really needed to take and the faster he got off this ship the better.

He listened at the door before he opened it, reluctant to be confronted by anyone, and slid out into the corridor. There were fresh bloodstains on the deck, drips and footprints smudged in red, smeared handprints on the walls. Christ.

LC stopped, caught between the need to run and a cold empty vacuum of feeling he caught from someone behind. He turned and saw Gallagher and Elliott struggling to hold up Hal Duncan between them, the big man drenched in blood and sagging, struggling to stay conscious. They pushed through into the medical bay and LC stared after them. He cursed and ran to catch up, every instinct screaming at him to run the other way and get off the ship.

They were hoisting Duncan up onto a bunk by the time he reached them, Gallagher stepping back, shocked.

"They're right behind me," Duncan gasped, words slurring. His face was a mass of bruises and LC was almost overwhelmed by the intense pain the big man was trying to shut down and overcome.

"We have to go," Duncan whispered and grasped at Elliott's arm. "They're coming." His jaw looked broken and LC could feel his frustration as he tried to get the words out. "I had to warn you. Donnelly thinks you betrayed him."

LC turned and dug around in the supply lockers for anything that looked like a trauma patch. He threw a pack to Elliott, trying to ignore the panicky confusion emanating from Gallagher and the cold despair surrounding Duncan.

Elliott pushed the big marine gently down onto the bed but Duncan struggled to sit, trying to look at Gallagher.

"McCabe's here," he said, voice breaking. "Gallagher, go. Get this ship away." He sagged back, closing his eyes. "They're right behind me."

Gallagher swore and touched LC's arm. "Luka, he's right. Come on, we need to get to the bridge."

Elliott nodded them away and calmly tended to Duncan, blood everywhere, IV lines trailing. LC couldn't help feeling that this is what the room must have looked like when they brought him back from the dockside on Poule.

He backed away and ran after Gallagher, calling Thom and Sean on an open urgent link.

"Is the ship ready to go?"

Sean answered first. "We're scheduled to leave in about an hour and a half. What's wrong?"

"We have to go now." He gave them a quick and concise rundown as he tried to keep up with Gallagher. It was easy to forget how serious the injury had been until he tried to move anywhere fast, then the wound in his thigh, which wasn't entirely healed, pulled like a bitch and his limbs felt like jelly.

"We're good," Thom sent from the engine room.

"DiMarco's drunk but I can get us out of dock," Sean sent. "Where are you?"

"Right here," he replied as they walked onto the bridge.

She looked at him in disgust. Gallagher hadn't questioned why he was up and about but both Sean and DiMarco looked surprised.

"Feeling better there, buddy?" DiMarco said with a laugh.

LC ignored him, slipping into the engineer's chair and hooking up with the ship without a word. He could sense Elliott in there too and the tech guy guided him through to a sitrep from the station. Donnelly and McCabe were dominating the docks, running roughshod over the security and approaching with a force bristling with heavy weapons.

LC threw the picture over to Sean and felt her ready the ship for departure with an increased urgency.

A deep rumble echoed through the hull of the Duck as grapples whipped free and the ship shifted.

Elliott broadened the scene and showed LC shields firing up to maximum, a couple of other ships undocking around them with weapons targeted.

"Oh shit," he muttered.

Elliott's voice was a calm and quiet whisper inside his head, "Tell them to set course and just fly. The shields will take care of anything these people can throw at us. I'll arrange jump."

"Give us warning this time, will you?"

Elliott didn't reply but a display appeared on one of the screens with a countdown timer. Four hours to jump.

LC relayed the message and sat back. So much for slipping off the ship quietly and disappearing.

They watched the shields deflect missiles and ignored the threats that Donnelly was broadcasting.

Elliott's countdown dropped abruptly to five seconds. Christ. LC warned Thom.

When they dropped out of jump, no ships followed them. DiMarco laughed. "Hell of an exit there, Gallagher."

LC could feel that Sean wasn't happy but was trying to reconfigure her plans on the hoof. She glanced around at him, furious but at the same time content that he was right there and she still had tight enough reins on him, wherever the hell they ended up.

He stood. "Gallagher, I'm going back to see if Elliott needs a hand."

Gallagher nodded. "Right, no problem." He looked confused for a moment then said, "Shouldn't you be in medical anyway?"

Elliott was leaning against one of the bunks with his arms folded by the time he got back down there. LC stared. Duncan didn't look good and he could feel the edge of a chill darkness creeping in.

Elliott turned and shook his head. "I'm sorry. There's nothing more I can do. There's too much damage. It was a miracle he made it this far."

LC could feel the big man slipping away. "There must be something you can do." He spun around, pulling open drawers and throwing out pouches and syringes. "Come on, Elliott, do something."

He could hear a frantic edge to his voice. The big marine had saved his life, and it was hard to stand aside and watch him die.

Elliott stood quietly. "I'm not a medic, LC, but I know when someone is too far gone."

"You saved me," he said awkwardly.

Elliott shook his head again. "No, I didn't."

LC felt cold inside, knowing exactly what he meant. "There must be something," he said again.

"He needs blood and plasma, LC, lots of it and we don't have enough. Apart from that, his injuries are too severe. He's taken a huge amount of punishment from someone. I couldn't even tell you how many broken bones and fractures there are. He's got a punctured lung and massive internal bleeding. The best I can do with what we have on board is give him an overdose of painkillers and sedatives. At least it will take the pain away."

LC blinked, the headache peaking again. "We can't just let him die. There must be something you can do to stabilise him. We'll find a colony with a hospital. Don't you have an isopod? Anything?"

"There's only one miracle cure for imminent death around here that I'm aware of, LC, and it's not in the medical locker."

LC backed away, staring at Duncan lying there. "We can't."

"I've seen accelerated regeneration before," Elliott said calmly. "Earth is renowned for it. They test regenerative drugs on entire battlefield units. But I've never seen anything like whatever it is you have in your body, LC."

"Elliott, god, no, you don't know what it's like. It's a fucking death sentence."

"He's going to die anyway."

"I can't do that to him. It would be worse."

"Would it?"

LC started to shiver, flashing back to the lab and the cold jab on his neck, the heat of the explosion on his back as they fled.

"He'll be better off dead than living with this," he said, voice quiet and unconvincing.

Elliott was impassive. "You should know." He looked LC straight in the eye. "It's your choice."

LC could see that Duncan's breathing was slowing, feel his system shutting down, the big man's essence fading. He shrugged out of his jacket suddenly. "What can we do? How do we do it?"

"It's in your blood. Sit down. I don't know how much we'll need."

19

The solitary candle was struggling, fighting and failing to push back the darkness. The Man moved his queen into a position to threaten NG's knight then sat back, still staring at the board.

The stifling heat in the room was almost unbearable. NG absently rubbed at the band around his wrist. There was no point looking at the watch; it always stopped when he entered this chamber but it felt like he'd been in there for hours.

The Man raised his eyes. "Colonel Jameson denies all knowledge of the research that was acquired from their laboratory?"

Jameson was Old Earth through and through and he'd been stubbornly guarded and obstructive every time NG had managed to speak to him. "He wasn't happy." That was an understatement. NG moved the knight to safety and reached for his wine. "He wanted a guarantee that we'd hand over their stolen property without poking our noses into it, was the way he put it."

That elicited a smile. "Earth dabbles in the very fabric of life without appreciating how close they are to burning their fingers," the Man said. "How old are you, NG?"

He paused with the goblet half way to his lips and returned the smile. "Older than I look."

The Man picked up his own goblet. "What price, do you think, is this galaxy prepared to pay for immortality?"

He hadn't meant to sleep. He'd watched as Elliott set up a transfusion system, watched as the guy drew blood and hooked it up to Duncan and somewhere along the process he must have keeled over because he couldn't remember anything else and he woke up curled on his side beneath a blanket.

Elliott hadn't bothered to give him an IV, probably thinking that Duncan needed any plasma they had left more than he did. His head was pounding and the muscle in his back twinged painfully as he twisted round to sit up.

Hal Duncan was sleeping peacefully on the opposite bunk, cleaned up and under clean sheets, breathing steady and colour starting to return.

LC checked the time on his wristband and watched the bioreadings scroll, meaningless numbers that were even more erratic than before.

He felt drained. It had only been three hours. The background sound of the ship's engines was a constant thrumming drone. They were flying but he didn't know where they were going, never mind how far out they were.

He didn't want to speak to anyone and he was done lying around in medical so he got up, grabbed his jacket and left, standing for a moment watching the big man's chest rise and fall and feeling the warm, passive calm of sleep emanate from his mind. It looked like he'd live but LC couldn't help the uneasy apprehension in the pit of his stomach at the thought of what they'd have to deal with when the big man woke up. When he'd been on the run with Hil, neither of them had realised what was going on. They thought he'd been poisoned with some kind of bioweapon. It had been excruciating, every cell in his body burning in agony, and they'd had people chasing after them. No chance to rest up and recover. They'd just had to run and hide until Hil had offered to take the heat and they'd split up.

LC rubbed his eyes. He needed a shower and a beer, not necessarily in that order.

There was no one around in the crew's quarters and he acquired a couple of beers by taking a detour to the mess. As he sat and drank the first, the implications of exactly what they'd done started to filter through. Sean had him tagged as her target but as far as he could pick up, she didn't know why apart from knowing that he'd run an unauthorised tab and the guild wanted him back. She didn't seem to have questioned what he could have been after that would warrant such an excessive bounty, so she probably didn't know about the lab.

DiMarco could prove to be trouble but only in so much that he knew people were out there offering money for information.

And Elliott knew about the virus, or whatever it was, and the price on his head but not necessarily about the guild.

He'd have to figure out how much to tell Hal Duncan of all this. Or he could just split and leave Duncan to live with it. If no one but Elliott knew, it might go no further. Who could tell?

LC finished the beer and dropped the bottle in the chute, taking the other one back to his cabin. He didn't mean to crash out again but woke up sprawled on his bunk with a headache. A fast cold shower didn't do much to clear his head and not knowing where they were going was starting to niggle. He wasn't a control freak like Hilyer but he had to leave next time they docked, no doubt about that; wherever and whenever it was, he was leaving.

There was no reply from Elliott when he tried to reach someone and Thom buzzed back quickly that he was busy and would talk later. Sean said she was in the mess and if he was hungry, she'd heat up a pack of soup for him. He wasn't but she refused to talk, saying she'd bring him up to speed if he got his ass down to the mess.

By the time he got there, she had a pack of tomato soup sitting on the table for him.

Sean pushed the pouch in front of him as he sat and reached a hand up to his forehead, feeling his temperature before he could swat her away.

"You feel hot," she said. "Should you be up?"

"Probably not."

"How's Hal?"

"He'll be fine. It wasn't as bad as it looked. So what's happening? Where are we headed?"

Sean smiled and switched to the Senson, a tight private link. "Some place called T72. DiMarco knows it. We're about three hours out. We're dropping off his cargo then heading to Erica."

Erica not Harbin.

LC snapped open the tube on the soup and took a sip. He hadn't eaten anything in a while and it was weird to feel the hot liquid hit his stomach.

"Why are we talking privately?" he sent back.

Sean was watching him, thinking of Hilyer again. 'Because we have a problem. DiMarco is bragging that he knows something about you that is worth thousands. He ran into a couple of bounty hunters on Sten's World and he recognised the image they were touting around. He obviously doesn't know how much the bounty is but it won't take him long to find out. We need to leave."

She said it matter of fact, as if it was agreed that he was going with her.

LC smiled and put down the pouch. "Sean, I'm not going with you," he sent through the connection.

"What else do I have to say to convince you, LC? What's the problem? You don't trust me, fine, that's probably smart of you. But it's NG who wants you back. Don't you guys all live and breathe guild? I'm offering you a fast ride back, as safe as you're going to get." She narrowed her eyes, thinking that she shouldn't say what she was about to. "I'll level with you, LC. It's my fault that things are so hot around you. The other bounty hunters, they're not tracking you. They're following me."

"One of your buddies tell you that?"

Sean flashed on the guy with the groomed stubble and he could feel her mixed feelings for the man. There was professional admiration but it was tinged with an uncomfortable aversion. That was interesting.

"No one knows I'm working for the Thieves' Guild," she sent. "The bounty on you is ridiculously high enough that a lot of people are after it and the easiest way for some of these lowlifes to have a go is to follow someone they know will find you. We're running out of time. I have a ship that can pick us up as soon as we dock. She's been following us. What's the harm in coming back with me?" She leaned forward. "What are you afraid of, LC?"

"I can take care of myself, Sean."

He finished the soup while she watched, listening in while she desperately tried to think of something she could say that would change his mind. He was about to stand when Thom walked into the mess, trying to scrub dirt out of his fingernails and distractedly running an argument through his head, trying to persuade himself that he'd done the right thing. It was a noisy intrusion and LC had to concentrate to dampen it down but Thom couldn't look either of them in the eye as he sat and it was hard not to think that the kid may have done something stupid that could affect them all.

Sean threw another pack of soup into the heater and asked LC if he wanted more. He shook his head, picking up that Sean was concerned about the kid too. As if things couldn't get more complicated.

She pulled three beers out of the fridge and opened them without asking. Thom took his without a word.

"The Lewis is playing up," the kid said eventually. "I've been trying to fix it without disturbing you, but…"

That wasn't what was bothering him. He was fixating on a conversation, a dressing down, running the words through his head and LC couldn't tell if it was recent or years old. He picked up that the kid felt bad lying to them. And when Thom ran through his head, clear as day – screw the mission, what the hell do I care, they can't force me to do that to anyone – LC almost choked on a mouthful of beer. He resisted the urge to throw the kid against the wall and pound some kind of confession out of him. God knows who 'they' were but Thom was working for someone. And LC had no inclination to stick around and find out who.

He stood up. "The drive will be fine," he muttered. "I'll take a look at it later," and he made his excuses, head pounding and needing space to think. It felt like the walls were closing in. He needed to cut loose and the sooner he could get off this ship, the better.

Duncan was still sleeping. LC settled quietly onto his own bunk and stretched out. Elliott had said Sean's ship had an AI so going with her and stealing the ship was probably out of the question. Going with her and persuading her to take him somewhere else was a possibility. If she genuinely wasn't interested in the bounty, he could start to work on her. Maybe she'd consider a diversion to Aston. He could introduce her to Pen and decide from there if he could go back to the guild.

It occurred to him that he hadn't been able to confront her about Hil. If he owned up and admitted who he was, he could ask what the hell she'd done with Hilyer. She might know if he was still alive.

He didn't realise he'd fallen asleep again until he became aware of a gentle nudging at his awareness.

"Elliott," he replied without opening his eyes.

He felt the amusement in Elliott's reply. "I thought you might like to see something interesting."

LC sat up, opening his eyes and startled to see Elliott sitting there between the two bunks.

"Jesus, Elliott," he whispered out loud, "why didn't you just wake me up?"

The tech guy smiled and leaned across to hand over a data board. It was playing footage from security cameras on the dockside, something hacked from station security. LC watched a figure that was obviously Thom walk hands in pockets up to a guarded airlock, flash an ID at the guards there and wait while they cycled the door.

"So?"

"Listen to this."

LC felt the connection switch and broaden as Elliott played back a recording through the link. He recognised Thom sounding defensive, "… I haven't had a chance," then a woman's voice, "Lieutenant Garrett, don't give me that. You've had plenty of time to corroborate the evidence. Find out where and find out how. Check in within the next hour and you'd better have something to report," clipped tones and no humour, military.

"There's more," Elliott said, "but you get the idea."

"Christ."

"The ship he went onto is registered with Earth, some phoney corporation that doesn't exist past some dubious documentation they filed with the station."

"So Thom is Earth military?"

"So it would appear, attached to some covert spec ops unit by the look of it."

"Why," LC sent, keeping to the link so as not to disturb the big marine, "why the hell is Earth running a covert operation on a shit-hole like Sten's World? There's nothing here."

"You know Gallagher's story?"

"The aliens?"

Elliott nodded. "He was shot down returning from a routine supply run to one of the mining colonies. He swears blind it was an alien vessel, out of nowhere, faster than anything he's ever seen, configured like nothing anyone has ever encountered before and it shot him down. Destroyed his ship and the AI he'd worked with for years. Gallagher was lucky to get away at all."

"Elliott, we've all heard his story. Are you saying it's true?"

He spread his arms with a little shrug. "Who knows? But it looks like Earth has a spec ops unit operating here in the Between and it looks like they've sent young Lieutenant Garret to check out Gallagher. Maybe they're looking for aliens."

LC couldn't help the smile that snuck out. He'd been sent to retrieve enough 'alien' artefacts in his career. They were some of the most valuable items out there and the corporations didn't believe such artefacts should languish in private collections unless it was their own. So if the owner refused to sell, the guild was sent in to acquire – all in the name of scientific progress. Most of it was junk. One piece had eaten through its hermetically-sealed container and then his backpack to give him second-degree burns before he'd realised something was wrong. God knows what that had been.

Elliott stood up. "I suppose they had to chase down Gallagher to see if there was anything in his story. He was making enough noise, telling anyone who'd listen. Lieutenant Thom Garrett is probably just here to confirm that it's bunkum. More probably they suspect the Wintrans of developing some new technology out here."

He patted LC's leg briefly as he passed, heading towards the door. "This has been a most entertaining crew, I must admit. The best the Duck has seen in a long time."

LC stared after him. "How many have you seen?"

Elliott walked out without answering.

"What's your story, Elliott?" LC fired after him. "You know all about the rest of us. You can listen in to a tight wire between Senson Sixes. That's hacking military grade shit."

The man was a black void of nothing that LC couldn't read or even sense. But that ability was at least one thing Elliott didn't know about and not something LC would admit to.

He didn't reply. LC rubbed the back of his neck. Whether Thom was here for Gallagher or not, he didn't want to be anywhere near military of any sort. Sean's offer was suddenly looking more and more tempting.

20

"Garrett?" the Man said, picking up the jug and swirling gently. "Why do I know that name?"

NG drained the last of his wine and pushed the goblet across the desk. "Old Earth," he said. "Military family. Generations of top brass. There's been a high ranking Garrett involved in every major Imperial military action for the last five hundred years."

"Same family?"

"As far as we can tell," NG said. Legal had had a field day digging into the history files. "Their latest prodigy vanished from all records two years ago."

"Are you sure it's him?"

NG watched as the Man topped up both cups from the jug.

"Our military and government contacts on Earth deny all knowledge of a Thomas Garrett," NG said. "But then they deny that they have a special operations unit nudging Wintran space out in the Between."

White tendrils of vapour crept upwards, dissipating into the darkness.

The Man set the jug aside. "They lie and deceive while the real enemy circles. How close are they to finding out the truth?"

NG gave a slight shrug of his shoulders. There were always rumours of alien sightings on both sides of the line. Gallagher was no exception.

The Man stood up. He reached down to nudge a pawn. "Circumstances conspire to gather these individuals to us," he said. "I understand Ms O'Brien came close to bringing Anderton back. What happened?"

Sean sat on the end of the bunk, cross-legged, holding a hand with two pairs, kings and fours, ace high. She was thinking she could raise the bet but decided to call instead. She was too cautious and way too impatient for poker; she had no feel for the finesse of it.

"What else did Hilyer say about me?" LC sent privately through the link. It was good to hear that Hil was safe, or at least had been safe when Sean left him at the guild. He didn't care that Elliott was probably listening in – there wasn't much the guy didn't know anyway.

"He said never to play you at poker."

LC grinned and laid out his hand of four queens.

Sean threw down her cards in disgust. "Why now?" she said. "What's changed?"

LC gathered the cards and shuffled, hard and fast, lining them up the way he wanted as she looked straight at him, not his hands.

"You're right," he said. "It's time to go but I need you to take me to Aston, not the Alsatia."

She smiled and shook her head. "No deal. I get paid once you're back at the guild. And I won't be happy that you're safe until I see you back there."

LC paused with the deck poised to be dealt. "What did Hil tell you about the guild?"

Sean narrowed her eyes. "Why?"

LC bit his lip and squinted back at her. "Because it wasn't just running an unauthorised tab that got us into trouble. We were set up. And someone at the guild must have been in on it."

She started to shake her head but realised the precarious position she was in. He could tell she absolutely appreciated the privilege he'd granted her in admitting who he was and she knew without any doubt that if he wanted to, he could lose her again. She was thinking that he could vanish into thin air if she so much as took her eyes off him.

He dealt the cards, four aces to Sean and a straight flush to himself.

She picked up the hand, stared at him for a moment than threw the cards face up onto the bunk. "Okay, I get it. You can do whatever the hell you want." She smiled. "But I found you and I'm taking you back. Aston is too dangerous."

LC laid his own hand out, five hearts from nine to king, and she laughed. "You know," she said, "everything everyone told me about you is true. I should have asked for more money. NG isn't paying me enough. Here, let me deal. And tell me why you think someone at the guild set you up. God, I need to know things like that if I'm going to keep you safe."

She took the deck and they pretended to play cards while he told her the whole story. For some reason that he didn't understand, once he started and she was sitting there listening, he couldn't stop and he spilled everything, more than he'd ever told anyone. Even Hil.

Except when he got to the part about the lab, he faltered and skipped over the rest. She didn't need to know about the virus and she didn't ask why the bounty was so high.

She went back to the bridge with an hour left before they were due in at T72.

LC snoozed, any unease at the thought that she knew about his life cancelled out by the idea of a free ride out with a bounty hunter watching his back. She'd told him she was getting paid standard rates by the guild – half a mill plus expenses and that's plenty, she'd said. If she had any intention of selling him out for the twenty six million, she was hiding it well.

He was woken up from deep sleep by an urgent call that broke through abruptly, no subtlety in getting his attention and a sharpness to Sean's voice that set his nerves on edge. "Change of plan," she said. "Get up to the bridge."

He hadn't meant to sleep and he sat up feeling rattled. He pulled his gun out from under the pillow and slid off the bed to see Hal Duncan watching, eyes open but bleary. The big ex-marine was cold and it looked like he had the shivers pretty badly. As LC watched, he tried to sit up. A vicious spike of pain shooting up his spine from the small of his back made the big man wince and made LC cringe in a physical manifestation of empathy that was eyewateringly real. He'd picked up on people's pain before, bad when they were close, but nothing to this degree. And this was pain he'd thought he was done with. Going through it a second time, even by proxy, just sucked.

"Hey," he said awkwardly.

"Hey," Duncan whispered back hoarsely. "Where am I?"

LC tucked his pistol behind his back and grabbed his jacket. "On the Duck. What do you remember?"

"McCabe shooting his mouth off to Mal Donnelly. Not much after that," he admitted. "I feel like shit. What happened?"

LC shrugged into his jacket and stuck his hands in his pockets, feeling uncomfortable. This guy would have died if they hadn't infected him with god knows what – how the hell was he supposed to explain what had happened? Hey, you'll live but the entire galaxy will be chasing after you to pin you down, liquidise your brain and inject it into rats.

"We left Sten's World," he said. "We probably won't be going back."

Duncan nodded, like he might have been remembering. "Jesus."

LC picked up flashes of intense anger, and an edge of something he couldn't fathom. A headache was starting to prickle behind his eyes.

"Where are we now?" Duncan asked, wincing as he tried to move again and thought better of it. He was pale, fighting an incredible amount of pain and pushing through it by sheer force of will. It was hard not to stare. LC had almost forgotten how bad it had been and his admiration for the man went up knowing what it must be taking for him to sit there not screaming in agony.

"Heading into some mining colony. We've got cargos to ditch and I suppose Gallagher will figure something out after that."

"McCabe's a son of a bitch," Duncan murmured. "I tried to tell Donnelly but he wouldn't listen."

LC didn't know what to say. Duncan was thinking that he should never have let Richardson go home. They'd fought together, the intense pain of loss going back a long way, memories of deafeningly heavy firepower and the punch of dust and shrapnel from explosions that were too close for comfort mingling with unyielding bonds of camaraderie that made the losses all the more painful.

Duncan closed his eyes and shivered. LC pulled the blanket from his own bunk and put it within reach.

"I have to go to the bridge," he said quietly and backed away. "Shout if you need anything."

The tension on the bridge was palpable. Thom was sitting in the engineer's chair, seething, trying to hold in an anger that had more to do with the dressing down he'd had than anything that was happening on the bridge. Sean was tapping at her console like it had given her a personal insult and DiMarco was standing with Gallagher, a hand on the older man's shoulder, reassuring him that it would be fine.

It didn't look fine.

"What's up?" LC said casually, walking up behind Thom and peering over his shoulder.

Thom shook his head. Sean didn't look up but she answered through the wire, "DiMarco failed to mention that T72 doesn't have an orbital. We're taking the ship down onto the planet. Gallagher is fraught, Thom isn't happy, Elliott reckons we'll be fine."

"And you?"

"My ship is going to meet us down there. We can switch when she lands. I'm not happy but it's the best we're going to be able to do."

"Why did you want me up here? Thom looks like he's got it under control."

"I want you close by. I'll explain to Gallagher as soon as we get there that we have to go. Elliott and Thom can cover for the rest of the trip."

He could feel that she was worried. The sudden change in plan following his unexpected outpouring of honesty had made her reassess. Now she knew for definite that he was him and he wasn't fighting her anymore, she wanted to go.

And she was uneasy about DiMarco, that was clear.

"We have a few minutes before we start to descend," she said out loud. "You'd better all buckle in."

Gallagher and DiMarco took their seats and LC slipped into one of the auxiliary chairs.

"It's a great place," the pilot said. "I'm sure I said there was no station. You must've not been listening to me, Seanie. Bill, I swear, you'll love it. I'm surprised you haven't been out here before. The people are great. They're in the middle of nowhere and they're always so chuffed to get a shipment, you can triple the price you ask and they'll pay it. Believe me."

"I know," Gallagher said distractedly, "it'll be fine." He was thinking that he just wanted to get done and get to Erica.

They dipped into a steep descent. LC sat back and closed his eyes. The Duck was one hell of an old ship to be putting through the stresses of landing on a planet.

He squinted and dug sunglasses out of his inside jacket pocket. Sean was standing next to him and she put a hand on his back, the gentle gesture he'd seen her use before. It sent a shiver down his spine and not an unpleasant one.

"Don't wander off," she warned, speaking through the link, and squinting herself as she stared off into the distance. "I don't like this."

They'd got a message from the surface just as they hit the atmosphere, warning them that the designated airfield at the colony was too small and they'd have to land in the desert. No real problem except the ship was now surrounded by a dozen vehicles and they didn't seem to be anywhere near the colony itself. DiMarco had shrugged it off as fine. "They'll pay extra," he'd said. "Trust me." And he'd walked out to meet the colonists. Gallagher had looked uneasily at LC, not wanting to leave the ship himself but thinking more and more that this had been a bad idea and desperately needing someone to go with the pilot to hear what was said. It had been wrenching to overhear and before he'd realised it, LC had jumped up and volunteered to just go hang out with DiMarco because he needed to stretch his legs and get some fresh for-real air. Sean had glowered at him and followed but as much as she was unimpressed, he caught the feeling that she wasn't trusting DiMarco either and thinking that it might be better to know first hand what was going on.

They followed the pilot down the ramp and watched as he waved, signalling to one of the vehicles. Its doors were thrown open and three guys got out, wearing desert gear but looking less like miners and more like mercenaries the closer they came.

The air was dry and hot and it reminded LC of Kheris. But it was good to walk on the soil of a planet, boots crunching on the uneven surface, even if it was a rocky dirt ball that brought back childhood nightmares.

DiMarco was greeted like a long-lost brother, lots of back slapping and hand shaking, and it was hard to tell if this was just a friendly meeting of business associates or something more. The pilot laughed and nodded to them. "Gentlemen, this is Luka Cole and Sean O'Brien, crew on the ship." He waved back towards the Duck, which was a looming mass behind them and as much as it was huge, LC couldn't help but feel that it was the vulnerable one there.

"The cargo's ready for unload," DiMarco said, rubbing his hands together. "Where's Tierney?"

They were directed towards another vehicle, set back from the rest, and as they approached, a door opened and a huge guy stepped out, standing away from the car with one hand inside his bulky jacket.

DiMarco stopped and turned. "Might be best if you guys wait here. It'll just take a minute but Tierney doesn't like strangers."

Sean stepped in close. "Don't screw us over, DiMarco."

He spread his hands with a smile. "Would I do that?"

LC looked back at the ship. Vehicles had backed up to the ramp and guys were trundling out loaders. Thom was back there with Gallagher to supervise from inside but whatever happened, they were outnumbered and he had a bad feeling this was looking less and less like a routine resupply.

DiMarco disappeared into the car. LC tried to keep track of

him, follow the thread of his thoughts but it merged with the ever-present background noise as the car door closed.

He scuffed his boots on the gravel and looked up at the big guy standing guard, who he could hear and who was thinking that it was a bit cooler today. Christ, if this was cooler, he didn't want to be out here when it was hot. He was sweltering. Head to foot ops kit wasn't the best gear for the desert. He should have taken his jacket off but he had the gun tucked into his belt at his back and if they had to run, he wanted his stuff with him.

Sean was standing beside him, running a quiet assessment of the situation through her mind. It was strange but it seemed like the more time he spent with someone, the clearer he could read their thoughts. She didn't know how long it would be before her ship would be here and she didn't like that there were so many guns openly on display.

LC didn't like that DiMarco was taking so long in the car.

When the doors opened, the pilot emerged first followed by a man in worn desert fatigues. He had a scar cutting his jawline and was thinking that DiMarco had done well for once. That in itself didn't mean anything but LC still didn't like the way the guy was looking at him and Sean.

There were no introductions.

"DiMarco tells me you have more than our cargo on board," the guy said, Wintran accent and the kind of voice that people listen to, not too loud but powerful. He didn't give them time to say anything. "We might be interested in negotiating a price for your full manifest. We don't often get ships out here and we have to take advantage of situations that present themselves, you understand."

There was the dilemma. Gallagher wouldn't want to lose his shipment, no matter how much these people offered.

LC was about to open his mouth to object but Sean got in first. "DiMarco doesn't have any authority to bargain. You'll need to speak to our captain. I'm sure you understand."

The man he assumed was Tierney nodded. "He'll deal with us. People don't tend to refuse our offers." He turned to DiMarco. "We don't have much time."

The pilot grinned and gestured towards the ship. "This way…"

LC tried to contact Elliott as they walked back to the Duck, unease growing at the sight of more vehicles arriving. There was no reply. He tried Thom and saw the kid raise his hand in casual acknowledgement from the top of the ramp as he connected. They'd started unloading the cargo, bulky loaders carrying the shipping boxes out to waiting flatbeds.

"Thom, warn Gallagher that these guys want the whole shipment," LC sent, keeping his voice calm. "They haven't mentioned a price yet but they want the whole lot. DiMarco's getting some kind of backhander – he's way too pleased with himself. Just tell Gallagher to watch himself and not agree if he isn't happy with whatever they offer."

"Do you want us to stop them unloading?"

"Only let them take the stuff that's theirs. Let's agree a price before they get anything else. Something's screwy with this whole set up. Do you know where Elliott is?"

He didn't.

"Okay, stay on the ramp," LC sent as they reached the ship and climbed up into the hold. "Let us know if anything happens out there."

They passed Thom and the kid just nodded and kept his position, casually watching the vehicles surrounding them, hands in his pockets like he was bored. "Are we expecting anything to happen?" he asked through the link.

"Just let us know if you see anything," LC replied, "and whatever happens, stay on the ship."

It was a relief to get back into the cool interior of the Duck. Sean introduced Gallagher to Tierney and suggested they go somewhere quiet to talk. "Stay with me," she warned LC through the wire. "Does this feel hinky to you?"

He caught her eye and shrugged. Everything had been hinky in his life since he'd got the message from Mendhel that Anya was missing.

She led them to the back of the cargo bay and through into an empty equipment storeroom. The big guy, plus another they picked up on the way, followed Tierney, bodyguarding from their stance. Why would a mining colony boss out in the middle of nowhere need bodyguards to negotiate the price on a cargo of domestic supplies?

The back of LC's neck was prickling and the buzz of noise in his head was increasing with the heightened tension he was picking up from all directions. He thought he'd been getting better at controlling it, dampening it down to the background, but it peaked with a voracity that sparked a pulsing headache. He stayed by the door, keeping it open and keeping an eye on the cargo bay.

"How much for the whole manifest?" Tierney said, straight to the point.

Gallagher shifted uneasily. "I've got a contract to take those supplies somewhere else," he said. "I'm sorry but..."

Tierney stopped him with a gesture. "Do you know what we mine here?"

Gallagher shook his head.

"Minerals, copper, diamonds... andirium. We can pay whatever you need for the full cargo. We have plenty of raw materials. What we don't have is supplies."

LC swapped a glance with Sean. No wonder DiMarco was so pleased with himself.

Gallagher shook his head again.

Something caught LC's eye out in the hold. He took a few steps back to increase the angle of his viewpoint just as there were shouts and the crash of a crate falling.

He heard Thom yell, "Hey," and footsteps thundering across the deck. Sean frowned and nodded at him. LC backed out and broke into a run, sending through the link, "Thom, what's going on?"

The kid didn't reply and LC saw why when he skidded to a halt, out in the open. A crate was lying in front of a loader, racks of weapons spilled out of its packaging onto the deck, rows of rifles and rockets glistening in the sunlight pouring in through the open bay doors. Thom was being held with a gun to his head.

"Hey," LC yelled and pulled out his pistol. Emotions were high and his head was throbbing with the clamour of indistinct voices. He thought he felt Gallagher run up alongside him, absolute dismay in a split second of frozen shock.

Trying to reach Elliott failed again and amongst the uproar of paranoia and anger and sheer disbelief that was pounding in his head from a dozen different people, LC sensed the presence of a body behind him a fraction too late to react as he was grabbed. The pistol was twisted out of his grip and he was pushed down to his knees.

21

It was hard to explain why Sean hadn't brought LC straight in. NG chose his words carefully, feeling the strained patience wearing thin.

"The Between is no place to linger," the Man said. "It's no surprise, is it not, that they became embroiled in the murky lives of the folk that infest it."

NG turned his attention back to the board. His bishop was in danger of being taken by a mere pawn. It was tempting to react but that was too obvious a move.

The Man was right. It wasn't surprising that LC had run into pirates. The raiders were getting more bold as tensions between Earth and Winter rose and the tenuous stability of the Between degenerated.

"Out loud, NG," the Man chided.

"There are whole colonies of pirates out there now," NG said. "It's a lucrative way of life. And seeing how most of the ships targeted are well-insured vessels belonging to the corporations, rich corporations, a lot of people are content to turn a blind eye, if not outright sympathise with the renegades."

He made his move, a white pawn stepping forward to threaten the black knight. Offensive not defensive, a dangerous strategy to attempt against the Man.

The Man smiled. "They are violent brigands," he said and moved his piece to safety.

"This is unfortunate," he heard Tierney say behind him.

LC tried to get up but the hand on his shoulder pushed down and the cold metal of a gun barrel was pushed against his neck. He could feel Gallagher seething.

He sent through the Senson, "Sean?"

"Right here," she sent back. "Don't move. Let's make this easy for them. We're fine and if all they want is the weapons and supplies, we can get out of this. Don't do anything stupid."

LC glanced over at Thom and could tell the kid had got the same message. He was twitching to fight back. They all were but Sean was right.

"Take them somewhere secure," Tierney said.

LC was hauled to his feet and turned around. Gallagher and Sean were pushed ahead, guns at their backs.

DiMarco led them up through the ship to the mess, standing aside and watching as they were searched in turn. Gallagher and Thom were clean but they took two knives and a small pistol from Sean. They took their time with LC, checking him twice with a wand and still missing the knife in his boot. He stood calmly while they frisked him, staring at DiMarco and wondering how the hell he hadn't seen it coming.

"Long time ago, huh?" he muttered.

The pilot shifted uneasily. "Nothing personal, Luka buddy." He turned to one of Tierney's men. "There's another one in the medical bay but he's in no state to move anywhere. Don't worry about him. And there's a tech guy who's probably on the bridge." He turned back into the room, leaning on the doorway. "Make yourselves comfortable – this might take a while."

Gallagher moved to step towards the pilot, squaring up to him. He was stopped by one of the men, a hefty palm on his chest, as the other two guys both raised their guns. LC took a step forward but Sean stopped him with a hand on his arm.

"Why?" Gallagher said simply, anger still bubbling beneath the surface.

DiMarco shrugged. "It's not what you think."

"You're a goddamned pirate."

DiMarco narrowed his eyes. "It's complicated. You wouldn't understand."

"Damned right I don't understand," Gallagher fumed. "Gun running, DiMarco? For pirates? For Christ's sake, didn't you think I had enough trouble?"

"You're not the only one with trouble," he said and left, followed by the other three who slammed the door shut behind them.

LC sat on the floor and stared at Thom who'd tucked himself in the opposite corner of the mess, tapping a hand incessantly on his knee. Sean passed round bottles of water from the fridge, LC refusing and asking for a beer instead. He was feeling flaky, head still pounding, and he needed the hit from the carbohydrate. She frowned but threw him a beer.

"Well, this is fun," she said.

Thom was quiet. LC tried Elliott again but there was no sign and there was nothing in the mess that he could hack into to get into the ship's systems.

Sean sat down. "It'll be fine. They just want the supplies," she said out loud, adding privately to LC, "This has nothing to do with us. Don't make it worse than it is."

"They haven't found Elliott," he sent back.

"He'll be hiding somewhere. What else can he do?"

"You might be surprised," he sent, regretting it as soon as he said it. His bizarre relationship with Elliott relied on them both keeping secrets.

"What does that mean?" Sean bounced back.

"Nothing, forget it." He was relieved that she didn't follow it up, attention focused as it was on their own immediate predicament.

He drank down half the beer. It didn't help as much as he was hoping. As much as Sean said this had nothing to do with them, the fact that DiMarco knew about the bounty was niggling at the back of his mind.

They hadn't caught Elliott so the tech guy could still help them and there was also Duncan, but he was probably in no state to move if the virus was running anything like it had with him. He'd spent the first three days in a delirious fever according to Hil. If Duncan was lucky, he'd start to stir in about four day's time. No good for them right now.

Gallagher sat on the sofa and rubbed his face with his hands. He looked up suddenly. "I've been shot down by bastard aliens, set up

169

by double-dealing bastard mobsters, attacked by corporate bastard mercenaries and hijacked by bastard pirates. Is there a pattern here, do you reckon?"

LC couldn't help but smile at the uncharacteristic outburst. He genuinely liked Gallagher. Mendhel had that same sense of self-deprecating humour. The smile faded and he felt the pang of loss deep inside. Mendhel had believed in him, despite everything everyone else at the guild had said when he'd arrived on their doorstep as a scrawny kid who'd known nothing but war. Mendhel had seen something in him and nurtured it, and he would have done anything for the man.

He looked up at Gallagher, who was scrubbing a hand over his head as if he could shake away the bad luck that was following him. LC bit his lip. He didn't owe these people anything but at the same time he was caught up with them in a way it was hard to explain, even to himself.

DiMarco came back after about an hour. LC had been itching to go walkabout, see if he could find Elliott, but Sean glared at him every time he stood up – and thinking about it, she was right. They were searching the ship and probably had thermal imaging out there. They'd catch him in an instant if he went crawling around the ducting vents of the ship.

The pilot leaned in and said, "Up and out, people. We're gonna take a little ride."

Gallagher folded his arms. "I'm not leaving my ship."

DiMarco opened the door further to show them that he wasn't alone – two guys armed with stubby assault rifles were standing in the corridor.

Thom got to his feet and walked out but Sean touched LC's arm. "Wait."

She wasn't happy and she was worried about Gallagher too. She whispered something in the older guy's ear and he nodded reluctantly and stood.

DiMarco smiled. "That's the smart thing."

"What about Hal?" she asked.

"He can stay here. He's too messed up to move. One of our guys will look after him. We're just going into town. Tierney wants to talk to you."

They were escorted off the ship and led towards a line of vehicles. It was hotter than it had been earlier, the sun higher in the sky and no hint of a breeze. LC put his sunglasses on and hung back, trying to gauge the scene. His headache had eased off but he didn't like the tension he was still picking up.

DiMarco dropped back. "You're with me, Luka buddy," and directed him away, separating him from the others.

Sean stopped but was persuaded along by a nudge from a rifle butt.

"I'm fine," LC sent to her. "It's DiMarco. What's he going to do?"

"What if he knows about the bounty?"

"He doesn't. Trust me, I'll be fine."

DiMarco stopped at a jeep and opened the door. LC climbed into the front seat and watched the others get into an array of battered vehicles painted in desert colours, an armed escort getting into each one.

It was hot in the jeep. No air con but windows that wound down or pushed open, real old style, the type of vehicle that had no dependence on electronics in case of EMP. LC pushed out the small corner window in the door and quickly checked the door pockets while DiMarco walked round. There was a bottle of water and a box of small bore ammunition but no weapons.

He was sitting quietly, looking out of the window when DiMarco got in and fired up the ignition. He drove off, spinning round and kicking up a cloud of dust to take the lead in their convoy.

"How much?" DiMarco said without looking at him, eyes on the dirt track ahead.

LC smiled without turning. "How much what?"

The pilot grinned. "Out here we're all running from something, Luka. You should think about staying – you have skills we could use. You can take care of yourself and I heard about the way you hacked into the station's systems on Poule to get us out of there."

"Don't believe everything Thom says."

DiMarco laughed and spun the jeep into a hard left turn, the wheels spinning on the desert floor and the vehicle bouncing over ruts in the rocky surface. "Five hundred thousand," he said, proud of it as if the price on his head was a badge of honour. "Wintran side."

"Twenty six million," LC said simply, still looking out of the window.

DiMarco laughed louder. "You're something else, buddy, you really are."

He could tell that the pilot thought he was joking, being flippant to avoid telling him the truth. DiMarco joked and drank to avoid thinking and it was easier to assume that was what other people did than it was to realise they might be serious. Whatever the hell had happened to him or whatever it was that he'd done, it was all buried way beneath the surface and far deeper than anything LC could read from the guy's mind, even sitting next to him.

They bounced across a dried out riverbed and veered right towards a range of mountains that loomed on the horizon. The side mirror was cracked but he could see in the few shards remaining that the other vehicles were keeping up behind them.

"I'm serious, Luka," DiMarco said suddenly. "Tierney isn't going to let Gallagher go. He'll offer him a choice – join us or else. How can we risk just letting you all go? There are too many people here that are safe only so long as no one knows where we are. You could do well here, Luka, I'm telling you. We need people like you. And Jiro appreciates the type of skills you have."

LC turned to look at him, one arm resting on the window. "You loaded guns onto Gallagher's ship, DiMarco. Do you know what would have happened if we'd been inspected before we left Sten's?"

"We do what we have to do, buddy. I'm sure you of all people understand that."

LC turned back to look out of the window. He wasn't going to stay. He definitely wasn't going to get caught up in someone else's fight. If Sean's ship was on her way here, he needed to make sure Gallagher was sorted and then they'd split. Simple.

As they got closer to the mountains, they passed small outposts on the road and a landing strip with huge sheds and a couple of ships lined up next to a rough and ready airfield. After that the buildings got more frequent and eventually they turned in towards a walled encampment nestled in the foothills. LC could see glints at regular intervals along the top of the ramparts.

They were stopped at a gate and armed guards stood with raised weapons while the vehicles were searched. DiMarco joked with them, knew them all by name and didn't for a minute relax until they were waved on their way.

The gate was secured behind them.

DiMarco blew out the breath he was holding and laughed. "Welcome to Tortuga," he said, throwing the steering wheel wildly as he manoeuvred fast through a maze of narrow dirt streets. The town was a mixture of old prefab popups, the type of metal and plastic structures the corporations used to drop planetside to create an instant colony, and even older stone buildings. It was an old settlement, camouflaged to merge in with the desert.

LC watched the windows flit by, occasional faces watching them pass. Add in some bomb craters and rubble and it would be just like home.

They drove to the centre of the town and stopped by a two-storey stone building with a flat roof and small square windows. LC turned to open the door of the jeep but DiMarco stopped him. "Jiro wants to see you. Listen to what he has to say," the pilot said, more sombrely than LC had ever heard him. "We need good people out here. It's tough. And anyway," his tone switched back again, "there's no one here can match me for the moonshine like you, buddy. Who else am I gonna drink with?"

"I haven't seen much hospitality so far."

"Yeah well, we have to be careful. See Tierney then we can kick back."

"What happens to Gallagher?"

"If he agrees to join us, he'll be free to run whatever routes he wants."

"For you?"

"Yes, for us. Jesus, Luka, we're not war criminals. We need to eat like anyone. Listen to what Tierney has to say. And if you can sway Gallagher, do – he hasn't really got a choice."

Sean glared at them as she stepped out of the vehicle. She looked cool. How could anyone look cool in this heat? LC watched her as she walked past without a word, following DiMarco into the building and drawing appreciative looks from all the men in the immediate vicinity. He smiled to himself; she'd already started manipulating Tierney and his men and they didn't even know it.

LC was nudged forward but he let the others go first, making sure they were all there before he went in himself. Why the hell he felt so responsible, he didn't know, but it was bugging the crap out of him.

They were led through into a back room that was sparsely furnished, two benches and a chair, rugs and throws on the walls and floor. DiMarco stood at the door and ushered them in, stopping LC before he could step foot in the room, saying quietly, "Think about what I said."

LC took off the sunglasses. Everyone in the room was looking at them and all of DiMarco's buddies were watching with weapons ready. "It's not that easy," he said.

The pilot gestured him to go inside. "It never is."

The door was closed and LC heard a bolt thrown. The room was stone, no windows and no way out. DiMarco knew there was a bounty but he hadn't been thinking about it. He'd been thinking about these people, children he knew here, and their survival. He was right. LC had exactly the right skills to thrive here. But he was guild, despite what had happened, and he needed to close the door on that and find Anya before he could settle somewhere else, if he could ever settle anywhere.

Sean was looking at him and she stretched a hand out along the bench she was sitting on.

He got the message and crossed the room to sit beside her. "Think about what?" she sent through the wire.

"He thinks we should join them."

"He thinks you should join them?"

LC leaned back and stretched out his leg. It was aching. "What can I say?" he sent back. "He recognises a thief when he sees one."

She was shocked. He felt it like a blow. His flippant comment had brought back to her in no uncertain terms what she was dealing with. He looked her in the eye and maintained the contact with a steady gaze. She had his file. There was almost nothing she didn't know about him, including the fact that he was the most successful operative the Thieves' Guild had handled in generations. He stole things. Hilyer used the term 'acquire' like that made what they did legitimate and they all hid within the confines of a guild that ran its operations like a slick corporate-government hybrid, beyond all rules and a law unto itself. But that didn't change what he was.

She broke eye contact and glared ahead at the wall, furious that she'd let herself get drawn in by him. LC almost laughed but stopped himself. Christ, he didn't want to piss her off even more. He wanted that ride out.

22

"And what do we know about this particular band of brigands?" the Man asked, picking up the half empty jug.

NG watched warily as the small bowl on the desk began to turn slowly. It almost felt like it was a test, provoking him into an attempt to halt its motion. He stared at it, wondering, not sure he really wanted any more wine.

"Jiro Tierney is wanted on both sides of the line," he said. "Piracy, extortion, kidnapping, fraud, homicide. Not someone to mess with." He looked back at the board. The bishop was still in a precarious position but he wasn't ready to back down. He moved one of his rooks instead. "Legal and Media have been tracing Tierney's movements. This is the first time anyone has had any solid evidence of his whereabouts in over five years."

Another pinch of powder went into the wine. The Man rubbed his thumb over his fingers and looked up. "Is he of value to us?"

"In monetary terms, no. In ability, he's a natural leader but not guild material." NG had no doubt on that. He wouldn't want Tierney anywhere near the guild or any of their people.

The Man nodded and gently moved his pawn to take NG's bishop. "And this pilot, DiMarco?"

The piece was the first major loss of the battle. NG nudged one of his pawns forward to threaten the Man's queen. Fight fire with fire. "DiMarco," he said, "is something else entirely."

Jiro Tierney came in about three long hours later flanked by two of his men who took up position on either side of the door.

"We need to talk," he said to Gallagher. "Here or in private, it's up to you."

Gallagher said with no hesitation, "We've got no secrets."

LC blinked and kept his gaze steady, straight ahead. Jesus, how ironic.

"Okay," Tierney said and sat on the only chair, far enough from them that his guys didn't get more twitchy but close enough that he was eye to eye. "I want your cargo but I didn't mean for it to go down like this. We're legitimate traders. We need supplies and we're willing to pay for them."

"You've taken my crew at gunpoint," Gallagher said quietly. "That's piracy."

"We're not pirates," Tierney said firmly. "We're…" He cast about for inspiration, "independent."

"Independent pirates?" LC said and got a shove in the ribs from Sean.

She murmured though the link, "Don't be an ass, Luka. We need to be invisible here, don't forget that."

Tierney smiled. "It's tough here in the Between. I'm sure you know how tough. For some of us, it's more difficult. I don't need to go into reasons, but I can assure you that we can't exist within the normal channels of society. We have no choice. We need to live and there are factions out there that don't want us to survive. We protect ourselves, no more than that."

Gallagher shook his head. "This isn't any way to trade, Tierney. We're hauliers. We ship anything anyone needs to wherever they need it. But we don't run guns. DiMarco was out of order and this is an act of piracy."

"I'm prepared to offer you a deal."

"No deals. We don't run guns."

"Hear me out." Tierney was sounding like a reasonable guy and LC wasn't picking up any contradicting emotions from the man. He seemed tired if anything, rubbing absently at the scar on his jawline. "We run a decent mining operation. The resources we have here are valuable. We've had trouble, I'll admit that, and we have a reputation that's hard to lose, that some people here don't want to lose. There are kids here now who don't know anything other than raiding. But I'm not sure that's how we want them to grow up. We have a good settlement here and managed right, we can trade and," he paused, then admitted, "and raid less."

Thom stood up. "So why the weapons?" he said, thinking that he was going to be screwed to the wall for letting this happen. By whom was a curious question and LC filed it away for a more opportune moment.

Tierney looked at the kid. "We have to protect ourselves." He looked back at Gallagher intently. "We need regular supplies. If we let you go, will you consider a regular run back here, no more questions, no mention that you're coming here to anyone on the rest of your run?"

Thom said incredulously, "If you let us go?"

The leader of the pirates ignored him. "DiMarco has vouched for you," he said to Gallagher. "I will trust your word if you give it."

LC could overhear Gallagher thinking that he wasn't that far removed from these guys, that he didn't fit in, he couldn't go back to Sten's World, why the hell not consider supplying a band of brigands if there was money in it that would help him get out to where he needed to be.

And LC couldn't help but think himself, who the hell was he to argue against it. He was an operative of the Thieves' Guild, a rogue operative at that. And the only safe haven he could think of to run to right now was Pen Halligan, head of one of the Between's most infamous and widespread criminal organisations. A colony of pirates gone soft was nothing compared to Pen.

"I'll think about it," Gallagher said. "How about showing some goodwill and letting us go?"

Tierney smiled. "It's best you stay here for now. For your own safety, you understand." He stood and looked round at them all, his gaze resting on LC and LC felt a chill from him. Not so soft after all.

"I'll get some food and drinks sent in," Tierney said and left.

Gallagher stood up as soon as he was gone. "I'm not doing it," he said suddenly. "I'm not a damned pirate. Does anyone have a problem with that?"

LC watched as the others all shifted awkwardly, no one liking to risk eye contact. Thom had something going on, something military and nothing to do with hauling cargo across the far ends of the Between. Sean was here for him and they were about to split. God knows who Elliott was but LC had the distinct impression that in some way the ship actually belonged more to the skinny tech guy than it did to Gallagher. And down to absolute basics, Gallagher himself only wanted to get back to Erica to chase down his aliens and prove his insane story – he didn't give a flying hoot about hauling cargo for anyone.

No one said a word and Gallagher sat down, decision made but LC could feel him fret, thinking this would give him an out from the connections he'd hated being part of at Sten's World. If Tierney paid, the skipper was trying to persuade himself, then he didn't care what he was hauling so long as he could get out to Erica and prove to everyone that he was right. Well, good luck to him.

It was a while later that the door opened again and DiMarco came in, followed by two guys carrying trays laden with sealed cartons and tubs – rations stolen from god knows where. DiMarco gave a short half whistle and beckoned to LC. "Luka."

LC gave Sean's knee a gentle squeeze where his hand seemed to have found itself and stood.

"Be careful," she sent.

"Always am."

Outside it was dark and there was a chill to the night. He followed DiMarco from the building and across the street. No armed guards, no weapons clattering. The pilot pulled his jacket in tight and turned around with a grin. "You wanted hospitality?"

There was a hint of burning incense and spice in the air that reminded LC of Aston.

"I'm not joining your band of pirates, DiMarco," he said with a smile, glad to be free of the confines of the room.

They crossed the dirt road and DiMarco led him through a twisting route of narrow alleyways between the buildings, emerging eventually into a courtyard that was lit by burning torches. Brightly coloured silk flags fluttered around the square and music filtered through on the breeze. The sweet scent of narcotics mixed with the incense.

"Wait until you try the hooch we have here," the pilot said, more content and at ease than LC had seen him on the ship or the orbitals. He felt at home and it was a feeling that LC knew he could fall into himself.

There was a bonfire blazing in the centre of the square. DiMarco circled around it, tousling the heads of the children that buzzed around them as they walked. They passed a woman carrying a tray crowded with baskets of sizzling dumplings and girls at a long bench topping up mugs from huge pitchers of steaming liquid. LC lingered but DiMarco laughed and pulled him along. "You want the serious stuff, my boy."

Any stuff would be fine. He was feeling low on energy and anything would do. People were staring at him and he had to remind himself to relax. There was nothing these people could do to him. He'd been in worse places.

On the far side of the fire, there were rows of benches and tables, half full of people talking loudly and drinking. DiMarco pushed his way through to the end table and gestured LC to sit.

"I'll be right back," he said and left with a grin.

LC edged around to the far side of the table and sat with his back against the stone wall of a building that was still warm from the heat of the day's sun. He stretched his leg out along the bench and sat back, a clear view across the courtyard. People at the other tables cast sideways glances in his direction and the children and girls were curious but there was no immediate threat. There was an underlying tension and a haze from the narcotics within the background buzz he was picking up but nothing he couldn't handle.

The sky was black above the glow of the bonfire. It felt good to be planetside. There was something about the feeling of a breeze that artificial aircon could never emulate.

He absently massaged his thigh as he let his gaze wander across the courtyard. The injury was healed but there was a slight ache there as if it had healed too quickly and the muscle was going to complain regardless. He was lucky to be alive, several times over, and sitting there watching DiMarco work his way back, stopping to talk and laugh with these people hidden away here it was hard not to think that maybe this was where it was supposed to end. He'd never fitted in at the guild, never understood that desperate need to chase for points in the standings. He was too reckless, self-destructive, a guild psych had told him once. God knows what they thought of him now.

"That leg still bothering you?" DiMarco said as he slid onto the bench opposite, placing three tiny shot glasses and a tall thin bottle of clear liquor onto the table.

LC shrugged and leaned forward to take a glass.

The pilot took care filling the ridiculously small receptacles. "Seanie has a thing for you, y'know. I can tell. She was glad you didn't die."

"I was glad I didn't die. For Christ's sake, DiMarco, how expensive is this stuff that we only get an ounce each?"

DiMarco laughed and raised his glass, waiting like that first time for LC to drink first. He obliged, tossing it back in one. It was like downing pure supercooled vapour that hit the back of his throat and wafted like a tendril down to hit his stomach and his bloodstream a fraction of a second later.

"Jesus," he muttered and slid the empty glass over for a refill.

DiMarco downed his own and poured out another two shots. "So what do you think of Tortuga?" he said with a nod towards the bonfire.

"I grew up in the desert," LC said, taking the glass and casually knocking back another shot of the liquor. "Couldn't wait to get out."

The pilot shook his head. "I don't buy that, Luka buddy. You live in a place like this, it gets into your blood. Look at those kids. They belong here. We all do. No matter where we wander off to, we all end up back here."

"I'm not staying, DiMarco," LC said and sat back. It was tempting. Too tempting. And the liquor was spreading a warmth through his limbs that he hadn't felt in a long time.

They sat in silence then, DiMarco keeping the glasses full and emanating a contentment that was contagious. A girl brought a small metal cup to the table filled with some kind of substance that she lit for them with a smile. Fumes rose from it in a wisp of smoke that swirled into the night air.

"What's Gallagher decided?" DiMarco said after a while, leaning forward to fill the third glass and glancing over into the crowd.

LC felt the forced nonchalance in the question. Tierney was walking towards them and the pilot wanted to know before his boss.

"He doesn't want to do it," LC said, "but I think he'll realise he needs to. Make sure Tierney doesn't screw him over."

"You say that like you're not going to be here, bud. Where do you seriously think you can go?"

There was a hint of a threat there, veiled and casual, but LC knew he wasn't being paranoid. DiMarco was thinking openly and confidently that this cocky kid sitting in front of him would join them or be thrown to the bounty hunters. There was no doubt there, just a vague curiosity at how much the price would be. How much they'd get for handing him in if it came to that.

LC smiled and sat up as Tierney joined them.

The man looked even more tired out than before. He rubbed a hand across his face and reached for the glass, raising it in a toast.

LC clinked glasses with them and drank. Tierney was a man of conflict, internal and external, and his mind was a dark whirlpool of mixed anxieties that set off a ticking pulse inside LC's head. He got the distinct impression that the man wanted to speak with DiMarco alone and at the same time welcomed the fact that LC was there so that he couldn't. It wasn't easy to be close to.

DiMarco leaned his elbows on the table and said, "Tough day?" LC picked up genuine emotion. Maybe the guy wasn't such a jerk after all.

Tierney growled. "Inventories." He was thinking, how damned smart do you need to be to run a stock check that matches the damned data on a board with the damned stock you have on a shelf? But he didn't want to bitch about his people in front of a newcomer. Diplomatic. Who would've thought it of a bunch of pirates?

DiMarco smiled and waved to someone across the courtyard to get their attention. The music was getting louder, a drum beating out a pulsing rhythm, and LC could feel the narcotic effect of the smoke rising from the metal cup tingling at the edges of his senses.

Steaming mugs and a basket of dumplings appeared on the table, the girls hanging around and flirting with DiMarco for a few moments before wandering back to serve other tables. The pilot watched them go then poured the last of the liquor into the tiny tumblers.

"To Tortuga," he said, the words slurring slightly.

They drank then Tierney leaned forward and looked intently at LC. "So what do we have here, DiMarco?"

LC felt that chill again. He didn't want anyone looking at him. Be invisible, Sean had said. He never tried to stand out, but he couldn't help it. Olivia called him incorrigible and Mendhel had always laughed and said he couldn't help himself. It was ironic – give him a tab to run and he vanished into thin air, put him with a group of people and he couldn't stand aside and watch, not if something was wrong, not if someone was pushing where they shouldn't.

DiMarco smiled, face creasing into that feral grin, and he pushed across the mugs. "Gallagher is going to fold," he said. "He'd be a fool not to. He wants to run cargo and you're offering to pay. It's a no-brainer, even to someone like him. There's no AI to interfere, the navigator is pretty good eye candy and the kid running the engine room seems capable enough."

"What about the other one," Tierney said, "the tech guy? What of him?"

DiMarco scowled.

LC had to stop himself laughing. Apparently they still hadn't found Elliott.

"The guy's a jerk," the pilot said. "Don't worry, we'll find him. I've got Tanzi pulling the ship apart. As far as Gallagher goes, he has a decent crew and I don't think he'll run to the authorities. He has his own reasons for wanting to be out here with no questions asked. Like the rest of us." He let that hang for a moment, then added, "Luka here has a bounty on his head worth ten thou a pop just for info."

Tierney knew. LC could tell they'd already been talking about him. And they'd worked out that ten thousand for information meant a bounty of at least two hundred thousand. He picked up the mug and sipped at the steaming liquid.

"We don't care what you did, Luka," Tierney said, slow and careful. "Most people here have a price on their heads. We live in the cracks between society and we only do what we have to do to survive. You could do well here."

It was some kind of ale in the mugs, cool and heavy, chilled by whatever was making the vapour. LC put the mug down on the table and traced a finger slowly around its rim.

He raised his eyes to meet theirs and said quietly, "I'm not staying," and knew instantly that it was the wrong thing to say.

23

"Never have we lost a field operative to the outside," the Man said. He swirled the wine in the jug, blood red liquid splashing. "Why now?"

"LC's different." NG pushed forward his empty goblet. "He always has been. He stayed with us as long as he did because of Mendhel."

They sat quietly as the Man filled the cups without a word. NG didn't know what else to say. Losing Mendhel had been difficult for everyone. It was the first time they'd lost an active handler. The repercussions in Acquisitions had been ferocious and as Earth and Winter had increased security, conditions outside became harder and everyone had started making mistakes, the handlers and the field-ops. Everyone had been shaken. And having Legal sniping at his back hadn't helped.

The Man pulled back his queen, easily moving her to safety. "It was your decision, was it not, to bring Legal to her new post?" he said softly.

The fumes from the wine had a bitter sweet edge. NG reached for his goblet. He ignored the question about Legal. "I don't think LC intended to run. He just didn't feel that he could come back. With good reason."

He drank, the hot liquor and the bite of the stimulant rushing into his system. He knew he was being defensive. It had been all too easy for everyone to condemn LC as soon as he disappeared but NG knew what it had been like out there. Sitting cosy on the Alsatia, the loudest dissenters had no idea.

He kept the pawn in pursuit of the queen, relentless in his reckless attack.

The Man moved his queen again and looked up. "Did you ever at any point think we'd really lost him for good?"

Tierney sat back and DiMarco laughed. They thought he was young and stupid, only Tierney wondering what he could have done to be worth that much to someone.

"We'll see," the pirate leader said, not so much threatening as matter of fact.

"Hey, Jiro, do you remember Tanyenko?" DiMarco said, picking up his mug. "Jesus, that guy didn't know what was good for him either."

Tierney let DiMarco talk and LC listened to their stories, sitting back casually watching as the courtyard became more crowded as night set in. They weren't trying to impress him or scare him, they were just swapping tales around a mug of ale. They had no idea where he could be from and no curiosity. The Thieves' Guild was little more than a folktale this far out, a rumour and myth that had no grounding in the lives of the people out here. He doubted that any of them would even have heard of the Alsatia.

The mugs were topped up twice, then replaced by cups and a jug of something hot and sweet, scented with some kind of herb.

LC was starting to think he was going to fall asleep right there at the table when a guy walked up, nervous looking, wringing his hands, standing awkwardly waiting to be invited to join them. The surge of anxiety threatened to set off a pulsing headache behind LC's eyes.

DiMarco and Tierney both sat up.

"For Christ's sake, Tanzi, sit down," DiMarco said, "and tell me you've ferreted out that jerk Elliott."

Tanzi sat, perching on the edge of the bench, squirming, and pulling a face like he was in pain. The guy really needed to learn some relaxation techniques.

"Elliott, Tanzi. Where the hell is he?" DiMarco said, less than subtle and not disguising his irritation.

"We don't know," the guy said timidly. "We've used every sensor we have and we've searched every inch of that vessel and there is no AI and no way anyone else is on board. I swear it."

"Could he have skipped out and run?" Tierney said.

Tanzi shook his head emphatically. "We've scanned the whole area. Are you even sure he exists?"

DiMarco snorted. "What? What the hell are you saying, Tanzi?"

The guy winced and LC had to concentrate not to wince along with him as his agitation peaked.

"We've reviewed footage," he said, looking from Tierney to DiMarco and back like he didn't know who he was more afraid of. "The captain, navigator, two engineers," he looked at LC, "DiMarco, and the guy in the medical bay – that's all we can see."

"The guy in the medical bay?" Tierney said, frowning.

DiMarco shook his head. "Passenger. What the hell do you mean, Tanzi, that's all you can see? Elliott was all over the ship. He was on the bridge. Tall, skinny guy." He glared at LC as if he was expecting back up.

LC didn't say a word.

Tanzi shrank into himself, shoulders bunched around his ears. "I'm just telling you what we found. That ship. It's like it's…" He stopped abruptly. Haunted, he was thinking.

LC almost laughed out loud, catching himself and coughing instead. Holy crap, that wasn't completely unexpected. He should have known Elliott would have been playing games. He picked up his cup and sipped at the tea.

"Like it's what?" DiMarco snapped.

"There's no AI," Tanzi said firmly, "we're sure of that. No electrobe activity, no AI core, no veins so no AI. But things happen…" He tailed off, unsure of himself again.

DiMarco stood up and walked round to stand next to the guy.

Tanzi shrank away. "I swear, DiMarco. It's like there's something invisible on that ship. Stuff moves. Doors are locked then they're not. We think we're making headway getting into the ship's systems then we'll suddenly get thrown out. If there was an AI, I could get it, but there isn't."

"It's Elliott, you moron," the pilot said. "He's fucking with you."

Tanzi looked across at Tierney. "We've checked and double checked. There's no living person on that ship." He bit his lip and looked like he was going to say something but was thinking better of it.

"What?" Tierney said in that soft but persuasive voice.

Tanzi squirmed. "People are starting to talk. You know what they're like when weird shit starts happening."

"For crying out loud, Tanzi, Elliott is the ship's tech guy. He can pull all sorts of crap." DiMarco looked round at Tierney. "That's all. He'll be holed up somewhere."

"There's no life signs," Tanzi argued. "I swear, we've swept the whole ship. There's no one on board and stuff happens and I'm starting to run out of people I can send in there. They're saying it's haunted."

There it was – he'd finally said it.

"I don't believe this," DiMarco said, exasperated. "I'll find him myself tomorrow. And I'll wring his scrawny neck."

LC smiled to himself. Elliott would think this was hilarious.

Tierney looked at Tanzi and said softly, "Find him," and the guy squirmed out of his seat and left, dismissed.

DiMarco was embarrassed and laughed it off, launching into more stories.

LC sat quietly and drank his tea. He was sitting drinking tea in the middle of the night with goddamned pirates. How civilised.

They talked for a while longer then Tierney made his excuses and left, more business to be taken care of despite the hour. DiMarco was still in the mood for talking and waved over more ale and dumplings. LC kept up easily, feigning an interest in the colony and DiMarco's people that turned disturbingly into a fairly genuine curiosity.

The crowd around the bonfire grew as the night wore on. LC felt almost comfortable there, picking up from a few of the guys watching them a wariness that he was a newcomer and had been sitting with Tierney like they were old friends, but there was nothing to worry about. DiMarco was actually not bad company.

LC still couldn't help glancing round every now and then. He caught a glimpse of two guys lurking at the far side of the courtyard, drinking and laughing with the girls but casting enough looks his way to catch his attention. They were both armed which in itself was nothing unusual but they were both watching him. It didn't take a lot of effort to scan the crowd around the courtyard, home in on them and figure out that they were bounty hunters. He swept back round and closed in on DiMarco. The pilot was calm, glad to be home. No hint of betrayal. Sean had said they were probably following her. They could have been here by pure random chance but maybe she was right. Anyhow, it was time to go.

It wasn't much later that DiMarco stood, stretched and offered to walk LC back to the safe house, not giving him any choice in the matter which was absolutely fine. The two bounty hunters watched them leave, watched the contingent of Tierney's men follow them and decided against trying anything. LC managed to not smile as he walked away.

As they moved further from the courtyard, the town got dark and quiet, a chill permeating the streets and only their footsteps breaking the silence. LC could still feel the cloudy edge from the liquor and the narcotics even as the virus worked to neutralise it all.

DiMarco complained the whole way about Elliott. It was funny. The guild had tricks and gizmos they used to disguise life signs, nothing available on the open market or even the black market but there was nothing ordinary about Elliott so it wasn't surprising the guy might have something like that. LC let the pilot rant and didn't bother to argue.

There were armed guards outside the house. DiMarco stopped and spoke quietly with them then opened the door for LC.

"Are we under house arrest?" LC said, not really expecting anything else.

"It's for your safety," DiMarco said dryly. "You've got free run of the house but don't try to go anywhere outside. You're under my protection here. I can't guarantee that someone else won't get ideas if they hear about you."

DiMarco left him there and the door was locked behind him. It was dark in the main room downstairs but a flicker of light was creeping under a door at the far end of the hallway and he could hear voices even though it was well past midnight.

He pushed through the door into the kitchen where the others were sitting nursing a jug and cups that looked like they'd come from the same shipment as the ones they'd had in the courtyard. They'd probably been raided from the same ship.

They all looked up as he stepped in. They were tired and expecting him to have news, but it wasn't really anything he wanted to share yet.

Sean poured him a cup of the tea and said, "So?"

He took a sip while he decided how much to say. It was more bitter than the stuff he'd been drinking at the courtyard.

"Are they going to let us go?" Gallagher said, slumped down with his arms folded on the table.

"No," LC said simply.

Gallagher groaned. Thom seemed calm, tired but calm, that training kicking in again. He was tired and wanting to sleep but not wanting to miss out on anything that might happen.

Sean seemed to realise that LC wasn't going to talk openly. She said, "Why don't we all get some sleep?" and sent to him privately, "What's going on?"

"What's the sleeping arrangements?" he sent back.

"Two rooms, one for you guys and one for me."

LC smiled. "Does your room have a window?"

Sean hid her smile with the cup as she took a sip of her tea. "Yes, it does."

LC rubbed his eyes and stood. "I'm goosed," he said out loud. "Let's all talk in the morning."

Sean followed his lead. As she eased her way past him, LC hooked a hand around her waist and fell into step with her, looking back over his shoulder at Gallagher and Thom with a wink.

"Yeah, subtle," she sent. "Watch where that hand is."

Up in the room, LC checked the window and threw his jacket on the bed. He stripped off layers down to one shirt and turned to see Sean watching him.

"There are bounty hunters here in town. They saw me," he said and knelt to tighten his bootlaces. "We need to go."

She was surprised, disturbed and relieved all at once. "Good. We're ready." We meaning her and her ship.

LC stood up. "I have to speak to Elliott first."

"Why?"

He crossed the room and opened the window. "Don't ask."

She put her hands on her hips. "I'll come with you." She was worrying about him. She'd been worrying all night and she didn't want to lose sight of him again. There was a disconcerting mix of emotions there that he didn't feel up to confronting.

He turned and leaned back on the stone window ledge, feeling the cool air through his thin shirt. "You won't be able to keep up," he said softly.

"If DiMarco knows about the price on your head, others will," Sean said. "You just said there are bounty hunters who know you're here. I can't let you risk your safety like this."

"You can't stop me."

Climbing up onto the roof was easy. And once up there, it wasn't difficult to find a route back to the wall, jumping across gaps and balancing his way across beams between the flat rooftops.

He tried not to think about Sean. She'd slammed the window shut behind him and had been fuming, feeling inept which wasn't something she was used to. She was thinking he was being reckless but he'd been accused of that so many times before, it was hardly going to make him stop.

Approaching the wall was more tricky. LC lay on the top of a flat-roofed house some distance away, watching the patrols and guard changes and timing the pattern. When he had it, he dropped down to street level and made his way through narrow alleyways to the edge of the town. There was a flat open killing ground running round behind the wall. He stood in the shadows of a building and watched. They were sticking to their routines strictly enough but with a casual air, not bothering to keep total blackout and talking loudly enough that voices were drifting through the night air.

LC picked his spot, timed the moment and ran, no noise, low profile, easily making it to the wall without attracting any attention. Climbing the wall itself was the most effort he'd exerted since getting shot and it was frustrating to feel the pull of weakness in the muscle but it was an easy up, nothing like the Wall in the Maze back on the Alsatia. He reached the top, stayed low for a moment listening then eased himself over the edge to climb down into the desert beyond.

He ran then, pacing himself and pushing it more than he should have done but it was good to feel the desert air in his lungs, dry and cool, feeling the oxygen flow. He ignored the ache deep in his right thigh and kept his stride steady and even.

He got half way out to the landing strip before he slowed to a walk. It was quiet out there, the black sky pierced by stars.

Something was different.

He stopped after a few steps and turned in a slow circle, feeling the quiet deep inside, and standing there he realised that it was the first time in a long time that he had nothing but a still and peaceful calm inside his head.

He was alone.

It was weird but he'd forgotten how this felt. He stood for a few long minutes, breathing slow and deep. It didn't take long for the sense of tranquillity to flutter and, having nothing to fight against, his own thoughts intruded with a passion, emotions he'd buried and refuted. And having the chance to think and feel on his own terms was suddenly more difficult than having to live with the constant intrusion of company. Christ, he was more screwed up than he'd realised.

He started walking and broke into a run again, pushing harder so it took all his concentration to keep breathing and keep his legs moving. He veered in a wide circle around the landing field and the outposts, not wanting to risk being spotted by any sentries, feeling the presence of the minds there as a vague encroachment, and he didn't stop until he reached the river channel. He took his time then, clambering down to the dry riverbed and picking his way across the boulder-strewn floor, catching his breath and giving his muscles a chance to recover. Considering how long he'd been out of action, he wasn't in bad shape and if anything he felt faster and fitter than he'd been even before the incident at the lab. Even the pulling in his thigh seemed to ease as he stretched out the muscle and made it work. It felt good.

It didn't take long after that to make his way to the plain where the Duck was resting, a tiny shadow on the horizon that grew as he got closer. It looked like there were only two vehicles outside, the loading ramp down but the internal cargo bay door firmly closed. LC slowed and circled round, taking his time and finally reaching out to Elliott through the Senson as he moved in.

There was no answer.

LC edged past the two jeeps once he was sure there was no one inside either of them, and worked his way up to the ship.

As he approached, the cargo bay door groaned gently and eased up slowly, just enough of a gap that he could crawl under. It slammed shut with an echo the instant he was through. He managed to snatch his fingertips clear and rolled to his feet, disappearing into the ship before Tierney's guys came to investigate.

He tried again.

There was still no reply and he walked carefully through the abandoned ship, making his way to the engine room, reckoning that was closer and not as much risk as trying to get to the bridge. The Duck was big and the skinny tech guy was probably sitting somewhere watching and laughing at the care LC was having to take to avoid Tierney's men.

"Elliott, if you can hear me, a hand here would be useful," he sent.

Nothing.

Maybe the guy didn't exist after all. Maybe the superstitious pirates were right. LC thought back to the touch of those cold dry hands and the black void surrounding the guy. What if he really was a ghost?

He stopped and listened. The ship was cold and he was only wearing a thin shirt. He shivered. It was ridiculous. Elliott had bandaged the wound in his thigh, stood there and stuck a needle in his arm. He hadn't imagined that. And regardless of what Gallagher and that guy Tanzi said, LC knew for a fact that there was an AI on board the Duck. And Elliott was hooked up with it somehow.

24

NG studied the board, running scenarios and potential consequences through his mind, thoughts guarded. He wished he could say he'd never doubted LC or Hil. With all the rumours and snatches of information that had wormed their way back to the Alsatia, it had been hard to consider that they would do anything to jeopardise the guild, but not impossible. He knew they could both be wayward and unpredictable, and no one had ever been able to temper LC's outright and blatant disregard for protocol and procedures, but it was never to the detriment of the guild. He should have trusted that.

He leaned forward and brought his own queen into play.

The Man nodded slowly. "Are you aware that Legal alleges that you have been fully aware of the whereabouts of Anderton and Hilyer all along?"

NG shrugged. He knew and he knew that no one had taken her rumour mongering seriously.

"There are also rumours," the Man said softly, "that you sent Anderton out specifically to find this mysterious ship."

NG raised his eyes. That one he hadn't come across. As much as he didn't believe in coincidences, and it really was an astonishing ship that LC had run into, he hadn't sent him there. Simple truth. "I'd be happy to take the credit but that's absurd."

The Man moved his knight, a simple retreat back to his own lines. "Serendipity or simply the latest in a stream of cascading events? Whatever the reason, this ship and its crew have come to our attention. We must not fail to capitalise upon this turn of fortune."

The engine control room was dark. LC stood for a moment, waiting for his eyes to adjust. No need for lights – these days he could see as well in almost total darkness as he could in daylight. He climbed down to the control room in the eerie silence amidst a mass of powered down machinery.

He slipped inside, grabbed a data board and sat on the floor in the far corner, one eye on the door. He initiated a full system check through the board and simultaneously used the Senson to link in with the ship, ploughing straight to the barrier. He pushed through, full force, no care to avoid the spike that flared back at him.

"Elliott, quit screwing around."

There was nothing, no reaction.

For a second LC thought he'd been thrown out but then he felt the connection change, a force pulling at his mind as if there was a hand around his throat squeezing. It dragged him in deeper.

"Jesus, Elliott, if you're in here, talk to me, you asshole."

He could feel every heartbeat, pounding and slow, one after the other. He couldn't break free. He closed his eyes and pushed back violently. He didn't like dealing with an AI at the best of times but trying to reach one that had already proved itself elusive and arrogantly defiant was something he didn't have a lot of patience for.

"Who are you, LC Anderton?" it whispered at him.

He relaxed then. "So you do exist. Where's Elliott?"

"Who are you running from, LC? Who is it that wants you so badly, Luka, that they've posted the highest bounty ever seen in human history? It's gone up again, if you care to know." It increased the pressure. "There are ships landing here every day – what are the chances someone is here with their eye on that much cash?"

"We don't have time to fuck about with mind games," he sent back. "Where's Elliott?"

It cast him out abruptly, leaving him gasping for air. He opened his eyes and sat back.

Son of a bitch. Elliott was sitting there in the chief engineer's seat, swinging it slightly from side to side.

"Your AI has a real attitude problem," LC said, looking up from his spot on the floor.

"You need talk," Elliott replied with a smile.

Funny. LC stood up. "I need your help." He pulled the stolen implant out of his pocket and held it up. "I need you to find out where this came from."

Elliott got a condensed version of the story, no mention of the guild and no mention of the enforced tab, just a vague outline of someone he cared about being in trouble and the implant being from the bastards that had caused it. And yeah, it was all connected to the damn virus.

If Elliott knew about the guild, he didn't say anything.

After that, LC headed to medical, reluctantly, needing to check on Duncan, out of guilt more than anything. He took beers and perched on the bunk opposite.

The big man had glucose dripping steadily into his bloodstream. LC was almost envious. He hadn't had that luxury. All they'd tried early on were painkillers, stronger and stronger drugs and whatever illegal substances Hilyer could get his hands on, without realising that they were having no effect because they were never going to have an effect.

Duncan tried to move and got an agonising stab of hot pain through every joint. "Shit!" he gasped. "How long is this supposed to last?"

LC kept his breathing even, riding the second-hand pain as best as he could manage. He sent silently to Elliott through the link, "How much have you told Hal?"

"Enough," Elliott sent back. "Are you in pain there?"

LC gritted his teeth. "No." There was no way he wanted Elliott to know more than he did already. "I'd just forgotten how bad it was."

"He's handling it better than you."

"You think?"

"I know. It seems to be adapting to his body much faster. You know I said it was mutating within your system? Seems like it's become used to being in the human body so Hal's not having such a fight with it. It's still not easy though. How long did you have to endure this?"

"I don't know, long enough." He couldn't help the edge of desperation. He looked over at Duncan and shrugged.

The big man pinched the top of his nose and LC felt the headache they were sharing spike. He couldn't remember when the buzzing in his head had started or when it had begun to separate out into distinct voices. Earlier than he'd realised at the time probably, because he'd been so screwed up at the beginning. But he didn't need to guess what was going through Duncan's mind; it was like some kind of insane audio feedback.

"Elliott told me I have you to thank. Is that true?" Duncan said.

"You might not thank me when you know what's going on," LC said. "What else has Elliott told you?"

"He said I would have died if you hadn't intervened."

"Did he say how I intervened?"

Duncan smiled despite the pain. "He said you have an unusual strain of some biological thing in your blood. It helps healing. What is it, something experimental?"

"You could say that." Christ, it felt like he was dancing along the edge of an abyss. How the hell was he supposed to explain what had happened without mentioning the guild? Elliott would be listening and as much as Hal Duncan seemed like a decent guy, he really didn't know him. And here they were, tied irrevocably and undeniably to each other.

"Whatever it is, I guess it works," Duncan said, "but these are hellish side effects."

That were going to get worse, LC thought. He rubbed a hand over his eyes. They felt hot and sore. He looked across at Duncan. "How's your head?"

"Buzzing like I have a nest of giant bees in there."

"Did Elliott say anything else?" LC asked, tentatively, not sure how to broach the subject of the bounty.

"He said not to say anything to anyone, that there might be repercussions. He said you had no choice."

"You saved my life on Poule. I couldn't stand aside and watch you die. You might wish I had."

"The 'repercussions' that bad, huh?"

"I have a bounty on my head worth more than twenty six million because of this. If anyone finds out you have it…"

"Shit."

They sat there in silence for a few long minutes. Then Duncan said again, "Shit." He leaned forward. "Who else knows about this?"

"Sean knows about the bounty but she doesn't know why."

"The gunshot wound to your leg – that really was as bad as it looked?"

"Yeah."

"Shit."

In amongst the overwhelming buzz of noise and pain, he overheard the big marine put two and two together. "She's a bounty hunter. For Christ's sake, Luka, why are you even still here?"

"Not many places left to run to. I said you might not be thanking me when you know the whole story."

"How much more is there?"

"Some."

Duncan closed his eyes. LC caught the edge of the pain and knew exactly how it felt – bone deep aches and knots that twinged too often to let you relax, your entire nervous system being torn apart and rebuilt one neuron at a time. He could feel his own energy sapping in sympathy.

"Where did it come from, this virus or whatever it is?"

No doubt Elliott's ears perked up wherever he was. "Don't ask me that yet, Hal," he said softly. "I promise I'll explain it sometime but not right now. I just need to sort Gallagher out then I'm leaving with Sean. It's up to you if you want to come with us."

It was still dark when he crept back into the town. There was a chill in the air and a vicious wind had whipped constantly at his back during the whole run in. He hadn't stopped once and his lungs were burning in a way that made him feel more alive than he had in a long time.

Elliott had taken the implant and said he'd see what he could do. It had taken a massive leap of faith and trust to hand it over and walk away. LC had half been hoping for an instant answer right there and then. Elliott had laughed and said he could have a go if LC didn't mind if the damn thing exploded but it would take some time to break into it without risking any damage.

He made his way easily past the guards on the wall and headed for the safe house. The town was quieter, no music or drums any more, just drifting sounds of voices and laughter as people made their way home. He avoided them, using the rooftops and staying in the shadows, getting back looking like it wouldn't be a problem, until he heard a scream.

He knew he shouldn't get involved, knew there were bounty hunters here who'd recognised him and knew he should keep his head down and get back to the safe house.

The girl screamed again, a frightened pleading that turned into a whimper. LC made his way over and knelt at the edge of the roof, watching and looking deep into the minds of the two men pinning her to the wall. She was one of the youngsters that had been serving drinks at the courtyard. The two men were transients. Scum that used the colony as a drop off point when it suited them, no allegiance to Tierney and no thoughts of anything other than their own gratification and gain. There was nothing there about the bounty.

They were pawing at the girl, both armed, both big guys.

LC dropped silently to the street and stood, waiting for them to spot him. The girl saw him first and opened her eyes wide. They turned. One had straggly blond dreadlocks and a shotgun in a holster across his back. He pulled it free as he stepped aside, a smile spreading as he looked LC up and down.

"What the hell do we have here?" he said, words slurring.

His buddy shoved the girl away, sending her sprawling into the dirt. He drew twin knives from his belt, a shit-eating grin on his face.

"Go home," LC said to the girl, maintaining eye contact with the thug without blinking. She backed away but stood watching. Dreadlocks with the shotgun was angling around. They were both high on narcotics and pumped for a fight.

LC relaxed and shifted his balance almost imperceptibly. He didn't let the eye contact slip. They were closing in slowly, one slightly ahead of the other, which was a mistake.

Dreadlocks glanced at his buddy and looked back to LC. "She's ours," he said with a grin and made his move too soon hefting the shotgun in a malicious jab aimed at LC's stomach. It was a move he used a lot and he was expecting LC to fold, winded, following it with a blow to the back of the head to put him down. LC could see the scene in the guy's head, feel the expectation that it would happen.

Time slowed and with lightning fast reflexes, LC stepped aside and simply wasn't there to be hit. He let the guy's arm and the butt of the shotgun pass into thin air and used the momentum against him, punching a fist hard and fast into his kidneys as he went past. The guy stumbled, and LC could almost feel the thug's mind taking valuable time to catch up with the sudden shift from what it thought was going to happen to the shock of the reality it was suddenly faced with.

LC continued his move to intercept a slicing blow from the second guy that was aimed at his throat. He swatted the lumbering attack aside, tapped the guy on the nose with just enough force to make his eyes water and ducked under and around behind, shoving the guy to keep his forward momentum going. They were both bigger than him by some way but they weren't expecting him to be trouble so they weren't thinking. He was used to training against the likes of guild recovery agents and Pen's team of ex-spec ops. And he'd always been fast even before the virus took a hold of his nervous system. These guys were amateurs with egos, not a good combination and LC wasn't in the mood to waste any more time.

Dreadlocks regained his balance and laughed off his mistake. He approached again, taunting and gesturing a come on with one hand while he swung the shotgun with the other.

LC backed away a step and the two men moved in simultaneously, no honour amongst pirates and no chance they were going to fool about any more taking a shot one at a time. But even if he hadn't been able to read the guys' minds, it wouldn't have taken much to pre-empt a stabbing thrust from the knife guy. LC avoided the blades easily even as he swung round to block a kick from the guy with the dreadlocks.

He casually blocked a few more strikes to gauge their timing then got the opening he wanted and spun with a kick that caught the knife guy on the side of the head. That one dealt with, LC turned to fend off another blow from the shotgun. He caught the gun and thrust back, hitting the guy in the nose with it. Blood spurted. LC twisted the shotgun free and swept the guy's feet out from under him, driving him down with a punch that put him out cold. Instinctively he spun quickly to block another attack but he knew before he'd finished the move that the kick had done enough to take the knifeman out of the fight. They were both flat out in the dust of the road.

LC stood for a moment, slowing his breathing. The whole fight had taken less than thirty seconds. He threw the shotgun aside and looked at the girl. "Go home," he said again.

She smiled shyly, turned and ran.

25

NG took a sip of the wine. He might have been imagining it but he was feeling more focused the more he drank.

"Never in our history have we faced more turmoil," the Man said, absently picking up the discarded bishop. "While our operatives fight for their lives, we fight for the very survival of the guild."

NG bit his lip, not exactly sure what to say.

The Man put the piece down and looked up, dark eyes catching the light from the flickering flame. "We are under seige from all sides. The Federation, the Assassins, and what of the Merchants? Has that situation been resolved?"

Media was swearing that it was but it was nowhere near that clear cut. NG shook his head. "No, no, it hasn't," he said and moved his remaining bishop to capture a pawn and threaten the Man's queen.

The Man sat quietly, waiting for him to clarify.

It was hard to explain without sounding like he was slating Media so NG kept it simple. "There are always individuals that believe they can undercut our price. There always will be."

"And the Merchants?" The Man was persistent. He pulled back the queen.

"Were foolish enough to believe they could blow us out of the water, was the way I heard it."

It was worse even than that sounded. The Merchants' Guild had gone beyond talking about it; they'd started offering acquisitions in the open market.

NG took another sip and placed the goblet on the desk. "Media is fooling herself if she thinks they've dropped it, whatever her contacts have told her." He moved his knight. "I've heard otherwise and I'm dealing with it."

Sean was waiting and let him back in through her window. There was a tray of rations on the table by the bed, the box opened and its contents spilled out, and a jug of tea that was still steaming. She poured him a cup and threw across a packet of biscuits.

"What's going on?"

LC perched on the bed. He was cold, the adrenaline wearing off fast. He pulled on an extra shirt and bit open the packet. "I just need to make sure Gallagher is okay then we can go." The biscuits were sweet and the tea was hot. It wasn't hooch but it helped warm him up.

Sean sat next to him and took one of the biscuits he offered, taking in the scuffed and grazed knuckles on his hand. She looked at him with that curious expression.

"Have you been fighting?"

He shrugged and she frowned.

"I thought it was Hil that gets into trouble."

"It's Hil that gets caught," he said.

The frown almost turned into a smile but Sean set her face into neutral. "Why are you so worried about Gallagher, LC? I know that's not like you."

He had to bite his tongue not to say that she didn't know him at all because he knew that she'd read his file. He wasn't exactly renowned for working well with people and Mendhel was the only person he'd ever respected enough to be able to take direct orders from. Mendhel had always given him the time and space to be himself.

"I owe someone," he said softly, "and it's a debt I can never repay. But that doesn't mean I can't set it right in some other way."

He could tell from her face that she understood and Mendhel's name flashed into her mind. She knew what had happened to his handler and she easily figured out for herself that Gallagher was way too much like Mendhel for him to be able to turn his back on the freighter captain.

"Do you know what your record shows?" Sean said.

"Which one?"

She smiled. "Your guild personnel record."

He knew exactly what it showed and he could see in her mind that she was torn between utmost respect and abject dismay thinking about the file she'd read.

"I was expecting you and Hil to be alike," she said, "from the stats and the notes I was given, but I'm not so sure now. You're both very different."

LC sipped at the tea and demolished a couple of biscuits. He didn't want to talk about the guild. He didn't know who he could trust there and even thinking that made his stomach cold. Sean genuinely believed that she could trust NG and she was reminding him about the guild because that's where she wanted his attention, not out here running around to god knows where.

"I need to go to Aston," he said. "I want to find Anya."

Sean sat quietly for a minute trying to decide if she could persuade him back to the guild. "I talked to people on the Alsatia, LC, and I know you have a helluva reputation but you don't need to prove anything to anyone."

"I don't care what people think," he said.

She looked at him intently. "I know. That's in your file too." She reached a hand out to touch his arm. "Just come with me, LC. The last I heard on the bounty was that it's going up. Someone wants you really badly, Luka. Dead or alive." She paused and he could hear the anguish running through her mind. "I don't want to lose you."

There was that warm feeling again and he couldn't help but smile.

She punched his arm. "Don't get ideas. I don't get paid unless I get you back there."

LC reached across for another packet of biscuits. "I can't let Anya down. I need to find out if she's still alive. I don't care what you think about NG, I can't go back to the guild until I know what's going on." He raised his eyes to look at her, defying her to argue with him.

"Why Aston?"

He stared at her, trying to figure how much to say. "There's someone there that I trust," he said finally, not wanting to say any more about Pen.

Sean shook her head. "Aston's too dangerous."

"Then take me to Redgate. Badger will be able to help us."

"It's too dangerous," she said again, and he could hear that she was running scenarios through her head – what if anyone else had their eye on the bounty, what if they were caught in the fighting, what if he was hurt again?

"Sean, I don't believe in what ifs," he said and she stared at him, slightly confused. Crap. He needed to be careful not to do that. "Help me with this," he added quickly, "then you can take me wherever the hell you want."

She told him to get some sleep and walked out, conversation over. For a brief moment, her mind had been completely open to him. She wasn't impressed, with herself as much as with him. It was obvious that she was used to running the show and it seemed like he'd set on edge every emotion she usually kept under wraps. He read easily from her mind that she had a strict don't get involved rule and he was pushing the boundaries. And he wasn't even trying.

He grabbed a blanket off the bed and dozed fitfully in a chair, fully dressed, boots on and a headache pulsing behind his eyes. It felt like it had been a handful of minutes when he heard the door open and Sean call softly to him.

"Tierney wants to see us. You want some breakfast?"

LC threw off the blanket and blinked. It was daylight outside. "What time is it?"

"Early. Come on, we have a pot of tea on the go."

What was it with the tea? LC scrubbed a hand through his hair, grabbed his jacket and followed her down the stairs, catching hold of her hand as they walked. Gallagher and Thom were sitting in the kitchen and both looked up at them as they entered.

LC could have sworn that Sean blushed.

She shook off his hand and sent, "Don't push it," through the wire at him as he sat.

He smiled and watched as she poured tea for them all and nudged across a plate of dry biscuits with slices of cold meat and some kind of cheese.

"Sean said you have to go," Gallagher said. "Is there anything I can do?"

For a second LC thought he meant was there anything Gallagher could do to stop him leaving but it wasn't – it was a genuine offer of help. He looked deeper for an instant, wondering what Sean had said to him but there was nothing else. She'd just told them that they had to leave for personal reasons. Gallagher would be alright. Elliott could take care of the Duck and would take care of Gallagher, LC had made sure of that.

He leaned forward and took a handful of biscuits. "I'm sorry, I don't have any choice."

"You went back to the ship?"

He nodded.

"How's Hal doing?"

"Good. He'll be fine."

"Do you think I should work with Tierney?" Gallagher said, trusting in him completely.

"Yes," LC said. "You have no choice."

They took their time over breakfast, light-hearted banter masking the tension.

Thom was nervous. Gallagher just wanted to get back to the ship. And Sean was thinking that LC was going to get himself killed, watching him out of the corner of her eye when she thought he wasn't looking.

He sat calmly, filled up on rations and drank tea.

When DiMarco burst into the room, it was clear it wasn't a social visit. LC jumped up, blinking away the onslaught of tension and raw aggression that hit his mind.

Sean stood immediately, angling round defensively to put herself between LC and the pilot.

"We're going now," DiMarco said. "Gallagher and Garrett through the front. You two come with me. Luka buddy, Jesus, why didn't you tell me?"

He was furious. Not hostile.

Sean stopped him with an outstretched hand. "Back off, DiMarco."

"Sean, sweetheart, I'm trying to save his ass. We've got vehicles front and back. Get out there and get to the Duck because I can't control what's going on here. Lucky for you," he said, pointing at LC, "Tierney has a soft spot for you otherwise he'd be in here himself hauling your butt out for that bounty."

Gallagher and Thom were looking from face to face, mouths open.

Crap.

"We've got to go," DiMarco said. He looked at Gallagher. "I took the liberty of dealing with Tierney on your behalf. You've got a crate of andirium. It's yours. He wants medical supplies in return. Is that a yes? Because if it's no, you're welcome to stand there and watch Luka here get himself busted by one of the dozen or so bounty hunters who are in there right now offering Tierney a piece of him." He paused and gestured towards the door. "We need to scram."

Gallagher and Thom were herded out towards the front. LC stopped at the door. Every time he'd run, it had been on his terms. He'd never trusted anyone except Hilyer to watch his back. And whatever happened here, he didn't want to drag anyone else into his mess.

DiMarco fixed him with a stare. "Don't argue, Luka, and don't even think of running off by yourself. We've got patrols out on full alert but I wouldn't trust even those bastards as far as I could throw them. They're as likely to nab you for that much money as the fucking bounty hunters. Two of my guys are driving. Now get out there or I'll tag your scrawny neck for myself."

The pilot was as open and honest as LC had ever picked up from him, genuine emotion. He nodded and they moved fast, out of the back door and into a jeep that was waiting, engine running, in the alley.

"Once we get in the ship, we'll be fine," DiMarco said, leaning round from the front seat as they drove off, tyres spinning in the dust. "Twenty six million? You're a real comedian, Luka."

The pilot had a value spinning round in his head that was more than twice that much. Holy shit. LC held onto the window frame, bracing himself and kicking in every ounce of training he had to keep calm, keep his heart rate down and focus.

He closed his eyes and scanned the area around the jeep as they careered recklessly through the narrow streets. The town was busy even this early and opening his mind to the rush of thoughts from every individual was almost overwhelming. He felt Sean take hold of his hand, vaguely heard her talking to DiMarco and the driver. A cacophony of emotion, thoughts and feelings flew by as they passed crowds of people, snippets of intentions flashing, mostly passive and personal irrelevancies but pricked every now and then by a spark of focused intent. It was impossible to pinpoint and his head began to pound, pain peaking each time they hit a pothole in the road.

He started to shut it out, caught a snatched view of the jeep through crosshairs and had no time to react as an explosion rocked the vehicle, sending it tumbling and crashing into a wall.

26

"This ridiculous bounty that the Federation has accepted..." the Man said.

NG glanced up at the Man, still semi-shrouded in darkness, giving nothing away. It felt like time stood still here in this claustrophobic chamber. As much as he understood the impossibilities of the physical universe, he hoped it stood still – a million strands of incidental connections and events were sparking out there, fast and furious, and he was sitting here playing chess.

"The terms of the officially sanctioned bounty are alive, as far as we can tell," he said. "The Assassins assured us that if they'd been hired, Anderton and Hilyer would be dead. That doesn't alter the rumours that there's someone out there prepared to pay a substantial amount if they're handed in dead rather than alive."

The Man moved his bishop into a position to threaten NG's rook. "A substantial amount?"

"It's up to eighty five million each." NG picked up his wine, resting the goblet on his knee and breathing in the vapours. He could save the rook but it would set him on the defensive and that wasn't somewhere he was prepared to go.

The Man drained his goblet and rested his hand on the jug. "I understand we're making progress in alleviating their interest in this misguided contract."

NG abandoned the rook to its fate and moved his knight into a position to threaten the Man's queen. "We are but that doesn't help LC and Hil in the field right now."

He lay stunned for a moment, crumpled against the window, all sound blurring into a vague background hum. Then Sean was screaming at him, shots were hitting the jeep and a hand was pulling at his arm.

DiMarco was yelling at him to go. LC twisted around, head spinning, trying to orientate himself. The jeep was on its side. The hand that had a grip on his arm pulled hard and he worked with it to free himself and climb up out of the smashed window, glass fragments crunching beneath him.

Sean pulled him out and into a run. They made it across the street, pushing past people who were staring at the wrecked jeep, and into an alleyway. Shots ricocheted off the walls around them sending fragments of stone flying.

"Don't say it," LC muttered as they ran. Sean's anger and frustration were beating at his efforts to stay focused. She was right – they should have been well gone by now, taken the chance to run when they had it. But he didn't work with ifs and buts and he shut her out.

They were followed, footsteps thundering behind them and loud yells echoing. He pulled Sean into a doorway, pushed her inside and pulled the door closed behind them. They ran through into a storage room, long aisles of shelving laden with boxes. The door crashed open behind them and canisters flew overhead hissing out smoke.

LC coughed and covered his nose and mouth with his sleeve. "Any of these guys friends of yours?" he sent to Sean, shoving her through a swing door. She wasn't impressed.

They burst out into a narrow alleyway. LC squinted through stinging eyes, spotting a door opposite and figuring that anywhere on the ground was going to be too hot. He pushed Sean towards it and they ran in to a long hallway, a set of steep stairs at its far end.

"Up," he sent.

She grabbed his arm and spun him around in front of her. "You first," she hissed. "I want you where I can see you."

He grinned and ran, taking the stairs two at a time, adrenaline pumping, sprinting around two landings and heading up to the roof.

If these guys were any good at their job, they should have

211

someone up here. LC paused at the top of the stairs and listened at the door. There were two.

He gestured back to Sean and whispered, "There are two guys out there but they're watching the street."

He could feel the depth of her frown as she tried to figure out how he knew. It was almost tempting to tell her but instead, he told her to wait and eased open the door.

He crept out into the sunlight, taking care to watch where his shadow fell, and worked his way silently round to the nearest. They were both lying prone against opposite edges of the flat roof watching the street. The first one he targeted had a gun in a holster at his side.

LC moved up on the man like a ghost, dropping to plant a knee in his back and grasp the gun in one smooth fluid motion. The pistol had the tell-tale orange tag on its magazine and he didn't hesitate in firing an FTH round at close range into the guy's back, rising and turning and firing at the one across the far side of the roof before the other man barely even realised there was a problem.

Sean was watching from the open doorway, glancing back down the stairs. She knew them and she knew that they operated with a third. LC ran over and retrieved the second guy's sidearm.

"Where will the other one be?" he said, running back into cover and handing one of the guns to Sean.

"Street level. Bannerman likes to get up close and personal." She wanted to ask him how he knew.

He could feel that the guys who'd chased them into the building were starting to climb the stairs. He edged past her and pulled the door closed. "We'd best stay up high then."

She leaned in close and whispered in his ear, "You're enjoying this."

He grinned. "Aren't you?"

They ran across the rooftops, LC thinking fast about a way out. At one point he tried to persuade Sean to let him go, there was no point in both of them running; they were after him not her. And anyway he could go faster if he was on his own and not having to worry if she could make a jump or keep in cover. She'd grabbed him and pushed him against a wall. "You're mine," she'd hissed. "Like it or not, LC, you're mine and none of these money-grubbing bastards are going to get their hands on you while I'm still breathing." He'd grinned at her and he'd felt her work hard to hold in a smile, thinking to herself, my god girl, what are you doing?

After that they'd had to slow down, taking it careful as more figures started appearing on the rooftops, watching or prowling.

Finally LC pulled Sean to a stop and they crouched in the shade of a ventilation shaft.

The hairs on the back of his neck were bristling. He couldn't distinguish any individual targeting them, there were too many threats in all directions, too many people searching and too many hiding and fearful for themselves. Christ, the town was flooded with bounty hunters and half the townsfolk probably had prices on their heads and even if they didn't match DiMarco's five hundred thousand, it was enough to make them nervous.

"This isn't going to work," he sent. "We need to find somewhere to lie low."

She nodded.

They waited until he was sure it was clear and made a run for the roof's edge.

They didn't make it. There was a yell. Shots.

LC dropped, rolled and fired at the guy running out behind them, turning without waiting to see if he'd hit and pushing up from the crouch into a sprint to catch up with Sean. Something hit him in the back and his knees buckled, lights sparking behind his eyes. He shut out the pain, staggered to his feet and looked up to see Sean crumple to the floor.

He spun around, fired at two of the guys coming at him and knew there was a third closing in. Something heavy hit the back of his head and a blow to his arm sent the gun flying. They moved in fast, two grabbing his arms and the other clamping a hand around his neck from behind.

LC dropped his head, slowed his breathing and relaxed every

muscle for a single heartbeat. Then he moved, lightning fast, precision blows, throwing his weight so fast they didn't have time to react. He took out the one on the left with an elbow to the solar plexus and a fist to the face, dropping to one knee. The guy at his back stumbled forward, off balance. LC dropped his shoulder and tucked in tight, throwing the guy's weight up over his head, turning fast to land a blow on the one struggling to hold onto his right arm. It connected with a crack and another blow put him down. LC spun and finished off the other guy with a kick.

All three were on the ground. He stood for a fraction of a second then looked round. He could sense more closing in, drawn by the sounds of fighting. He glanced over at Sean, made an agonising decision and ran.

He made it back to the cover of the ventilation shaft before anyone else appeared on the roof. He ducked down. He kept his heart rate low and controlled, sensing the essence of the searchers like pinpoints of bright light flowing and ebbing all around. No need for elaborate technology. The focus of the moment made him realise it like never before. He could sense lifeforms and that gave him an insight he'd never had from any gizmo or gadget. He looked briefly into each mind, flitting from one to the next in a dizzying spiral. It was powerful, another kind of invincibility, hypnotic and intoxicating.

The ones close had heard the shots but didn't know where he was.

He tracked them as they got close, a door crashing open on the far side of the roof and footsteps crunching through the layer of dust. There were two of them, both bulky men, armed and moving with a tight focus that marked them as professionals. They saw Sean lying motionless and moved over to her, an exclamation of recognition hitting both minds as they looked down at her.

That changed everything.

The intense hate that emanated from them hit LC with an almost physical blow. He edged round to gain a line of sight, a cold chill settling deep inside. He sent an urgent and demanding query through the Senson and felt her stir slightly, the shock of the FTH still resonating.

One of them kicked her viciously.

LC twitched.

"Kill the bitch," the other one said, cold and malevolent, an edge of satisfaction in his mind as he looked down at Sean through black shades. He was older, close cropped grey hair and a silver badge at his belt that was glinting in the sun.

The younger guy pulled out a knife and nicked his thumb along its edge, a smile creasing his tanned face.

LC stepped out and yelled, "Hey," no thought in the plan other than to stop them.

They looked up in unison, Sean forgotten in a heartbeat and eyes narrowing, identifying him instantly as their target just from his silhouette, proximity to O'Brien and lack of a weapon. It was weird but LC felt like he'd met them before.

Two guns snapped up, aimed directly at him in a slick synchronised motion. He turned and ran.

A rush of adrenaline got him to the edge of the roof, full on sprint, no slowing down as he closed in on the edge. He jumped, time slowed, and he hit the next roof, taking the impact in his knees, tucking into a roll and letting the momentum take him on into a staggering run.

They were following.

LC crossed the roof and veered left, running to the edge and crouching, pausing and listening, very aware that he could just as easily run headlong into a bounty hunter as run away from them. The two at his back didn't hesitate at the jump and very quickly he had no choice but to drop down to street level.

He ran.

An FTH round hit him between the shoulder blades. He stumbled against the wall, shook it off and ran, pain flashing behind his eyes. He couldn't count how many more shots hit him. One caught him in the back of the head and finally he went down.

Out cold.

27

The Man's hand hovered over his queen, thumb rubbing over his fingers.

NG watched. There was nothing resting on the outcome of this game but he couldn't help feeling it was a test of his ability and judgement, not merely at chess but at running the guild. He was being reckless but every move was a calculated risk, the same as every move he'd made to defend his field operatives.

The Man looked up. "Such as hiring O'Brien to track him down? A stroke of genius," he said and paused, "but she led them to him."

"They would have found him anyway," NG said. Sean had covered her own tracks adequately enough. LC had simply run out of places to run to. And ultimately run out of time.

He finished the last of his wine and rested the goblet back onto his knee. The guild had sent extraction agents to T72 as soon as they'd received word that LC and Sean were there but it was already too late.

"It's hard to lose good people," the Man said softly, and swept his queen across the board to take one of NG's pawns, an outright and confrontational attack. Another one down.

NG stared at the board.

It was hard to lose anyone.

Coming round was a painful return to awareness. He was lying on a bench, in a vehicle, he realised, travelling at speed over an uneven surface. His hands were restrained, knees and ankles bound, and a persistent throbbing pain was pulsing in the back of his neck.

It felt like his eyeballs were on fire. They must have kicked him while he was down because his ribs were hurting and one eye was swollen and wouldn't open.

He blinked the other one and a gun barrel was pushed up under his jaw line.

"We have ourselves a live one," someone said.

There was a laugh.

His heart was pounding. He worked on slowing it down and keeping his breathing steady. He was shielded somehow, so no chance to use the Senson.

It was just him and the two bounty hunters.

The younger guy was driving, the older one watching him. LC looked into their minds and felt nothing but professional pride, greed for the bounty and intense satisfaction at having beaten the rest, Sean most of all. They didn't care who he was, just that he was the one. And they were sure; they'd run a retina scan. Christ, how much did these people know about him?

He wriggled slightly to test the restraints around his wrists and got a slap to the head.

The older guy leaned down and held a remote device in front of LC's face, making a show of pushing down on the control.

A stabbing needle of agony drove through the back of his neck into his spine, unrelenting and excruciating. He curled up, squeezed his eyes shut and tried to take it and bundle the pain away but it magnified. It lasted a second longer than unbearable then vanished.

He took a slow breath and lay still.

The message was clear – don't try anything.

They had him. Caught. First time in his career.

Shit.

The vehicle skidded to a halt.

The throbbing pulse sparking into his spine started up again, just intense enough to take his attention off anything but keeping conscious.

Doors slammed. They sliced through the restraints holding his legs and he was pulled out into the sun and dragged into a short run in the open before they were back inside. He was thrown down into a cage-like cell, arms pulled tight behind his back as the restraints were tied to something. Breathing was difficult and he started to think ribs might be broken.

He didn't fight them. There'd be a way out but he knew he needed to bide his time. He could feel from their heightened emotions that they'd kill him given half a reason. They knew the bounty was higher if he was delivered alive, a lot higher, but they knew it was a risk and they weren't entirely sure it was a risk they were prepared to take, not with that kind of cash at stake. It was only the older guy arguing that he wanted to deliver this sucker still breathing that was keeping him alive.

A hand pinned his head to the floor and a sharp pain pierced the top edge of his left ear.

Once done, the guy stood, kicked him hard and left. The door slammed shut.

LC lay quietly, listening. He was cold. They'd stripped him of his jacket, belt and boots. And he wasn't sure but it felt like they'd ripped the wristband off his arm. The restraints clamped around his wrists were hefty, tight, with no room to manoeuvre. The virus was doing its best to compensate for the physical damage but the constant pulse that was throbbing in his neck in time with his heartbeat was draining every ounce of his energy, his system struggling to deal with it.

He could hear the two men talking, a third voice joining in. He couldn't feel any trace of another living entity so he reckoned he was on a ship with an AI. They were gearing up to leave.

It was hard not to panic.

And it was hard not to regret being so stupid as to give himself up. What the hell had he been thinking?

But coming back to it time and again, he couldn't have stood there and watched them kill her.

He felt the engines start up, a deep vibration through the deck.

He had no tools, no tricks and no way to reach anyone.

Lying there, breathing slowly and keeping still, listening to the engines fire up, LC realised that this was the closest he'd come to finding out who was behind this. Somewhere along the line, these guys would hand him in to the people who had sent them into that lab.

His heart started pounding, adrenaline pumping. It wasn't exactly what he'd planned when he'd decided it was time to stop running.

He reached out desperately, a sweeping scan as far as he'd ever tried, looking for Sean or DiMarco, any essence that he could recognise. There were other people near by but no one he knew. It made his head hurt and he spiralled into grey for a while, coming round to sounds of shouting and banging.

The engines were quiet, the ship still. The two bounty hunters were arguing, with each other and with their AI.

LC struggled into a half sitting position, feeling a rush of aggression from the younger guy. They had their golden ticket and all they had to do was deliver it, he was thinking, and the damned ship went into shut down on this godforsaken rock.

Something was wrong with the AI.

And the two bounty hunters knew there were people who'd fight them for him. "We should kill the bastard now," LC heard one of them say, "and get the hell out of here. I'd settle for ten million."

There were sounds of a struggle then the young guy appeared at the cell, a rifle in his hand and as he swung it up into an aim, LC knew where he'd seen them before. The last time it had been in near dark, running through the claustrophobic accessways of Sten's World station. Someone had intervened so he could get away.

This time he tensed, nowhere to go, looking down the barrel of the rifle, feeling the desperation, knowing the guy wasn't going to let him escape again.

There was a crash. A gunshot. The bounty hunter fell, LC recoiling from that black pop of void.

Hal Duncan ran past without a word, Thom following, both of them armed and running the rescue mission with military precision, tight and focused with pinpoint accuracy.

Thom glanced in, saw him and stopped, slamming open the bolts on the cage.

There were more shots from inside the ship. A burst of automatic gunfire followed by the loud retort of Duncan's gun. Two shots then silence.

Thom knelt by LC's side. "Are you alright?"

"I'm fine now," LC muttered, trying to stop the shaking in his limbs, twisting round to give Thom room to free his hands. "Nice timing. How the hell did you know where I was?"

"Elliott's been tracking you. He screwed with their AI somehow. Sean's on her way in. We need to get out. There are others coming."

The manacles snapped open. LC rubbed his wrists and tried to flex some feeling back into his shoulders as Thom sliced through the other restraints with a knife. He whispered a thanks and tore the patch off his neck, trying to stand and reach out to Sean at the same time. He didn't quite manage either.

"Oh crap," he said faintly, "I have something in my neck," feeling like he was going to pass out.

Thom reached around gently and pulled the device out, a spike of pain sending LC's senses reeling. He greyed out again, heard Duncan demanding his attention and thought he felt Sean close by. Then he was being pulled up and led out, Duncan on one side, Thom on the other.

The deck was cold beneath his bare feet.

"Wait," he mumbled, "I need my stuff."

"We've got it," Sean said from somewhere. "Come on, we have to go."

He smiled stupidly and let them walk him out into the sun and across towards a vehicle.

Halfway there he realised half the pain he was feeling wasn't his own. He looked sideways at Duncan. "Hal, what are you even doing up?"

The big man looked pale and clammy. He glanced at LC, gave the briefest smile, eyes rolling up into his head, and fell backwards, crashing to the floor.

DiMarco had the engine running. They bundled Duncan into the jeep and crowded in, Sean sitting close and keeping a firm grip on

LC's arm like she was damned if she was going to lose him again. At least this time, she was thinking, the bastards were dead – she shouldn't have left them alive on Sten's World. It had been Sean who'd saved him. He stared at her, that realisation making his heart skip a beat.

They set off before the doors were closed, careering away from the airfield and into the desert.

It was a rough ride. LC closed his eyes, shutting out the massive mix of emotion from the others, not quite believing he was home free until the jeep tipped sharply up a ramp and into the cold darkness of the Duck's hold.

The cargo bay door slammed shut.

It was hard to drum up the energy to move. LC heard the jeep's doors open and half opened one eye.

DiMarco twisted round from the driver's seat. "Hey, the gang's all here," he said with a grin. "C'mon kid, give me a hand to get the big guy up to medical." He winked at LC.

Christ, the jerk was setting him up to be alone with Sean. And from what he was picking up from Sean's current state of mind, that was the last thing he needed.

Thom and DiMarco helped Duncan out and left, footsteps echoing across the hold.

LC geared up to move, needing to leave with the others, but Sean squeezed his arm.

"I need to talk to you," she said quietly.

She was angry.

"Sean, I feel like crap."

She faltered at that, taking in the bruises and reaching a hand up to touch his ear. He flinched away but not before she'd pulled gently at the tiny metal tag pierced through the edge there.

He pushed her hand away. "I know I screwed up," he said. "I know you're pissed. And I know you want to leave. But there's something I have to do first." He got out of the jeep and leaned back in, resting his weight wearily against the door. "Where's my stuff?"

Sean stood with her arms folded, watching as he struggled into his boots. The knife was gone. That sucked more than anything.

"You're going to get yourself killed," she said.

LC ignored her as he shrugged awkwardly into his jacket, ribs complaining. Sean stared at him as he quickly checked each pocket. They'd stripped out everything and they had taken his wristband. He turned and met her gaze. "Sean, in everything you've read in my file and everyone you've talked to about me, where did you ever get the impression that I give a shit?"

She scowled and stuck her hands in her pockets as if she needed to restrain herself from slapping him. She was furious. He could read her as easily as if she was yelling at him. She was fuming, angry at him and angry at herself for falling for someone who was a target, purely a pay-on-delivery, don't get involved, no emotions attached target. Who had a butt that was way too cute to ignore, a look in his eyes that she'd die for and dimples in his cheeks when he smiled at her that made her melt.

He couldn't help the grin that slipped out. He stepped in close and for a second he thought she was going to kiss him but she frowned instead.

"You and Hilyer are exactly the same," she said in a voice that was little more than a soft whisper. "You're pathologically incapable of appreciating the danger you're in. It's institutionally ingrained in you. I thought it was arrogance but it's not, is it? You can't see it. You really don't see it. Your guild gives you the perfect cover. You don't exist so you don't need to care."

He could feel her heart beating. He stared into her eyes and looked deep into her mind, seeing the plan she was trying to convince herself was the only way they were going to get out of this alive. Her ship was on its way in. And she was thinking that if she risked alienating him so that he hated her then fine – at least he'd be alive.

Her fingers tightened around the autoinjector in her pocket. She raised the other hand up to his neck with a gentle touch that sent shivers down his spine. He blinked slowly and moved closer, leaning in to kiss her, feeling her respond, feeling her want the moment to last. He increased the pressure, her lips soft against his, and reached into her pocket gently to steal the injector away from her grasp.

She tensed.

LC pulled back and held it up between them. He quickly tumbled the injector around his fingertips until it was the right way round then stabbed it into his neck, feeling the ampoule pulse whatever the hell she was trying to dose him with into his bloodstream.

She was too slow to react to stop him.

He felt the drug dissipate, filtering through his system in the same hazy way that the realisation of what he'd just revealed to her started to dawn on him. He pulled her close again and whispered into her ear, "Now we've got that out of the way, I need you to trust me. Let me do this then I'll go with you wherever you want. I told you that."

He left Sean in the cargo bay, staring after him and wondering what had just happened. He was wondering what had just happened.

He made it up to the crew quarters, feeling his internal temperature rising fast, heart racing and hands shaking. He slipped into his cabin, stripped and stood in a cold shower, letting the icy water stream over him until he was numb. He leaned his head against the cubicle wall and let the water pour down his back. God, he'd never been caught before. Except for that one time on Kheris, which hadn't been his fault. This time he'd given himself up willingly. For Sean. And knowing that he'd do it again in a heartbeat scared the crap out of him.

28

"How tender are the emotions of these creatures." The Man refilled the goblets.

NG tried not to smile. The Man had always found it hard to fathom the intricacies of human relationships. And the field operatives out of everyone tended to fall wholeheartedly into complex and volatile partnerships.

Not surprising considering what they did every day.

"LC was lucky that he had good people around him," he said. It was hard to admit, none of them being guild, that they'd been there for him when there wasn't a guild agent in sight.

He leaned forward, ignoring the peril the rook was in to move his bishop.

The Man lifted his goblet and drank deeply. "Is this development with O'Brien likely to compromise our use of her in the future?" he said and moved his own bishop to take the rook.

"There is no development," NG said, watching another of his key pieces fall to the side. "LC has half a dozen girls on the go at any one time. He can't help it. He doesn't go looking for it. At the time, they were in a difficult situation. Heightened emotions lead to irrational actions. LC's never been caught before. Sean rescued him. Given his nature, he had no choice but to fall for her."

DiMarco knocked at the door and came in without waiting.

LC looked up, half dressed and trying to figure out if he could be bothered to lace his boots.

"Jesus," the pilot said, "Luka, you look like shit."

LC looked down at the black bruises colouring all round his chest and left hand side. He pulled on a shirt.

DiMarco sprawled on the bunk. "Why didn't you tell me?"

"How could I?"

"I told you, I'm not going to hand you in – however much you're worth. Jesus Christ, eighty five million. What the hell did you do to earn that kind of attention?"

LC rooted around in his locker for another shirt. He was chilling down fast. He found the thick, long sleeved shirt he'd been wearing the night they'd hit the lab. It had tiny shrapnel holes in the back but he'd kept it because it was one of his favourites. It was clean, it was warm and it had a hood. He shrugged into it and turned to look at the pilot.

"I need to go to Redgate. This andirium Gallagher has – will he be able to sell it there?"

DiMarco laughed. "Redgate? Jesus, Luka buddy, you have a death wish."

LC pulled a holdall out and dug in it for his spare tool kit, guild standard and nothing flash but it would do if he got stuck somewhere. He palmed it into his pocket. "I know someone there – it's the only safe place I can think of."

"That's the first time I ever heard Redgate called safe." DiMarco yawned and stood up. "Yes, he'll be able to sell it there and he'll be able to sell it for a fortune. Gallagher wants to see you by the way. So does Seanie. You're mister popular today, Luka." He walked out, throwing in a casual, "We're leaving as soon as the kid gets the engines warmed up. You want to go to Redgate, you'd better get in there and persuade Gallagher why he should risk his ship for your ass." He stopped at the door and looked back in. "You need to lose that tag, buddy. Eighty five million, Jesus."

LC touched a hand to his ear self-consciously. The pilot laughed and disappeared.

Walking down the corridor to Gallagher's office was like walking the dark hallway to see the Chief. Mendhel had always softened the way and LC didn't get the severe chewings out that Hilyer got regularly but even so, it was never a good thing to be summoned to that room.

Bill Gallagher was a teddy bear compared to the Chief but LC paused at the door and hesitated to knock. He'd already checked that the captain was alone; Sean was on the bridge and Thom was in the engine room. He thought about getting a beer first and took a step away but the door opened and Elliott walked out, holding the door open for LC to go inside.

The tech guy initiated a private link through the Senson as LC walked past. "I've cleared the way for you," he sent. "I've told Gallagher I can get us safely down to the surface on Redgate. I can't wait to see why you want to go there. And I've got an answer for you when you're ready."

He walked off, leaving LC stranded by the open door. He should have known Elliott would be listening in.

Gallagher beckoned him into the office.

"Sit down," he said softly.

There was nothing personal in the small cabin. Nothing on the desk and bare shelves.

LC sat. "I'm sorry," he said. "I should have…"

Gallagher hushed him with a raised hand. "Not necessary. We look after each other here and you've earned a place on this ship." He leaned on the desk. "We need to leave. Tierney said he's grateful that you helped his niece but he can't do much else to protect us if we stay any longer. We have three of his guys on board plus DiMarco, so I'm his whatever I decide. You need to go to Redgate?"

LC stared, cheating and reading the surface of Gallagher's mind before he replied. The old guy was resigned. DiMarco had promised him a run to Erica once they'd brought medical supplies back to Tierney and Elliott had suggested that a call into Redgate with the andirium might bring enough revenue to make the whole run profitable. It said a lot about Gallagher that he really didn't care in the slightest why LC had such a massive price on his head. LC had saved his life and that was good enough for him, and although he was slightly disconcerted by the fact that he had the most wanted fugitive in the whole galaxy on board his ship, he seemed to be handling it well.

LC nodded.

"We'll take you there. Sean's told me she needs to leave with you," Gallagher said. "Is that right? Are you good with that?" He was wondering what Sean's interest was. He wasn't stupid, nowhere near as naive as people assumed he was, and he was genuinely worried about LC's welfare. It was strange to realise that there was a place here where he was so welcome.

"It's fine," he said unconvincingly, hearing the waver in his voice as he said it.

Gallagher stood up. "Luka, whatever you've got going on, I don't want to know. But we'll all do anything we can to help, okay?"

LC nodded again and stood.

Gallagher walked round and slapped him softly on the back, genuine concern in his mind and a lingering regret that this kid standing in front of him looking so vulnerable had to leave. "Sean's looking for you," he said, steering LC out of the office. "Think about staying if you can."

Sean started querying the Senson as soon as he left Gallagher's office. He ignored her, looked briefly in on Duncan who was sleeping and hooked up to the glucose drip, and headed for the engine room, grabbing beers on the way.

The klaxons for the countdown to launch started sounding as he worked his way to the control room. Thom was in there watching the boards.

LC stashed the beer bottles, sat down and strapped in, leaving the restraints loose to ease the pressure across his chest.

"I'll take this shift," the kid said, half a question in the way he said it.

LC nodded and sat back with his eyes closed, feeling the vibration of the engines change.

It was an uncomfortable ride. Thom fretted the whole way and as soon as his anxiety started to make LC feel like maybe a lot more could go wrong with space flight than he'd ever appreciated, he shut it all out and worked on lowering his heart rate, which was still too high and erratic. After effects from the FTH, he reckoned. Nothing to do with Sean.

They made orbit with no problems. Thom blew out the breath he was holding as they eased into the steady flight configuration to make clearance distance. LC opened one eye and glanced over at him.

Thom stood up and stretched. "God, this is a big ship," he said. He looked down at LC. "You're not an engineer, are you?"

LC shook his head nonchalantly. He unhooked the restraints and swung the chair around, reaching out two beers. He popped them open and handed one to Thom. "And you're not just an engineer, are you?"

Thom frowned, embarrassed. "Is it that obvious?"

LC didn't comment. He didn't want to talk about himself so he wasn't going to push the kid into revealing anything he didn't want to. The beer was cold and the sugar hit well overdue.

Thom sat down and leaned forward earnestly. "Is it true?"

"What?"

"The bounty on you. Is it true you're worth eighty five million?"

LC smiled and gave a brief shrug of his shoulders. "Last I heard it was twenty six."

The kid was fascinated. "What did you do?"

"I was set up." He rubbed his eye and held the cold bottle against his cheek. The swelling was going down but his cheekbone was still sore.

When he looked up, Thom was still staring, itching to ask how he'd been set up, what could be so bad that someone would set that kind of price on his head.

"Who do you work for, Thom?"

He watched the reaction and went deep into the kid's mind as Thom tried to figure out what to say.

"It's complicated," he said eventually, flashing on orders and arguments, uniforms and rank. Nothing to do with LC, that was certain.

"Just don't do anything to hurt Gallagher," LC said.

"Good god, I wouldn't. I'm here to look out for him." Thom shut up abruptly as if he'd said too much.

They sat quietly for a while then Thom turned back to the boards and started running checks. LC stood up. "Don't worry so much, kiddo. Life's too short."

He left the control room and climbed up to one of the subsidiary terminals deep inside the engine room. If Sean came looking for him, there was no way she'd find him in here. He settled down and hooked in, looking for Elliott. He couldn't face hitting the barrier with his nervous system still trembling the way it was so he waited patiently until the AI turned its attention to him.

It didn't take long.

"That was a close one, Mr Anderton."

"Yeah. Where's Elliott?"

"He's busy – calculating jump. To Redgate. Who is it that you know on Redgate, LC Anderton?"

"I need to speak to Elliott."

It pulled him in closer, blocking the way out.

"Who is it there that you think can help you, LC?"

Breathing got really hard, sparks of pain jabbing through his broken ribs. He tried to push back but the connection felt too vague to grasp with any power. He sent instead, "How did you manage to persuade DiMarco that you don't exist?"

"We told Gallagher, he told DiMarco. No one else has encountered me, why should they doubt the ship's own tech guy when he denies my existence." It increased the pressure. "I'm your little secret, LC."

The link began to blur, lights flashing behind his eyes in time with his erratic heartbeat.

"Who are you going to see on Redgate, LC?"

"Screw you," he managed to send and passed out.

He dreamed about Kheris, the heat and the dust, kneeling in the dirt with his hands tied behind his back, a gun to his head and soldiers screaming at him. A cold hand touched his neck and he almost screamed, waking in a cold sweat to see Elliott leaning over him.

He scrambled backwards and bumped up against the bulkhead,

using it to get up into a half sitting position. "Shit, Elliott. Your AI is vicious."

The tech guy rocked back on his heels and regarded LC with a curious look. "You should be more careful," he said.

LC tried to control his breathing. "You said you had an answer."

"You should be in medical," Elliott said. "Your stats look precarious, LC. That was a close one back there."

"Yeah, that's what your AI said. Thanks for finding me." He meant to say it sincerely but it came out with a touch of suspicion.

Elliott smiled. "You're welcome."

LC shifted his weight, feeling trapped. "The implant, Elliott. You said you had an answer?"

Elliott stood and reached out his hand. LC took it and let the skinny tech guy pull him up onto his feet. It took him a minute to get his balance.

"Zang," Elliott said.

The word didn't register. "What?" he muttered.

"Zang Enterprises. The implant was from a woman who worked for Zang Enterprises. A Wintran corporation. Big into bioweapons, I believe."

LC stared, stomach clenching in a cold knot. It was a Wintran corporation that had sent them into the lab, that had killed Mendhel at the safe house on Earth. The lab had been on a planet firmly inside Earth controlled space.

Elliott started to walk away. "Why Redgate, LC?" he said casually.

"Do you know where they are?" LC asked, ignoring Elliott's question and holding an arm against the bulkhead to stop himself swaying.

"Zang?" Elliott turned round to face him again. "They have facilities all over the place. Headquarters on Winter itself, bases on planets right the way out to the Between. Your friend could be anywhere. Who are you going to see on Redgate, LC?"

If getting back to Aston was out of the question, then Badger was his only chance of finding out what was going on. LC felt the blood drain from his face. Badger was the guild's deepest undercover field agent and he'd come close to leading a bunch of complete strangers right to him.

Elliott laughed. "In your own time, LC. But if you want my help, there's only so much I can do if you only give me half the story." He turned away again. "I should thank you, Luka. I've been thinking of going back to Redgate for a long time. I haven't been in the middle of a war zone in years."

LC woke from a nightmare, breathing fast. It took a moment to realise where he was and a second more to realise he wasn't alone.

He sat up, hand reaching under the pillow.

Sean was leaning around the door, not sure of his reaction and not entirely sure of her own feelings. He'd managed to avoid her for the whole trip, swapping six hour shifts with Thom and napping in the engine room to stay out of the way. He'd split once they were on the run in towards Redgate, needing some sleep which hadn't come easy even in his own bunk.

"Hey," Sean said softly.

She took a step into the cabin. She was holding something behind her back and for a second he thought she was going to try the injector again. God knows why because there was nowhere they could go. She brought her hand round quickly though and offered him a knife, hilt first.

He took it, heart quickening as he recognised it.

"I'm sorry," she said quietly, standing there awkwardly.

She didn't know what to say, thinking that she'd lost any chance of getting him to trust her, wondering why the hell he'd given himself up for her and regretting that she'd ever agreed to the job. She was wishing she'd never met him. That wasn't easy to overhear.

She gestured towards the knife. "I know how important that is to you. I'm sorry I didn't have time to look for the rest of your stuff."

LC rubbed his bare right wrist. He didn't know how she knew what he'd done on the roof but she was trying to figure out what it meant.

He shook his head, confused, gripping the knife tightly. "It's fine. Thank you. I thought I'd lost this."

"I thought I'd lost you," she said and wished she hadn't as soon as the words were out.

He stood up and pulled her close. She didn't resist and he held her tightly, breathing in the scent of her hair and feeling her heart pounding against his chest.

"This isn't just a job any more," she whispered, "and I don't know if I can do it."

She was tying herself in knots inside. She was thinking that he was the most valuable target she'd ever been given, the most extraordinary guy she'd ever met and the most difficult she'd ever tried to understand. He could feel the exasperation that was tearing at her.

She pulled back and stared into his eyes. "Why did you give yourself up on the roof? They could have killed you."

"They were going to kill you. What was I supposed to do?"

She leaned her head on his shoulder. "What are we supposed to do now?"

"We go to Redgate and get Badger to help us find the bastards that did this. I know who it was. I just need to find them. Find Anya."

"And then what?"

"Find out who it was in the guild that set us up. I'm done running, Sean."

They stood for a moment then she pulled away again, fixing a resolve deep inside that he wasn't completely sure he was reading right. "Redgate is going to be difficult," she said, back to business as if nothing had happened. "It was bad enough when I was there with Hil but we're getting reports that the Merchants have pulled out of the airfield. So not only has the only neutral way down to the surface gone but it's the target of the heaviest fighting Redgate has seen in years. There's a no fly zone around the city and a twenty-four hour curfew on the ground. The situation down there looks to be deteriorating so we need to be in and out fast. Elliott says he can get us down undetected. North Shore, right?"

She didn't wait for him to confirm. "We're getting maps and scans uploaded now. Hal will come with us to find Badger. He swears he's fit enough and said you'll get yourself in trouble if he's not watching you. Thom's staying here with Gallagher. DiMarco will shift the andirium – he says he knows people here. We'll have to trust him. The weather's worse too, total blizzard, so dress warm." She reached up to his ear. "We need to do something about this."

LC brushed off her hand and tugged at the metal tag. "Can you get it off?"

"Not here, but I can reprogramme the information burnt onto it. You'll belong to me." She smiled.

Oh god, what had he got himself into?

29

The candle was flickering, wax threatening to flood the wick. The chamber felt very dark.

"Redgate?" the Man said, with disdain. "If ever a concentration of living beings was doomed to self-destruct, it was Redgate." He lined up the discarded pieces in an immaculately neat line, perfectly parallel to the edge of the board.

NG watched, absently rubbing a hand across his chest. He hadn't handled the situation on Redgate well and he was still sore from the encounter.

The Man nudged the captured white bishop into line. "You knew the Merchants were vying for a confrontation with us." He looked up. "How did you leave it with Ballack?"

NG moved one of his pawns. "He was very amenable once the misunderstanding had been cleared up. He said he was going to pull the Merchants out of there because the place wasn't profitable for them any more."

It was that simple.

"It's never that simple," the Man said. "That fool Ballack pulled his operation out of Redgate because he lost control of the game he'd been playing. You know that he was selling arms to both sides?"

The wax spilt over the edge of the candle, cascading in streams. The flame flared, pushing back the darkness.

NG nodded. He'd been lucky to get out alive.

The Man reached for his queen and changed his mind, sitting back to consider the board. "Ballack's problem was that someone somewhere else decided that Redgate was worth a substantial investment and flooded the place with weapons. They lit the fuse to the powder keg."

An hour of running through the snow amidst a rocket bombardment and LC crouched in a doorway wondering what the hell he'd got them all into. He'd tried to argue with Sean to let him go alone but she was adamant. Duncan was just as stubborn.

They'd made it down to the surface safely, no gun ships or missile emplacements targeting them as they descended, Elliott obnoxiously smug about the stealth capacity of the big freighter. That was another curiosity to be filed away for future reference. They'd landed on an abandoned highway about ten miles north of the river, as close to the city as they dared. Night was setting in fast. DiMarco and his guys had taken the jeep and the andirium. LC had taken a quick look at the map of the city that Elliott had compiled and they'd left the safety of the Duck, making a run through the snowstorm into the maze of battered and bombed out high-rise tenement blocks.

It was slow going. The bombings had started about twenty minutes in.

A missile hit the building across the street, debris flying, the blast sending the billowing snow into a flurry. He turned away, covering his head with his arms, shielding Sean as she sheltered against the door. He'd always come in through the airfield before, using the tunnels to get to the North Shore. He didn't know this side of the city that well and the white out was making it hard to match the streets to the map in his head. And it had never been this volatile.

"At least there are no bounty hunters after your butt out here," Sean sent through the wire.

Funny.

Redgate had seemed like such a good idea at the time.

Duncan ran in and grabbed LC's shoulder. "We need to move," he yelled, "we've got vehicles incoming."

They ran out into the snow and hugged the wall, ducking into a side street to get off the main road. Drifts were piling up on the pavement, building up against the walls and kerbs. His ribs were still sore but LC felt more alive than he had in a long time. He knew who they were now and having a name gave him focus. It felt like he'd turned the hunt around. It wasn't easy to run in the snow but it felt good to be out in the cold, feeling the chill across his face and the wind cutting into the back of his neck.

He moved faster than was safe, skidding on patches of ice where the snow cover was thin and sliding wherever he could, racing ahead to scout out the way. He headed for the river, taking turns from memory and veering away from any sounds, gunfire echoing eerily though the gaps between the tall buildings. He could feel Sean some distance behind, twitching whenever she lost sight of him. Duncan was behind her, moving more steadily, glancing back and walking backwards regularly to make sure no one was following. For someone who'd never been a team player, LC was surprised at himself. It felt good.

They made good time and managed to avoid trouble until they reached the river. An icy wind was blowing in off the dark frozen expanse of water. Flashing lights glinted through the blizzard and snatches of angry voices drifted on the wind.

They stopped in the shadow of the buildings that fronted onto the main road running parallel with the river. It was quiet to the west, some kind of roadblock to the east where they needed to go.

A shell hit the street behind them, the rumble of the explosion rocking the pavement. They all ducked as debris rained down.

"Shit," Duncan muttered. LC could feel that the big man was fighting to ignore a headache that was building. The marine was thinking it had been a while since he'd been on the ground in the middle of a conflict like this. And the last time, he'd had a platoon of marines at his back and an armoured unit on call. "Who the hell is this guy Badger?"

"He's a friend," Sean said before LC could think of an answer. She stamped her feet and blew on her hands. "And he can help us."

"No one can know we're here right? How the hell do we get past that?" Duncan said.

LC edged out and took a look. He could feel too many people closing in from all directions to double back and too many in front to make a run for it. The river was the only quiet void of peace.

"The river," he said. "If we can get across the road, we can jump the fence and drop down to the riverside path. We'll be able to sneak past. They don't know we're here – they're looking for rebels."

He turned to see Duncan staring at him. The big man wanted to ask how they were expecting Badger to help them and was wondering what the hell Sean was doing here. They'd just rescued LC from a pair of bounty hunters and here he was gallivanting around with another at his side like he was best buddies with the girl.

LC felt the headache spike.

"Just trust me," he said quietly.

Duncan frowned.

Sean pushed between them. "Come on, boys," she said, "let's get the hell out of this storm."

She looked both ways and ran out, vanishing into the falling snow. LC took a step out to follow and caught a hit of desperate emotion that punched through the darkness. Vehicle engines roared and gunfire erupted to their left.

Duncan hissed, "Wait," behind him but Sean was already out there, exposed, and LC ran after her, feeling the vehicle bearing down on them. The crack of a rifle shot and the sound of glass shattering cut through the air. He felt a black tug of vacuum, a quick instant of nothing that hit his centre, and the sound of the car changed, wheels screaming as it skidded on the ice. He could see Sean up ahead, stopping and looking around, a realisation of horror as she realised the driver was dead and the vehicle was slewing across the road right towards her.

LC didn't even think. Inhumanly fast reflexes sparked and he sprinted, bundled into her and shoved her aside, momentum carrying them out of the way, a fraction of a second too late.

The car hit and he relaxed every muscle as he was bounced up against the windscreen, rolling with it and expecting the car to crash into the fence and pitch him onto the road. It hit the fence and didn't stop. He felt it fall away from under him. There was a crash and then he was falling. He hit hard ice, right hand taking the brunt of the impact. The ice cracked and he plunged into icy water, every inch of breath forced out of his lungs with the shock. He sank, feeling the mass of the car sinking beside him.

It felt like his heart stopped.

There was a brief instant of nothing. Echoing, detached from reality nothing. Then his entire system reset with a burst of energy and he kicked for the surface, muscles straining.

He could hear Sean sending a steady, "Talk to me, LC," through the wire.

"I'm fine," he sent back. "Shit, this river is cold."

He bumped up against a solid surface and worked his way to the edge of the ice, splashing up to the surface and sucking in a breath of freezing air that stabbed needles of ice into his chest. Someone grabbed the back of his jacket and hauled him out.

He lay on his back for a second, shivering, then rolled over and doubled up, coughing. He couldn't help the laugh that slipped out, half hysterical and completely inappropriate. Soft white snowflakes drifted down past his nose.

Sean knelt close and whispered in his ear, "You're insane." She hugged him, trying to stop the shivers but he was soaked through.

He looked up and used her to pull himself to his feet.

Duncan was watching the path up ahead. "We need to move," he said. "How far is it?"

It wasn't far and once they'd crept past the roadblock, it didn't take long to work their way away from the river and into Badger's district.

They ran at a steady pace, keeping close together. LC was struggling to stop the shivers, every bit of him wet and cold, joints beginning to seize up. Sean urged him along, taking his arm and rubbing heat into his back as they ran.

It was quieter in the narrow streets leading to Badger's place and it was a relief to finally make it to his door. Sean pressed the buzzer and for a long drawn out moment, LC had the sinking feeling that something was wrong when the door didn't open. He was fumbling to get his tool kit out when the lock clicked. Sean pushed it open and pushed him inside.

"Don't be alarmed by anything," she warned Duncan, stepping confidently in behind him.

LC stood trembling and dripping onto the floor. It took an eternity for the blue beams to scan him, longer than ever before.

"Come on, Badger, don't be a dick," he called out, about at the end of his patience.

The beams lingered then faded. Sean passed the security test in seconds, Duncan only a little while longer. Badger had a twisted sense of humour.

They made their way inside, doors opening ahead of them as they approached and it was only when LC pushed his way into Badger's den that he realised something really was wrong.

The room was dark and quiet, monitors off, equipment on standby, only a gentle hum from the emergency systems that were still operational breaking the silence.

LC had never known Badger leave his gear powered down before, not to this extent.

"He's not here," he said.

Sean edged past. "I'm sure he'll be back soon." She headed for the bathroom. It was weird to see her so familiar with a place that was so sacred to the guild.

The sound of banging was followed by running water. "Get those wet clothes off," she yelled back at him.

LC shrugged out of his sodden jacket, trying to shield the broken fingers on his right hand. His whole arm was throbbing, chest sore and head pounding but it was good to be somewhere safe at last.

"Make yourself at home," he said to Duncan.

The big man took his coat off and pulled out a chair at the table. He looked around and leaned forward. "It's a hell of a time to bring this up, bud," he whispered, "but you and I need to talk."

"Not here," LC muttered.

"Yes, here. You want to tell me why it feels like my chest is on fire, why it feels like it was me that got hit by that car, like it was me in that river?" He was massaging his right hand, kneading the fingers.

LC stared at the floor. He couldn't explain.

"Try," Duncan hissed.

It felt like he'd been punched in the chest even though he was expecting it. He turned his head and looked Duncan directly in the eyes, wondering what he could say. How the hell did you tell someone you could read their mind, see their innermost thoughts, feel every emotion and hurt they were feeling?

The big man stared back, disbelief in his eyes.

'You are shitting me,' Duncan thought.

'Wish I was,' LC thought back, trying to figure out if thinking that way was the same or different to using the Senson. It was different, he decided, not as clear, more hazy. With the Senson you knew without doubt that someone was communicating with you via a distinct connection, tagged with whatever priorities and encryptions you decided you needed, tight as a wire strung between you both. Reading someone's mind was more confusing; he'd been sensing Duncan's thoughts for weeks, to hear him send a thought directly was very odd.

'Shit, I thought I was going insane. Who else knows?' he heard Duncan think, whether to him or not, he couldn't tell.

"No one," LC said quietly, out loud to avoid confusion. "Absolutely no one. No one alive anyway."

Sean yelled him to get his ass into the bathroom and she helped him out of his wet clothing, fretting at the bruises, throwing his stuff in the drier and leaving him to it once she saw that he was alright.

LC stood in the torrent of hot water, closing his eyes and keeping his breathing slow and steady. He felt drained, wrung out trying to keep track of what he'd revealed to whom. He felt exposed. Sean knew that he couldn't have known about the injector in her pocket and she knew he shouldn't have been able to withstand the shot he'd been stupid enough to punch into his neck right in front of her. It was only that she felt caught out and guilty that was stopping her from giving him a hard time about it.

And now Duncan not only knew about the virus, he knew about the side effects. It felt like the secret was out and LC had no control over it any more. He wasn't even planning on telling anyone at the guild about it. He hadn't been able to imagine how he could even tell Hilyer or Pen. He'd known Hal Duncan for five minutes and now the man knew his most intimate and dangerous secret. And it could cost both of them their lives.

His clothes were dry by the time he was done and the smell of hot chilli was wafting in from the kitchen.

Sean and Duncan were sitting at the table, weapons spread out on a cloth. Sean stood up as he approached. "Food won't be long," she said and moved close, adding quietly, "Is there any chance Badger has left? Could something have happened?"

LC shrugged. "He never powers his stuff down," he admitted, "but all the security systems are still up and running so if he's gone, he intends to come back. I'm sorry, this could have been a waste of time."

She squeezed his shoulder and sent through the wire, "LC, I know we can trust NG. Come back with me."

He shook his head, feeling more and more with Badger missing that the guild was the last place he wanted to be. "Go get warmed up," he sent back. "We'll eat then get back. I want to try Aston next."

She started to object but he turned away, pulling a first aid kit from a drawer and sinking into the chair she'd vacated.

Duncan waited until she'd gone then looked up. LC ignored him, strapping three of the fingers on his right hand, aware that the big man was watching him intently as he pulled the bindings tight.

'I felt that as you hit the ice,' Duncan thought, clenching and unclenching his right hand, thinking that his own fingers were still aching. "What happens if one of us gets seriously hurt?"

'I could shoot you and tell you how it felt.'

Duncan gave a wry smile. He was thinking about the driver of the car by the river. He'd felt it, felt that void as the guy had died, same as when he'd killed the bounty hunters on Tortuga.

LC shrugged it off. 'Don't think about it.'

Duncan swore silently to himself, deftly disassembling his gun for cleaning. "We need to get back to the Duck before it gets even worse out there," he said out loud, while carefully wiping dry each individual component of his gun. "Whoever this Badger guy is, he's not here." He picked up another pistol and clicked a magazine into it. "Can you shoot left-handed?"

LC nodded.

The big marine passed him the handgun and continued to clean the weapons. He looked right at home. "So what is it?" he asked casually without looking up. "Assassins or thieves?"

It came out of the blue and LC blinked in surprise, heart thumping. "What?"

The big marine turned and folded his arms, leaning back. He stared at LC, dark eyes piercing. "This guild of yours, what is it? What are you, LC, assassin or thief?"

30

"I take it the Merchants denied any move against us."

NG was nursing the goblet of wine, feeling the warm fumes haze their way into his bloodstream. "It didn't come up," he said, "but Ballack was uncomfortable that I was there."

The Man laced his fingers together and closed his eyes. "I have initiated the establishment of a new coalition that will attempt to hold Redgate's space port under an independent banner. It should be easier for you the next time you need to send people there."

NG sat perfectly still, keeping his breathing steady. It wasn't often the Man spoke of his other involvements. He knew the Man had interests throughout the galaxy, but NG wasn't privileged to any of the details. And he didn't ask. The Thieves' Guild took his full attention.

"The one you call Badger?" the Man asked, eyes still closed.

"Still missing. He got out in time though. He'll be in touch when he feels it's safe."

The Man shook his head slightly. He was thinking that he didn't want to be this close to the individuals of the guild, the minutiae of everyday life and its dramas too cumbersome for him to waste time trying to comprehend.

NG kept his own mind neutral. The Man had been purposeful in letting him overhear it.

"I understand why you care so much," the Man said, finally opening his eyes and leaning forward. "But the sooner the fallout from this escapade settles, the better for us all. There is so much more at risk than humanity can imagine and there will be losses."

He reached for the queen and swept her forward to capture the rook and place NG's king in check.

Damn.

Duncan didn't move and didn't shift his gaze. LC sat quietly for a long minute. The gun was heavy in his hand.

It was hard not to stand and walk away, realising that every thought that crossed his mind was wide open to the man sitting there so casually in front of him. He didn't know how to shut him out. He'd learned how to shut out other people's constant bombardment of thoughts when he wanted to but he had no defences against someone else listening in to his.

"It doesn't matter," he said finally. "I can't go back."

He could feel that Duncan was getting stronger. Elliott had been right; the virus seemed to have adjusted much quicker than it had in him.

"You saved my life," Duncan said softly. "I don't care where you're from, Luka, or what you are. But I do need to know what's going on if I'm going to be able to help us stay alive and stay ahead of the game here. I'm in this shit as deep as you are. You have to talk to me. And you have to trust me, whatever else you've got going on."

LC took a deep breath. It felt as if his chest was going to burst, adrenaline pumping and heart racing. He hadn't told Sean everything but Hal was right; he had a right to know.

The big man was still staring.

LC bit his lip trying to figure out what to say first. "I need a beer," he muttered and pushed away from the table.

The fridge was well stocked, all long-lasting pouches and bottles, nothing fresh so maybe Badger had planned to go away. He grabbed three beers and wandered back into the den. His head was starting to pound and he couldn't tell if the ache in his chest was from the broken ribs or a chill in his lungs from the river.

Duncan ignored the beer. "Why are we here?" he said. "That would be a good place to start."

LC popped his bottle open and drank down most of it trying to decide what to say. He wanted Badger to tell him where to find Zang, tell him who in that organisation had initiated the tab and the price on his head afterwards.

'Initiated what?' Duncan thought.

LC looked up over the beer bottle, eyes hooded, flashing back to the scene on Earth, corporate suits holding a gun to Mendhel's head and threatening to kill his daughter if they didn't take the job.

'Who's Mendhel?' Duncan sent softly.

LC frowned. He didn't want to go there. He didn't want to explain any of this to anyone. 'My handler,' he found himself thinking. 'He's dead. They killed him because we didn't get the package back to them.'

'The virus?'

LC shrugged. 'I don't know if they really even knew what they were sending us to steal.'

Duncan thought to himself, Thieves' Guild then. LC closed his eyes and leaned forward on the table, dropping his head onto his folded arms. It didn't matter. He wasn't going back. How the hell was he supposed to introduce Hal Duncan to NG?

'Who's NG?' Duncan asked.

LC shook his head, burrowing deeper into his sleeve.

'Who's us then?' Duncan thought, wanting to know who else was caught up in this drama he'd found himself in. 'Who were you with? This is important, Luka.'

'Zach Hilyer,' LC replied reluctantly. Duncan needed to know to assess the situation and it was only fair considering. 'He's another field-op. We went in together. I was hit with the virus and he split to take the heat away from me. I don't know where he is.'

'He wouldn't give you up?'

LC opened his eyes and looked at the marine with disbelief. 'Never.'

Duncan looked unimpressed. 'Yeah,' he sent, 'I know how long never lasts when special forces gets their hands on someone.'

LC shrugged. Hil wouldn't give him up.

They sat quietly then and he finished the beer, reaching across for a second. Duncan looked on disapproving, thinking that he drank too much; the big guy had never let his men near alcohol in the middle of a mission.

'Try it,' LC thought.

'What?'

'Try it.' He drank, feeling the hit as the virus ripped apart the molecular carbohydrate chains turning the alcohol into fuel. The ache in his chest started to ease as his body used the energy to heal the damage.

Duncan picked up on it. 'You're shitting me.' He frowned, reaching for the third bottle. He popped it open and raised the bottle to his lips, a questioning glance flashing across his eyes as he tipped it up.

'Can't get drunk,' LC thought at him. 'Believe me, I've tried.'

He rested his head down again. He didn't mean to sleep and the nightmare that snatched at his subconscious left his heart racing. It couldn't have been for long but he woke to find Duncan gone and Sean there by his side.

She rested her hand on the back of his neck, massaging gently with warm fingers as he stirred.

"How do you feel?" she said softly.

"Like I was hit by a car."

She was thinking about Hilyer, how Hil had fallen asleep at the table too. She stroked his neck. The last time she was here she was still looking for him. And she couldn't quite believe that she was now sitting next to him, that she had the infamous LC Anderton right here beside her.

He twisted round slightly to look at her. It was suddenly difficult to tell if the personal feelings he was picking up from her were real or some kind of wacky idolisation.

She smiled and it was even more confusing.

The sound of the shower cut off. Sean leaned in close. "We can't go to Aston, LC. It would be suicide."

He knew she was right. It had been hard enough last time and Pen had been furious that he was taking such risks. "I don't know where else to go."

She sighed and stood, briefly touching the tag in his ear, thinking that she couldn't lose him again. "Well, this is probably the safest place we can be right now," she said. "Let's take our time and figure out what's going to be best."

She gave his shoulder a squeeze and wandered off to the kitchen.

LC sat up, muscles he hadn't realised he'd pulled aching stiffly. She was right again. Out of everywhere he'd run since it had all gone to hell, this was the closest he'd been to the guild. He looked round at Badger's gear, neatly stacked boards and racks of dormant monitors and sensors. The data wall that was usually streaming with information and maps was inert.

He wasn't worried about Badger. He'd never known the guy to work amidst anything but total chaos. Badger had had time to tidy – there was no way he'd left quickly or unexpectedly.

It didn't take long to fire up some of the main systems. A lot of Badger's kit was completely inaccessible, even to the field-ops. But LC had a couple of ins. He grabbed a data board and a beer and slouched on the sofa, taking his time to get comfortable. He could hear Sean and Duncan moving about in the kitchen. He shut them out and delved deep, resting the board by his side and using the Senson to connect remotely, managing to make a smooth link to query Badger's system without too much trouble.

It recognised him – that made it easier. And Badger had left a few signposts specifically for him as if he'd wanted to make sure LC got the update if he made it here. Scanning through it all was hard going, made harder when he realised how much trouble he was in, how deep this all went.

He surfaced with a jolt, adrenaline pumping. Sean was watching, Duncan trying not to. LC looked across at them both, breathing hard. They'd finished eating, hadn't liked to disturb him and had left his food in the kitchen. He hadn't realised he'd been in there that long.

He ditched completely out of the system and shut it all down, swinging around to sit on the edge of the sofa, rubbing the back of his neck.

He got his breathing under control and looked over at them. "I need to give myself up," he said, decision made.

Sean stared, confused, not sure how much she could say in front of Hal Duncan. The big man had caught some of it but not all. He kept his mouth shut.

"Why?" she said finally, cautiously, not sure what he meant by that, who he was intending giving himself up to.

"Hilyer's missing," he said.

It was worse than that. At least two of the guild's extraction agents had gone awol, the guild had lost track of Hil even though he was supposed to be under surveillance and NG had initiated a Black Rogue Seven alert on them all. LC had never even heard of that level of alert, Black was bad enough. The guild had teams out with orders to apprehend and detain, extreme force approved towards any outside agency that interfered. The Thieves' Guild never outwardly sanctioned hostilities towards anyone.

LC rubbed at his eye. That was what spooked him – the thought that whatever he and Hilyer had got themselves caught up in had far wider reaching consequences than they'd ever stopped to appreciate.

Badger had left a week or so ago and he'd made sure that the message was loud and clear if LC got here; don't go back to the Alsatia, trust no one and for god's sake, don't get caught. This place suddenly seemed a lot less safe.

Sean stood up, gathering bowls. "You need to eat," she said, like that would solve everything. She went to the kitchen, trying desperately not to over-react and throw him onto the floor in cuffs.

LC left the board he'd been using on the sofa and wandered over to the table. He had a headache pinching at the back of his mind.

"You need beer," Duncan said and pushed over a bottle from a stash lined up in neat rows. Half of them were empty already. "Worse than you thought?"

LC nodded and sat, spinning the beer bottle around on its base. He should have known with the bounty spiralling up to such stupid levels.

'Bud, excuse me for thinking this,' the big marine thought, 'but isn't Sean a bounty hunter? Has she not caught up with you already?'

LC popped open the beer. Duncan needed to know. He had no choice but to open up. 'Sean's working for the guild.'

'Ah.'

She came back with a bowl of chilli for LC and a packet of chips that she threw to Duncan. She sat down and stared defiantly at LC.

'And she wants to take you back?'

LC took a mouthful of chilli. 'Yep.'

'And you want to give yourself up how exactly?'

LC took another slow mouthful of chilli and washed it down with beer. They were both looking intently at him. "I can't go back to the guild," he said.

Sean sucked in a breath and glared at him, total disbelief that he'd mention the guild in front of anyone.

"It's fine," he said casually, waving towards the big marine with the spoon. "Hal knows."

She was thinking that he was out of his mind. She couldn't have been more wrong. For the first time, he knew what he had to do. Ploughing through the information Badger had left for him to find, it was obvious that no one in the guild knew how to find the people who had taken Anya, forced them to take the tab and set the bounty when they'd failed. He knew exactly how to find them. He'd realised when he was lying on the floor of the bounty hunters' ship, he just hadn't been in a fit state to act on it. Now he was and he was going to do it.

Duncan gave a small smile and shook his head.

"What?" Sean said suspiciously.

LC pushed away the bowl. "I need to find Anya to finish this," he said. "I know who has her. I give myself up to a bounty hunter and they'll take me right to them."

"You're out of your mind," she said. "You give yourself up to one of these money-grubbing bastards and they'll take you right to the nearest processing centre, alive if they decide that keeping you that way is worth the hassle, and then you'll be lucky if you ever see the light of day again."

"They want the package, Sean. It's Zang Enterprises, some

249

Wintran corporation. They don't want me or Hil, they want the package they sent us to steal."

That took her by surprise. She sat back, uncomfortable that Duncan was hearing any of this, disturbed that the big man knew about the guild and completely unsure what to say. From the look on Duncan's face, he was picking all that up too.

"Do you have it?" she said awkwardly.

LC nodded. She'd never asked before. It hadn't been part of her brief and she was furious with herself that she hadn't considered its importance when LC had first mentioned it. She couldn't help thinking about Hil. She knew they'd run an unauthorised tab but that was all NG had said, and Hilyer had been too screwed up with amnesia to tell her anything else. It hadn't occurred to her that all this could be about an actual package somewhere.

Duncan leaned forward. "Is there any chance they might have got their hands on Hilyer?"

It was possible that Hil was safe somewhere. Then again he could be dead or strung up in a bounty hunter's hold. "Even if they have," he said, "all they want is the package. If I can get to them, I can offer it in exchange. You follow and get me out, with Anya and Hil if he's there."

Sean went pale, biting her tongue as the memory of a conversation skipped through her mind.

"What?" LC said, knowing fine well what she was thinking, flashing back at her bounty hunter buddy bragging that she wasn't the only one with a private contract. He hadn't said who he was working for but he'd derided the suckers who were playing for the open bounty and it was only now that LC was talking about the corporation that had done this that Sean put it together.

Oh god, he heard her think, McKenzie's working for Zang.

"No," she said. "No way."

31

NG sipped at his wine, keeping calm and working out the convoluted consequences of each possible move.

The Man was watching his reaction. "I understand you initiated a Rogue Seven?"

"We had no choice," he said, leaning in to move the king to safety. "We suspected a breach in security. It's hard to send extraction teams into a situation when one or more of their own may turn and stab them in the back."

It had been hard for everyone. Unprecedented.

The Man reached to move one of his knights. "And speaking of a knife between the shoulder blades, where are we with the Assassins?"

NG raised his eyes. He'd sent out a scale of alerts that had never been seen before, the Thieves' Guild pulling its weight in every corner of the galaxy and the repercussions still resonating. "Still unresolved," he said reluctantly, slightly grudgingly, diplomacy not always his strong point, not when he had people actively in danger. Not when he had idiots like Ballack and the Merchants taking potshots. The Assassins' Guild and its threats were not to be taken lightly but he wasn't going to let it spook anyone.

"You rattled cages, NG. You should not have been surprised that it caused alarm in so many quarters." The Man picked up his goblet and swirled it. "Did O'Brien know what Anderton intended to do?"

"Presumably but she'd stopped reporting to us by then."

It took an age to get out of the city centre, taking care to avoid trouble. Sean had refused to be drawn into a debate and she'd simply said he was a damned fool.

It didn't matter; he'd made up his mind.

They'd waited until dark then secured Badger's place and ventured back out into the storm.

LC was finding it hard to concentrate, getting irregular bursts from Duncan, unintentional at times and conversational at others like he was experimenting with it. LC threw comments back, trying his best to keep a grip on shielding his mind the rest of the time with no idea if it was working. They were all soaked through again and chilled to the bone by the time they reached the ship.

The jeep was back in the hold and Elliott told them to ready for launch as soon as they set foot on board. "No hurry," he sent. "There's just a division or two of troops heading this way."

LC went to the engine room out of habit more than anything. The klaxons began to sound before he made it, the engines firing up for launch and the ship's mass beginning to shift as he ran into the control room and fell into the chair. Thom looked round apologetically.

"How much did DiMarco make on the andirium?" LC said, struggling to fasten the restraints as they took off.

"Enough," Thom said with a grin. "Gallagher's offered to split the profit with us all. Did you find the guy you were looking for?"

LC shook his head. "No, but I've got a plan. Where are we going, do you know?"

"Somewhere to buy medical supplies."

There was a bang from within the depths of the engine room. They looked at each other and back at the console, the kid punching up data with dismay. The ship was moving fast, accelerating hard. LC reached across, turned up the heat in the tiny control room, sat back and closed his eyes.

They made orbit and eased into a steady flight path. His clothes had pretty much dried out so LC offered to sit watch while the kid went to make some repairs. He kept one eye on the numbers scrolling across the monitors and tried to work out the flaws in his plan. Handing himself in would be easy. Figuring out a way to stay alive was more tricky. It made his head hurt.

He was finding it tough to stay awake by the time Thom got

back, about another hour to jump and a couple of the primary systems still goosed. The kid tossed a spanner to LC and slumped in the other chair. "You're going to have to give me a hand," he said, wiping a black smudge across his cheek. "The primary cooling system is struggling and the secondary is shot. I honestly don't know how this bucket manages to keep flying."

They were knee-deep in grease and components from the stripped down coolant unit when Sean appeared. LC was leaning in headfirst, up to the waist, balancing on one foot and trying to reach a damned valve that Thom was directing him to when he felt her approach. He caught the emotion, a thought she'd be horrified to share at the sight of him leaning over, and the spanner fumbled out of his grip to bounce clattering into the depths of the drive.

He rested his head on the conduit that had been hampering him and couldn't help the grin or the flush that flashed across his face.

Thom yelled up that he had it and LC sent a quick, ' Give us a minute," to Sean and climbed right in, twisting over the pipe to reach the valve and ease it open by hand.

She waited patiently while they finished up. From the grin Thom gave, it was obvious that the kid guessed she wanted LC alone and he offered to take the next watch, disappearing back to the control room.

Once he'd gone, Sean stepped in close.

"I didn't get to thank you for what you did on that roof," she said quietly. "I couldn't move but I heard what they said. It was a mistake to give yourself up, LC, a really stupid mistake, but you saved my life, so thank you." She was hoping he'd kiss her again so he did, taking her by surprise and taken aback himself when she pulled away, trying to keep some distance between them. Even when he could read her mind, he didn't understand her.

She put a hand gently against his chest. "I've been thinking," she said, a look in her eyes warning him not to argue. "If we're going to do this, we do it my way. And you have to trust me."

She paused, expecting him to protest. He didn't.

"I know someone we can use," she said. "He's a snake and I don't like him, much less trust him, but I have a feeling he might be working directly for the corporation that set you up. He's an arrogant son of a bitch and I'll be honest with you, when I work with him you won't like it. But I can offer him a deal he won't be able to refuse. He'll take us right to them."

Gallagher said his goodbyes uneasily. "Are you sure about this?"

LC looked up. Whenever he used to take off on a tab, he left the Alsatia with no ceremony, a brief shake of the hand from Mendhel once they'd covered all the data and he'd split. He wasn't used to any fuss. Gallagher was standing there trying not to mist up. It wasn't making it any easier.

Sean touched a hand to his arm in a gentle nudge. She'd already stowed her gear on board her tiny ship, Edinburgh. It didn't even fill a quarter of the Duck's hold. They'd brought her on board once they were on route to Medway, once they'd decided that was the best place for Gallagher to get his medical supplies and Sean to call in McKenzie. Medway was firmly in Wintran-controlled space, the least volatile planet they could get to quickly. Sean had asked him the same question before she'd gone onto the station to meet the bounty hunter and make her proposition. She hadn't liked the answer any more than Gallagher was going to now. She'd fixed that resolve again and disappeared onto Medway's orbital. LC had scampered down to the engine room and hooked up with Elliott, who was already deep inside the station's systems, to listen in to the conversation. He was desperately hoping that he hadn't misjudged her and he wanted to hear first hand what she said to the guy. It hadn't taken long for McKenzie to find her and sidle in there beside her at the bar. And it hadn't taken long for Sean to persuade him that yes, she had their target safely tucked up on board her ship and no, she wasn't completely content to hand him in for the measly half a million she'd agreed to like a chump before she'd realised how much he was really worth.

McKenzie was a jerk. LC had watched while Sean flattered and teased, easily winding him around her little finger. She'd been very convincing.

Elliott had laughed at the discomfort LC couldn't hide. "You don't have to go through with this," the tech guy had said softly. "We could go now, take the Duck and disappear. No one would ever find you." It had been a tempting thought and watching Sean flirt shamelessly with a guy who wanted his scalp had almost sent LC off the edge. But running wasn't an option any more. Not when he knew that Hilyer was missing. Not when Anya was still out there somewhere. And especially not when he heard McKenzie brag that Zang had contracted him for the job because they knew no one else could manage it. "And face it, Seanie," he'd breathed into her ear, "you're here now asking for my help because you can't handle him."

She'd smiled and sent back through the wire to LC, "How about we take this one step further and take the eighty five million for ourselves?"

She'd come back on board fuming, told him to stash any gear he didn't want to lose and advised him to put on something warm. "McKenzie keeps his holding pen cold," she'd said.

He'd left his jacket in his cabin, pulled on a thick shirt and handed Sean his knife in a show of absolute trust in her that he was glad didn't go unnoticed.

Gallagher shifted awkwardly. Hal Duncan stepped in and clasped LC on the shoulder. "We'll see you back at Tortuga, bud," he said, no doubt in his voice and a private message for LC to take care of himself sent through a thought that pierced into LC's mind.

He nodded and followed Sean onto the ship, refusing to let a pang of hesitation creep in. Edinburgh was polite and curious. He strapped in to the passenger's seat and scuffed his feet against the console, feeling weirdly like he was a prisoner already. Sean seemed to sense it and reached across to squeeze his knee.

"Trust me," she said and turned away to make preparations to leave. Edinburgh manoeuvred herself deftly out of the Duck and they dropped down to the planet. LC closed his eyes and slowed his breathing carefully, ribs still not completely healed and a tightness there that had more to do with the tension of playing the part than the injury he'd picked up when he'd been caught for real.

Sean didn't bother with any superfluous chatter. It was strange to see her in her own environment. She was completely in control for the first time since they'd met and he couldn't resist the urge to delve into her mind to make sure she wasn't planning on just flying out and heading straight for the Alsatia.

They didn't. They made a smooth descent and landed at a nondescript airfield on the outskirts of a small township, checking in with McKenzie on the way.

Sean busied herself securing the ship and repacking her holdall. LC sat and watched, feeling a rising tension as Sean avoided looking at him. She took a deep breath before she finally turned to face him, bag hoisted onto her shoulder and a set of plasticuffs in her hand.

"We need to make it look good," she said, a hint of apology tingeing the determination in her voice. "And unwrap the bindings on your hand. I wouldn't have given you the chance to do that."

LC stood calmly, heart thumping, and pulled the strapping off his fingers. He held his hands out, wrists up. "Front or back?"

She took hold of his arm and twisted gently, easing behind him. "Always behind the back," she said with a smile. "We know what you guys can do."

He let her secure the cuffs around his wrists. She pulled them tight, not caring too much to take care, and turned to face him. She held up a small device that looked hideously like the one the bounty hunters had stuck in his neck. "You have to trust me," she said again. "This needs to look good."

"Do you have to make it look that good?" LC muttered and flinched as she placed the device on the back of his neck again. It adhered with a spike of intense pain.

She flicked the metal tag pierced through the edge of his ear. "From here on in, Luka," she said, "we have to make it look better than good because if McKenzie thinks anything is amiss here, he'll kill you." She stroked a hand along his jawline. "Just be glad you have enough bruises already to make this look real. I'd hate to have to bust up this pretty face of yours."

She pushed him out into the grey overcast daylight of Medway and they made the short walk across to McKenzie's ramp. His ship was bigger than Edinburgh, slick and flash looking, weapons subtly but obviously placed on its hull. Sean had a confidence in her step that was completely at odds with the nerves he could feel fluttering inside her. She was very good. She'd worked on these terms with McKenzie before but never with such a lot at stake, never with someone she cared so much about. My god, she was thinking, she'd never cared so much about anyone in her life, never mind a target. LC couldn't help the cocky smile that snuck out as McKenzie greeted them.

It slipped as the guy moved close to Sean and rubbed hips with her, nudging her aside to grab LC's arm and shove him up against the bulkhead. "So this is the badass the whole galaxy is after?" he said. The slick accent and strong scent of sickly cologne almost made LC gag. "Well done, Seanie, well done girl. You've done all the checks? I thought he was supposed to have green eyes."

"It's him, Mac. Trust me. And keep him intact, for god's sake – I want the full bounty."

McKenzie smiled, taking in the bruise under LC's eye. "Seanie, I'm not the one who rough-handles the merchandise," he said and pushed LC ahead of him into the ship. Sean followed them, casual but alert, giving the impression that she was eager to wrap up the job and not a hint of any attachment.

LC didn't resist even when McKenzie banged him up against a door. "It's been one hell of a chase, Sean," the bounty hunter said. "One of the best in a long time. I heard this guy was supposed to be real fiery. How the hell did you get him so docile?"

LC watched out of the corner of his eye as Sean nonchalantly threw something to the guy. He couldn't help tensing as he realised what it was. McKenzie caught it, gave an appreciative grunt and LC's knees buckled as the bastard used the remote to flick the device onto full power.

His vision greyed out and it felt like his heart was going to burst out of his chest. Make it look good? Shit, he didn't have much choice. It snapped off abruptly and he was only half aware of being hauled back up to his feet.

McKenzie laughed. Sean brushed past them, willing LC to be calm and just take it. She rested a hand on McKenzie's back. "He's mine, Mac," she whispered. "And he knows it."

An uncomfortable mix of emotions rose in the man, pride, envy, an edge of lust. LC almost cringed. McKenzie was obsessed with Sean and she didn't realise it, or if she suspected she didn't realise the full strength of it. They may have made a real mistake here.

McKenzie laughed again, forced that time, and held LC against the closed door. A cold jab hit his neck and his knees threatened to go again as the drug coursed into his system. The virus snatched at it, sending his head spinning and heart pounding. He felt it start to neutralise, overheard McKenzie think viciously that this would send the sucker to lala land for the trip and realised he couldn't just stand there. Tempting as it was, there was no way he could give away the fact it was having no effect.

He crumpled, deadweight to the deck.

He felt Sean rush back to him, kneeling. "God, McKenzie, what have you given him?" She was thinking about the trauma patch and the allergies that hadn't been mentioned in his file.

Fingers pushed against LC's neck and they reassured themselves that he was still alive.

"Shit," McKenzie said, "it doesn't usually kick in that fast."

32

The Man stood, staring at the chessboard for a long momen- before walking away from the desk.

"One man," he said from across the room. "One man set these events into motion. You say you had no choice but to react with a Rogue Seven. Was it worth it?"

Hundreds of the guild's deep cover agents and sleepers had been compromised. No, it hadn't been worth it but it had been about more than just finding his two field operatives alive.

NG decided his next move. "Ultimately, yes," he said. The Man's perception of time was very different to that of the rest of this galaxy. A disaster on any normal scale was merely an inconvenience for him.

"Maybe so," the Man said, returning and settling back into his chair. He looked up.

It felt as if the temperature in the room had increased a notch. NG reached for his knight and moved it, taking a pawn and placing the Man's king in check.

The Man immediately moved his piece to safety. "How is it that such foolish actions from a man like Zang Tsu Po can cause such widespread anguish and permeating turbulence?"

NG sat quietly. Zang wasn't a fool and the Man knew it. No one got to be that powerful without extraordinary vision and drive. Zang had chanced upon knowledge of a development in bioengineering that he literally could not live without, and he'd mobilised his entire organisation and vast wealth to get his hands on it.

But Zang had crossed the Thieves' Guild and that was never going to be acceptable.

Whatever the cost.

It was a short trip but it seemed to last forever. LC used the time to rest, ease his heart rate and heal. It wasn't that different from hitching a lift to a regular tab. He settled in and snoozed, as comfortable as he could manage with his wrists and ankles tied and a band across his chest keeping him firmly in place.

They'd locked him in a tiny cell, securely restrained to a bench. It was touching that Sean had made sure he was breathing alright and loosened the ties as soon as McKenzie left. So she hadn't completely turned into the cold and ruthless bounty hunter she was making herself out to be. She'd felt his pulse again before she'd left, lingering as she held a finger against his neck. He didn't really want them to know he was awake so he'd kept quiet.

They made one jump. He listened in on their conversations, casual flirting with an edge of professional competition that was almost brutal. They didn't hide the fact that they didn't trust each other. McKenzie hadn't told Sean where they were going and from what LC could pick up, the ship's systems were sealed from her. She teased McKenzie for being paranoid and she was right, LC didn't like it, didn't like the way she spoke to the man in that provocative tone and as much as he knew it was an act, there were moments when he couldn't help but doubt her. It was a lousy way to have to work.

He tried to stay impassive. Sean checked on him a couple of times, worried that he was cold. He was. And concerned that the drugs McKenzie was doping him with were too strong. They weren't, even though he got the distinct impression that the bounty hunter was double dosing to make sure LC stayed under and didn't cause a problem.

McKenzie was a vindictive son of a bitch. He had an instinct for inflicting pain, leaning a hand on LC's chest as he topped up the sedative, hitting the exact spot where the ribs were still sore. LC took it all without flinching. He could read the man clearly enough without having to go too deep into his twisted mind. McKenzie wasn't going to kill him and he wasn't thinking of double-crossing Sean – far from it, he was hoping this job would lead onto more between them. And he'd persuaded himself that Sean had come to him because she wanted to share the notoriety of bringing in the highest value target in history with him, tie their renown together forever, irrevocably.

It took more self-constraint than LC thought he possessed to listen in to it.

He woke as a jab hit his neck, warmth spreading through his bloodstream, stimulant rather than sedative, not that it made a difference to the virus. The ship was quiet and still. He hadn't meant to sleep and the edge of a nightmare clawed at his memory.

"Hey sleepy," Sean sent through the wire, fumbling to release the restraints. Her hands were cold and, as much as she was hiding it, she was emanating a nervous tension that pulsed behind LC's eyes. She freed his wrists quickly and he reached to untie the strap around his chest as she moved to his ankles.

"We're at the facility," she sent.

He sat up, stretching some life back into his muscles. She helped him up and retied his hands. "I don't want you incapacitated if we get in trouble. You can get out of these?"

He gave her a look that didn't need explaining. "Any chance of a weapon?"

She tried to hold in a smile. "Don't push it."

He calmed his breathing, beginning to feel the depth of that intense focus he got before going out on a tab. This time he was walking right into the lion's den – in the company of one bounty hunter who would settle for a fraction of the bounty if it came to handing him in dead rather than not at all, and another who was so scared she was losing her edge that she was thinking she'd rather knock him unconscious than risk kissing him again.

He leaned in and kissed her. She swatted him away and sent an awkward, "God, LC, McKenzie might be watching."

"He isn't."

Sean frowned and took hold of his hands, pretending to check the restraints. "I know I don't need to say this but don't do anything stupid when we get into this place," she sent without looking up.

LC could feel her heart pounding.

She touched his chest and he could feel her feeling his own heartbeat.

"I only get paid if you're alive," she sent, raising her eyes to meet his. "Stay alive. Okay?"

They left the ship and walked through a long tunnel into a sterile entry terminal, efficient, cold and impersonal. Sean and McKenzie were both wearing silver badges on their belts and they flashed documents that got them past the first two checkpoints with no trouble. The third took longer.

LC was on his best behaviour, head down, avoiding eye contact. McKenzie had refused to relinquish the remote to Sean and a persistent throbbing emanated from the device. Somewhere along the way the virus had begun to compensate and it wasn't so much painful as distracting. It was like the FTH rounds – the more he was exposed, the more his system seemed able to adapt. He managed to keep his breathing steady and scanned ahead just far enough to anticipate trouble. The facility was on a high alert, heightened security, and it was hard not to panic. His plan to dupe them with the lure of the package seemed flimsy in the face of the armed guards watching them troop through security barriers laced with bio-sensors.

Sean was nervous. McKenzie was arrogantly anticipating the notoriety this was going to attract. The woman at the third desk looked at them as if she'd seen this a million times.

"You don't understand," McKenzie said, smiling, "I have a delivery for Fiorrentino."

LC shifted awkwardly, hands bound, standing there in public as McKenzie referred to him as a delivery. Sean placed her hand on his back. He wasn't sure if it was to reassure him or warn him not to react.

"I've logged it," the woman said. She glanced at LC and spoke to McKenzie. "You want to leave him with us, we'll make sure he gets delivered."

LC looked into her mind as she turned back to her console. It wasn't the first time they'd accepted live merchandise for processing.

It made him feel cold inside. He'd been sent on tabs across the entire galaxy to steal thousands of items, never once anything living or sentient.

McKenzie leaned on her desk. "Payment on delivery."

"Then you'll have to wait," she said without looking up. "Mr Fiorrentino is busy."

It wasn't the reception McKenzie had been expecting. He laughed. "Get your boss over here, lady. You have no idea what you're dealing with."

She did look up then, eyes flashing to the side. A guard sidled up next to McKenzie and put a hand on his shoulder.

The bounty hunter turned. "Get your hand off me," he murmured, "or I'll break your arm."

Sean had set her mind into neutral, ignoring her buddy's behaviour and rubbing LC's back. McKenzie was a jerk but she was using him and she wasn't going to let herself feel embarrassed by him.

The woman held up her hand, staying the guard. "We have procedures, sir. I've logged your arrival. Mr Fiorrentino is in a meeting that is not to be disturbed. He'll be informed that you're here as soon as he is finished there."

An urgent alarm sounded from her console.

The guards all tensed in unison, anxious glances and an automatic alertness sparking in each mind.

LC felt his stomach backflip.

The woman snapped. "Sir," she said, corporate courtesy through clenched teeth, "please wait in our lounge. I'm sure Mr Fiorrentino will be with you as soon as he is free." She looked back at her console and muttered, "This is all we need."

Security upped another level while they were being ushered into a waiting area. McKenzie scowled, activated the remote out of spite, and helped himself to a drink from a hospitality counter at the far end of the room.

LC sat. He closed his eyes, feeling the virus working overtime to shut down the pain receptors, trying to be patient and not pull out the damned device himself. He felt Sean sit next to him.

"Something's wrong," she sent.

"Yeah," he managed to send back, "your buddy is a psychopath."

She stared puzzled, then reached to the back of his neck. A stab of intense agony shot into his spine as the device disengaged. He thought he was going to throw up.

"This is the highest contract posted in history," she sent. "I thought we'd be hustled right in."

LC leaned forward, resting his elbows on his knees and his head in his hands, the nausea easing slowly. "The staff out there don't know anything about me or the contract," he sent back. "Whatever's going on, it's off the record. It's not normal business for these people."

Sean didn't question how he was so sure of that. It had been evident in the desk clerk's mind. The alert that had come in was nothing to do with him. And she hadn't had anything on her system to make her spark up priority treatment for McKenzie when he walked in to deliver the guy her bosses had tagged with a price tag of eighty five million. It almost made him feel inconsequential again, like nothing was really going on and if he wanted he could walk right out of there and get on with his life.

Except he knew that wasn't true. And he knew that these people, with their shiny facility and plush carpets, tying themselves in knots with tight assed bureaucracy, were the ones who had killed Mendhel. He didn't want to walk out – he wanted to meet them head on.

McKenzie paced over. "Can you believe this?" He laughed. "We chase all over the galaxy looking for this little shit and we get told to wait when we turn up to deliver him. God, these people live in a different world."

He was embarrassed and trying to brush it off. He'd expected this Fiorrentino guy to come running. He was a hair's breadth from flipping out.

LC slouched back in the chair. Sean recognised the danger signs and stood, taking McKenzie's arm and leading him back to the bar. She fussed over making him a drink, standing close and flirting.

LC ignored them. He skipped from mind to mind looking for someone who knew what was going on, why the security status was so high, and trying to get behind the veneer of slick corporate operations.

He caught the message from the orbital as soon as it hit the security desk. He stood up as Sean turned to look at him, a curse on her lips and a transmission from Edinburgh echoing in her mind.

"Tell Edinburgh to go," he sent. "Now."

Tremors of a deep underground blast reverberated through the floor. A klaxon started wailing.

McKenzie turned, glass half full in his hand. "What's going on?"

"Three warships just entered orbit," Sean said.

Another blast shook the complex, closer to the surface. Dust shook down from the ceiling.

"What the hell?" McKenzie said and pulled out a gun. He strode up to LC and grabbed his arm. "Sean, come on. I know where Fiorrentino's office is. Goddamn these people. We're not leaving until we get paid." He thrust the gun into LC's back and pushed him out.

"Go with it," LC sent to Sean. "We want to find this guy, right?"

Out in the terminal, it was chaos. As they ran through, the shockwave of an explosion hit them from behind, sending them stumbling, glass blowing out around them, debris billowing into the open area. McKenzie cursed and hauled LC to his feet, dragging him towards a set of double glass doors. Sean ran alongside them.

"LC," she sent, "we're in trouble here. Edinburgh says they're shooting down any ships that try to leave and they're dropping ground troops. If we don't get out now, we might not be able to."

"Is it too much to hope this might not be anything to do with us?"

"This is a Wintran planet, LC. And Edinburgh reckons those are Earth warships. You tell me."

She wasn't impressed. It hadn't even occurred to him to mention it. He'd skipped over the incident in the lab when he'd spilled his guts to her. He hadn't made the connection himself until Elliott had told him about Zang. Even then, the implications of a Wintran corporation sending them to steal from an Earth-run military facility hadn't exactly sunk in. He ducked as another bomb hit the terminal behind them, dust and glass showering down. It was obvious enough now. Shit.

33

"War," the Man said, "is inevitable and these fools squabble over their petty insecurities."

NG took a sip of the wine and placed his goblet back on the desk, cautiously inviting a refill. He was beyond tired. One more wouldn't make a difference. "Zang Tsu Po thought he'd managed to steal the secret of eternal life. Colonel Jameson wasn't going to let their hard-earned research go into enemy hands that easily."

The Man frowned, studying the board. "They had no idea what they had their hands on."

NG sat forward. LC and Hil had both taken the fight right to their enemies. They'd been trained well and it wasn't too difficult to feel proud of the way they'd handled themselves. "Media thinks a conflict could be advantageous," he said. "War between Earth and Winter could accelerate some of the developments we've been seeding."

The Man looked up. "It will divide and dilute. Survival of the fittest is void once you equip the combatants with weapons capable of genocide. Men are fools and warfare makes them unpredictable."

Humanity had been doing fine for millennia but NG didn't say that. He didn't know exactly where his boss had come from but the Man had never set in motion any action that was anything but preservation of the human race in the face of some unknown enemy to come. As much as the Man berated the abilities and tendencies of humans, he had only that one purpose. And it was difficult for a mere mortal to comprehend when more immediate enemies were to hand.

"We can't help but fight back when we're threatened," NG said and moved his queen, the most important and influential piece on the board, into the lion's den to place the Man's king in check.

The Man's face was expressionless as he leaned over to take her with his knight.

The bomb bursts intensified. It felt like they were hitting the complex with deep penetrating bunker busters as well as surface blasts.

McKenzie pushed him through into a circular atrium and hustled him towards a wide staircase that spiralled down into the facility.

A recorded voice began to advise all personnel to evacuate, people rushing past them in the opposite direction, frantically heading for the terminal and a way out. A flood of panicked emotion hit LC with an almost physical force. He struggled to shut them all out.

"Mac, this is a bad idea," Sean yelled.

Another blast rumbled deep below them. The lights flickered and died, blue emergency lighting casting an eerie glow.

"I'm not leaving until I get paid, Seanie," the bounty hunter yelled back, keeping a firm grip on LC's arm and tugging him close whenever anyone bumped into them.

It was tempting to snap out of the cuffs and punch the guy to the ground, but McKenzie knew who this Fiorrentino guy was and they didn't so LC kept calm and bottled it up for later.

They made it down three levels before they got word from Edinburgh that ground troops were entering the facility.

"McKenzie, wait," Sean shouted. "This is suicide. We do not want to get caught down here."

Gunfire echoed down from above. McKenzie stopped as if to get his bearings, hand resting on his badge as if it gave him immunity.

"We have business to finish, Sean. I would bet half the bounty that these guys," he gestured upwards, "are here to get their hands on him. I intend to collect before they have the chance." He looked around. "One more level down then we take the west wing."

Sean conceded at a nudge from LC. He wanted to find them, not run away.

They moved quickly. The west wing off the circular atrium was dark, no power and no people.

McKenzie took them the wrong way a couple of times, cursing, then found the office he was looking for. He shoved LC inside.

It was deserted.

McKenzie swore violently and kicked at a chair.

LC laughed. "What did you expect? That they'd be sitting here waiting for you?"

The bounty hunter grabbed him and threw a hefty right fist that smashed into LC's face, connecting with the cheekbone that hadn't totally recovered and sending him tumbling back against the wall.

He twisted his hands free from the cuffs as he fell and braced himself to fight back, vision clearing to look up as McKenzie pulled a gun on him, twitching to pull the trigger.

Sean didn't hesitate to floor her bounty hunter buddy with a fast blow to the back of the head. McKenzie collapsed in a heap, gun skittering away from his hand.

"You're mad," she said, helping LC up. "He could have killed you. Now what?"

He threw the cuffs off to the side and blotted his hand against his cheek. "Now we find out where they are."

The emergency power was maintaining enough of the complex's crucial systems that it didn't take too long to hack in. LC broke through the superficial barriers and worked fast to get into the secure areas, figuring out quickly why security was so high and tagging Fiorrentino's ID codes to try to track the guy.

His heart was pounding by the time he was done and he broke free, cursing.

"Hilyer's here," he said, standing up. "That's what the fucking important meeting was. Christ. Come on. We need to find this Fiorrentino guy."

"Where's Hil?" Sean said.

"I don't know. With him maybe. I don't know but this guy's our only lead. C'mon."

Sean followed him out. The corridor was beginning to fill with smoke. She pulled a pistol from a holster, checked the magazine and nudged it into his hand. He took it but held it loosely by his side.

He ran on ahead, sensing that she was following. One look at the internal layout of the complex while he was in their system had been enough for him to anticipate the most probable route the guy would take to escape, an executive core offset from the central shaft. The personnel safety and security system that tracked the location of every ID badge had shown Fiorrentino to be deep down in the levels that were just numbered, anonymous, not labelled with anything that made sense, like they wanted to keep it all buried and secretive. If he used the lift, they'd be lucky to catch him. If the power to that had been hit, he'd be taking the emergency stairs and they'd have a chance.

Another blast rocked the complex. LC began to sense people up ahead before he heard the shouts and screams. He closed off his mind, coldly refusing entry to the heat of fear and panic. He slowed and edged against the wall, aware of Sean close behind doing the same.

Thin beams of red laser sights bounced through the haze of darkness and smoke. There was gunfire and he faltered as a punch of void hit his mind. There was another and another, again and again, multiple hits. He couldn't isolate them, couldn't block them out and it felt like he'd been kicked in the head. He stumbled to his knees, vision narrowing as a chill darkness closed in. He felt his entire system shutting down, body going into shock. He grasped his hands to his head and curled up as the onslaught continued.

"What's wrong?" Sean hissed through the wire.

He couldn't move.

Sean grabbed his arm and hauled him to his feet, dragging him back.

He was trembling as Sean pushed him into an office and away from the door. He sank to the floor, trying desperately to block it all out. He felt cold, bone deep cold, a black hollow consuming his entire being from the inside out.

Sean was fussing, checking his pulse, thinking it was an after-effect of the device or McKenzie's drugs. He felt a sharp jab on his neck, warmth spreading to fend off the chill. He felt the virus seize every molecule of the drug, every blood cell coursing through his veins to fight back.

Sean brushed a hand across his forehead.

"I'm fine," he mumbled, feeling far from it, pushing her away.

He stood up, knees still shaky. "C'mon, we need to get to that stairwell."

"Not that way, we don't. Is there another way?"

He thought fast and nodded, feeling sick. "Up. There's a secure access to the AI trunking."

They checked that it was clear before stepping out and tracking back until LC found the access. He knelt, took the toolkit that Sean slipped to him and worked the lock, fingers shaking and concentration screwed. It was a bitch to bust open. It took way too long, working with gunfire closing in and a nagging at the base of his skull that was threatening to overwhelm again.

Running a tab was always covert, in and out. Alone. Peaceful.

It made him feel like a fraud – like he could work magic when all the elements were perfectly set for him but he was screwed if there was so much as a hint of a distraction. And this was one hell of a distraction, that pop of void hitting the core of his being every time someone died.

He'd lost it. He fumbled the lock again and had to start over. Mendhel would laugh and tell him to go find a woman, chill out and come the hell back with a better attitude if he could see him now. He felt a lump form in the back of his throat. What the hell would happen if someone he cared for died right in front of him? He felt the shakes start, and it was nothing physical, not the way it used to be. This was raw, black emotion. And he didn't know how to control it. Not surrounded by this whirlwind of chaos.

Sean rubbed a hand across the back of his shoulders.

He closed his eyes. No choice but to shut it out and, with something bordering on desperation, he withdrew and concentrated, simply trying to block it out completely. For once in his life, intuition wasn't going to cut it and he had to take control. He had no idea what he was doing but somehow it seemed to be working as the overwhelming darkness receded.

He focused again on the mechanism and the lock clicked. He pushed against the panel with his forehead, took a deep breath and squeezed in, climbing up into the crawl space between levels. He made his way along, heading in the general direction as fast as he could, trying to make sure Sean was keeping up behind him and trying not to flake out, breathing difficult and tears in his eyes blurring his vision.

There were troops sweeping through the entire complex. Deep rumbles echoed through the pipelines and conduits. McKenzie was right – there was no way this attack was coincidence.

He led Sean up through the substructure, racing Fiorrentino to the surface. LC was anticipating where the guy was going, no time to hook back in to the security system to check, and running on pure, desperate instinct.

It was going to be close.

They made it to ground level and he listened for a second before dropping down from a maintenance hatch into a wide open concourse. It was dark, eerie white light reflecting in through the broken remnants of shattered windows from floodlights illuminating the airstrip. He glanced around, opening his mind a fraction to scan for company. Sean landed next to him, gun out, casting around herself, not liking that they were out in the open, exposed.

LC flinched as he picked up a surge of emotion heading in. He shoved Sean into a run and they made it to the shadows on the edge of the dome before a door crashed open and a group of corporate suits appeared, dishevelled, herded by a unit of soldiers in dark nondescript uniforms who were moving with the coordinated precision of experienced bodyguards.

"That's him," LC sent to Sean through the wire, recognising the man from the files. Fiorrentino was looking rough, shirt bloodstained and barely holding in an immense anger. "And that's Anya."

She was struggling to keep up, pulled along by a guy who was holding her arm. LC stared. It felt like a fist gripped his heart and squeezed tight. Mendhel had never let them get as close as they wanted, warning him off the first time they'd met as kids. LC hadn't even seen her in almost three years. Except for that night on Earth, in the storm, where they'd been shown the recording of her pleading them to help.

He twitched as the soldier dragged her forward. Sean placed a hand on his wrist, holding him back.

"Don't do anything stupid," she sent. "I don't see Hil, do you?"

LC shook his head. He could feel Sean beside him slowly taking items from her belt. She squeezed his hand and placed two grenades in his palm. "Make sure you throw them far enough, we don't want to get caught in the blast."

The soldiers were leading the group across the centre of the open area. LC edged around, waited for Sean's signal and tossed in the concussion grenades. The dome lit up and echoed with the clatter of bodies and weapons hitting the floor.

LC ran. He skidded to a halt, sliding in beside Anya, and gently pulled her away from the grasp of the soldier lying next to her. He had absolute confidence that Sean was covering him. He picked Anya up, cradling her head against his shoulder, and carried her away.

It was cold outside. They huddled in the shelter of the doorway watching gunships fly low over the complex, searchlights sweeping in wild arcs, knowing that troops could be running out after them any minute.

He could smell Anya's hair, a soft perfume amidst the scent of smoke.

They paused, waited for a break and ran, making it to the shelter of a bombed out hangar and hunkering down as another beam of bright light cut up the darkness in front of them. Anya stirred as LC set her down. He brushed a strand of hair away from her face, aware that Sean was watching them with mixed emotions.

"Hey," he said quietly as the woman Mendhel's little girl had grown into opened her eyes. She was stunning, beautiful, even though her face was smeared with dirt and soot. He didn't even know where she'd been living the past few years. Mendhel had always just said she was fine, and they'd respected his privacy.

She blinked and reached a hesitant hand to touch his cheek as if she didn't believe he was real. "LC," she whispered. "It's you. It's really you."

Sean stood and looked around. "LC," she sent privately, "we have a real problem. Edinburgh can't make it back in here."

He glanced up, hadn't even thought that far ahead. He took hold of Anya's hand and said softly, "Where's Hil, Anya?"

Dismay crossed her face. LC resisted looking into her mind. His head was still pounding. He didn't know how he was keeping it at bay but whatever he was doing was making it more bearable. He didn't dare risk trying anything that could make him lose it again. He couldn't bear the thought of letting that onslaught back in.

Anya sucked in a shaky breath. "He's dead, LC. They killed him."

34

NG watched as the Man moved the fallen queen to join the neat row of discarded figures at the edge of the board.

"In everything you've ever taught me," NG said, "the hardest is that we sometimes have to make sacrifices."

"It is never easy," the Man said gently.

The flame of the candle was down to a small burning ember and the darkness was closing in.

NG rubbed a hand across his eyes. "If we'd known earlier that it was Zang who was behind this we could have protected our people more. We could have hit harder with more precision."

"Hindsight," the Man said. "Never look back and never question what may have been, NG. What is, is. We learn and we look forward."

He poured the rest of the wine from the jug into the two cups, vapour trails winding lazily up to disappear into the darkness surrounding them.

NG reached for his goblet, looking at the configuration of pieces arrayed on the chequered board between them. It was over.

"We've lost some good people," he said quietly.

"We have," the Man said, raising his goblet, "and we will lose more before this is finished."

NG raised his own. It was never going to be finished. Zang Tsu Po had precipitated events faster than the Man had liked but it was only in the direction that Earth and Winter had been heading anyway. The guild was caught between two powerful factions and was the only chance humanity had to survive the coming onslaught that had nothing to do with either side.

He looked from piece to piece, his two knights poised in readiness, and moved his bishop to trap the Man's king in a final sweeping attack. Checkmate.

It didn't register. Sean put a hand on his shoulder.

"What the hell was Hil even doing here?" LC said, more harshly than he intended, shivering, feeling that shock begin to encroach again.

Anya blinked long eyelashes at him. "He came here for me, LC. I knew you'd get the package. I knew you'd come to rescue me."

He was vaguely aware of Sean moving away. She was uncomfortable and he couldn't help but feel her own dismay. She'd liked Hil.

LC rubbed a hand across his eyes. He'd always known it was possible that Hil could be in trouble but to be so close...

He sat back, rubble digging into his back.

Anya lifted her hand to his face again, gently tracing the bruising under his eye. "I knew you'd do it for me."

A gunship roared overhead, sweeping round and flying over the low domes of the complex, explosions blossoming out beneath as it passed. LC flinched, grabbing Anya and shielding her, heat flaring and fragments flying around them. The pop of dark void hit him again and again.

"Sean?" he managed to send frantically. He didn't want to lose her too.

"I'm fine," she sent back. "We need to go, LC. We have to get away from here."

He wavered, finding it hard to move, limbs feeling weak as the cold darkness of so many deaths spread over him. He couldn't keep it out.

An arm gripped his shoulders gently and drew him away.

"What's wrong with him?" he heard Anya say, sounding distant.

I wish I knew, Sean was thinking, close up, breaking through his barriers. She was worried about him. A jab hit his neck. "I can't give you any more of this," she breathed into his ear.

He could feel the explosions in the depths of the complex below them, each shock of void hitting hard. He tried to shut it out, feeling sick, wanting to sink to the floor and curl into a ball until it was over.

"LC, Luka, come on. Look at me."

He struggled to open his eyes. "We need to get away from here," he muttered.

Sean nodded. "Yes, we do."

She told them to wait and ran off into the darkness. He didn't know where she found the car, but she warned him as she approached, lights off, that it was her.

They had to help him up and he huddled in the back shivering, Anya beside him, clutching his hand.

Sean drove fast, avoiding the sweep of the searchlights, bumping over rough ground to get away from the horror of the massacre.

He'd felt the violent passing of every individual that had died in there. It was ironic – he'd come here wishing revenge on the people who had killed Mendhel and he'd seen it, living every moment of it with them. Dying with them.

It felt like he'd never stop shaking. He stared out of the window to the horizon, starting to feel more in control as they increased the distance.

Sean avoided the roads, the neatly landscaped area around the base giving way to rough scrubland that stretched across the top of the plateau. It got peaceful fast, the sky an inky black once they left the artificial lights of the corporate complex.

There was a small copse of trees ahead and LC fixated on that dark shape as Sean swerved the vehicle towards it.

She pulled up and killed the engine. "We need to wait here," she said.

Anya squeezed LC's hand. "Wait for what?"

Sean looked back at them. "The ship that's coming down for us."

LC sent privately, "Edinburgh? I thought you said she couldn't make it. Aren't they still shooting down everything?"

"Yes, they are. I didn't mean Edinburgh. It's the Duck. Elliott's been shielding us – how did you think we got out of that compound without anyone chasing us?"

LC sat in the back of the car with one arm around Anya who was leaning on him and still grasping his hand as if she was afraid to let go.

Sean got out, leaving the door open and letting a damp, cold breeze creep in. His internal temperature dropped another notch but he still felt too nauseous to move to close it.

Sean paced around the vehicle, talking to Edinburgh. He didn't try to listen in, head too delicate, clear of the constant barrage but sore.

Anya stirred. "I knew you'd do it for me," she murmured.

"Of course we did," he said softly. "We weren't going to leave you there."

"I told them," she said, still half dazed from the effects of the concussion grenades.

Something jarred. He resisted taking a look inside her mind, hesitant to risk losing the level of control he was barely managing. "What did you tell them, Anya?"

"That you'd get it for me."

"Get it?" A cold chill settled in the pit of his stomach. "How did they know about us, Anya?"

She nuzzled into his shoulder. "MJ told them," she said innocently, groggily. "MJ and Kase."

The chill twisted into a knot. LC looked up. Sean was watching, leaning on the open door.

"MJ and Kase?" she sent through the wire.

"Extraction agents," he sent back, struggling to keep his heart rate steady.

"Guild extraction agents?"

He nodded, the knot gnawing deeper inside. "They're missing, awol." Martha and Kase. Christ. They'd pulled his ass out of the fire too many times to count. It was almost impossible to see them betraying the guild, even harder to see them setting Mendhel up to be killed. "MJ is Hil's ex-girlfriend. They've had an on-off thing going for years."

"And what? They're working for Zang?"

Martha had got Hil killed. LC shivered. "I don't know if I can go back, Sean."

She hesitated, as if she didn't know how far she could push him. "NG needs to know."

"He probably does by now. He might have known all along."

She frowned, looking at Anya nestled there against him, unconscious after everything she'd been through, vulnerable and pushing all LC's buttons. "You have to trust him, Luka. You said it yourself, you're done running. Please LC, it's time to go back."

The sound of the waves crashing against the natural barrier of the breakwater was hypnotic. It was warm and dry, the mid-summer heat lasting into late afternoon.

LC sat on the end of the rocky outcrop, feeling the cool spray mist his face each time a wave broke. He was finally warm right through.

Sean was back at the cabin, close enough for him to sense her there, far enough for it to feel like he was alone.

They'd left the Duck at Aston. It had been hard to leave Anya but sending her to Pen was the only way he'd know she was safe. Gallagher had been happy enough to detour and Hal Duncan had offered to take her down to the planet. LC had sent a message to Pen then split with Sean and Edinburgh.

He knew he had to go in. It was never going to be the same, not without Mendhel and Hil, but the guild wasn't going to let him disappear, tempting as it was to try to convince Sean to vanish with him. He'd tried anyway and she'd compromised – a few days alone at a place she went to pains to make sure no one could find. And as soon as they'd landed, she'd sent Edinburgh to fetch NG. LC had read it in her mind, along with an intense regret that she had to deliver him to the Alsatia at all.

He stretched his legs out and leaned back, feeling the sun on his face. He'd heard the roar of engines as they landed a little while back. Any minute now NG would walk up and that would be it.

NG was the Man's right hand. NG was the guild.

LC was rogue. No one ever walked away from the guild and this panicked feeling of having been caught finally was worse than when he'd screwed up badly enough to end up in the hands of the bounty hunters on Tortuga. It took a massive inner strength to keep his heart rate low and steady, breathing deep and calm as he watched the waves build and crest.

He became aware of someone approaching from the headland behind him and closed his eyes, reaching out cautiously to read their intention. What he felt hit deep and he got to his feet and turned, shading his eyes to look out down the length of the breakwater.

Hilyer was limping, something almost like guilt fluttering around his mind, an apprehension like he couldn't really believe it was LC there in front of him and an awkward agitation that he didn't know how much LC knew.

Damn, it was good to see him.

Hil grinned as soon as he was close enough to see it was him. "Hey, LC," he sent through the Senson, "NG says get your butt back to the guild – he has a job for us."

"I was thinking a few more days by the sea," he sent back with a grin. "A few beers, tequila…"

He stood and watched as Hilyer walked up and they stood slightly apart for a second, looking at each other, grinning like idiots. Hil had a scar on his forehead and was favouring his left hand side, meds dampening the sharp edge of pain that LC was picking up.

"It's good to see you," Hil said quietly.

"It's good to see you're alive."

"And kicking." Hil grinned again and stepped forward, grabbing LC in a hug. They slapped each other on the back. Awkward. As close as they'd always been since they were kids, they'd never been hugging types.

LC pulled away. "You look like shit. What happened?"

"Crashed Skye – she's okay. Got screwed by the guild. Started a war. How about you?"

Hil was being flippant and trying desperately to figure out how to say that Mendhel was dead.

"I know about Mend," LC said softly.

They stood in silence for a while then Hil gave up trying to stay standing and eased himself down onto the rocks. They sat on the edge of the breakwater and looked out to sea, watching the sunlight glint off the surface of the water. LC shut out the confusion milling around Hil and resisted the urge to read the whole story direct from his mind. He didn't need to – Hil would fill him in when he was ready.

It was peaceful and it felt like the universe had given up chasing them, even if only for a few moments.

"Pen took care of the guy who killed him," Hil said eventually.

"Good," LC said. "I found Anya. I sent her to Pen. She should be safe there."

Hil snapped his head round to stare, a pop of shock hitting his mind that LC couldn't avoid.

"You did what?" Hil said sharply.

LC blinked, confused at the emotions he was picking up. "What?" he said hesitantly.

"Anya," Hil said with dismay. "When did you see Anya?"

"About a week ago. I sent her to Pen. She'll be safe. I trust the people I left her with."

Hilyer was still staring. LC couldn't help but look, seeing her face in his mind, hearing her words resound around Hil's thoughts, 'You forced me to this. And all I want now is that package'.

The cold knot stabbed deep inside. "Hil?" he said and listened, detached, as Hil told him everything Anya had thrown at him in a small room deep in the bowels of Zang's underground complex.

"She told me you were dead," LC said quietly when he'd finished, trying to think back, trying to figure out how he'd missed it. He hadn't even thought to look into her mind; even once they'd got clear of the death and destruction that was screwing him up so badly, he hadn't once considered looking into her thoughts.

"She's barking mad," Hil said, anger stinging deep inside from the betrayal. He picked up a pebble and tossed it up and down in his hand.

"What about MJ? Anya said it was Martha and Kase that set us up. Was that another lie?"

Hil rubbed at the scar on his forehead. "I wish it was. LC, I don't know. Kase is dead. MJ killed him." He looked up sheepishly. "He was about to shoot me. She wasn't working for Zang but she's not guild either. I don't know if she ever has been. NG thinks she's been some kind of plant the whole time she's been with us."

It was hard to overhear the distress Hil was keeping locked up inside thinking about her. MJ had got Hil out of there alive. They'd probably been there when he was there with Sean.

It was absurd.

"What do we do now?" he said.

Hil shrugged and threw the pebble into the sea. "Go back. What else can we do? NG wants to talk to you. He's waiting with Sean." He grinned again and flicked a finger at the metal tag in LC's ear. "I told Sean she'd never catch you."

"She didn't," LC said, a tad too indignantly. He smiled. "Can you believe I gave myself up to a pair of bounty hunters so they wouldn't kill her? I must be insane."

Hil laughed then looked across thoughtfully. "She said you've had a really rough time."

LC shrugged, knowing that Hil wouldn't ask him outright about the lab, about the bioweapon they'd been sent to steal. "I'm over the worst of it," he lied, not wanting to think about what had happened to him while Earth was annihilating Zang's facility. He was dreading going back to the Alsatia. There was no way he wouldn't be hauled into Medical to get checked over. That wasn't going to be fun.

Hil looked him in the eye, serious still. "We've been assigned to Quinn," he said. "The Man has plans for some kind of special projects team. You and me. Off the list. If they ever decide to let you out again."

The sun was setting by the time they set off back to the cabin, long shadows stretching out behind them as they walked. Hilyer was struggling, holding a hand to his side as if he had a stitch. He laughed it off and called ahead to Sean to say they were coming in. It was odd to hear Hil talk to her like that, as if they'd known each other for years. LC felt a step removed from reality, like things were happening all around and he had no part in it, no say in anything.

It was only as the cabin came into sight and he saw NG and Sean sitting on the porch that he started to feel, for the first time in as long as he could remember, that it was going to work out, that everything could be okay.

Sean stood and waved as she saw them, heading inside and leaving NG to wait for them, a strong, warm presence watching them approach. There was no enmity there at all, just calm camaraderie, but even so LC's heart started to pound. Hil clapped him gently on the back and followed Sean inside.

"Sit down," NG said gently, an invitation rather than an order. Hilyer had said they were here alone, no guild agents, no grunts from Security, no question that LC wouldn't come back with them.

LC sat on the step, trying not to think.

He almost flinched as NG placed a hand briefly on the back of his neck but that fleeting touch was reassuring, a spark of warmth in the connection that was so relieving he felt his eyes almost well up. All the anxiety vanished in an instant.

He blinked and they both sat there, staring straight ahead out towards the sea.

"It's good to see you're alive, LC," NG said finally, softly, non-threatening, no trace of anger or retribution.

LC almost faltered then. Mendhel wasn't and that was his fault.

"We know what happened, Luka. You had no choice. We know it's been a hard time, and believe me, the guild hasn't had an easy time of it either, but we want you back."

He didn't know what to say. He wanted to blurt it all out but that was a whole different dilemma. Going back to the guild was one thing, admitting to NG that he had the package, that he was the package, was impossible to contemplate.

He dropped his eyes and stared at the floor, counted pebbles and scuffed the toes of his boots against each other.

He heard NG ask about the package. That was what it all came back to. NG wanted to know where it was and the lie was on the tip of LC's tongue. But you didn't lie to NG. No one ever lied to NG.

"I don't know where it is," he lied.

He felt NG's surprise, became painfully aware that NG turned slowly to stare at him. Shocked.

LC turned his head to look at NG, adrenaline pumping. He closed down his mind, as much as he'd ever managed to do, breathing difficult, heart beating fast.

"You didn't say that out loud, did you?" he said, voice almost a whisper.

'What happened out there, Luka?' he heard NG say inside his head, direct thoughts, not through any artificial connection.

This changed everything. It felt like the entire universe shrank to that tiny cabin perched on a small piece of coastline on some abandoned planet in the Between.

He felt his face flush. He was caught between absolute horror that he'd been discovered and immense relief that he wasn't alone.

NG stood up. "Come on, let's walk."

Walking gave LC a chance to do something other than fold in on himself. NG was smart and he knew how to get the best out of his people, LC had always known that. As much as it was Mendhel who'd rescued him from the firing squad on Kheris, it was NG who had welcomed him into the guild with no questions and no doubt.

"Talk to me, LC."

"What do you want me to say?" He flashed back to the lab, getting hit with the virus, the after effects, almost dying after getting shot on Poule, sharing the void of each death at the massacre – a whirlwind of painful memories that left him doubled over, gasping for breath.

He felt a rush of healing warmth stronger than any drugs he'd ever used as NG held a hand against the back of his neck.

"The Earth lab was destroyed after you got away," NG said quietly. "And chances are Zang didn't know exactly what it was he was sending you in there for. Does anyone else know?"

LC hesitated and that in itself gave NG his answer.

"We need to bring them in. Do you understand?"

He nodded reluctantly, wondering how the hell Elliott and Duncan were going to react to the guild.

"Anya's with Pen," he said.

NG nodded. "We'll deal with Anya." He paused. The sun was an orange ball dropping below the horizon behind him. "Are you ready to come back?"

LC bit his lip. It was a rhetorical question and he knew it. He didn't really have much of a choice.

"Good," NG said. "There's someone I need you to talk to."

35

The Man drained his goblet and placed it slowly on the desk, reaching a hand gently to knock over his king, graceful in defeat. "How much of this is known?"

NG sipped at the last few drops of his own wine. "Nothing."

The kid was in quarantine. No one knew anything.

The Man stared at NG. 'How strong is he?' he thought, sending the question clearly and directly into NG's mind.

'He's had to learn quickly and alone,' NG sent back. 'With training, he could be more capable than me.'

That wasn't easy to admit but he could sense it.

"And where is the girl?" the Man said, switching back to spoken words.

NG bit his lip. Anya had fooled them all.

"She betrayed us," the Man said. "She needs to be dealt with." He leaned forward. "Zang Tsu Po is a worry. The bounty has doubled. He acts directly against us." He leaned forward and said again, "Where is he?"

"Vanished," NG said, finishing the last of the wine. "Jameson is looking for him, Ostraban is looking for him, we have people on it and we have people watching them. With tensions this high and emotions this charged on both sides of the line, there aren't many places to hide."

"We have enemies, NG," the Man said softly. "We must take care. Zang's wild actions are making him more dangerous than we anticipated. Find him."

A massive fist punched into the side of NG's face. He felt blood vessels burst, sparks flaring behind his eyes.

He'd felt the intention behind the blow before he felt the force of it but he was restrained, upright, arms bound behind his back, ankles manacled to the legs of the chair he was sitting on. A cloth blindfold was tied around his eyes and a needle stuck in his arm was dripping what he recognised as Banitol into his bloodstream.

He was about as far from the safety of the guild as it was possible to get.

Another blow to the jaw sent his senses reeling. When sounds started to filter back into his awareness, they were of weapons being readied, a distant beeping and harsh voices. Footsteps echoed.

Cold water hit his face. He lifted his head slowly and spat blood off to the side.

"Let's try again," a voice said, up close, quiet. Earth accent and a mind that was cold and dark. "Where are they?"

"I don't know what you're talking about," he said softly with a faint smile, keeping his heart rate under control and feeling the Banitol spread its tendrils into his subconscious.

A hand slapped him across the back of the head.

He felt the guy in front lean in close and whisper, "Come on now, you're in no position to act dumb."

He blinked, feeling the rough cloth against his eyelashes. They'd hit him hard when they'd taken him down and the dull pounding at the base of his skull was getting steadily worse.

"You're making a mistake," he said calmly, just loud enough for the other three in the room to hear. He was aware of four more, patrolling outside. For hired muscle they were above average, he'd give them that. He'd goaded them until they'd knocked him unconscious and they still hadn't slipped up. On the whole, the situation wasn't going well.

He sensed a presence move close in by his side and felt a slight tug on the needle taped to the crook of his elbow. A sharp jab hit the side of his neck, another drug on top of the crap they were already pumping into his veins to get him to talk.

It would take more than that.

He let his head drop and heart rate slow, hearing the echoing beep of their monitors respond with a shrill alarm.

He drew back from attempting to get anything from them. It was tough enough trying to neutralise the drugs filtering into his system and dampen down the pain. He had no idea where he was, where they'd taken him, but it didn't have the feel of a medical facility. It felt more like an aircraft hangar. Cold and empty with a lingering smell of engine oil.

And it was doubtful that anyone at the guild even knew he was missing.

HARSH REALITIES

THIEVES' GUILD: BOOK THREE

COMING SOON

www.6e.net